Praise for Richard Montanari's

THE ST

"Richard Montanari's writing is both terrifying and lyrical, a killer combination that makes him a true standout in the crowded thriller market. A master storyteller at his very best." — Tess Gerritsen

"The latest Balzano and Byrne mystery is full of surprises and dark shadows — literal dark shadows, as part of the story concerns a long-shuttered mental asylum and a former inmate who uses it to explore the catacombs beneath the city. Fans of this tightly written series will definitely enjoy this one, and the Balzano and Byrne books work pretty nicely as standalones, too, so familiarity with the earlier books is not necessary." — David Pitt, *Booklist*

"Montanari weaves a mesmerizing tale." — Lisa Gardner

"Gripping, gothic horror.... Few contemporary crime writers can deliver psycho thrillers with such power, panache, and pitch-perfect pacing.... If you haven't yet latched on to Richard Montanari's fast-paced, atmospheric crime thrillers, then get ready to be bowled over... and seriously scared." — *Blackpool Gazette* (UK)

"A master storyteller. Be prepared to stay up all night."
— James Ellroy

"A writer whose prose can capture quite extraordinary subtleties.... One of the best in the business." — Thomas H. Cook

"*The Stolen Ones* is a police procedural with a dash of the thriller and touches of horror stories." —Jack Batten, *Toronto Star*

"Innovative....Plot-driven and compelling with hints of horror and parapsychology, this thriller is less of a whodunit and more of an exploration of character and motive. Readers needn't have read the first six novels in the series to appreciate this one; adventurous crime-fiction and thriller readers and fans of Keith Ablow, John Katzenbach, and Thomas Harris's Hannibal Lecter novels should enjoy." —Carolann Curry, *Library Journal*

THE
STOLEN
ONES

THE
STOLEN
ONES

RICHARD MONTANARI

MULHOLLAND BOOKS

LITTLE, BROWN AND COMPANY

NEW YORK   BOSTON   LONDON

Mulholland Books / Little, Brown and Company
Hachette Book Group
1290 Avenue of the Americas, New York, NY 10104
mulhollandbooks.com

First published in hardcover in North America by Mulholland Books, February 2014
First Mulholland Books paperback edition, April 2015
Originally published in Great Britain by Sphere, July 2013

Mulholland Books is an imprint of Little, Brown and Company, a division of Hachette Book Group, Inc. The Mulholland Books name and logo are trademarks of Hachette Book Group, Inc.

The publisher is not responsible for websites (or their content) that are not owned by the publisher.

The Hachette Speakers Bureau provides a wide range of authors for speaking events. To find out more, go to hachettespeakersbureau.com or call (866) 376-6591.

Library of Congress Cataloging-in-Publication Data
Montanari, Richard.
    The Stolen Ones / Richard Montanari.—First North American edition.
    pages cm
    ISBN 978-0-316-24470-1 (HC) / 978-0-316-24471-8 (PB)
    1. Detectives—Fiction. 2. Murder—Investigation—Fiction. I. Title.
    PS3563.O5384 S86 2014
    813'.54—dc23   2013032882

10 9 8 7 6 5 4 3 2 1

RRD-C

Printed in the United States of America

For Amanda, Gina and Michelle
Ex tenebris lux

THE
STOLEN
ONES

The first thing the hunter saw was the shadow, a long silhouette stamped on milk-blue snow, rising near a copse of maples halfway across the field.

It was deep twilight, mid-March, and the ground had not yet given up its game, nor the night its quarry. Certainly nothing of this size.

The hunter walked cautiously forward, his boots crunching the crust of frozen earth beneath him. The sound echoed across the valley, and was soon met by the cry of a nesting barn owl, a mournful plea that reminded him of the girl, of the night everything changed.

The mountain fell silent.

As the hunter closed the distance to the trees, the shadow reappeared, became a man — a big man — now standing no more than ten yards away.

The hunter tried to raise his crossbow, but could not lift his arms. He'd had this paralysis once before, a thousand sleepless nights ago, back when he wore a gold shield on his chest, back when he was a hunter of men. On that night he'd all but paid for this failing with his life.

The big man stepped into a pond of moonlight, and the hunter saw his face for the first time in three years.

"My God," the hunter said. *"You."*

"I found it."

At first the hunter thought the man was speaking another language. It had been that long since he'd heard a voice not his own. The three words soon reached his memory. He tried to purge them, to rid himself of their power, but the words had already begun to tunnel into his past, his soul.

The hunter dropped his weapon, fell to his knees, and began to scream.

Before long the moon was once again clothed in shadow, and his screams became the wind.

ONE

1

In the city beneath the city, through these hollow black halls where dead souls murmur and the seasons do not change, he moves, silent as dust.

By day he walks the city above. He is the man in the shabby overcoat on the bus, the man in the gray workman's coveralls, the man who holds the door for you, touching a finger to the brim of his cap if you are a woman, offering a tactful dip of the chin if you are a man.

There is something in his manner that remembers another time, something formal and reserved. It is not politeness or courtesy, nor could it be described as politesse—although most people who met him would, if asked, comment on his courtly fashion.

It is by night he has seen the very heart of human vice, and knows that it is his own. It is by night he moves through his warren of stone corridors and shabby rooms, bearing witness to assignations in quiet basement chambers. It is by night he wanders the dream arcade.

His name is Luther.

He first killed a man when he was twelve years old.

He has never stopped.

On this late winter morning, five days before the ground will tremble beneath the bulk of the giant machines, he waits third in line at the City Fresh Market on West Oxford Street.

The old woman stands in front of him. He considers her purchases: five boxes of Jell-O, various flavors; a quart of Half and Half; angel-hair pasta; a jar of smooth peanut butter.

Cancer food, *he thinks.*

There is a small hole at the back of her cardigan, a starfish of threads peeking out. Through it he can see a tear in the fabric of her blouse. It is where she cut out the label, perhaps because it irritated her skin. Her shoes are sturdy, round at heel, tightly laced. Her fingernails are scrubbed and clipped short. She wears no jewelry.

He watches as she scrutinizes each entry on the cashier's LCD screen, oblivious—or, more likely indifferent—to the fact that she is holding up the line. He remembers this about her, this obstinacy. Transaction completed, she takes her bagged groceries, walks a few steps toward the exit, scanning the register receipt, making sure she has not been cheated.

He has watched her over the years, watched as lines furrowed her face, watched as spots blossomed on her hands, watched as her gait slowed to an arthritic shuffle. What had once passed for regal comportment, an imperious manner that shunned intimacy or acquaintance at any level, has become a scowling, ill-mannered dotage.

As the woman nears the exit she puts down her bags, buttons her coat. She is being observed, but not just by the tall man behind her.

There is a boy of seventeen standing near the Red Box video rental machine—loitering, witnessing, looking for some sort of opportunity.

When the woman picks up her bags she drops her credit card onto the floor. She does not notice.

The boy does.

Träumen Sie?
    Yes.
Where are you?
    Tallinn. In the Old City.
What is the year?
    It is 1958, nineteen years adrift from the end of the first
    independence. It is five days before Christmas. Food is scarce,
    but there is still joy in the lights.

Where will you go?
   To Läänemaa. I am to meet a man.
Who is this man?
   A blind man, a Baltic German. He is a thief. He preys upon the
   elderly who have little to begin with. He stole something from a
   friend, and I will have it back this night.
How is this possible? How would a blind man be able to do this?
   He does not yet know of his blindness.

*Luther shadows the thief at a discrete distance, down West Oxford Street
to Marston Street, then south. Many of the buildings on this bleak and
desolate block are boarded, abandoned.*

   *Before they reach Jefferson Street the thief ducks into an alley, shoul-
ders a door.*

   *Luther follows. When his shadow darkens the wall opposite the splin-
tered doorway the thief notices. He spins around, startled.*

   They are alone.

   "You have something that does not belong to you," Luther says.

   *The thief looks him up and down, assessing his size and strength,
searching for the telltale bulge that signals a handgun. Seeing none, he is
emboldened. "D' fuck are you?"*

   "Just a ragged stranger."

   *The thief glances at the doorway, back. Recognition alights. "I remem-
ber you. You was at the store."*

   *Luther does not correct the thief's deplorable grammar. He remains
silent. The thief takes a step back. Not a defensive move, but rather a
gauging of range.*

   "What you want, man?" the thief asks. "I got business."

   "What business would that be?"

   *"Not your business, motherfucker." The thief slowly moves his right
hand toward his back pocket. "Maybe I take what you got. Maybe I fuck
you up, pendejo."*

"Perhaps so."

Another few inches toward the pocket. Nervous now. "You talk fucked up, man. Where you from?"

"I am from everywhere and nowhere. I am from right beneath your feet."

The thief looks at the floor, as if the answer might be there, as if there might suddenly appear a dog-eared Baedeker.

When he looks up, the man standing before him removes his overcoat, takes the felt cap from his back pocket, slips it onto his head. What had only moments ago been curiosity becomes something else, something of nightmares. The thief's eyes roam the man—the tattered brown suit, the frayed sleeves, the patch pockets crudely sewn, the missing button. The bloodstains.

In one fluid motion the thief reaches into his back pocket, retrieves a semiautomatic pistol, a black 9mm Hi-Point. Before he can clear it, the weapon is slapped from his hand, and he is brought roughly to the floor.

With the thief subdued, Luther takes a few moments, steps away, picks up the weapon. He checks the magazine, chambers a round. "What were you going to do with this?" he asks.

The thief has yet to catch his breath. When he does, he says, "Nothing."

Luther places the handgun on a wooden pallet near his feet.

"My name is Luther," he says. "I think it is important for you to know this."

The thief says nothing.

"I say this because I know, from experience, that what happens in this room will be a turning point in your life, a story you will repeat many times over, and that people will ask you: 'What was this man's name?'"

"I don't need to know who you are."

"Well, this is merely what I am called," Luther says. "It is not who I am."

"Just take my shit, man. I didn't mean what I said before. I wasn't going to shoot you."

Luther nods. "Let me ask you a question. When you sleep at night, or when you nap in the afternoon after a particularly good meal, do you dream?"

"What?"

"It is a simple question. Do you dream?"

"I don't. . yeah. I dream."

"Some people say they do not, but the truth is we all dream. What these people mean to say is that they do not often remember *their dreams."*

Luther crosses the room, leans against the far wall. The thief glances at the handgun on the pallet. His eyes say he will never make it.

"Let me give you an example," Luther says. "Do you know how sometimes, when you are dreaming, it begins as one thing, and then magically—for dreaming truly is in the realm of magic—it becomes something else? Something other?"

The thief remains silent.

"In the dream you are, let us say, a famous matador. You are in the ring with the beast, being cheered by thousands. You wave the muleta, *you ready your* espada *for the kill.*

"Then, suddenly, you have the ability to fly, to soar above the crowd, to cast your shadow on the countryside, to taste the salt of the sea. Such dreams, I suggest to you, are difficult to leave behind. For most of us it is such a disappointment to awaken, to relinquish such godlike powers, only to discover that we are still, simply, ourselves. Still bound by this mortal coil."

Luther takes a few steps toward the door, glances into the alley, continues.

"When I left the house today, the situation in which we find ourselves was not my dream. I suspect, however, that it was yours."

"No, man," the thief says. "It wasn't. Just let me—"

"And yet you brought with you this fearsome weapon."

"It's for protection."

"From whom? Old women with credit cards?"

The thief looks at his hands. "I wasn't going to use it."

"I understand," Luther says. "In the broadest sense, I believe this to be true. And that is why this may end well for you after all."

A light returns to the thief's eyes. "What I gotta do?"

Luther approaches him, crouches down. "There is a dream about a blind man. Do you know it?"

The thief shakes his head.

"They say to dream about blindness means that there is a truth about yourself you refuse to accept, or that you have lost your way in life. I believe this applies to you."

The thief begins to tremble.

"I am here to help you find your way, Jaak Männik."

"Who?"

Luther does not answer. He picks up the thief's handgun, then reaches beneath his jacket, and pulls out a long, bone-handled knife.

"No," the thief says. "You can't do this."

"You are right. That is why you will do it to yourself. You will take your eyes, as the matador wields his espada, and by this you will finally see."

"You're fucking crazy, man!"

"That is not for you or I to determine," Luther says. He finds an oily rag on the floor, hands it to the thief. "For the blood."

"No, man. You can't—"

"Now, this is a delicate undertaking. Extreme care must be taken. If you push the knife in too deeply, you will sever the optic nerve, yes, but you may run it into your frontal lobe. If you do it, there is the possibility— quite a good possibility, as I understand it—that you will live. If I do it, I fear you will not. I cannot make the choice for you."

Luther stands.

"Do you see that old calendar on the wall behind me?" Luther asks.

The thief looks over. There is a yellowed calendar hanging on a nail. January 2008. "Yeah."

"Do you see the date for January fifteen?"

The thief just nods.

Without another word Luther spins quickly around and fires the weapon, hitting the small square for 15 January dead center. He turns back to the thief, hands him the knife, handle first. He steps away.

"So, tell me. Which dream do you choose?" *Luther asks.* "To live many more years as a blind man, or to die in this terrible place?"

Luther smells the sharp tang of urine as the young man fouls himself In the chill of this unheated room, vapor rises from the thief's lap.

"If … if I do this, you won't kill me?"

"I will not," *Luther says.* "You have my word." *He glances at his watch.* "But you must do it in the next thirty seconds. Beyond that, I cannot make any promises."

The thief takes a deep breath, releases it in four or five small gusts. He slowly turns the knife toward himself.

"I can't do it!"

"Twenty-five seconds."

The thief begins to sob. The knife shakes in his hand as he brings it closer to his face. He raises his other hand to steady himself, and stares at the blade as one might consider a burning rosary, an abacus of sins.

"Twenty seconds."

The thief begins to pray.

"Dios te salve, Maria."

"Fifteen seconds."

"Llena eres de gracia."

"Ten seconds."

"El Señor es contigo."

"Five seconds."

At the moment the tip of the blade pierces his left eye, the 11:05 SEPTA carrying twenty-one passengers roars to a stop outside. The thief's screams are swallowed by the whet of steel on steel, plumed inside the release of exhaust.

When the knife falls from the thief's hand, there is only silence.

* * *

The thief—whose name was Ezequiel Rivera "Cheque" Marquez—had always thought that when death came it would be accompanied by a bright white light, or the sound of angels singing. When his mother died at the age of thirty-one in an osteopathic hospital in Camden, New Jersey, it was what he wanted to believe. It was possible that all eight-year-olds want to believe this.

For Cheque Marquez the moment wasn't anything like that. Death wasn't an angel in a long flowing gown.

Death was a man in a tattered brown suit.

One hour later Luther stands across the street from the old woman's house. He watches as she sweeps the dead leaves from her porch, marveling at how small she is, how big she had at one time seemed to him.

He knows that the next time he sees her it will be in her bedroom, her ruched and cloying boudoir with its peeling wallpaper and brown mice and generic powders, a visit during which he will return the credit card to her wallet.

Nothing can be out of place over the course of the coming days. Everything must be as it has always been. Luther had not planned on dealing with the thief, but if the old woman's card was missing, it might change everything. It might mean they would begin to scrutinize this, her penultimate day.

He's already visited her home, three times sitting at the foot of her bed as she fitfully slept, chased by what demons he could only imagine. Perhaps he was one of those demons. Perhaps the woman knows that, when her time comes, it will be him.

In the end, someone always comes.

2

Detective Jessica Balzano found herself in a brightly lit room, sitting upright, her left hand high in the air, the clatter of street noise drifting in from a window behind her. At first she thought she was alone, but soon realized there were people all around her. She didn't see them, but she knew they were there in the way you know anything when you're dreaming, the way you know that, while danger may lurk in every shadow, it is only dream-danger, and you will not be harmed. All you have to do is wake up, and it will be gone.

But this wasn't a dream. Somehow, she was in a classroom. With her hand raised. And there were at least a dozen people staring at her.

Real people.

"Ms. Balzano?" someone said.

The man at the front of the classroom, the man who seemed to know her name, was thin and pale, about sixty. He wore a pilled blue cardigan with epaulets, beige corduroy slacks, cupped at the knees. There was a half-smile on his face, as if he had done this before, as if this were an inside joke he was sharing with everyone.

Everyone except Jessica Balzano.

Before Jessica could respond it all came rushing toward her in a hot, mortifying wave. She was not in bed in her small, comfortable South Philly row house, her husband Vincent next to her, her two children safely asleep in their rooms on the third floor. She was, instead, in school — specifically, her second year of law school.

Jessica had known it was going to be like this, but she had no idea it would be like *this*. She'd had the feeling this might happen one day, and it finally had. She'd fallen asleep in class.

She put down her hand, her mind a kaleidoscope of questions. What class was this, again? *Contracts? Torts? Civil procedure?*

Not a clue.

She glanced at the chalkboard, saw a quote from Louis Nizer: *In cross-examination, as in fishing, nothing is more ungainly than a fisherman pulled into the water by his catch.*

No help there.

"Ms. Balzano?" the professor said. "False imprisonment?"

God bless him, she thought. He'd repeated the question for her benefit.

Jessica said, "The three elements of false imprisonment are: willful detention, detention without consent, and unlawful detention."

"Very good," her teacher said with a wink. He'd been a law professor for more than twenty-five years. Jessica was not the first student ever to nod off in class. She would not be the last.

Jessica reached under the table and pinched the web of flesh between the thumb and forefinger on her right hand, almost to the point of drawing blood. It was an old trick she'd been taught by her Field Training Officer her first year out of the academy, a trick to keep her awake when she worked last-out, the eleven p.m. to seven a.m. shift.

For the next forty minutes Jessica tried every trick she'd ever learned to regain wakefulness. Thankfully, the professor didn't call on her again, and somehow she made it to the end of class.

On the way to her car, Jessica noticed a small group of students from her class walking across the parking lot at Cecil B. Moore and Broad Street. They all looked about twenty—wide awake, happy, fully caffeinated by life. Jessica wanted to shoot them.

"Hey, Jessica," one of them said. His name was Jason Cole, and he held the unofficial title of cutest boy in class, a class in which there was a lot of competition for that honor. "Nice save back there."

"Thanks."

"For a minute there I thought you were going to wash."

You have no idea, Jessica thought. "Not a chance," she said. She unlocked her car. "I've had tougher cases."

Jason smiled. He had braces, which somehow made him cuter. "We're going to Starbucks for a study jam," he added. "Want to come with?"

They all knew she was a police officer, of course, a homicide detective at that. They also knew she was juggling three lives—cop, mother, student—living days haphazardly constructed around a curriculum of early-morning, late-evening and weekend classes. Jessica desperately wanted to feel sorry for herself about this, but she knew it was nothing special for many people her age who were attending college. The truth was, she just wanted to go home and finish the nap she'd begun in the classroom. She couldn't do that. In addition to the thousand other things she needed to accomplish, she was staring down the barrel of a full twelve-hour shift.

It was her first day back after a two-week sabbatical.

"Gotta go to work," Jessica said. "Maybe next time."

Jason gave her a thumbs-up. "We'll save you a seat."

Jessica slipped into her car, the fatigue a living thing within her. She glanced at her law books on the seat, and not for the first time in the past eighteen months wondered how she got here.

She was currently working in the SIU division of the homicide unit four days a week—a generous offer allowed by her captain, cleared with the inspector and, most importantly, with her husband, Vincent— and getting about five hours of sleep per night. It was one thing when you were a twenty-two-year-old grad student; quite another when you were on the osteoporosis side of thirty-five.

Of the three divisions in the PPD Homicide Unit—the Line Squad, the Special Investigations Unit, and the Fugitive Squad—SIU was the least demanding, at least in terms of immediacy and the need for over-time. Although the physical and emotional rigors of working cold cases could be just as demanding as working fresh homicides, the days tended to be a little more structured, and the need to get the ball rolling—and hopefully make an arrest—in the first forty-eight hours was not there.

Still, this was the path she had chosen. She recalled the moment she'd chosen it, as well. She had been thirteen, and had visited City Hall with her brother, Michael. They went to watch their father—then Sergeant Peter Giovanni—testify in Judge Liam McManus's courtroom.

On that day Jessica sat in the back row, watching the proceedings, observing as the two lawyers went head to head. Having grown up in a police family, she knew that there were many jobs upon which the carriage of justice depended—cops, judges, forensic specialists, medical examiners. But for some reason she was instantly drawn to this stage, this rarefied arena where, if everyone else did their job, it would all come down to the clear, clinical thinking of two people to build a case for either guilt or innocence.

Young Jessica Giovanni was hooked, her future fully mapped by the time she and her brother and their father sat down to lunch at Frank Clements Tavern, which was then located across the street from the original Bookbinder's. As Jessica ate her cheesesteak she watched in something close to awe as defense lawyers, prosecutors and judges—even a future Pennsylvania supreme court justice—all mingled in the smoky, storied bar, many of them stopping by the table to chat with her father.

On that day the scheme was set in motion: Michael would be the police officer; Jessica would be the ADA. That was the plan. Theirs would be the South Philly version of *Law & Order*. Peter Giovanni—one of the most decorated officers in the history of the PPD, who eventually retired with the rank of lieutenant—would play the crusty former cop who tended his San Marzano tomatoes in the garden, supplying moral support and pithy wisecracks.

Everything went according to blueprint, until that horrible day in 1991 when Michael was killed in Kuwait, a Marine fighting in Desert Storm.

In that instant Michael Giovanni, Jessica's beautiful brother—her protector, confidante and greatest hero—was gone.

Jessica recalled sitting with her father the night they learned of Michael's death, how mightily her father tried not to cry in front of her. A week later, as she knelt next to Michael's casket, she knew that her dreams of being a lawyer would be put on hold, perhaps forever, that *she* would be the one to follow in her father's footsteps. Over the ensuing years she had never regretted her decision to enter the academy, not once, but she knew that if she was ever going to get her law degree, now was the time.

She wasn't certain she would even take the bar exam upon completion of her studies, but she knew that, at the very least, she owed it to her brother to try.

Jessica started her car, glanced at her watch. It was five minutes to noon. She had five minutes to get to the Roundhouse. In Philly traffic. She opened the glove compartment, found a Twix. High calorie, nutrient-free sugar.

Yes.

Candy bar in hand, Detective Jessica Balzano pulled out into the traffic on Broad Street thinking: if God was smiling down on her this day—and she was blessed in so many ways that she couldn't expect anything else from God, not anytime soon—she would be home and in bed around midnight.

God wasn't listening.

Whan Jessica reached the Roundhouse, the police administration building at Eighth and Race streets, the duty room was all but deserted. Homicide detectives working day work, the shift from seven a.m. to four p.m., were out on the street. The few who remained were working the phones, the fax machine, the computers, or just trying to look busy to the day watch commander, having hit dead ends in their investigations.

By the time Jessica removed her coat and sat down she saw Sergeant Dana Westbrook walking purposefully across the duty room in her direction. A former Marine, still in her early fifties, Westbrook cut an imposing figure, despite her five-foot-four frame. Since taking over the job as day watch supervisor from the retired Ike Buchanan she had proven herself more than capable in what was, and would most likely always be, a boys' club. The fact that Dana Westbrook could bench press her own weight plus twenty didn't hurt.

As Westbrook got closer, Jessica saw the look on her boss's face. It was a look that said: *job.*

No rest for the righteous, Jessica thought.

Other than a few loose ends that needed to be clipped and sorted on a murder case she and her partner had just closed, there was nothing on her plate.

That, it appeared, was about to change.

"Hey, Sarge," Jessica said.

"Morning, Jess."

Jessica stole a glance at the wall clock. It was technically afternoon. She wondered if Dana Westbrook was taking a shot, or just offering that greeting out of habit. "What's up?"

Westbrook held up a thin folder, a folder that looked curiously like a binder. The binder—often referred to as the murder book—was the Bible of a homicide investigation. A fresh binder was opened the day the investigation began, and by the time the investigation was closed, if it was closed, every piece of paper—summaries, witness statements, autopsies and toxicology reports, ballistics, crime scene and collateral photographs, even the handwritten notes from the investigating detective's work—was contained between its covers. Sure, there were backup systems in place, forensic data recorded onto hard drives in various laboratories, but the most referred to set of documents in a murder investigation was in the binder.

"We've got an open unsolved," Westbrook said. "About a month old."

"You want me to be lead on this?" Jessica asked.

Westbrook nodded.

"What's the new information?"

When a fresh homicide is investigated there is a great push, not only from detectives and brass in the homicide unit, but also from the crime scene unit, and all collateral laboratory divisions. The concept of the first forty-eight hours being critical in a homicide investigation was no cliché. Witnesses got amnesia, nature began to take back its evidence, suspects found the wind. The sad truth was, if solid leads were not generated in the first week or so, a case began to cool. Within a month it was cold.

"There isn't really a new lead," Westbrook said. "Nothing solid anyway. After the lead investigator visited the crime scene, and made an initial report, the victim's house was sealed."

Jessica didn't understand. Crime scenes were always sealed. At least until it was cleared by the investigators.

"I'm not sure I follow," Jessica said.

"When I say sealed, I mean the property was sealed by court order, by the victim's lawyer. It seems the victim had only one living relative, a distant cousin living in New York, a cousin he apparently didn't exactly get along with. The victim died intestate, which means the cousin would get whatever money and possessions he had. She had her lawyer meet the investigator at the crime scene on the day of the murder. When they left the apartment was sealed."

"So the victim was not killed in his residence."

"No," Westbrook said. "The body was found in a park in the Northeast."

"So why now?"

"The DA's office was able to get the victim's apartment unsealed." Westbrook put down a small envelope. "Here's the address and a key to the front door." She held up the binder. "Everything else is in here." Dana Westbrook put the binder down on the desk. What should have been about an inch thick appeared to contain no more than three or four documents.

"It looks a little thin, Sarge," Jessica said.

Westbrook looked at the floor for a moment, then back up. "There are a few missing files," she said. "Most of them, in fact."

"I don't understand. Why are they missing?"

Westbrook smoothed the front of her sweater. "This was one of John Garcia's last cases," she said.

And Jessica understood.

4

The dead man's name was Robert August Freitag. On the day of his murder he was unmarried, had no children, and was five days shy of his fifty-seventh birthday. He was five foot seven, weighed 166 pounds. He had brown hair, brown eyes.

When Jessica opened the binder, the first thing she saw was a picture of the victim, an executive-type headshot most likely taken for an annual report or a company website. Robert Freitag was a pleasant-looking middle-aged man, just sprouting gray around the temples. In the photograph he wore a blue sport coat, white shirt and a green and white striped tie, as well as aviator-style bifocals.

According to the summary, on the evening of February 20, 2013, Robert Freitag—who worked as a logistics manager for a company called CycleLife—walked from his home on Almond Street, in the Port Richmond section of the city, to a small convenience store on Allegheny Avenue. While there he purchased a loaf of whole-wheat bread, two cans of candied yams, a package of votive candles and a Snickers. Surveillance cameras showed him leaving the store at 6:22 p.m.

No one saw him alive again.

While Jessica was certain that a neighborhood interview had been conducted—a canvass of residents and shop employees spanning a one- or two-block radius of the victim's home—there were no statements in the binder. Nor was there an autopsy protocol. Freitag's body had been cremated within a week of his murder.

There were no crime scene photographs in the binder, but there was a brief description of the scene. Robert Freitag's body was discovered by an early morning jogger, sitting on an old wooden chair in the middle of a field in Priory Park, a densely forested parcel in Northeast Philadelphia, just a few blocks from the Delaware River.

Jessica had to read the brief twice. According to the summary, and the ME's ruling, the cause of death was loss of blood due to a massive fissure fracture of the skull.

The truth was that someone took a ten-inch-long, rusted piece of steel, and drove it into the back of Freitag's skull.

An officer in the Firearms and Ballistics Unit identified the murder weapon as a railroad spike.

CSU had lifted and analyzed a number of footwear impressions in the snow around the victim's body. Their closest guess was a European size 46, which fell between a US 12 and 13. The presumptive determination was a European work boot, brand unknown. The pattern did not show up in any of the reference databases. Because there were no other footprints in the thin layer of snow, it was presumed that the killer carried Robert Freitag to the center of the field. Adding Freitag's weight, the killer was thought to be between 170 and 200 pounds, based on the depth of the imprint.

The killer's height, race, gender and age were unknown, which narrowed the suspect pool to approximately 40 percent of the adult population of Philadelphia.

Jessica looked in the large envelope Dana Westbrook had left on the desk. In it was a videotape of the crime scene.

The lead investigator on the case was a veteran detective named John Garcia. While investigating the Freitag case, Garcia collapsed in the lobby of the Roundhouse one morning and was rushed to the hospital. He was diagnosed with a brain tumor, and emergency surgery was performed.

The surgery was unsuccessful. John Garcia died on the operating table.

Although they were not what either of them would have called close friends, Jessica had liked John Garcia, had worked a few cases with him over the years.

In the months leading up to his collapse and subsequent surgery, Jessica—along with a number of other detectives in the squad—had noticed Garcia's increasingly odd behavior, the unfinished sentences, the strange non sequiturs. No one spoke of it. Everyone chalked it up to fatigue.

And while Garcia's behavior was the sad result of the tumor growing in his brain, nowhere was his disconnected logic more evident than in the case notes for the Robert Freitag homicide. More accurately, what case notes there were. There were only three torn pages in the binder. On each were a series of drawings, casual doodles of flowers, trains and animals, childlike renderings of houses with smoke curling from their chimneys in long corkscrews.

The murder book for Robert Freitag should have contained dozens of synopses and witness statements. Instead, it held just a few pages of gibberish. It was not much to go on.

Jessica closed the binder, put it on the chair next to her. She looked out the window at the parking lot behind the Roundhouse, at the ceaseless cold rain, a question circling her mind. And that question was: *Why?*

For the most part, in any homicide investigation, *why* runs a close third after *who* and *when*. Quite often, just by reading the first few lines of a summary, Jessica could tell why someone was murdered. Unknown to the casual observer, a majority of the homicides committed in Philadelphia occurred within a small group of people who were in the game—drugs, vice, prostitution, gangs. There was, of course, a great deal of overlap. And while Jessica and just about every homicide cop she knew—with a few notable exceptions—took every murder on their patch seriously, it was when the average citizen was murdered that the motive moved front and center.

In the case of Robert Freitag, the how, when and where were scientific fact. He had been killed on February 20, 2013, somewhere between eleven p.m. and midnight, in an open field in a park in Northeast Philadelphia. What little forensics there were from the ME and CSU concluded that Priory Park was the primary offense location.

Many times, with Philadelphia's numerous parks, the area was used as a dumping ground, making it the secondary site. Apparently there was evidence that pinpointed the park as the place where Freitag was killed. It just wasn't in the book.

Jessica looked at the last piece of paper in the binder. It was a printout of the dead man's financials. In life, the man had been somewhat of an enigma. In death, his affairs were far more straightforward. His estate, what little there was, had been left to his sole relative, a distant cousin living in Forest Hills, New York, a woman named Edna Walsh.

In addition to whatever valuables were in his apartment, Freitag had left behind two CD accounts, totaling six thousand dollars, plus a money market account worth, at the time of his murder, just over two thousand. He did not own a car, and had paid off the mortgage on his home three years earlier.

Jessica looked at the videotape on the desk. She didn't want to watch it. She knew she had to.

She picked up the tape, crossed the duty room to the small room next to Interview A, the cluttered space that held the four monitors and VCRs. She slipped the tape out of its sleeve, put it in the machine, pressed PLAY.

The first shot in the video was the time and date stamp, along with victim's name and location of the scene. A few seconds later the video began to roll. It was handheld, moving toward an object sitting in the middle of the field, about thirty yards away—an object Jessica knew to be a dead human being. The body was sitting up on an old wooden chair, covered with a translucent plastic sheet.

As the camera moved closer to the body Jessica saw that the sheet was held down in the front by a pair of large stones. In the back someone, probably an officer for the crime scene unit, had fashioned a pair of stakes out of thick tree branches. As the camera focused on the victim, Jessica could see the flesh beneath the plastic—a filmy wash of pink and red and brown.

Every so often snowflakes would land on the lens, and the videographer would reach around to clean it. During one of these shots, the camera caught two CSU officers, young guys huddling inside their PPD issue rain jackets, stamping their feet, blowing into their gloved hands. At the moment they looked to be rethinking their career choices.

Jessica had been there, considered that.

"Okay," someone on the tape said. It sounded like John Garcia.

One of the officers reached down and removed the two rocks holding down the plastic sheet. He then grabbed the sheet by those two corners. The other officer pulled up the stakes behind the victim and held those corners. They both looked off camera, presumably at the lead detective. Slowly, the two CSU officers lifted the plastic sheet. They held it over the victim's head, doing their best to shield him from the snow, which looked to be turning to sleet.

When the sheet cleared the victim's head, Jessica saw him for the first time. It was an image that would stalk her dreams for a long time.

She knew that Robert Freitag was fifty-six years old at the time of his death, but it was almost impossible to tell by looking at his face. Or what was left of his face. There was very little about it that was still recognizable as human. His head had swollen to almost twice its normal size. Where his nose had been was now an amorphous mass of dark blue and purple tissue. Both of his eyes were distended and open so widely that the eyelids had split. A green viscous substance had formed over the top of his eyes, a substance that had begun to freeze in the rapidly dropping temperature. He wore what appeared to be a long-sleeve white shirt, now a mass of dried blood and flecks of mottled flesh.

As the camera circled the body Jessica saw the murder weapon for the first time. As horrible as it sounded on paper, it was worse to see. The railroad spike sticking out of the victim's head had split the man's skull nearly in two. Broken pieces of skull were frozen to the bisected flaps of torn scalp. Flesh clung to the back of the man's collar.

Jessica was suddenly glad, perhaps for the first time in her life, that she had skipped lunch.

As the camera's field of vision returned to the front of the body, Jessica saw something she had not noticed the first time, something so incongruous to the drab, wintry setting she wondered how she had missed it. There, peeking out of the victim's clasped hands, was what appeared to be a dried flower. A white flower with a yellow center. She stopped the tape, scanned the evidence log. All of Freitag's clothing, as well as the murder weapon and the chair in which he sat, were cataloged by CSU. There was no mention of a flower.

Jessica looked more closely at the screen. She was by no means knowledgeable about flowers—indeed, she had a notorious black thumb when it came to plants both indoor and outdoor, had been known to kill plants with a dirty look—so she made a note to get a printout of this angle from the video recording.

She hit PLAY once again. Before the video ended, the camera panned across the area where John Garcia stood. For a brief moment Garcia looked straight at the lens, and Jessica felt her heart flutter. It had only been a month or so since she had seen him, but in that time he had moved to that area of her heart reserved for people who had passed on.

She rewound the tape, let it play. When the camera once more found John's face, Jessica hit PAUSE.

In the background, slightly out of focus, was the body of Robert August Freitag. In the foreground was the detective tasked with finding the man's killer. Jessica knew that, forty-eight hours after this video was made, John, too, would be dead.

Jessica saw the puzzlement in the man's eyes—the confusion caused by the insidious malignancy in his brain—but also saw the kindness. John Garcia had been the gentlest of souls.

Jessica hit the eject button, removed the tape from the machine, put it back in the envelope, thinking: *We've got your back now, John. Rest well, my friend.*

Back at her desk, Jessica picked up the small envelope containing the door key she would need to gain entrance into the victim's house. As she slipped on her coat she saw Dana Westbrook crossing the duty room.

"Sarge, have you seen Kevin?"

Westbrook pointed in the general direction of Northeast Philadelphia, and said: "He's already at the scene. He's waiting for you."

"At the crime scene?"

Westbrook nodded. "At the crime scene."

5

Detective Kevin Francis Byrne stood in the cold rain, at the edge of the field, thinking: *All killing grounds are the same.*

If there was one truth he had learned in his many years working homicides, it was that a place where murder is done—whether it be an inner-city tenement, a Chestnut Hill mansion, a lush, green field— never again holds a sense of peace. What had once been pristine land was forever lost to madness.

For Byrne it was more than that. In his time as a homicide detective he had witnessed the grim residue of violence, the broken lives, the yoke of suspicion and hatred and distrust. Neighborhoods never forgot.

Byrne had long ago given up the notion of closure as it applied to the family of the victim. For the police and the courts and the politicians closure meant one thing: a number on a ComStat report, a headline in the paper, a campaign slogan. For survivors, it was a nightmare that never found the morning.

At times Byrne forgot simple things—he'd once left a pair of dress shirts at a dry cleaner's for over a year—but he recalled in rich detail every case he had ever worked, every notification he'd ever made. He often drove through the city and got a feeling when he passed the scene of a murder, felt the hair on his arms bristle. For more than twenty years—since he himself had been pronounced dead for more than a minute, only to come back to life—he'd had these intuitions, these vague feelings that led him down dark paths.

On this day, standing in a place where murder was done, Byrne saw that there were no flowers, no wreaths, no crosses, no remembrance of the evil that had been loosed here. The field probably looked as it had a hundred years earlier.

It was not.

Byrne walked the grid as he imagined it, the path by which Robert Freitag had come to this place.

When he had read the files in the binder, such as it was, the first thing he noticed was that there was no hand-drawn sketch of the crime scene. Even in this age of iPads and Nexus tablets, the most frequently used method of detailing a murder scene was still a pencil and a yellow legal pad. If you were a real up-and-comer you bought your own grid paper.

Whether John Garcia was capable of such a thing, so close to the very end of his life, was unknown.

Byrne wondered what it looked like from the inside for Garcia. Byrne had twice been shot in the head. The first time, he was just grazed by the bullet. The second time it was much more serious. He was extremely fortunate that there was no lasting damage, but his lot in life, for the rest of his life, was to undergo a yearly MRI. The prevailing theory, at least as far as his neurologists went, was that the MRI was just precautionary. The truth was that Kevin Byrne was at risk for a litany of neurological maladies, not the least of which were aneurysms and tumors.

Many a night—too many, if truth were told—he had stayed up, cruising the internet for horror stories that involved aneurysms and tumors, especially the warning signs. Usually, for the first few days after those Bushmills-fueled research sessions, he was certain that he exhibited nine out of ten symptoms.

Lately, there had been one sign that lingered. It was probably something that he should contact his doctors about, but he hadn't had the courage to do so.

At this moment, at the edge of this frozen field, there was a scent in the air, something Byrne was certain no one else could smell. Part of him hoped there was a reasonable explanation for it. Part of him feared there was not.

Byrne closed his eyes and breathed deeply. There could be no doubt. The smell brought him to a time and a place he could not see; a flood of sensory input he knew was part of a memory not his own.

There, beneath the odor of sack cloth and human waste, was the smell of wet straw.

6

Priory Park, in the northeast section of the city, was tucked between Frankford Avenue and the banks of the Delaware River. The heavily wooded 62-acre tract acquired its name from the monastery that had once stood on the grounds in the early 1800s. All but one of the buildings had long since been razed, leaving only a small stone chapel near the northwestern corner. Threaded through the dense trees was a tributary of the Poquessing Creek, which emptied into the Delaware River, just a few hundred yards from the eastern edge of the park.

When Jessica turned onto Chancel Lane she saw the solitary figure standing at the edge of the southern section of the park. Although it had only been two weeks since she had seen him, it seemed like a longer period of time. When you work as closely as she and Byrne did, time apart was, in many ways, the same as time apart in a marriage. At first it was a welcome respite, but after a while, when the people around you didn't quite get what you were saying, didn't see things quite the same way you did, you began to miss that person, to miss the shorthand. More than once, over the past two weeks, Jessica had seen or heard or read something, and one of her first reactions was to tell her partner about it.

She had her husband Vincent, of course, but Vincent Balzano was as different from Kevin Byrne as he could be. Except for the brooding part. What complemented Jessica's own personality in her marriage also worked with her partnership as a homicide detective. It carried the same basic statute, as well.

You could both be crazy, you could both be temperamental, just not at the same time.

Byrne had been injured on a case the previous year, and had spent a long time on medical leave, the longest time he had been off the job in his entire time on the force. Many in the unit were certain he would retire, but one day he showed up at the Roundhouse, as if nothing ever happened, and he and Jessica were soon on a new case.

But Jessica, who arguably knew him better than anyone in the squad, maybe in the world, had noticed a change. While he was not one of those detectives always ready to deliver some wisecrack, he did have his moments. Still, he seemed more serious in the past six months. Maybe serious was the wrong word. He seemed a bit more introspective.

Seeing him standing at the edge of the field, silhouetted in the gray mist, he looked more solitary than ever.

The rain was unremitting. As always, Jessica had her umbrella—the big London Fog Auto Stick she'd gotten as a Christmas present from Vincent, Sophie and Carlos last year— in the trunk of the car. Why she did this, she would never know. How hard was it to keep an umbrella in the back seat?

As she parked she noticed that Byrne was holding one of those small umbrellas you pick up on Market Street for five dollars when you're caught on the street without one. It barely reached halfway to his shoulders. It was mostly serving to keep his head relatively dry. One good gust, though, and it would invert. And the wind was starting to blow. Jessica grabbed her notepad, tucked it inside her coat, clicked her pen three times, which had somehow become a habit years ago, as if she were Dorothy and wore ruby slippers. She put her pen away, took a deep breath knowing she was going to get soaked, opened the door and sprinted to the back of the car. Within seconds she had the trunk open, and her umbrella out and unfurled.

She crossed the road, walked over to where Byrne stood.

"Hey, partner," she said.

Byrne turned to look at her. Any fear she'd had about him and his dark moods evaporated in an instant. His eyes were a bright emerald, like always.

"Hey."

"Not much of an umbrella."

Byrne smiled. "No substitute for quality," he said. "Welcome back."

"Thanks." Jessica pointed to the field. "Did you walk it off?"

It was a perfunctory question. She knew he had.

"Yeah." He pointed to an area about thirty feet in from the road. "The body was found right there."

"What about the binder?" Jessica asked. "Are you up to speed?"

"As much as I can be."

"Did you make much out of John's notes?"

"Not really," Byrne said.

John Garcia did not work with a partner, so there was no one to ask about these things. His strange doodles, it seemed, would forever remain a mystery.

"And there's no lead on where the missing files are?" Byrne asked.

"No. Before I left the office I looked at every binder in that drawer, plus the drawers above and below it. They're not in there." Jessica put her umbrella over the two of them just as a gust of wind cut across the open field, soaking them both with frigid rain. They huddled a few inches closer to each other.

"Did you watch the video?" Jessica asked.

Byrne shook his head. He knew that Jessica would watch it, and tell him if there was anything he needed to know. There wasn't.

"I made a few calls before I left," Jessica said. "I asked for backup copies to some of the files that are missing. They're on the way."

These files included the autopsy and the toxicology reports, as well as a detailed report from the Firearms Unit on the murder weapon.

There were digital copies of all this material, of course, but it would take a while. Although the murder of Robert Freitag was an open/ unsolved, it was technically a cold case. There had been more than thirty homicides in the City of Brotherly Love since then, and every victim deserved the attention of all divisions in those crucial first few days.

Jessica looked out over Priory Park. "Is it too late to turn in my badge today?"

Byrne smiled. "You can do it, but I don't think you'll get a full refund. And then there's that restocking fee."

"It's always something." She glanced at her watch. She was wet and cold and ready to move inside. She knew that her partner needed time at the crime scene, even one as cold and wet as this. She asked anyway. "Ready to head back?"

"Sure."

"You want to follow me?"

"No, I'll ride with you. I want to come back here later, make a lap around the park. Look for vantage points."

The nearest houses were just to the west. Although the view from those houses was almost certainly obscured by a deep tree line, it was probably worth checking out. If John Garcia had driven up there, and talked to some of the residents, the notes were not in the binder. They would have to re-canvass, although conducting a neighborhood interview a month after a crime rarely yielded anything useful.

The missing files, combined with John Garcia's notes, meant that they were not even starting at square one, but before square one. They didn't even have the benefit of a dead body or crime scene to work.

The killing ground had long ago disclosed its secrets.

Twenty minutes later, Jessica and Byrne turned onto Almond Street. Jessica pulled over in front of Robert Freitag's row house, put the car in park.

Neither detective wanted to leave the warmth of the car.

"I forgot to ask," Byrne said. "How's school?"

Jessica shook her head. "Don't ask."

"That bad?"

"I fell asleep in class."

"Sleep was pretty much my default position when I was in school."

"With your hand raised?"

"No," Byrne said. "I think you win that one. Then again, I never raised my hand." He pointed to the pile of texts on the front seat of Jessica's car. "Has anyone offered to carry your books?"

"*Please.* I have pantyhose older than these kids."

"Jess, you have a ponytail. You don't look a day older than any of them."

Jessica cut the engine. "You are a fabulous liar," she said. "Have you ever considered going to law school?"

Byrne smiled. "And give up show business?"

The address was a two-story stone-front structure, third from the corner, 1920s vintage. There were four sandstone steps up to the front door, which shared a white awning with the house next to it. The two sidewalk-level basement windows were glass blocked. The front windows had security bars, as did most of the houses on the street.

Jessica opened the screen door. Across the interior doorjamb was a bright orange PPD sticker, signed by John Garcia two days before he died.

The sticker was intact. No one had been inside Robert Freitag's house since that day.

Jessica took out the envelope she had gotten from Dana Westbrook, tore it open, dumped the key into her hand. She slipped the key in the lock.

As she opened the door she turned to her partner.

"So, you don't have a new case yet?"

Byrne shook his head. "Philly behaved last night."

"Imagine that."

7

J essica had always thought that loneliness had a smell, a grim and silent airlessness that said that the occupant of a space drew a distinct line between inside—where he lived his solitary existence—and the rest of the world.

Robert Freitag's small row house was just such a place. From the moment she entered Jessica could sense Freitag's seclusion, his desire to be shut off from others.

Against the wall to the left was an inexpensive sofa; to the right, at a precise ninety-degree angle, a matching chair. The coffee table had a pair of remotes aligned perfectly next to each other, along with a candy dish with three pinwheel candies in it.

The wall unit across from the sofa held a twenty-seven-inch LCD television. On either side were books, mostly paperbacks on top, with two rows of hardcovers on the bottom. At first glance Jessica could see that many were novels popular in the eighties and nineties. Jessica wondered if the books had come with the house.

Above the couch was a generic landscape print, something you might see on the wall at a budget interstate motel. There was nothing else on the walls in the living room or the attached dining room.

Jessica and Byrne fell into a familiar rhythm: Byrne headed downstairs, Jessica went up.

On the second floor were two bedrooms and a bathroom. Jessica walked down the short hallway to the first bedroom. It was empty, save for a pair of laundry baskets. One of the hampers held a pair of blue bath towels. The other, a white undershirt and a pair of boxer shorts.

The bathroom was as tidy as the rest of the house. Jessica opened the medicine cabinet: Tylenol, Listerine, Arid Extra Dry, dental floss. No prescription medications.

She walked down the hall to the other bedroom.

A bed, a dresser and a small vanity. A month of passing street traffic had shaken loose dust. A thin film covered all the smooth surfaces in the room.

Inside the closet were two dark suits, a pair of navy sport coats, a half-dozen or so short-sleeve dress shirts, just as many striped ties. There were a pair of V-neck sweaters on the shelf, along with a 1970s-vintage Samsonite suitcase. Jessica took down the suitcase, put it on the bed, snapped it open. The case was empty, save for a small plastic bag with travel-sized bottles of shampoo, conditioner and body lotion. All appeared unused. Jessica put the suitcase back on the shelf. She checked the pockets on all the items of clothing, found nothing.

No matter how many times she did this, Jessica always felt as if she were violating the rights of the victim. While she had no problem frisking a suspect, and subsequently going through their possessions, when the items belonged to the victim it was different. She often thought about what her own closets and drawers and suitcases would yield.

She opened the drawers in the dresser. Socks in one drawer, underwear in another, T-shirts in yet another. Robert Freitag's was a life of mathematical order.

Jessica walked back downstairs, stepped into the kitchen. Like the rest of the house, it was way too clean. The refrigerator door handle had no smudges, the kitchen drawer that held the cutlery and carving knives held no crumbs. The house was not spotless, but it was close.

As Jessica moved from room to room she took dozens of pictures, mostly for her own reference. She never printed them off, for the simple reason that they might become mixed in with official crime scene photos, and in this era of PhotoShop it would leave the door open for a savvy defense attorney to have all photographic evidence come under suspicion.

While Jessica was upstairs, Byrne had taken the contents of the small living-room desk and spread it out on the dining-room table.

"Anything in the basement?" Jessica asked.

Byrne shook his head. "Washer and dryer, a Christmas tree in a box, a folded treadmill. That's about it."

Jessica stepped into the dining area. On the table was a soup bowl with a coffee mug upside down on it. Next to these items was a folded linen napkin and a silver spoon. All were clean, perhaps set up for a meal Robert Freitag would not live to enjoy. The spoon looked to be a commemorative, with something etched into the handle. She pointed to the papers on the table.

"This is all that was in the desk?" she asked.

Byrne nodded.

Freitag's personal papers were as tidy and minimal as everything else in his life — a checkbook, a neatly bound stack of electric and gas bills, a few paper-clipped coupons for nearby Chinese takeout and dry cleaners. As far as they knew, Robert Freitag had no computer, no cell phone, no pager. This was the extent of his interaction with the outside world. There were no personal letters, no birthday or Christmas cards.

Jessica flipped through the check register, found the expected: utilities, insurance, income tax, doctor's and dentist bills. She made note of the doctor and dentist names.

The only thing left to search were the books on the bookshelves.

They crossed the living room in silence. Byrne took the shelves to the left; Jessica, the right. The paperbacks on the shelves — mostly worn, secondhand copies — were popular novels: Stephen King, John

Grisham, Tom Clancy. Jessica flipped through them, one by one, found nothing.

"Jess," Byrne said. "Look at this."

Byrne had in his hands a yellow hardcover book. It was an old book club edition. The cover was ripped in a few places. It was titled *Dreams and Memory.*

"Never read it."

"Me neither," Byrne said. "Waiting for the movie."

"Anything inside?"

Byrne riffled the pages. "Nothing," he said. "But it is inscribed." He opened the book, turned to the title page. On the left-hand side was a brief inscription. It was written in blue ink, with a flourish.

Perchance to dream

"Just the inscription? No name signed?"

"No," Byrne said.

"Looks like a textbook," Jessica said. "Doesn't really fit with the other reading material in the house, does it?"

"No, it doesn't."

Byrne turned back to the title page, then flipped to the copyright page. The book was first published in 1976.

"I didn't see any inscriptions in any of the other books," Jessica said. "Did you?"

"No. This is the only one."

Byrne looked at the inscription for a few more moments, opened the book to the back. There, drawn in pencil on the last blank page, was a series of geometric shapes. One long rectangle, with a much smaller rectangle to the left, as well as a small square at the top of the page, drawn in perspective. He showed the page to Jessica. "Mean anything to you?"

Jessica looked at the drawings. "Not a clue."

Byrne glanced at the inscription once again, then put the book back on the shelf. They were done. They knew nothing more than they had when they walked into this house, or at least nothing that would point them to the person who had so brutally murdered Robert August Freitag.

"This guy was a ghost," Jessica said.

"Yeah, but why?" Byrne replied. "How?"

Jessica thought about it. She wondered how many people in her city, any city, live their lives like this. No ripples, no tracks. Before leaving the Roundhouse she'd done an online search on the man, and come up with nothing. In this day and age it was virtually impossible to leave no digital footprint whatsoever. But Robert Freitag had done it.

"If he was so ordinary, why did someone put a railroad spike through his head?" Byrne said.

For now, that remained the most important question.

As they prepared to leave, Byrne walked to the end of the living room. He glanced down the short hallway leading to the kitchen.

Like everything else in the house there was a thin layer of dust on the baseboards. In the center of the hallway the dust looked to be lighter in color. Almost white.

"You see that?" Byrne asked, pointing to the powder on the floor.

"Yeah," Jessica said. "It looks like it might have come from the light fixture."

Without a word, Jessica returned to the dining room, retrieved one of the chairs. She put it under the light fixture, climbed onto it. Steadying herself with one hand on the ceiling, she slipped a finger behind the plate and gently pulled downward. The frame opened easily. She unclipped both sides, handed the lens and plate to Byrne. She looked up.

"Um, partner?" Jessica asked. "I'm no expert, but shouldn't there be something up here with wires and sockets and light bulbs in it?"

"You would think."

There was no fixture recessed into the ceiling, just a rough cut hole in the drywall and a metal frame. Jessica positioned herself on the chair, felt around the opening. After a few moments she found something.

"There's a box."

For a moment Jessica thought about getting the crime scene unit out to handle the removal of whatever was in the ceiling, considering that, in this day and age, anything and everything was possible, including booby-trapped boxes in a dead man's ceiling. On the other hand, this was not technically a crime scene and, besides, Jessica had already reflexively grabbed the box before she could stop herself. She edged it toward the opening, bringing with it more than a little dust.

"Steady me," Jessica said.

Byrne put a hand on her back as Jessica got on her tiptoes. She removed the box—an old Nike shoebox with a large rubber band around the middle. She handed it to Byrne, then climbed off the chair, brushed herself down. They walked into the small dining area.

Byrne took out his cell phone and took a few pictures of the box. He then gently slid off the rubber band, opened it. As he did this, Jessica found that she was holding her breath.

Inside the box, on top, was a five-by-eight-inch white envelope. The envelope was sealed, with a signature across the flap. The very careful hand of the signature was Robert A. Freitag. Byrne removed the envelope, placed it on the table. Beneath the envelope was a layer of newspaper. Byrne removed the folded page of the newspaper, set it next to the box.

"Oh, *hello*," Jessica said. There, on the bottom of the box, were six rubber-banded stacks of cash, all with one-hundred-dollar bills on top.

Jessica looked at Byrne, back. It was a look they each knew well, one that said that something—although, at the moment, they had no idea what—had changed. Before touching the money, Byrne took photographs of everything *in situ*.

With his gloved hands he gently picked up the stacks of bills, thumbed through them. They were all one-hundred-dollar notes.

"The bills are old," Byrne said. "Non-sequential."

He carefully put the stacks back in the box.

When he was finished, Jessica picked up the envelope, held it up to the light. Inside she saw the silhouette of what appeared to be rectangular pieces of cardboard, perhaps three-by-five inches in size.

Jessica took out her knife, a four-inch serrated Gerber she was rarely without. She looked at Byrne. "Shall we?"

"We came to the fair," Byrne said. "Might as well ride the rides."

It was something they probably should have waited to do back at the Roundhouse but, having found this material, neither wanted to wait. Jessica flicked open the razor-sharp blade, slit the bottom of the envelope, carefully preserving the signature across the flap. She gently shook the contents onto the dining-room table.

As she had surmised, the rectangles inside the envelope were photographs. One by one, Byrne flipped them over.

They were old pictures, edges curled by time, the color all but leached to sepia. But it wasn't the age of the photographs that drew Jessica's interest, as well as her partner's, it was the content.

The photographs were of nude people.

One showed a woman, clearly in her fifties or sixties. She sat on the edge of a steel-frame cot, staring at something on the floor. On her small, sagging breasts was some sort of dark liquid. Another photo was of two men, also in their sixties, fondling each other against the backdrop of a painted cement wall. A third was of a couple on a bed, a man and a woman, with three nude men watching their sex act, each at some stage of tumescence. In that photograph, the men were only visible from the neck down. One photograph was a close-up of someone's face, very blurred, with an open door in the background.

There was nothing remotely erotic about the pictures. If anything, they were ugly and exploitative; candid snapshots of people who had either no idea they were being photographed or no interest in stopping the practice.

Byrne flipped the photographs over. There was nothing written on the backs—no dates, times, names. One was stained with something light brown, perhaps a partial coffee cup ring.

He stacked the photographs, took a paper evidence bag from his pocket, slid the photographs inside. He took out a second evidence bag, and put in it the envelope in which the pictures were contained. In this bag he also put one of Robert Freitag's voided checks for later comparison of signatures.

Jessica picked up the sheet of newspaper that had been between the envelope and the bands of cash. She unfolded it. It was from the *Philadelphia Inquirer,* the front page of the Metro section, dated two weeks before Robert Freitag had been found murdered.

She scanned the page. The articles were local to Philly—a city councilman in some kind of tax trouble, the announcement of condominiums in the Northeast, a pair of girls from Conshohocken were accepted into a prestigious piano competition, along with a handful of ads. None of the articles were circled, no words underlined, nothing had been clipped.

"You see anything there?" Byrne asked.

Jessica scanned both sides again, just for good measure. "Nothing."

"Well, these photographs look a lot older than a month. If Freitag was the one who put this page in here back in February, he didn't do it by accident. It wasn't used to wrap anything delicate. This meant something to him."

While it was obvious that Robert Freitag wanted to keep the contents of this box secret—if, indeed, it was Freitag who had placed the box in the ceiling—the question was: did these photographs, and the money, have anything to do with why the man had been murdered? Had he taken these pictures? Was he one of the men in the background? Was his murderer one of the people photographed? Or were these just a prurient, albeit grotesque, hobby?

Just as important, if not more so, was the money, which looked to be more than thirty thousand dollars. Had Freitag embezzled it? If so, why hadn't his murderer come here and torn the place apart looking for it? Had John Garcia cleaned the place up during his one and only visit?

These were questions neither detective had to ask aloud. They would collect the photographs, and cash, put it all into the chain of evidence, and have it processed.

Robert Freitag's secrets were now part of the record.

Sorry, Mrs. Edna Walsh of Forest Hills, New York, Jessica thought. *This part of your loving relative's estate will be tied up for a while longer. Maybe forever.*

As she buttoned her coat, and tried to brace herself for the icy rain, Jessica glanced around the small, forlorn house. Somehow, since the discovery of these ugly pictures, the atmosphere had morphed from one of loneliness into one of despair. She wanted a hot shower. She turned back to her partner.

"So, I can understand hiding the stash of cash, and I can understand not wanting to leave those pictures on the coffee table, but why that page from the *Inquirer*?"

"Good question, Counselor."

Jessica smiled. *Counselor.* She wondered if she would ever earn that title.

"And why those pictures?" Jessica asked. "There isn't anything remotely like them in the whole house. No *Playboy*, no *Penthouse*, no *Hustler*. Do they still publish *Hustler*?"

"I wouldn't know."

"Uh huh."

The photographs and the money now added a sense of direction to the case. Perhaps Robert Freitag was not just at the wrong place at the wrong time after all, an ordinary man who just happened, by the luck of the draw, to cross paths with a madman, someone who would pound a railroad spike into his skull. The elements of money and sex—as it were—had just entered the room.

Jessica once more pulled from the shelf the copy of *Dreams and Memory*. She opened it, looked at the inscription.

Perchance to dream

Before returning it to the shelf, Jessica glanced at the last page. "Kevin."

Byrne crossed the room. Jessica held up the book. "These drawings," she said. "These three shapes."

Byrne glanced at the book, then down the hallway in which they had found the hidden box in the ceiling. There could be no mistake. The hallway, the light switch to the left, and the square light fixture above.

"It's a drawing of the hallway and the fixture," Byrne said.

"Sure looks like it."

"It's as if he left a little treasure map for us," Byrne said. "He wanted us to find that box."

"My thoughts exactly, partner." Jessica took out a paper evidence bag, and slipped the book inside, adding one more piece of this ever-growing puzzle.

On the way out to the car Jessica noticed that the front door of the row house next door was open.

She got Byrne's attention, then knocked on the screen door. The woman who answered the door was in her late twenties, and had about her the harried look of someone trying to wrangle young children.

As Jessica introduced herself she heard screaming in the background, accompanied by the loud soundtrack of *Finding Nemo*. She told the woman she would be brief. She asked what the woman knew about Robert Freitag.

"I told the other detective that I saw him the night that he disappeared."

Jessica wanted to correct the woman on Robert Freitag's ultimate fate, but there was no need. "So, you saw him on February twentieth?"

"Was that when it was?"

"Yes."

"I only know this because Robert would usually get home the same time my husband gets home. The kids are always at the door waiting for Howard. They're watching the street, I'm watching them. That's how I know."

"So Mr. Freitag came home that day at the regular time?" Jessica asked.

The woman nodded. "Yeah. When Howard got home that night I asked him to run up to the store and get a few things. I met him on the porch and gave him a shopping list. I looked up and saw Robert walking down the street."

"Which direction was he coming from?"

"That way. Like always." She pointed toward Allegheny Avenue.

"Was he with anyone?"

"It's hard to remember clearly now, but I don't think so. I'm not sure I ever saw him with anyone."

"What about his hands?" Jessica asked. "Was he carrying anything?"

The woman shrugged. "Sorry. I just can't remember. I don't think so."

"Do you recall what he was wearing?"

"Not really. Probably something black or gray. He was a pretty drab guy." She brought a hand to her mouth. "I'm sorry. That wasn't very kind."

"It's okay," Jessica said. She made a few notes. "Did your husband know Mr. Freitag well?"

"No. He didn't care too much for the guy."

"How so?"

"Well, it's not that he didn't like him. He didn't really know him. It's just that he found him a little ... creepy."

"Creepy in what way?"

"He called him a Gloomy Gus."

"He called him 'Gus' because of Robert's middle name?" Jessica asked.

The woman blushed. Admitting this would mean that she probably had scanned the man's mail, and knew Freitag's middle name was August. "No," she said. "It's just an expression his parents used to use."

Jessica put her notepad away. "Okay," she said. "Again, we thank you for your time."

"Oh, you're welcome. I'm just glad that we're going to have new neighbors."

"Neighbors?" Jessica asked.

"Yes, new tenants are moving in next door."

"There are new tenants moving into Robert's house?"

"I'm pretty sure," she said. "Aren't there?"

"I don't know," Jessica said. "What makes you think someone is moving in next door?"

"Well, I heard someone in there. I heard talking."

Jessica glanced at Byrne, then back at the woman. "When did you hear this?"

The woman thought for a few moments. "A couple of days ago. Maybe a week. I just remember thinking to myself that it was a good thing, you know? That the place would be occupied. Less likely for it to be broken into, things like that."

"You heard talking coming from this house?" Jessica asked, pointing to Robert's house. "You're certain it was coming from here?"

"Well, I was until now." She gestured to the row house on the other side. "I know that Kate and Jennie—they're the two girls who live on the other side—are not home during the day, so it couldn't have come from there. So, yeah, I'm sure."

Jessica made the mental note. "Could you tell if it was the radio or television, or maybe a CD?"

The woman shrugged. "No. Sorry."

"Not a problem," Jessica said. She handed the woman a card. "If you think of anything else, please give us a call."

"Sure thing."

Jessica and Byrne walked down to the avenue, around the corner, then down the alleyway behind the houses. When they got to Freitag's house Jessica looked closely at the seal over the back door. It was intact. She took the seal out of her pocket, the one she had cut off the front door when they arrived, and held it up next to the sticker on the back door. She compared signatures. They were identical.

There were bars over the windows, and seals on the only two doors.

"So how did she hear anything coming from this place?" Jessica asked as they walked back to the car.

"Good question," Byrne said. "On the other hand, it's a wonder she hears anything at all with that brood."

As they reached the corner the rain picked up again. Jessica was frozen to the bone.

"Let's get this stuff to the ID Unit, and then over to documents," she said. "Then we'll go talk to Freitag's former co-workers at CycleLife."

While Byrne bundled the material into the trunk of the Taurus, Jessica closed the front door to Robert Freitag's home, turned the key in the lock. She peeled a fresh sticker, smoothed it in place, signed it.

She stood on the front steps for a few moments, looking both ways down the street, at the dozens of row houses, the scores of lives. She wondered what secrets were hidden in these houses, how many of them dreams, how many of them nightmares.

8

Sixteen years earlier

I heard something," Bean whispered. "I know it."

"No you didn't."

"I did *so*, Tuff." Bean threw off her covers, sat on the edge of her bed. "I did hear something. In my *ears*."

Tuff flipped on the nightstand lamp. Part of her lot in life was taking care of her little sister when she got scared, which seemed to be all the time these days. She glanced at the clock. It was after midnight. If Mom saw the light under their door they were *so* dead. "What did you hear?"

Bean shrugged.

"Okay, then. Where did it come from? Under the bed?"

Bean shook her head.

"Outside?"

"No."

Resigned, Tuff sat up, fluffed a pillow behind her. "Then where?"

Bean pointed one small finger in the direction of the closet.

Tuff looked at the closet, back. This was their routine, and had been almost every night since Bean turned four, nearly six months earlier. That's when the fear began. That was when their father had died in an accident at his work. That's when their mother started hiding the brown bottles in the house.

"There's no one in there, Bean."

Bean nodded feverishly, meaning: *Oh yes there is, there most certainly* is *someone in there.*

Tuff got up, put on her slippers, padded over to the window, made a dramatic effort to lift it. "See? The window is closed and locked. Locked up *really* tight. Want to try?"

Bean shook her head. Tuff again tried to lift the sash. As expected, it didn't budge. She tapped twice on the intact glass. "We're on the second floor. How would anyone get in here?"

Bean shrugged.

Tuff crossed the room, sat on the edge of her bed. She looked into her sister's clear blue eyes. Their life before their father died suddenly seemed like a million years ago.

"You know I wouldn't let anything happen to you, don't you?"

Bean looked away, at the closet, shrugged again. Tuff put a hand under her sister's chin, gently turned her head back. "Don't you?"

This time Bean nodded. "I know."

"Good."

Tuff pulled back the covers. Bean got into bed. Tuff then bunched the sheets under her sister's chin. She picked up Bean's three favorite bears and aligned them against the wall, a little stuffed army to protect against all invaders: foreign, domestic and imaginary.

"We've got to get to sleep," Tuff said. "Mom's gonna brain us." She picked up a book from the nightstand. It was *Goodnight, Moon* by Margaret Wise Brown, one of Bean's favorites. "Want a story first?"

Bean shook her head. Tuff put the book back on the nightstand. She knew what she had to do. If she didn't, this would go on all night.

"You want me to check the closet?" she asked.

Bean nodded.

Tuff smiled. "You are the biggest scaredy-cat in the world, you know that?"

Bean curled her fingers. "Yes."

Tuff brushed her sister's fine blond hair from her forehead, gave her a kiss on the cheek, stood up and crossed the room.

"Ready?"

Bean covered her eyes. "No."

"Gonna do it anyway."

With a dramatic flourish Tuff opened the door to the closet, just to show her little sister that the only things inside were their clothes and their toys. Just like always.

But this time it wasn't true.

This time there *was* a man inside the closet.

A tall man in ragged clothes.

9

On the way to the crime lab Jessica and Byrne stopped first at the Roundhouse to have the photographs they'd found in Robert Freitag's attic processed for fingerprints. They also signed the cash into evidence, and locked it down.

The Forensic Lab was a state-of-the-art, heavily fortified building at 8th and Poplar streets. In the basement was the Firearms Identification Unit; on the first floor was the Crime Scene Unit, Document Examination Unit, the Chem lab—mostly used for the identification of drugs — as well as Criminalistics, which handled the processing of hair and fiber. The first floor was also home to the DNA lab.

Firearms, Documents and CSU personnel were all sworn law enforcement officers. Everyone else was a civilian.

Of all the section directors, no one was more flamboyant, or dedicated, than Sergeant Helmut Rohmer. Standing around six-five, he had recently shaved his head, and presented himself as a soft-spoken, lab-dwelling version of Shrek. He was also known for his black T-shirt collection, a wardrobe accessory rumored to be in the hundreds. Today he wore a shirt with the slogan: PART OF THE PROBLEM.

He insisted you called him Hell.

When Jessica and Byrne walked into the room, Hell Rohmer had on large, over-the-ear headphones, eyes closed, feet up on his desk.

Jessica stepped closer, gently tapped Hell on the foot.

The big man nearly levitated.

Red-faced, Hell Rohmer scrambled to his feet, knocking over his chair. He turned off his MP3 player, took off his headphones, put them away.

"Uh, hey, detectives. I didn't see you come in." He righted his chair.

"Didn't mean to scare you," Jessica said. This wasn't entirely true. "How is Doni?"

Donatella Rohmer was Hell's daughter from his first marriage. If Jessica recalled correctly, she was about twelve or thirteen now.

Composing himself, Hell straightened a few things on the desk. "Well, Doni thinks I'm a dinosaur. Everything her father says and does is totally stupid. Do they ever get over that?"

Jessica had no idea. She certainly hoped so. Her daughter, Sophie, was just entering that phase. Hell looked to Byrne for an answer.

"They do," Byrne said. "Colleen used to feel that way about me. Now she thinks I'm the coolest. She bought me an iPhone 5 for my birthday."

"Sweet."

"Now if I could just learn how to use it."

"Can't help you there," Hell said. "I use Windows at work, of course, but at home I'm a Penguin."

Jessica and Byrne just stared.

"That's what they call Linux users. Penguins."

Getting no further reaction, Hell leaned back against the examining table. "So, to what do I owe the pleasure?"

Byrne took out the paper evidence bag containing the photographs. He opened the flap, shook the pictures onto the examining table.

Hell glanced at the photograph on top, the picture of the nude older woman on the rusted cot. "I see," he said. "At least you *have* a social life."

One by one Hell turned over the photographs, each one more disturbing than the previous. When he got to the last picture—the one with the couple on the bed, being watched by the trio of men—Jessica heard him draw a quick breath. "Wow."

"My thoughts exactly," Byrne said.

Hell looked up at the two detectives. "What's the job?"

Jessica gave Hell a brief rundown on the Robert Freitag homicide.

"A railroad spike?" Hell asked. "Really?"

"Yeah," Jessica said. "Rusty, no less."

Hell took a moment to absorb this. He pointed at the photographs. "And where did you find these?"

"In the victim's house," Jessica said. "They were in a shoebox, hidden in the ceiling."

"Was it humid up there?"

"Not particularly. It seemed pretty dry."

"Were they inside anything?" Hell asked. "By that I mean, were they in a plastic bag, or wrapped in newspaper?"

"They were in a plain white envelope," Jessica said. "It was sealed."

"Did you bring it?"

"We did."

Hell picked up one of the photographs. "I take it these have been processed."

"Yes," Jessica said.

"Who did them?"

"Tommy D."

Hell Rohmer nodded with something close to reverence. "He's good."

It was true. Tom DeMarco was the best print man in the PPD.

"He said he'd red line them for us," Jessica added. A red line was a rush job. Jessica said this to give Hell a sense of urgency on the job, even though she had no idea if this material — these strange and grotesque pictures — was evidentiary or not.

Hell smiled. "By *us* you mean *you,* right?"

"What can I say? Tommy likes me."

"Jezebel."

Hell angled the overhead light, studied the specimens before him. He put his hands on his hips, his standard posture when standing at the precipice of a new puzzle.

"What can you tell us off the top?" Jessica asked.

"Well, they're Polaroids, of course," Hell said.

Holding the pictures by the edges, Hell spread out the photographs on the table. He rearranged them twice, perhaps looking for the order in which they were taken. In the harsh light of the document room the images were even uglier than before.

"I'd say they were mid-seventies vintage," Hell said. "Maybe a little later. The film is certainly pre-SX70."

"What do you mean?" Jessica asked. "What's SX70?"

Hell looked slapped. "Don't you remember those great Polaroid commercials for the SX70? *The age of miracles . . . a pocket-size, folding, electronically controlled, motor-driven, single-lens reflex camera that quite simply does the impossible.*"

Jessica did not respond.

"Uh, Laurence Olivier?" Hell added.

Laurence Olivier did commercials? Jessica thought. "Oh yeah," she lied. "I remember."

Hell shook his head, put on a pair of linen gloves. He held one of the photographs up to the light, one with an edge peeling away from the backing. "See this right here? These photos are mounted. Back in those days you bought the pack of film, and in the box were eight or ten of these self-adhesive boards for mounting. Before that, instant film had a curling problem."

Hell brought the photograph to his nose, sniffed it. Neither Jessica nor Byrne said a word. Hell put the picture back on the table.

"My father used to have a couple of Polaroid cameras back in the day," Hell said. "His favorite, the one we always took to Cape May, was one of the old 250s, the kind with the projected frame lines and automatic parallax compensation. Great camera. Wish I still had it."

Hell zoned for a moment. He did this from time to time, adrift on some techno reverie. You had to wait him out.

"Hell," Jessica finally said.

"Instant *film,* man. Think of everything that changed because of it. Dr. Land was a genius."

Jessica glanced at the dreadful photographs on the table. She wasn't so sure that Dr. Land had this in mind. "He was awesome," she said. "And this exact film?"

"Right," Hell said, returning to the moment. "This looks like the 108 series. Low ASA. I think it was about seventy-five in those days. This guy didn't use a flash, see. That's why they're kind of dark."

"Any chance of finding out where it was purchased?" Jessica asked.

"The 108 film?"

"Yeah."

"It was only the most popular Polaroid film *ever.* I think they produced it for forty years or so. So, the long answer to your question is no. It was sold all over the world. They switched over to PolaColor for the SX70, but the 108 was still widely available."

"Is there any way to tell when the photographs were taken?"

Hell smiled. "There's *always* a way. But that would take some time and testing. I *can* tell you that this film isn't available anymore, at least not in stores. They stopped selling it around 2003. But that doesn't mean that someone didn't keep the camera, and store some film."

"It would still be usable?" Jessica asked. "The film, I mean."

"Sure, as long as it wasn't exposed to extreme temperatures or light."

Hell turned the photos over, angled the swing arm lamp. "But on first blush I would have to say these pictures are at least ten years old. The yellowing on the backing tells me these were taken and—if you'll excuse the expression—mounted a long time ago."

Hell once more turned the photos over, faceup. "It looks like we have some serious fingerprints on these. Best surface on earth for processing."

It was true. Glossy, nonporous surfaces were the latent expert's dream but, in Jessica's time on the job, she'd seen prints lifted and processed from any number of unlikely surfaces—cigarettes, orange peels, rocks, even bedsheets. Unfortunately, determining the age of a fingerprint was not as exact a science.

"I can hang on to these, right?" Hell asked.

"Sure," Byrne said.

"I might be able to narrow down the year this release of film hit the market. That should get us closer to when they were taken."

Byrne reached forward, picked up one of the pictures, the one with the blurred face in the foreground, and the lighted doorway behind. He slipped a tissue out of the box on the counter, wiped the photograph clean of the fingerprint powder. "I'll sign this one out."

Byrne was referring to the chain of evidence logs. They had no idea if any of this even *was* evidence, but it never hurt to go by the book. Jessica wondered if and when a moment such as this would ever play out for her in a courtroom.

Signing out was a euphemism that went back to the earliest days of law enforcement in Philadelphia. These days, everything got a barcode.

Byrne put the photo into a paper evidence bag; Hell coded it. For the most part, the PPD, as well as departments across the country, used paper for their evidence storage and transport, especially when dealing with fluid evidence, due to the possibility of mold. Once evidence had been tested, it went into plastic, to prevent cross-contamination.

Byrne reached into his briefcase, took out a second evidence bag, handed it to Hell.

"This was the envelope that contained the photographs," he said.

Hell removed the contents of the bag, studied it for a moment. "So, someone signed along the flap in case someone else opened it."

"That's what we figured."

"And that's why you opened it at the bottom," Hell said. "You guys are super sleuths."

"All in a day," Byrne said. "There's an exemplar of our victim's signature on a voided check in there. They look the same to me, but we wanted you to take a look at it."

"You got it. You know I love handwriting."

A good portion of what document examiners did involved handwriting. Nobody was better at it than Hell Rohmer.

"I've got a few things in the pipeline for this afternoon, but I'll get on this right after."

"Thanks, Hell."

Jessica turned at the door to the lab, glanced back.

The big man was standing over a pile of old photographs, an entire world of scientific possibilities now open to him.

10

CycleLife LLC was located in the back of a redbrick, two-suite professional building on an industrial parkway in the southeast section of the city.

On the way, Jessica did a search on her iPhone, and found the company's website. According to the site, CycleLife was a provider of reclining lift chairs, walkers, grab bars, shower chairs, bath lifts, scooters, ramps and other healthcare products. While the company's headquarters were in Philadelphia, there were catalog stores in Allentown and York.

When they pulled into the parking lot there were only two vehicles: a white delivery van and a red Kia Rio. The van had the CycleLife logo on the door.

On the way to the building they met a woman coming out. She was in her early forties, and wore a smart navy blue suit, white blouse. She also appeared to be in a hurry.

Byrne took out his ID wallet, opened it, introduced himself, then Jessica.

The woman nodded at both of them, but she couldn't shake hands because her hands were full with binders, catalogs, a pair of telephone directories, as well as a pair of tote bags, each bulging with papers.

"Your name, ma'am?"

"Oh, I'm sorry," she said. "I'm Karen Jacobs."

Byrne gestured to the nameplate next to the door. "Do you work for CycleLife?"

"Yes," she said. "I'm the national accounts manager."

"We'd like to ask you a few questions, if you have a moment."

It was clear that the woman did *not* have a moment — rush hour was in full thrum, and there was a good chance this woman needed to get home, make dinner, corral the children, etc. Jessica could relate. But Kevin Byrne had a way of posing this particular question, especially to women, that broke down the barrier.

When Jessica saw the woman's shoulders relax, she knew Karen Jacobs was resigned.

"Is this about Robert?" she asked

"Which Robert would that be?" Byrne asked.

"Freitag," the woman said. "Robert Freitag. That's why you're here, isn't it?"

"It is."

"We don't get too many visits from the police."

Byrne smiled. "That's probably a good thing."

"No offense."

Byrne just nodded.

"Did you catch the person who did it?" she asked.

Jessica noticed that the woman used *person,* not *man.* Most people said *the man* or *the guy* who did it.

"Not yet," Byrne said. "We're working on it."

The woman looked a bit longingly at her car, then back at the two detectives. "Well, we might as well go inside." She turned to the door. "If that's okay."

"That will be fine," Byrne said.

The woman tried to balance the books and folders in her hands, attempting to get to the right key on the ring.

"Let me take those for you," Byrne said.

The woman hesitated, as if she might be carrying highly sensitive material, then handed it all over to Byrne. "Thanks."

A few moments later she unlocked the double glass door, stepped inside. As they entered, Jessica noticed Byrne watching the woman. Karen Jacobs, as harried as she was at that moment, as end of the day disheveled, was not an unattractive woman.

When she disappeared into a small alcove off the reception area, and punched a few numbers into the alarm system's key pad, Jessica nudged her partner, whispered: "You never carry *my* books."

They sat in the small, fluorescent-lit waiting area. Two sofas facing each other, one chair, a pair of glass-topped end tables, along with a coffee table arrayed with industry trade magazines: *Sports 'N Spokes, AAH, New Mobility.*

"I talked to the other detective right after...after it happened," Jacobs said. "I told him everything I knew."

"That would be Detective Garcia," Byrne said.

"Yes. I still have his card. Doesn't he work for the police anymore?"

"No, ma'am," Byrne said. "Detective Garcia passed away."

Jessica watched the woman closely when Byrne said this. Karen Jacobs was by no means a suspect in the murder of Robert Freitag, but the way people took news of a person's death said quite a bit about them.

On hearing the information the woman's face lost a little color. "I'm so sorry. I didn't know."

"Of course," Byrne said. "He was a good man, and a good detective. And now Detective Balzano and I have taken over the investigation."

Karen Jacobs just nodded. She snuck a glance at the wall clock.

"How long did Mr. Freitag work here?" Byrne asked.

The woman thought for a few moments. "Just over five years, I think. I can get his work records if you like."

"That would be very helpful," Byrne said. "We'll get them before we leave."

"I'm afraid they're not here."

Byrne looked up from his notepad. "You don't have them here?"

"No. They're kept off site. I can have them faxed to you in an hour or so if you give me your fax number."

Byrne handed her a card. "Do you recall where Mr. Freitag worked before coming here?"

"I'm pretty sure he worked as an accounts manager at Aetna for a while, but I couldn't confirm that unless I looked it up."

"How many people are employed here now?"

"There are just six of us. We really need at least two more people, but the economy being the way it is…"

"Has Mr. Freitag's position been filled?"

"Oh my, yes. Even a company this size needs a logistics manager."

Byrne made a few notes. "How well did you know Robert?"

Jessica was waiting for *Mr. Freitag* to become *Robert*. Right on schedule.

"Not very well at all, really, considering how often I saw him. He was pretty much a loner."

"How so?"

The woman gestured to the walls around them. "As you can see, we're not a big company. At least in the brick and mortar sense. Most of our sales are online and catalog sales. We maintain a warehouse in Newark and ship worldwide from there."

Byrne nodded, waited.

"What I'm getting at is that we work in pretty close quarters, and there tend not to be a lot of secrets. We know who is dragging because of a late night, who has a lousy diet, who is sick, who's in love."

"And you're saying that Robert didn't make friends here?"

"Let me put it this way, one year—I think this was the second year Robert worked for us—we bought him one of those oversized birthday cards, the kind with the pop-up characters in the middle. The only reason we knew it was his birthday was because it was on his application. He would never tell anyone something that personal." Karen Jacobs rearranged herself on the chair, crossed her legs, continued her story. "Anyway, we gave the card to him at lunch that day and, in Robert's inimitable style, he reddened a bit, mumbled a thanks, gathered together his uneaten sandwich and left the break room in a hurry."

Both Jessica and Byrne sensed there was more to the story. They remained silent.

"The next day Alonzo—that's Alonzo Mayweather, our IT guy—was dumping some shredded documents into the big recycling bin out back, when he saw some material in the bin, some red shredded cardboard. He moved some of the paper aside and saw that the big birthday card had been shredded. Not only had Robert shredded the card, but he then tried to put it on the bottom of the bin so no one would see it. Weird, huh?"

A bit antisocial, Jessica thought, certainly ungracious, but not particularly weird. And she knew weird.

"Why didn't he just take it home and throw it out when he got there?" Karen Jacobs added.

It was a rhetorical question, but Byrne responded to it anyway. "I'm afraid I can't answer that, ma'am."

"Well, needless to say, we never bought him another card, never acknowledged his birthdays in any way."

This partially explained the dearth of cards at Robert Freitag's house. If he got them, it seemed, he didn't even bring them inside.

Byrne continued the standard line of questioning, taking sparse notes. There wasn't much to write.

"Can you think of anyone who might have had a problem with Robert?" Byrne asked. "Someone he owed money, or someone who owed him money?"

She thought a moment. "No. I don't think he ever gambled, and I'm sure he was never involved in drugs or anything like that."

You can never be sure about drugs, Jessica thought, but decided to take this woman's word for it.

"What about personal relationships? Girlfriends, a jealous boyfriend?"

At the word boyfriend, the woman smiled. "Robert wasn't gay, if that's what you mean."

Jessica was pretty sure Byrne meant Robert Freitag may have been dating a woman who had a jealous boyfriend. Byrne let it ride.

"Is there anyone here, other than yourself, who might have had a closer relationship with Mr. Freitag?" he asked.

She took a moment. "Not really. He was impossible to get to know."

Byrne made another note. "Was there ever any money missing from your business accounts? Any unauthorized withdrawals?"

It seemed as if this question came as a bit of a shock. "You mean CycleLife accounts?"

"Yes."

"Are you saying Robert took money from the company?"

"I'm not saying that at all," Byrne said. "We just have to explore every possibility."

Karen Jacobs shrugged. "Not that I know of. Again, we're a small company. If something like that happened I would know about it."

"Did Robert have access to the accounts?"

"No. Only the owner, Mr. Larson, has access. He signs every check." At this she pointed to a photograph on the wall, a picture of a white-haired man shaking hands with a woman in a wheelchair.

Byrne glanced at Jessica, who shook her head. She had no questions. They both stood; the woman followed suit, straightened her skirt.

"We thank you for your time," Byrne said.

"You are most welcome." The woman glanced at her watch. She

had all but missed rush hour. "I'll probably get home about the same time."

"We don't want to keep you any longer," Byrne said. "Can we get that list of employees now?"

"Of course." She crossed over to the reception desk, hit a few keys on the computer keyboard. Seconds later the laser printer came to life. Karen Jacobs grabbed the sheet, handed it to Byrne.

"Thanks," Byrne said. "You'll have that other information faxed to us? Mr. Freitag's application and resume?"

The woman held up her cell phone. "I'll call them straightaway."

"I just have one other question," Byrne said.

"Sure."

"When you met with Detective Garcia, did he ask a lot of the same questions I asked you?"

She thought about it. "Not really. To be quite honest, I didn't really understand some of the things he was talking about."

"Can you give us an example?"

"Well, he asked me about Robert's last day of work, and whether or not he seemed troubled or agitated that day. When I told him nothing seemed out of the ordinary, he just stared at me for the longest time."

"Then what happened?"

"Nothing for a little while. Then he asked if I would turn the music up."

"The music?"

"Yes. The odd thing was, there wasn't any music playing. We sometimes play easy listening through the intercom speakers, but we didn't have it on that day."

Byrne glanced at Jessica, back at Karen Jacobs. He buttoned his coat, put his notebook in his pocket.

"Can you think of anything else about Robert?" he asked at the door.

She thought for a few moments. "Not really. Like I said, Robert was pretty much a closed book. You might be able to find something in the stuff we took out of his desk, if you'd like to take a look at it."

Jessica looked at Byrne, then back at Karen Jacobs. "You still have the contents of his desk?"

"Yes," she said. "It's all in a box in our storeroom. We figured someone in his family would come for it. No one ever did. There isn't much."

"Did you show Detective Garcia Robert's desk when he was here?" Jessica asked.

"No."

"And why is that?"

"Well, two reasons, to be perfectly honest, Detective. One, it was a bit of a shock having just learned that Robert had been murdered. That was a first for me, and I hope it's a last."

"Of course," Jessica said. "And the second reason?"

Karen Jacobs shrugged. "Detective Garcia never asked."

They stood in the parking lot of the industrial park. The rain had let up for the moment, but the occasional drop signaled a return. The white, legal-document-size cardboard box was on the hood of the car.

"Makes you wonder what else John didn't ask," Jessica said.

"Yes, it does."

Jessica opened the box, looked inside. The woman was right. There wasn't much in there—a stapler, a tape dispenser, a pair of local Philadelphia yellow page directories, along with a white pages directory. There was also a flip-over desk calendar. Jessica took the calendar out of the box and put it on the hood of the car. She began to page through the days.

"Are there any entries around February twentieth?" Byrne asked.

Jessica checked. The page for February 20, the day Robert Freitag was murdered, was gone. As were the pages for the previous six days. The nearest calendar page was for February 13. Jessica took out her Maglite, angled the beam on that page. There were indentations on the page, as if something had been written on the page above it.

"Can you read what's there?" Byrne asked.

"Hard to tell."

"Wish we had a pencil."

"I think we do," Jessica said. She rummaged in the white box, soon produced an unsharpened pencil, as well as a desktop pencil sharpener. The manual kind, not the electric kind.

"Thank God our friend Robert was old-school," Byrne said.

While Byrne held the sharpener, Jessica put a tip on the pencil, blew on it. She then gently rubbed the graphite over the serrations on the calendar page. Just like in the old movies, an image began to appear. When she was done she aimed her Maglite on the page.

"Looks like JCD 10K 8P." Jessica handed the calendar to Byrne. "What do you think?"

Byrne scanned the entry. "Well, Robert didn't really look like a runner to me, so I'm thinking this 10K doesn't refer to a race."

"Not too many races start at eight p.m., either."

"Good point."

"JCD," Jessica said. "Any bells?"

"Not yet," Byrne said. "Check the list of CycleLife employees. See if any of the initials sync."

Jessica took out the list, scanned it. "Nothing. There's a Judith, but her last name is Blaylock." She looked back at the calendar page.

"Let's assume, for the moment, he wrote this on February fourteenth," Byrne said.

"Six days before his murder," Jessica said.

"So, Freitag goes to meet with this JCD, gets the money, words are exchanged, confidences are betrayed, and six days later he's killed."

"Okay, but why wasn't his place tossed?" Jessica asked.

Byrne thought for a few moments. "Spitballing here. Let's assume further, for the moment, that the killer wanted to make a point."

"Yeah," Jessica said. "But to whom?"

Byrne raised an eyebrow. "To *whom?* You sound like a lawyer."

"Get used to it."

"Of course, this would mean Freitag was connected to some criminal enterprise, or at least some very dangerous skullduggery."

"He doesn't strike me as a guy who was mobbed up."

Byrne picked up the pencil, rubbed a little more graphite on the page, gently blew it off. They saw nothing they hadn't seen the first time.

"How come this always works perfectly in the movies?" Jessica asked.

"Everything works perfectly in the movies. If it doesn't, they just reshoot it."

"Cary Grant had no problems doing this in *North by Northwest*."

"I guess I'm no Cary Grant."

"Sure you are." Jessica took the pad from Byrne. Even with her Maglite, it was impossible to tell whether it was 10K or 10E. Now she was starting to doubt the JCD initials. She put the calendar back in the box. "I'm sure Hell will have an idea or two about this."

Byrne glanced at his watch. "He's gone for the day."

Jessica knew what Byrne meant. Seeing as how this was a cold case, there could only be so many demands made on forensic personnel, especially as it related to overtime.

Jessica tapped the printout they'd gotten from Karen Jacobs. "Let's run these names."

11

Detective Joshua Bontrager was a veteran of nearly seven years in the PPD Homicide Unit. Before that, he had worked in the Traffic Unit. He had been called up to Homicide to work on a case that took investigators into his home county of Berks, a case that called upon Josh's unique qualifications, credentials no other homicide detective in Philadelphia—or for that matter most of the world—could provide. Josh Bontrager had grown up in an Amish family.

And while he had left the church before entering the academy, in the time Jessica had known him he had transformed from a country boy into a streetwise detective, capable of holding his own with the hard realities of investigating homicides in a city like Philadelphia.

There was, however, one vestige of his former life that was hard for anyone in the squad to believe. In his entire time in the homicide unit, no one had ever heard Josh Bontrager swear. Not once. He'd come close a few times, switching over to *darn* or *heck* or *shoot* at the last second.

And if there was a record made to be broken, this was the one. A universal trait for law enforcement worldwide was the ability to curse creatively and at prodigious length. There had been a pool ongoing for years about when Josh Bontrager would utter his first *fuck*.

If you heard Josh Bontrager come close to swearing, but not pull the trigger, you had to add a dollar to the pot. The pool was over six hundred dollars, with no limit in sight. If you were in the room, and closest to the pot when it happened, you got the money, which would certainly be donated to your favorite charity, which, by default, was the Police Athletic League.

As Jessica and Byrne walked into the duty room they saw Josh Bontrager poring over a binder, lost in thought.

"Joshua Bontrager!" Jessica said.

Bontrager jumped a foot. "What?"

"Are you growing a beard?"

Josh Bontrager was very fair, and his beard was sandy, almost blond. He turned a scarlet red. "It's not a beard, it's, you know, a goatee."

"Same thing, isn't it?"

Bontrager reflexively stroked his chin. "Well, not really. Amish men grow beards."

"I thought you were Amish."

"Not technically. Not anymore."

Jessica gave him a few angles. "It looks really good. Really sexy."

Another blush. With Josh Bontrager it was like flipping a light switch. On. Off. There was no setting for medium. "Thanks."

Jessica let him off the hook. She pointed to the binder on the desk. "What do you have?" she asked.

"Got a victim down on North Marston, first floor of an abandoned building," Bontrager said. He pulled a few crime scene photographs out of the envelope. "The victim was stabbed in the eyes."

"The ME said that's the cause of death?"

Bontrager nodded. "He believes it was some kind of very long knife that was pushed into the guy's eyes so deeply it went right into the victim's brain."

"Lovely," Jessica said.

"He's thinking an eight-inch blade, but thin."

Jessica looked at the photographs. They were horrifying. The victim was a white or Hispanic male, perhaps in his late teens. He was slumped against a graffiti-covered wall, near the door. There were thick washes of blood down his face onto what had been, at one time, a light-colored shirt.

What had once been his eyes were now purplish-black holes.

"Any ID on the victim?" Byrne asked.

"Not yet. There are a lot of cars parked on the street. We're running them now."

"Are you thinking he was a gangbanger?"

Bontrager shook his head. "It doesn't look like it. No gang tats."

"Any witnesses?" Byrne asked.

Bontrager slipped the crime scene photos back into the binder. "Mass amnesia. Like always."

"Did you canvass already?"

"Yeah. Neighborhood interviews are done. The first round, anyway."

"If you need any warm bodies," Byrne added.

"Thanks."

Conducting neighborhood interviews were always, at the very least, a two-stage process. In a city like Philadelphia, or any large city populated by people working all three shifts, it was in a detective's best interest to revisit the scene, staggering the time window by four, eight and twelve hours. At least half the doors you knocked on at any given time went unanswered, but might be answered later in the day. More than one case had broken wide open with a re-canvass.

"Flying solo on this?" Byrne asked.

Bontrager shook his head. "Working with Maria."

Maria Caruso was a very attractive younger detective. Everyone knew that Josh had a crush on her—more accurately, he was boots over buckles in love—but no one knew if the two were seeing each other. While it wasn't prohibited by the brass, it was better to keep such things a secret. You never knew what might compromise a trial if and when it came to that.

Bontrager glanced at his watch. "Gotta hit the street," he said. "We need to get this guy identified before the whole darn case starts getting cold."

Jessica glanced at Byrne. *Darn*. When Josh left the duty room they each took out a dollar, opened the file cabinet drawer, and put them in the kitty.

The fact that Josh Bontrager had picked up a fresh homicide meant that Byrne was next up on the wheel, the ever-turning mandala that brought detectives back up to the top of the order, regardless of whether or not they had closed their other cases. As a veteran, Byrne did not have to physically man the desk in the duty room, but he would be on call until the next case came in. And the next case always came in. History proved that forty-eight hours without a suspicious death in Philadelphia County had not passed in more than three decades.

At seven o'clock Jessica ran the names of the employees of CycleLife. Of the six employees who worked at the company during Robert Freitag's tenure as logistics manager — whatever *that* was, Jessica made a mental note to look it up — not one of them had a record on NCIC, the National Crime Information Center, or the Philadelphia equivalent, PCIC. One man, Alonzo Mayweather, the man who found Freitag's birthday card shredded in the recycling bin, seemed to have a problem keeping his car under fifty-five. He'd gotten eleven moving violations in the past six years, and had his license suspended for six months, since reinstated.

That was it. No killers, no boogeymen. At least none in the employ of CycleLife LLC. Or, if there was a killer in their midst, they'd managed to never commit even a misdemeanor offense. Considering the vitriol with which Robert Freitag met his demise, that was unlikely.

Jessica then did a search, looking for different uses for railroad spikes. She learned that some people used spikes to literally and figuratively "tie down" their property—guarding against foreclosure, eviction or even harassment—by pounding a spike in all four corners of their property. She also discovered that there was some ancestral significance to the use of iron, traced to a Congolese religion in which the spirit of a violent warrior was embodied in iron.

Jessica wrote. *iron + ritual?* in her notes.

The other search she did was for the flower that was found in Robert Freitag's hands. Because they did not have the flower itself to work with, finding a match from a database of flowers indigenous to this part of the world proved to be more than daunting. Jessica made a note to take the printout of the freeze-frame to local florists. If that didn't pan out, she would search for someone at one of Philadelphia's myriad colleges and universities.

She was just about to run Google searches on the employees of CycleLife, hoping to pick up something not contained in their less than larcenous noncriminal histories, when she saw Byrne crossing the duty room, documents in hand.

She gave him a brief rundown on what she had found in her NCIC search, as well as the data on the railroad spike.

"Do you think this might be a ritual killing?"

Jessica shrugged. "Right now it's as good a theory as any." She pointed to the documents. "What do you have?"

"Talked to a guy at Amtrak," he said. "He says a lot of the time, although it's not company policy, the people who work on the tracks just toss the old spikes on the side of the track when they replace them with new ones."

"They don't bring them in for scrap?"

"They've started doing that in the last few years, but he said a spike as old and rusty as our murder weapon could have come from anywhere. No identifying characteristics."

"Shit," Jessica said.

"Plus one. What about the flower?"

"Nothing yet." She held up the color printout of the flower, a four-X enlargement of the image taken from the videotape. "Recognize it?"

Byrne scanned the photo. "Not a clue," he said. "Did you run it by Dana?"

Dana Westbrook was the in-house expert on things horticultural. Her office was a virtual conservatory of healthy plants. "Yeah," Jessica said. "She said it didn't look familiar. She's bringing in a half-dozen books tomorrow."

"By the way, I ran into Tommy D on the way up," Byrne said. "I've got good news and weird news."

"Can you tell me them both at once?"

"What's the fun in that?"

"You're right," Jessica said. "You pick."

"Okay." Byrne held up a sheet. "We've got hits on the fingerprints that were on those photographs."

"But we're not happy."

"Not yet," Byrne said. "There were four good matches. All six-pointers. All four hits were men with criminal records."

"By criminal I take it you don't mean serial jaywalking."

Byrne glanced at the sheet. "No. We've got two ag assaults, one attempt to lure, two armed robberies, assorted and sundry burglaries."

Now her partner had her undivided attention. "So, we're talking jailhouse porn, right?"

"Probably."

They had a number of photographs bearing fingerprints of men with criminal records. There was a good chance that the pictures were passed around a county jail or state prison.

"So, why were they in Robert Freitag's attic?" Jessica asked.

"You mean *our* Robert Freitag, a man who did not even have a speeding ticket in his life, as far as we know. Robert Freitag who never spent so much as a single night in a drunk tank?"

"Himself."

"I don't know," Byrne said. "Yet."

Jessica tried to make the connection. Nothing jumped. She looked back at her partner. "There's more, isn't there?"

"Oh yeah."

"All right," Jessica said. "I'm sitting."

"These men? The ones who handled the photographs?"

"What about them?"

Byrne put the files on the desk, one by one, and said: "They're all dead."

12

Sixteen years earlier

How many nights had the man come to visit? It was all a blur. Tuff could not remember. He was younger than she'd originally thought. Maybe just an older teenager. At first she'd thought him to be as old as their father—their *late* father he was called, although neither Bean nor Tuff knew what that meant, he wasn't *late,* he was *gone*—who had died at the age of thirty-four.

But Tuff recalled with clarity the first night the man had visited. On that first night, after she opened the closet door, she was so scared she could not move. Or speak. She wanted to run out of the room, but she knew she could not leave her sister in the bedroom with the tall man in ragged clothes.

In the end, she simply backed up from the closet until she felt her bed hit the back of her legs. She didn't need any help sitting down. Her legs felt as if they had turned to water.

The man stepped out of the closet, and sat down in the chair that was pulled up to the small desk next to the window. At first he didn't say anything. It was almost as if he were in some kind of trance.

There was something about him, the way he looked at Tuff and Bean, that made them feel safe. For some reason, they weren't afraid. At least, Bean wasn't. And that was pretty amazing. Bean was usually very frightened of strangers.

When this man finally talked, he knew things about them. He knew that Bean had gotten her nickname because she liked string beans. *No* little kids liked string beans. And she was only called Bean around the house. Not at her preschool, or anywhere else. Just by Mom and Dad and Tuff.

How could he know these things unless he was a friend?

After that night, Tuff forgot how many times he came to visit. She was sure there were nights when she didn't even wake up. She seemed to remember Bean talking to the man, but later wasn't sure if she had dreamed this.

Just as she recalled the first time the man came to visit, she remembered with clarity the last time. On the last night Tuff fell asleep to the sound of his voice, the taste of apple juice and something bitter on her tongue.

That was the first night she had the dreams, dreams of walking through dark caves, hearing the sounds of cars and people as a soft, distant echo. In the dream the man in the ragged clothes took her and Bean to meet another man, a man in a white jacket.

A man who stood in shadows.

Tuff knew that she'd had dreams before, but not like this. This was so real; it was as if she wasn't dreaming at all, as if it was actually *happening*. She felt the dampness on her skin, felt the chill in the air, saw crooked shadows on glistening stone.

It wasn't until many years later, when the dreams returned, that Tuff began to understand who the raggedy man was, how he had stepped into their lives from darkness, and how, if she were to ever be free, she would have to follow him back there.

13

Byrne sat alone in a booth at a Point Breeze dive, nursing his second Jim Beam. There were a number of cop bars he frequented, but some nights he just didn't want the company, the shop talk.

He took out his phone, navigated over to the photo folder, began scrolling through the pictures he had taken that day, one after another. When he reached the last photo he began again at the beginning.

Thirty thousand in cash.

A handful of ugly photographs.

A page from the *Inquirer.*

For a moment Byrne had considered that Freitag had wrapped something delicate in the newspaper, stashed it in the box, then removed the item, leaving the paper behind. He rather quickly ruled this out because of how neatly folded the paper was.

No. Robert Freitag—and Byrne was all but certain it was Freitag who stashed the shoebox in the ceiling—had kept that page from the newspaper for a reason.

Because the newspaper page had been entered into evidence, Byrne had made copies, front and back, before leaving the Roundhouse.

He reached into his pocket, pulled out the sheets, spread them on the table. There were a total of seven articles. A wolf-dog had been captured in Pennypack Park. An article about how Germantown

Avenue draws history buffs. A piece about new condominiums in the Northeast. He was just about to read the second page when his phone rang.

He checked the number on the caller ID. It was his father. A little late for Paddy Byrne, but he was known to watch the fights on HBO. He clicked on. "Hey, Da."

"There's a problem."

Since Byrne had been a child, he had only heard this phrase from his father twice before. Once, when his father had a union meeting, a union meeting at which Padraig Byrne was up for election, an election he ultimately won. On the way to the union hall, though, in five feet of snow, the Pontiac was dead. The other time was when Byrne's mother was diagnosed with cancer.

Three times in one life meant something bad. This was serious.

"What's wrong?"

"My blood pressure."

Byrne knew it. He felt the cold shiver rise from his feet into his chest. He fished around in his pocket for his car keys. He considered which hospital would be closest to his father's house. He couldn't think of a single one. "What are you talking about?"

"My blood pressure," his father repeated. "Something's wrong with it."

Oh, man, Byrne thought. Besides himself, Padraig Byrne was the last person he knew who would even think about dealing with something like cholesterol or blood pressure, or anything that might have anything to do with good health. Unless he had to. Which reminded him that his yearly MRI was coming up soon.

Padraig Byrne had been a longshoreman all his working life, had survived on cheesesteaks, Tastykakes and Harp Lager. Health was a side issue. Like flood insurance.

"What about it?" Byrne asked.

"It's twenty-seven over eight."

The numbers were all wrong. They didn't even make sense. *"What?"*

"My blood pressure is twenty-seven over eight," Padraig said. "I'm looking right at it."

"I don't understand." There was a long pause, a silence that filled Byrne with dread. "Da?"

Mercifully, his father soon responded. "What's it supposed to be?"

"What do you mean?"

"What's my blood pressure supposed to be?"

The previous year Byrne had bought his father a top-of-the-line cuff blood pressure monitor, along with books on low-sodium cooking and the low-cholesterol diet. When Byrne took the blood pressure monitor out of the package, he had read the small brochure—printed in English, Spanish, Portuguese and French—about how to use the device, and what the readings should be, complete with an age and weight chart. Like all things medical, all things health-related, Byrne couldn't remember a word or a single number. Now that it mattered.

"I don't know," Byrne said. "Are you sure about those numbers?"

"Son," Padraig said, with a tone that suggested Byrne was still a child, still sitting deliriously naked in the small rubber pool behind their house on Reed Street. "Did I not say I was looking right at it?"

Byrne knew the tone. His father was sure about something, and would not be challenged. "Where are you?"

"Where *am* I?" his father asked. "I'm home. Where do you think I am? Miami?"

"In the house. Where in the *house?*"

"Ah, okay," Padraig said. "I'm in the kitchen. What's the difference?"

"Is the monitor plugged into the outlet next to the bowl on the sideboard?"

"Where else?"

"Da," Byrne said in relief, "that outlet is on a dimmer switch."

Silence.

Then, from his father: "It is?"

The Irish, Byrne thought. Sometimes he wondered how the Irish ever ran this city. "Yes. The outlet in the kitchen, the one next to the bowl. It's on a dimmer. It's the round switch in the hallway leading to the living room."

"A dimmer?"

"Yep."

"Hang on."

Byrne heard the phone being put down, his father scuffing across the kitchen. A full minute later he picked up the phone.

"I have it plugged into the outlet next to the stove now. Hang on." Byrne heard the plastic rustle, then the cuff pump hold, deflate, hiss. "Let me see here. All right. It's one hundred eighteen over eighty. Better?"

"Better."

"Ah, okay," Padraig said. "Christ, am I stupid."

"No you're not," Byrne said. "It could have happened to anyone."

Byrne said this, but at the moment he could not think of a single person.

They said their goodbyes, entreating each other, as always, to be safe.

Byrne called for another drink.

14

Luther walked down the narrow lane between two buildings on Frankford Avenue, reached into the pocket of his overcoat, extracted a ring of keys. He looked both ways down the short passageway and, seeing himself alone and unobserved, headed down the three steps. He slipped the key into the lock, opened the door, and stepped inside.

He could not turn on a light because there was no electricity in this three-room basement apartment, a flat he had rented two years earlier, paying two years' rent—plus security deposit—in advance, in cash. He knew that this was not the way real estate transactions were generally conducted, but he had long ago learned the power of cash. The building's owner did not hesitate a second before shaking on the deal.

Luther knew this man conducted deals such as this in many parts of the city. He had followed him for two weeks, observing the man offering and accepting white envelopes on street corners, in diners, and between car windows in indoor parking lots. Luther requested that no lease or paperwork exist on this transaction.

The man was more than happy to oblige.

There was no furniture in the apartment, and thus nothing to trip over, so Luther only needed a small LED flashlight to negotiate his way to the small closet that contained the water heater. Or, more accurately, had at one time contained the water heater.

He opened the door to the closet, stepped inside, closed the door behind him. Overhead was a large vent, once used as a cold-air return. Luther took the vent out of the ceiling. He grabbed the iron bar he had installed years earlier and pulled himself into the crawl space. Once there he replaced the grill and tapped it into place.

Few people knew about the vast network of catacombs beneath the city of Philadelphia, and how they were all interconnected with the nearly three thousand miles of sewer lines, some more than twenty-four feet in diameter. As a young boy, Luther had mind-printed the intricate and venous corridors that allowed him to move through the city unde-tected. It was in this place he felt most at home.

In many ways, it was the only home he'd ever had.

At some points, in North Philadelphia, the tunnels were more than thirty feet below the surface of the roads. Down there, Luther could tell when it was raining. He could tell when traffic was heavy, when it was dusk or dawn, when the air above was suffused with fog.

There were dangers here, but Luther knew where to hide. Only twice, when Philadelphia fell victim to sudden rainstorms, had he been caught off guard by a flash flood that had been channeled through the storm sewers to the Delaware River.

He walked down a narrow, low-ceilinged corridor, beneath Grant Ave-nue, sidestepping the thin river of rainwater flowing over the old cobble-stones. He slipped through an opening into a catacomb that was just beneath a building that once housed a massive commercial kitchen. Even these many years after the last meals had been prepared, the air smelled of onions and animal fat. Beneath that, the sickly-sweet smell of spun sugar.

He walked the long black hallway, beneath the ceaseless hum of the expressway far overhead. When he came to the main door he removed his shoes, as silence here was paramount. He gently opened the door and stepped into the brightly lit room.

He sat for a while on the edge of the bed, marveling, as always, at the miracle of it all. He did not know anything about love — indeed, he wouldn't know how to differentiate it from any of the other emo-tions other people felt — but he knew peace, and that was what he called love.

15

When Byrne returned home, at just after one, he took off his suit coat and tie, poured himself a short whiskey. He turned off the lights, opened the blinds, and positioned a chair in front of the window overlooking the street.

He thought about Robert Freitag.

According to some people, probably most people, Freitag was a man of small consequence. When Byrne was a young cop he would probably have thought so, as well. But if his more than two decades in homicide had taught him anything it was that there was no glamour in death, that we were all peers in the morgue.

In life there were people who were wealthier than Robert Freitag, people who were taller, stronger, better looking, certainly more powerful. Byrne believed that to care about anybody, any murder victim, you had to care about them all. Yes, some cases were higher profile than others, mostly due to media exposure, or political pressure put on the department. At some point Byrne began to resist that pressure, even to push back against it.

The Robert Freitags of the world deserved his best effort. The man certainly received the killer's best.

But if Freitag was such a nobody, why was he such a somebody to the man who took his life? The crime was too vicious, too staged, to be random.

He took the Polaroid out of his shirt pocket, held it in the dark. He ran his finger over the glossy surface, thought about the fear Freitag must have felt in those final moments. Byrne wondered how long it had been since he himself had been truly afraid. Working the Line Squad in homicide was not about putting yourself in danger on a daily basis, although he'd been injured too many times to make that a hard and fast rule.

He supposed the only things he feared now were for his daughter's safety, and not just growing old, but growing old alone.

Byrne drained his glass, poured himself another inch. He glanced out the window, at the traffic moving up his street. He had taken to doing this of late, speculating as to where these people were going, wondering if the person he sought was passing just beneath his sill.

He looked at his watch, angling the face toward the street lamp. Even though he knew his father was asleep, he thought about calling him. It was too late. And although he had been putting it off for a long time, he knew it was probably time to move a little closer to where his father lived. There were no guarantees in this life, no warranties. They had X amount of years left together, and nobody knew what that number was.

Byrne put the Polaroid back into a shirt pocket, killed the whiskey, walked into the bedroom. He lay down on the bed, closed his eyes, just for a few moments.

Soon, the day overtook him, and he was fast asleep.

In his dream he walked down a long black hallway, followed by the sound of hard soled shoes on a wet stone. Every time he turned to see who was following him, there was no one there.

But still, as before, the smell of wet straw.

16

Jessica's only class of the day was Criminal Law. It started at 6:45 a.m., and lasted one hour. This time, she was ready for it. She had gotten up at just after five, made lunch for Sophie and Carlos, made sure Vincent was alive and well and awake, and gotten in a twenty-minute run up Reed Street to Fourth, down to Dickinson, then back to Moyamensing.

In the cold drizzle the run was exhilarating.

Now, sitting in the classroom—her final lecture on the subject—she was wide awake, and ready for anything.

For the first time in a long time she felt she could do this.

The four men whose fingerprints were lifted from the photographs they'd found in Robert Freitag's ceiling—the four dead men—were all small-time criminals, each having met their demise as the result of consorting with the wrong people. Two of the men were killed during the commission of a felony—one during a robbery attempt at a gas station in Portsmouth, New Hampshire; one during a home invasion in Fort Lauderdale. The remaining two men died in prison—one in Coyote Ridge Correctional Facility in Washington State, and the other in Los Lunas in New Mexico. According to their records, none of the four men had been in the same institution at the same time, nor was any connection to Robert Freitag established. Besides the fact that the most recent of these deaths occurred in 1989, and was unlikely to be reinvestigated, all four cases were well out of the jurisdiction of the Philadelphia Police Department.

Jessica put all this data into the Freitag case's ever-growing binder, moving it, for the moment, to a back burner.

At just after nine the fax came in. If Jessica had learned anything in her time on the job, it was that things take longer than they do. Karen Jacobs, who promised to get this information to them the previous day, wrote an apologetic note on the cover sheet of the fax.

It was what it was. The wheels turned at their own pace.

Jessica began to skim the two-page fax, which included Robert Freitag's resume and job application to CycleLife, when she spotted Byrne crossing the duty room, two large Starbucks cups in hand.

"There is a special place for you in heaven," she said.

"I've got about three hundred thousand years in Purgatory to do first," Byrne said. "But thanks."

Jessica opened her coffee to cool. She glanced at the assignment desk, back. "Still no case?"

"I checked the sheet. Two shootings in South Philly, a stabbing in Nicetown. All three vics hanging on."

One of the oldest axioms in homicide was that a murder was just an aggravated assault gone wrong. Until a suspicious death happened, the cases belonged to the divisional detectives.

Still, every time a phone rang, every detective—or at least those near the top of the wheel—looked toward the center of the room.

Jessica sipped her coffee, crossed the duty room, made a copy of the fax. She returned, handed one of the copies to Byrne. They both scanned the resume.

"Like the woman said, before Robert worked for CycleLife he worked for Aetna as an accounts manager, then before that he worked for Merck."

"All healthcare related," Byrne said.

"He graduated from West Philadelphia High School, then got an associate's degree in Medical Assisting at Community College of Philadelphia."

"More healthcare."

"Interesting," Jessica said, tapping the bottom of the first page. "There's a four-year gap from nineteen ninety-two to 'ninety-six."

"There's nothing there."

"Nothing," Jessica said. "Don't people usually put something down, figuring their potential employer is going to ask? Something like 'traveled in South America to find myself' or 'took time off when kids were small'?"

"Well, we know he didn't *do* time," Byrne said. "He wasn't trying to leave a stint in Graterford off his CV."

"Have we put in a call to this cousin of his?"

"I called the lawyer this morning," Byrne said. "Nothing back yet."

"And I'm not seeing where this guy would have made enough money to stash thirty-one grand in a shoebox." Jessica flipped a page, looked at the second sheet. She sat upright. "Look at this. The name and address he put in for Emergency Contact."

Byrne glanced at the bottom of the page. "J. C. Delacroix." He looked at Jessica. "JCD."

"As in JCD 10K."

"Or 10E."

Byrne rolled his chair over to a computer terminal, punched in the information. A few seconds later he turned the monitor. He had looked up the address on Google Maps. It was the second to last house in a block of row houses in Brewerytown.

"I don't think this address has a 10E. I'm going with 10K, as in ten grand," Byrne said. "Let's go see what J. C. Delacroix has to say about it."

As they got ready to leave, Jessica glanced back at Robert Freitag's resume, at the missing entry spanning 1992 to 1996, wondering: *What happened during those four years?*

17

The house was located on a narrow street in the Brewerytown section of North Philadelphia, a neighborhood pleated between the east bank of the Schuylkill River and 25th Street. To the north was Cecil B. Moore Avenue; to the south, Parrish Street. An unofficial district, Brewerytown got its nickname from the many breweries that flourished along the river during the late nineteenth century.

The house was a painted brick trinity with a white wrought-iron railing leading up the two steps to the small porch.

When Jessica rang the doorbell she noticed holes drilled above and below the two windows to the right of the door. It appeared there had, at one time, been bars over the windows. While the area was not a high crime area, she didn't believe it was gentrified to the point where dropping your guard was a good idea.

After ringing the bell for the third time, Jessica and Byrne took a step back, checked the upstairs and downstairs windows for movement. They found none.

Seeing as the row house was the second address from the corner, they walked to the cross street, then left, and found an alley running between the houses. They headed down the alley and saw a gate leading to the back of Delacroix's house. In the tiny back patio was a man with earbuds firmly in place, working on what appeared to be a container garden. The air was thick with the smell of compost.

Jessica knocked on the gate, even though she was certain the man could not hear her. He didn't. She waved a hand until she caught his eye. He immediately looked over and removed the earbuds. Even from a few feet away Jessica heard that he was listening to some heavy metal rock. The man was in his fifties, fighting the good fight against a paunch, had a receding hairline. He wore faded Levi's and an orange down vest. At first Jessica thought the music sounded a little young for him, but then had to remind herself that the seventies was forty years ago. The truth was, some people who listened to AC/DC looked like this guy.

"Hi," the man said. "I didn't see you standing there."

"Not a problem," Jessica said. "We rang the bell a few times."

The man nodded. He gestured to the seven or eight redwood planters on the ground in front of him. "Just getting the soil ready for the season," he said. He then pointed at the rather intricate trellis that grew up the north side of his small terrace. It was constructed out of electrical conduit and what appeared to be fishing line. "The plight of the Philadelphia gardener," he added. "Vertical gardening."

Jessica was familiar with the technique. Growing up on Catharine Street with their minuscule backyard, her father grew his tomatoes and cucumbers on stakes that seemed to reach the clouds. Of course, she was much smaller then.

"Are you Mr. Delacroix?" Jessica asked.

"Yes," the man said. "I am." He took off his gardening gloves and unlatched the gate. "What can I do for you?"

Jessica produced her ID. "My name is Detective Jessica Balzano. This is my partner, Detective Byrne."

The man looked between them a few times. "Police?"

"Yes, sir," Jessica said. "We just need to ask you a few questions."

The man turned in place, looking for somewhere to put his gloves. There were two small tables where he could've put them, but he seemed a little flustered. Not felony flustered, but rather not used to talking to police flustered.

"May we come in?" Jessica asked.

The man returned to the moment. "Yes, of course," he said. He opened the gate. "Please, please."

Jessica and Byrne walked a few feet across the back patio, and into the house. Like many row houses of this type, they entered a small kitchen, which gave way to a short hallway leading to the dining room and living room beyond. They gathered in the living room.

"May I ask your full name, sir?" Jessica asked.

"James Delacroix," the man said.

"Is there a middle name?"

"Sorry. It's Charles," he said. "I rarely use it."

Jessica made a note, underlined it. JCD.

"Mr. Delacroix, are you acquainted with a man named Robert Freitag?" As she asked the question, Jessica watched the man for some tic of recognition. She saw none.

"I'm sorry," Delacroix said, "could you repeat that name for me, please?"

"Freitag," Jessica said. "Robert Freitag." She spelled the last name for him.

Delacroix looked up and slightly to the right. It was an indicator that he really was thinking about his answer, not trying to cook one.

"No," he said. "That name is not familiar to me."

"May I ask where you are employed, Mr. Delacroix?"

"I work at the FlexPro Group."

"What is your position there?"

"I work in Quality and Compliance."

"Have you ever worked for, or with, a company called CycleLife?"

Again, a look at the ceiling, and to the right. He shook his head.

"Sorry, that doesn't ring a bell either." He leaned against the wall, but instead of crossing his arms—a classic signal of shutting down— he put his hands into his pockets. Backing off, but not shutting down. "I think this is the part in every cop show ever made where the guy asks what this is all about," he said with a nervous smile. "Am I allowed to ask what this is about?"

Jessica returned the smile. Half of it anyway. "Mr. Delacroix, we're with the homicide division, and we're investigating a murder."

The word reached him like a low-level electrical shock.

"A murder?"

"Yes, sir."

"Of this Robert…"

"Freitag," Jessica said. "Yes, Mr. Delacroix. Robert Freitag was murdered in February."

"Why would you think I would know anything about this? I've never heard of the man."

"We're getting to that, sir," Jessica said. "So, once again, the name CycleLife means nothing to you?"

"No."

"Might you have run across CycleLife in your job at FlexPro? I understand your company is in the pharmaceutical business."

With this, the repeat of the question he had answered earlier, he began to shut down. He crossed his arms.

"I am abso*lutely* certain."

Jessica believed him. While she was questioning Delacroix, Jessica saw Byrne looking around the living room. She caught his eye, and saw that he wanted to jump in. It was standard procedure for them. When a witness, even a potential witness, began to retreat, they tag-teamed him.

Byrne gestured to the photographs over the couch. They were large, professionally matted and framed black-and-white photographs, grouped into two rows of four. Jessica recognized most of the photographs as Philadelphia landmarks, shot at unique angles.

"These are very good," Byrne said. "Are you the photographer?"

Jessica glanced at Delacroix. He kept his arms crossed, but she could see him begin to soften.

"Yes," he said. "I dabble. A little."

Byrne crossed the living room to get a closer look at the photographs. "These are much better than dabbling," he said. He pointed to the photograph in the upper right-hand corner, a low-angle shot of what looked like a pyramid. "Is this Beth Sholom?"

Delacroix uncrossed his arms. "Yes it is," he said. "You know the area?"

"Philadelphia born and bred," Byrne said. "Although I don't get out to Elkins Park as much as I'd like to."

Delacroix crossed the room. "I shot this at high noon. The sun was dead center, and cast no shadow."

For the next few minutes, as the two men discussed the photographs, Jessica glanced around the living room and dining room. The space was nowhere near as Spartan as Robert Freitag's living quarters. This place was sloppy, but comfortable—books stacked in a corner, remote controls on the couch, a rolled-up bag of Doritos rubber-banded on the coffee table. Through the opening into the kitchen Jessica saw a day's worth of dishes in the sink. She looked at the steps leading to the second floor. They were being watched by a rather portly tabby cat. Jessica usually smelled cat litter, but her nose was still filled with the scent of compost from the backyard.

"You know, Beth Sholom was Frank Lloyd Wright's only synagogue," Delacroix said.

"I didn't know that," Byrne replied.

Jessica glanced at Delacroix as he rocked back on his heels a little. Byrne had him. She knew this the way she knew that Byrne knew full well that morsel of Frank Lloyd Wright minutiae.

"If you don't mind my asking, what cameras do you use?" Byrne asked. "I'm shopping for one for my daughter. Totally clueless."

Now they were in Delacroix's wheelhouse. "I have a few," he said. "My go-to is a Nikon D60. It's not the newest, but it's never let me down."

"Nice," Byrne said. "Are you all digital now?"

Delacroix smiled. "No, I'm still hanging on to my AE-1."

"The old Canon?"

"That's the one."

Jessica had a feeling she knew where her partner was going with this. She was right.

"What about Polaroids?" Byrne asked.

Delacroix shook his head. "No," he said. "I donated a pair of Polaroids to the city schools about ten years ago. Digital photography has really made all photography instant photography. I was only keeping them as artifacts anyway."

Byrne just nodded. He glanced at Jessica, effectively tossing her the ball.

"Mr. Delacroix, we don't want to take up any more of your time. So, just so we're sure, you're positive you've never met a man named Robert Freitag?"

"I just can't remember that name. I'm sorry."

"Would it surprise you to learn that, on an application for a position at CycleLife LLC, five years ago, Mr. Freitag named you as an emergency contact?"

Delacroix looked shocked. "It would surprise me a great deal. I'm not sure why he would do that. I don't know him."

Jessica reached into her portfolio, and pulled out the fax they had been sent by Karen Jacobs. She handed it to Delacroix. He reached into one of his trouser pockets, retrieved an eyeglass case. He opened the case, slipped on his glasses, and his gaze began to move down the page.

"It's right at the bottom, Mr. Delacroix," Jessica said.

Delacroix looked at the bottom of the page. He mumbled the last few lines until he got to his name and address. "Ah, okay. I see what happened here. This isn't me."

"Sir?"

"It says J. C. Delacroix. This is my sister: Joan Catherine."

"Your sister lives here?"

"Yes. No. Well, she *used* to live here. It was right after her divorce, and she went back to her maiden name. I still get some of her mail."

"I take it that she never mentioned Mr. Freitag to you, is that correct?"

"No. But that's not unusual. We don't really move in the same circles."

"I see," Jessica said. She noticed a photograph on the wall next to the passageway to the kitchen. It was a picture of a younger James Delacroix and a woman, perhaps ten years older, who looked like a family member.

"Is this your sister?" Jessica asked, pointing to the photo.

"Yes," he said. "That was taken in Atlantic City."

"It's very important we speak with her. Do you have her contact information handy?"

"I can do better than that," Delacroix said. "She lives right across the street." He glanced at his watch. "She's probably home now. I'll give her a call."

Before Jessica could step in and ask the man not to make the call — it was always better in situations such as this to catch a potential witness off guard — he had his cell phone on, flipped open, and a speed-dial number punched in. Jessica glanced at Byrne. He was already looking out the front window.

"Hey, Joanie," Delacroix said. "You busy?"

Delacroix crossed the room and looked out the window with Byrne. Jessica could see the living-room lights on in the row house directly across the street.

"Well, you're not going to believe this, but the jig is finally up." Delacroix looked at Jessica, winked. "The police are here, and they're asking questions." Delacroix listened for a few moments. In that time

Jessica saw the curtains part across the street, and the silhouette of a woman appear. "Yes, it appears they have finally caught up with you." Delacroix looked out the window, waved. The woman across the street waved back. "No, it's nothing serious. Okay. Sure."

He handed the phone to Jessica. She took it.

"Ms. Delacroix?"

"Yes?"

"My name is Jessica Balzano; I'm with the Philadelphia Police Department. We just need a minute of your time. Would it be okay if we stopped by now?"

There was a slight hesitation, but not long enough for any bells to ring.

"Yes, I suppose that would be okay," the woman said. "I'm just doing laundry."

"I understand. We promise not to keep you too long."

"We?"

"My partner and I."

Another pause. "Okay."

"Great," Jessica said. "We'll see you in a bit."

Jessica handed the phone back to James Delacroix. He put it to his ear for a moment, but said nothing. Apparently, his sister had hung up.

Jessica buttoned her coat. "Mr. Delacroix, we're sorry for the inconvenience. And again, there's nothing to be alarmed about. Most of our job is really rather routine. We have to cover all angles and all bases."

"I understand."

"If you'd like we could stop back after we speak to your sister."

"That would set my mind at ease."

"Happy to do it."

Delacroix showed them to the door, and watched as they crossed the street.

* * *

While Jessica climbed the few steps, Byrne stood back, on the sidewalk, checking the front of the house. There were matching lace curtains in all the windows.

Jessica opened the screen, knocked. When she did, the door opened. It was already slightly ajar. She knocked again, inched the door open further. "Ms. Delacroix? It's Detective Balzano."

"Just come on in," a voice called out, perhaps from the basement. "I'm finishing a load. Make yourself at home. I won't be long."

"Thanks," Jessica said. She and Byrne stepped inside, closed the door.

Where James Delacroix's house had been unmistakably masculine, Joan Catherine Delacroix's house was clearly a woman's house, but not frilly in any way. The furniture was slipcovered in a floral pattern; the walls were a pale yellow. The dining-room table—an older, well-preserved rosewood with curved legs that reminded Jessica of her grandmother's table—bore a crystal bowl of waxed fruit.

After a few minutes or so, they heard the washer or dryer beep, signaling the end of a cycle. When the woman did not bring her basket of laundry up the stairs, Byrne went to the top of the stairs, peered down.

"Ms. Delacroix, do you need a hand with the laundry?"

No answer.

"Ms. Delacroix?"

Still no reply. Byrne looked at Jessica, then back down the stairs. "Is everything okay, ma'am?"

Nothing.

"I'm coming down."

Jessica heard Byrne begin to descend the steps. There was no other sound in the house. Jessica then heard Byrne call the woman's name one more time. She heard no response. Byrne returned from the basement.

"She's not down there," he said.

"What do you mean she's not down there?"

"I mean she's not down there. There's only the one main room and two smaller rooms, and I cleared them all. She's not there."

"No exterior doors?"

"None."

Instinctively, Jessica looked at the ceiling, at the second floor. "You think she went upstairs?"

"It's possible."

"Not really," Jessica said. "We would have seen her make the turn on the steps. We would have heard her."

"You would think."

"Is her laundry still in the basement?"

Byrne nodded. "It's in the basket, still warm." He walked over to the stairwell. "I'm going to check upstairs," he said. "This makes no sense."

While Byrne went upstairs Jessica checked the back door. It was closed and locked with a deadbolt. There was no key in the lock. The curtains on the door were open. Jessica moved to the front of the house, opened the front door, stepped out on the stoop. She looked both ways on the street. There were no pedestrians.

When Jessica heard Byrne return to the living room she stepped inside, closed the door. "Anything?"

Byrne shook his head. "She's not here."

The two detectives stared at each other for a few moments, lost in their own thoughts. It wasn't as if they had just wandered into the woman's house uninvited. Jessica had talked to her, and the woman seemed receptive to an interview.

All told, it was fewer than two minutes between the phone call and the time they entered the house. The woman's own brother had run interference for them, so it wasn't exactly a sandbagging, or an interrogation.

That said, the woman and her role in all this was just nudged the slightest bit from witness to person of interest.

"Do you want to call him or should I?" Byrne asked.

Byrne was, of course, talking about James Delacroix.

"I'll call him," Jessica said.

She took out her iPhone, found Delacroix's number, called it. Within a few rings he answered.

"Hello?"

"Mr. Delacroix, this is Jessica Balzano once again. Is your sister there, by any chance?"

Pause. "My sister? Here?"

"Yes, sir. Has she stopped by in the last few minutes?"

"What do you mean? I thought you were at her house."

"We are," Jessica said. "Before we were able to talk to her, it seems, she slipped out."

The line was silent for a few uneasy moments. "I don't understand."

"Neither do we, Mr. Delacroix. Would it be possible for you to come over here please?"

Another pause, longer than the first. Jessica gripped her phone tightly. Before she could lose her temper, Delacroix said: "I'll be right there."

While waiting for James Delacroix, Jessica and Byrne poked around the woman's belongings. In terms of procedure, this was not technically a crime scene, not by any means, and they were not permitted by law to do any kind of search, even a cursory search that involved the opening of drawers, closets, and the like. But, being two veteran detectives, the temptations were all but overwhelming.

"Do you think she's in the wind?" Jessica asked.

"Maybe, but it doesn't add up. When you talked to her on the phone you didn't mention Freitag's name, did you?"

"No," Jessica said. "I didn't."

"And neither did her brother when he called her. So she would have no way of knowing what we wanted to talk about."

"Unless, of course, she had something to hide regarding her relationship with Freitag, or had some knowledge of what happened to him."

Byrne absorbed this for a moment.

A few minutes later James Delacroix came walking up the steps, opened the door to his sister's house, and slipped inside.

"Sorry it took me so long," he said. "I made a few calls to Joan's friends."

"Any luck?" Jessica asked.

Delacroix shook his head. "No. She has a friend, Molly Fowler, who lives two streets over. Joan has been known to cut through the vacant lot across the street when she visits Molly. I thought that's what happened. But Molly said she hasn't seen Joan in a few weeks."

"And no one else has seen her or heard from her?"

"No," he said. "I also called her phone twice. I got her voice mail."

"Did it ring a few times or click over to voice mail immediately?" Jessica asked this in the hope of determining whether the woman was on her phone at the time. With many systems, if you were on the phone, it routed to voice mail after one ring. Sometimes without ringing at all.

"It rang a few times," Delacroix said. "You didn't hear it ring in the house, did you?"

Jessica shook her head. "No."

At this, Delacroix put his hands on his hips, glanced at the floor, adrift in thought.

"Has she ever done anything like this before?" Byrne asked.

Delacroix looked up. "What do you mean by *anything like this?*" he replied, with more than a little hostility.

"What I mean, Mr. Delacroix, is perhaps your sister is so busy that she forgot she had another appointment when she agreed to speak with us. I meant nothing more."

Delacroix maintained his rigid posture. "If you're asking if my sister is senile, or has dementia, or early onset Alzheimer's, the answer to all three questions is no. She's sharp as a tack. Sharper than I am. She does my taxes."

"Good," Byrne said. "That's what we figured. Had to ask."

Delacroix softened his position a bit. "So, can you walk me through this again? You came over here and then what?"

"When we came over the door was open, we pushed on it, knocked on the jamb."

"Did my sister come to the door?"

"No," Jessica said. "I called out her name, identified myself. She yelled up from the basement, and said she was just finishing up with her laundry."

"So you didn't actually meet her."

It was more a statement than a question. And more than a little accusatory. "No, sir, we didn't," Jessica replied. "She said she would be up in a few minutes and for us to make ourselves at home."

"Do you mind if I take a look downstairs?" Delacroix asked.

"Of course not," Byrne said.

Without any hesitation James Delacroix quickly crossed the living room, ran noisily down the steps. "Joanie?" he yelled. No response. Jessica could hear the man moving things around down there. A few moments later he trundled back up the steps.

"Did you look upstairs?" Delacroix asked.

"Yes," Jessica said. "We did."

Delacroix sat down heavily in one of the armchairs. "I don't like this," he said. "This isn't right. This is unlike Joan. I don't like this at all."

"Mr. Delacroix, there's absolutely no reason to suspect that anything might be wrong with your sister," Byrne said. "There are probably a dozen plausible explanations as to why she stepped out."

"You don't understand. I know some people think my sister is a little demanding, and that perhaps she has some sort of . . . *mean* streak, but it's not true. And the one thing about Joan you should know is that she takes her responsibilities very seriously. If she has an appointment, even a casual appointment, she is there. When she said she would talk to you, she meant it. She wouldn't just walk out."

Unless she had something to hide, Jessica thought.

Delacroix tapped his fingers on the arms of the chair. "At what point does a person become a missing person?" he asked.

"We're a long way away from that," Byrne said.

Delacroix stopped tapping. "What should we do?"

"What we should do now is take a quick walk around the neighborhood. If I remember correctly there are a few stores and small restaurants in these blocks. It's entirely possible your sister popped out to a bodega for a bottle of fabric softener, or a coffee to go, and is on her way back right now."

The look on Delacroix's face said that he did not believe this.

"We'll need to lock the place up," Byrne added. "Do you have keys?"

For a moment it appeared the question had not registered. Then, James Delacroix snapped back, stood up, fished around in his pocket. "Yes," he said. "I have keys for the front and back."

"The back door is a deadbolt key lock, am I right about that?" Jessica asked.

Delacroix nodded. "Yes, Joan always keeps it locked, and she never leaves the key in the lock. She has this vision of someone punching through the glass, taking the key out and opening the door from the outside. She always keeps that deadbolt key in a drawer somewhere." He held up a key ring. "But I have a copy."

Jessica had tried the back door, found it secured. That's why this disappearance was so mysterious. Joan Delacroix would have had to come up the stairs from the basement, walked down the short hallway to the kitchen, through the kitchen to the back door, turned the key in the lock, stepped through the door, and locked the door from the outside, all without making a sound. It wasn't possible.

"I'm going to check the back door, then we'll go," Delacroix said.

As James Delacroix walked into the kitchen Jessica met Byrne's gaze. What had begun as a routine interview had just ratcheted up the investigation one notch. Maybe two.

Having checked the rear entrance, Delacroix walked back into the living room.

"What about a car?" Byrne asked. "Does she own a car?"

"No," Delacroix said. "She takes SEPTA. If it's a long distance, she borrows my car, or I drive her."

"Did you check to see if your car is gone?"

"Of course."

Jessica, Byrne and James Delacroix walked the neighborhood, covering five streets in all directions. No one had seen Joan Delacroix.

It had now been a little over an hour since the woman had simply vanished.

While Jessica and Byrne were waiting for James Delacroix to return they heard a scream coming from behind the woman's row house.

"Oh my God!"

Jessica and Byrne ran to the corner, around to the alley. There they found James Delacroix leaning against the wall, a few doors down from his sister's house, white as a ghost.

"God *no*," he said.

Jessica was just about to ask what he was talking about, when the man pointed to the ground. There, on the cracked concrete, just a few feet away, was a pearl clip-on earring.

Byrne moved forward, put a hand on James Delacroix's shoulder, easing the man back a step or two. "Are you saying that this belongs to your sister, Mr. Delacroix?"

The man nodded, began to hyperventilate.

Jessica stepped forward, knelt down. The earring was an inexpensive gold tone metal, with a swirl of what were most likely faux pearls.

It wasn't particularly stylish, or expensive, but the earring itself was not what drew Jessica's attention, or kept it there, bringing with it a chill that skittered down her spine.

The earring was covered in blood.

18

With sector cars from the 22nd District parked at either end of the alley, and a patrol officer at the front door to Joan Delacroix's house, Jessica and Byrne tried to walk James Delacroix through his sister's daily routine. Understandably, the man was all but inconsolable, and therefore not much help in the process.

Every few seconds, as they stood chatting in his living room, Delacroix cast an expectant glance toward the front window.

"There's no reason to believe your sister is seriously injured, Mr. Delacroix," Byrne said. "Let's take this one step at a time."

Delacroix looked up, his frightened eyes finding Byrne. "I don't know what to do. Should I try calling her again?"

"We can handle that. What's your sister's number?"

Delacroix told him. While Byrne stepped away to try the call, Jessica continued. She pointed to the picture on the wall. "Do you have another picture of your sister besides this one?" she asked.

"A picture? Why?"

"We'd like to make copies and get it out to patrol officers in the district."

Delacroix got up from the chair, crossed to the dining room. He opened one of the drawers in the hutch, pulled out an eight-by-ten photo, handed it to Jessica. In it, Joan Delacroix wore a nurse's uniform.

"How recent is this picture?" Jessica asked.

"I don't know," Delacroix said. "Maybe ten years old."

"Do you have anything more recent?"

At this, Byrne stepped into the room from the kitchen. He shook his head. He had not gotten hold of the woman.

"No, I..." Delacroix began. "We don't do a lot of things where we take pictures anymore."

"That's okay," Jessica said. "This picture will be fine."

"Wait," he said. "I do have a recent picture. It's on my laptop. I took it with my phone at a fundraiser a month or so ago. Joan didn't want to be in it, but I snapped it anyway."

Delacroix took his laptop out of its case, connected it to a printer that was on the buffet in the dining room. He tapped a few keys. Moments later, the photograph began to print. It was a high-quality color print, followed by a second copy. Delacroix handed one each to Jessica and Byrne.

As Delacroix was going to close his laptop, he suddenly stopped. "I just thought of something."

"What's that?" Jessica asked.

"Her phone. The one we've been calling."

"What about it?"

"I bought her an iPhone last year. She really doesn't use it much, but she always has it with her."

"I'm not following."

"We set up this app on the phone. Joan sometimes loses track of her phone, and she's pretty paranoid about leaving it somewhere and having someone else have access to her data."

"You're saying this app is set up?"

"Yes," Delacroix said. "Find My iPhone. If she has it with her, we can find where she is."

Delacroix sat down at the dining-room table. He tapped a few keys on his laptop, navigated to the right screen. He put in an ID and a password. Moments later another screen displayed a map of the greater Philadelphia area. Delacroix tapped a few more keys. The area of the map became a section of the Northeast.

In the center was a small icon.

When Jessica saw the location her blood ran cold. She glanced at Byrne. He saw it too. Without a word spoken they both knew what they had to do. Byrne would stay with Delacroix; she would make the call.

Jessica stepped out of the row house, onto the street. She got on the phone. In seconds she had Dana Westbrook on the line.

"What's up, Jess?"

"Sarge, we need sector cars at Priory Park."

"How many?" Westbrook asked.

"All of them."

19

Luther sat in the late-afternoon gloom.

The old woman had not said a word to him, not even to ask why. She *knew* why. He had searched her house three times, on his previous visits, looking for anything that would tie her to the hospital—newsletters, patient lists, medication protocols, anything. He'd found nothing. But that didn't mean she didn't have something somewhere else.

Luther knew all about cubby holes and secret places.

Removing her from the house had been a challenge, but not one with which he was unfamiliar. He had taken her out of the basement through the crawl space—a portal he had used for entries on his previous visits—then up into an abandoned shoe store five buildings down.

As a shadow moved to his right, Luther looked over to see that the policeman stood no more than three feet from him. He tensed for a moment, the bone-handle knife now slick in his grip. The danger soon passed.

Luther quickly arranged the table, descended the steps. A few minutes later he watched the flame begin to caper and dance. In the dream he was in a small village in Harju County. In that place two men were lashed to a roof beam in a stable—local men who loaned money to farmers at a usurious rate. Soon the green countryside became the dank basement of G10. In this dream Luther saw flames ripping up the back of soiled hospital gowns, scarlet harpies on blackening flesh. It stirred something inside him.

Earlier in the day the doctor, dead these many years, had stepped forward from the shadows, and told him what needed to be done. The digging machines were finally near, and when they turned over the ground all secrets would be revealed. This could not be. Each body told a story, and each story would lead to ruin.

"Do you understand what you must do?" the doctor had asked.

"Yes," Luther said.

"Do you know the dreams?"

Luther had closed his eyes, and in his mind walked the dream arcade, the long colonnade of bright exhibits, the carefully mounted dioramas of the dead.

"I do."

When it was time, when the air began to shimmer, Luther rose to his feet, crossed the room, and stole into a darkness deeper than midnight.

20

When Jessica and Byrne arrived at Priory Park, for the second time in as many days, they were met by two units from the 8th District. Jessica stopped the car, put it in park, kept it running. Byrne was out of the vehicle like a shot. He spoke to one of the patrol officers, then returned to the car.

"We've got cars at all four corners of the park. We've got two on the avenue, two on Chancel Lane."

"Anybody see anything?" Jessica asked.

Byrne shook his head. "No."

Jessica emerged from the car, slowly turned 360, looking for something, anything that looked out of place. She saw nothing. She reached in the car, retrieved her two-way radio, pointed to the tree line at the northwest section of the park, about one hundred yards away.

"I'm going to head up there," she said.

"I'll take the southern end," Byrne replied.

Both Jessica and Byrne had grabbed department-issue rain slickers out of the trunk of the car before heading to the park. It turned out to be a wise decision. As Jessica began heading across the open field she put up the hood on her slicker, pulled the cord tightly around her chin. The good news was that she had worn her boots. However, she had not brought gloves. She had been out of the car less than a minute and already her hands were freezing.

They had not said much on the drive to Priory Park. There was no concrete reason to think that Joan Delacroix was a victim of extreme violence. Not yet. There might be a number of plausible explanations for fresh blood on her earring. Neither Jessica nor Byrne really believed that. They wanted to, but their experience pointed them in the other direction.

When Jessica stepped into the wooded area she was somewhat shielded from the rain by the canopy of trees. She took out her flashlight, ran it along the ground. She saw no footprints.

When she'd gone twenty yards or so, toward the creek, she saw it. It was so incongruous sitting on top of the dead pine needles and composting leaves that she had to look twice. She almost walked by it.

But there was no mistake. It was the woman's other earring.

Jessica keyed her radio. "You better get up here, Kevin. Have the officers circle around to the northwest section of the park."

Jessica put the two-way radio in her pocket, reached beneath her rain slicker, and drew her weapon. The only sound was the steady rain, and the pounding of her heart. A few moments later she heard footfalls. She spun around to see Byrne making his way through the trees.

Jessica pointed to the earring on the ground. Byrne drew his weapon, held it at his side. Standing a few yards apart, the two detectives began to make their way through the pines. When they got to the clearing, and the southern bank of the creek, they saw her.

"Oh my God," Jessica said.

The body of Joan Delacroix was lying, faceup, on the muddy creek bed. Her feet were in the frigid water, her arms straight out to her sides. On each of her hands was placed a large rock. Even from twenty feet away Jessica could see that the right side of the woman's skull had been all but crushed. She also saw something that made the scene even more surreal.

The woman's shoes—a pair of white Rockport walkers with rubber soles—were on the wrong feet.

Jessica turned away, fighting the emotion, the nausea and revulsion. She glanced over at Byrne. He stood in the clearing, in the freezing rain, eyes closed. He seemed to be searching the air for a scent.

*   *   *

The park looked like an armed camp. At least a dozen sector cars flashed. There were no fewer than six CSU officers walking a tight grid around the creek bed, every so often placing small yellow markers at what might have been evidence.

The rain continued to pour, hampering efforts to maintain the integrity of the scene.

Byrne stood in the downpour, now holding an umbrella, his gaze locked on the woman's body. They would have to wait for an investigator from the medical examiner's office to move or cover the corpse. It was just one further indignity for the victim to bear.

While they waited, Detective Kevin Byrne stood guard, just a few feet away. The wheel, once more, had turned.

He had his new case.

Jessica sat in the Taurus, heater on full blast. She couldn't get warm or dry. Someone had brought hot coffee, which, in the few minutes since she had opened the container, had gone tepid. She drank it anyway. She was just about to once more brave the elements when her cell phone rang. It was Dana Westbrook.

"What's going on, Sarge?"

"How bad is it, Jess?"

Jessica glanced at the supine form of the woman through the trees. "As bad as it gets."

"I'm en route," Westbrook said. "I've got Inspector Mostow with me."

Jessica hadn't even considered the fallout until she heard that an inspector was coming to the scene. There was always a command presence at the scene of every homicide, but rarely did it reach this level. The truth was that a citizen had been abducted and brutally murdered right under the noses of two city detectives. It would be red meat for the local media.

Jessica said nothing.

"There's something else you should know," Westbrook added.

"What is it?"

"I just got a call from the supervisor in the 22nd. He's on scene at that Brewerytown address."

This did not make sense. If anyone was dispatched to that house it should've been divisional detectives. Either way, it would soon be considered a crime scene, and folded into the murder investigation of Joan Delacroix.

"I don't understand," Jessica said. "You're talking about the house where Joan Delacroix lived?"

"Yes."

"What about it?"

Jessica heard Dana Westbrook take a deep breath, release it. "It's burning to the ground."

TWO

21

1948 — Tallinn, Estonia

The predator watched the boy from across the square. The boy seemed a natural leader, taking charge midfield, kicking the ball to a teammate instead of reaching for glory each time he neared the goal. On the field he was surefooted, almost balletic in his movement.

Alas, when the game was over, the boy's team lost 2 to 1.

The boy remained behind while his teammates congregated at the other end of the field. He sat on a bench, reading from a paperbound book.

The predator approached.

"That was a very good game," he said.

The boy looked up. His eyes were brown, his hair a deep chestnut, his features delicate. "We lost."

"I know," the predator said. "This sometimes happens, despite our best efforts."

The boy considered this. "Perhaps it was not my best effort, then."

The predator smiled. "How old are you?"

"I am nine."

"You are big for your age."

The boy said nothing.

"I used to play for the national team," the predator said. "When I was much younger, of course."

The boy just listened.

"I can teach you a few things. Particularly your first touch. It is probably the game's most important, yet underrated, skill. Would you like to learn?"

"Yes. Very much."

The predator looked around. "We shouldn't do it here." He pointed to the far end of the field. "The other boys will see, and then it will not be our secret."

"I know a place," the boy said. "It is very quiet there."

They rose from the bench, crossed the avenue. It was midsummer, and the breeze from the Gulf brought with it a welcome coolness.

They walked a narrow path through Lillepi Park. When they came to a small clearing they stopped. The boy reached into his bag, removed the soccer ball, placed it at the predator's feet.

The predator put down his shoulder bag, took off his shirt. He now wore only a sleeveless tunic.

"You look very strong," the boy said.

"Would you like to see?"

The boy nodded.

The predator lifted the boy effortlessly into the air. When he put him back on the ground he brought him very close, close enough to smell the boy's shampoo. It smelled of cinnamon. He ran a hand through the boy's hair. The boy did not resist or pull away.

"Show me things," the boy said. "There is a larger clearing, just over here."

The predator looked around. The dell was a little too exposed for his liking. Still, the boy was beautiful. He followed.

"What is your name?" the predator asked.

"Eduard."

"That is a wonderful name. Quite regal."

They came to a small, sun-drenched glade. To the right, the predator saw something unexpected. There was a small burial site, with three crudely made cruciform. "Look at this," the predator said. "It seems someone has buried their pets in Lillepi Park."

The predator stepped forward, bent over, and saw that there were names written on the markers. Dr. Andrus Kross. Marta Kross. Kaisa Kross.

"Dr. Andrus Kross," the predator said. "I know this name. How odd that it would be—"

At first, the predator reacted to the cut as if he had merely caught the front of his clothing on a briar. When he looked down, and saw his tunic sliced side to side, and the blood begin to pour forth, he knew what had happened. The boy stood a few feet away, a razor-sharp bone-handle knife in hand.

The predator fell to the ground.

The boy, whose full name was Eduard Olev Kross—son of Andrus and Marta, brother to Kaisa—took a small cruet of the man's blood. Before he stepped away he ran the knife once more along the wound. The predator's intestines now glistened in the afternoon sun.

"They say that stomach wounds are particularly painful," the boy said. He pulled up the three makeshift stakes, put them in his bag. His father and mother and sister were not buried here. They were, instead, in a mass grave in Võru, murdered by the hand of the man now bleeding out in front of him. "They say it can take a long time to die."

The boy, who was twelve years old, not nine, slung his bag over his shoulder.

"What will you think about in your last moments, Major Abendrof?" the boy asked.

As he lay dying, the predator turned his head to see the boy standing in the dell. In the half-light of his passage the predator thought he saw something in the boy's eyes he had never before seen in one so young, a malevolence that seemed to swirl within like a dark squall.

Ten minutes later, as storm clouds gathered over the Gulf of Finland, the predator was dead.

1977—Philadelphia, Pennsylvania

White Rita sat on the floor, her back to the wall, her legs splayed. The water pooled on the filthy linoleum beneath her. She was called White Rita because there were two other women named Rita in her ward. One of them was black, the other was mute. They were Black Rita and Silent Rita.

White Rita had managed to conceal her pregnancy from staff and fellow inpatients for all eight months. Many nights she tried to rewind her thoughts—this is how she thought of her mind, as a large tape recorder—to recall who the father might have been. She could not remember.

In the Long Hallway—which functioned, among other things, as a patient transport corridor—White Rita sat near the T-junction with the Echo Hallway. People always yelled in the Echo Hallway, just to hear the reverberation, so when White Rita screamed, no one paid her any mind. Hours later, it seemed—there were no windows in the Long Hallway, so it was impossible to tell if it was night or day—White Rita looked between her legs and saw a baby.

Someone had left a baby.

The night nurse was a man in his mid-fifties, a former medic in the Army. He had served in the 12th Field Hospital in France, in the grime and chaos of the French Naval Hospital, which had first been overrun by the Germans, then the Allies in the liberation of Cherbourg.

When he gained employment at the hospital in Philadelphia, in the early 1950s, he encountered more than a few men he had helped patch up in Cherbourg, most of them in the contingent of POWs who were not transportable when the 68th Medical Group cleared out. He often wondered, seeing these men in their near catatonic states, if it hadn't been a mistake to save them.

When the intern brought the newborn baby to the clinic, the night nurse looked into the baby's eyes, and felt something he had never felt before. Childless and unmarried, he had never considered what it would be like to care for a child.

He cleaned the newborn, swaddled it in gauze. The intern who had brought the baby said he had found it in the Long Hallway, near the entrance to the catacombs. This probably meant the baby belonged to one of the women who was a ward of the state.

The night nurse wondered: *What kind of a future will this boy have?* There was a good chance he would be raised in some filthy group home, end up in prison. Or, worse, come right back here to this hell on earth.

There were plenty of places to hide a baby in a complex the depth and breadth of the hospital: cubby holes, dumbwaiters, patient transfer hallways, eaves, attics. How hard could it be? There were hundreds, perhaps thousands, of men and women who were all but ghosts to the staff and administration. Many went unwashed, their open sores untreated for weeks.

He looked again at the baby's eyes. He wondered what to call him. He was a firm believer that a person became the name they were given. His mother had been born in Norway and, although she mispronounced her only son's name right up until the day she died—calling him *Looter,* a source of ridicule from the few childhood friends he'd had—he always loved his name, and it had served him well enough in his fifty-four years.

He decided right there and then that the baby would have his name.

He would be called Luther.

1982—Northeastern Estonia

The two dead men lay at the bottom of the quarry, their pants around their ankles, their naked buttocks in blunt, pink relief to the blinding white of the limestone.

The killer stood at the top of the gorge. He did not hear the four men approach.

By the time he turned around, the largest of the men—a lumbering giant in an ill-fitting Soviet Army infantry uniform—raised the butt of his ancient Mosin Nagant rifle and slammed it into the killer's chin. The killer sagged, but was prevented from tumbling into the pit by the two other soldiers.

The fourth man in the group, older than the soldiers by more than three decades, took a handkerchief from his pocket. He draped it over his right hand, put it beneath the killer's chin. He turned the nearly unconscious man's head, a man he had been pursuing for more than twenty years.

"Hulkur," the man said, using the killer's provincial appellation, an Estonian word meaning *vagabond*. "We meet at last."

1990—Jämejala, Estonia

In the eight years Eduard Kross had been in the storied mental hospital in rural Parsti Parish, he had not spoken a word. He was said to have committed more than one hundred murders in his decades-long spree. His path of evil stretched from the Gulf of Finland to the forests of Riga.

For thirty-four years—from the moment he had all but disemboweled the man he held responsible for the murders of his mother, father and sister—Eduard Kross was a wraith, moving at night, never seen by anyone who would live to tell of the man in the sackcloth suit and floppy felt hat.

The doctor was young—young for this facility, where the average age of physicians seemed to be in the sixties.

His name was Dr. Godehard Kirsch.

Among the mostly Estonian hospital staff there was little known about Kirsch, but there were many suppositions. One about which there was little doubt was that he was the sole heir of a very wealthy family—his late grandfather had made his millions with Gustav von Bohlen und Halbach, a Prussian who had the good fortune to marry into the Krupp family in 1906—and the foresight to move his fortune into Swiss accounts before the war.

Among the other rumors was that months before his arrival in Estonia Dr. Kirsch had ordered a series of therapies begun on Eduard Kross, therapies that included testing with various combinations of medications to artificially induce dreams.

"This is he?" Kirsch asked, looking through the mirrored-glass portal into Eduard Kross's padded room.

"Yes," the nurse administrator said. Riina was a sturdy, rawboned woman in her late forties, by all benchmarks unattractive, with a broad forehead and a man's jaw. In her time as nurse administrator of the clinic she had met a number of men like this Dr. Kirsch, officious overeducated men practicing fringe science, lording their doctorates and wealth over staff like some Teutonic *Hochmeister*. Yes, he had the letters MD after his name, but this did not, nor had it ever, impressed Riina.

Because she was free from the strictures of games played between attractive women and the men with whom they dealt, she was able to speak her mind. As often as not it got her into trouble, which was probably why she did not work at one of the larger clinics in Tallinn or Parnu.

"How long has he been here?" Kirsch asked.

Riina knew that the doctor knew the answer to this question. She had for many years wondered why they played this game. She proffered a smile. "Just over eight years."

"And what has been his progress?"

Riina nearly laughed, but refrained. Laughing would be unprofessional. "There has been no progress, Doctor. We are not equipped or funded for rehabilitation or even the most basic regimen of behavioral therapy."

"Then what is it you do here, *Lapsehoidja* Riina?"

The title he gave her was an insult. It meant *babysitter* not *nurse*. Riina put her clipboard down on the desk, squared herself in front of the doctor. He was only an inch or so taller than she, but they were nearly eye to eye. She waited until the doctor turned his eyes to hers.

"Dr. Kirsch, we are a warehouse—a crumbling provincial warehouse at that—for the criminally insane. No more, no less. We bathe them, clean up their shit and vomit, intercede when their violent impulses outlast their medication, and bolt them down at night. What do *you* do, Dr. Kirsch?"

The doctor proceeded, unfazed. "What is his protocol?"

Riina turned a page on her clipboard. "900 mg Lithium, thrice daily."

The doctor pulled on his coat, slipped on his expensive leather gloves. He handed her a thin sheaf of documents. "I have accepted a position in the United States. Philadelphia, to be precise. Mr. Kross will be coming with me. We have much to learn from him."

Riina glanced at the form on top. "I've heard nothing of this."

Without looking at her he produced another document, one that appeared to be a patient transfer to a yellow house in Novosibirsk, a gulag by any measure.

Riina knew what it meant.

"It's my understanding that he has not yet said a word," Kirsch said.

Riina filed the forms, like a good little *lapsehoidja*.

"He talks," she said.

The doctor turned at the door, a look of surprise on his face. "He talks?"

"Yes," Riina replied. She slammed shut the file cabinet drawer, sat on the edge of her desk, shook a cigarette from the pack, took her time lighting it.

Time was her only weapon.

Finally she said: "But only in his sleep."

1990—Philadelphia, Pennsylvania

At the hospital, the one they called Cold River, Luther's world was the catacombs that linked the buildings far belowground, miles of long stone corridors lighted by dim fixtures caged in steel. Luther gave each hallway a name, as if they were streets in the city above. The only time he saw other boys and girls his age—there were not supposed to be patients under eighteen, but Luther knew of many who were—was when there were the infrequent staff picnics, mostly in summer.

Luther didn't like the sunshine.

The catacombs took him from patient wards to doctors' quarters, from the nurses' buildings to the cafeteria, where he ate the surplus food until he was fit to burst.

Before his death from stomach cancer three years earlier, Big Luther—the man who had clandestinely cared for Luther until the boy could wander the halls at Cold River without fear of discovery or expulsion—had taught him to read in the small inpatient library. Quite often Luther had to skip sections of the books due to the feces and food smeared on the pages.

From discarded correspondence and memos, Luther learned about all the different ailments treated in his hospital: the organic psychoses (senility and syphilis), the toxic psychoses (alcohol), the affective psychoses (manic depressives), even neurological conditions like hemiplegia and chorea.

Luther did not know which of these he had. Perhaps he had them all.

Luther was not the only child ever to be born inside the vast complex of Cold River. Not by far. With the many hundreds of patients who were wards of the county and state, many of whom suffered from a litany of psychological disorders, sexual assaults were commonplace. More than once Luther had tended to newborn babies he found discarded like so much refuse around the buildings and grounds, only to have them die from exposure, or, when discovered, be taken away and sent to the proper facility. In his years at Cold River, the number of babies for which he cared, even for as short a period as days, numbered in the dozens.

It was well known among both staff and patients that many male patients over the years had themselves committed to Cold River because of the availability of free food and sex.

When Luther was twelve, one of the patients, a bipolar named Hubert Tilton, was kept by a wall in the Long Hallway for a full year, his arms and feet restrained, his food and waste traveling through tubes, looking much the same to Luther. Luther watched him from the unused nurse's station nearby, every week making a drawing of the man as he wasted away. Sometimes Luther would read to the man at night. Hubert never responded, but Luther could tell that the old man liked the adventure tales of Jack London.

One day Luther showed up at the usual time, only to find Hubert and his bed gone. He went back to his room, a storage room off the Echo Hallway, but not before stealing a stapler from the reception desk outside the Chief Steward's office.

That night, by flashlight, Luther stapled together all his drawings of Hubert Tilton, and made a flip book.

From then on, depending on which way Luther flipped the book, Hubert would live or die, all at Luther's command.

In the spring there was excitement, but Luther did not know why. He eventually learned that there were two men coming: one doctor, one patient. They would be living in the new building, G10.

Luther thought that it was a terribly big building for only two people.

They had to be great men, indeed.

1992 — Philadelphia, Pennsylvania

Upon his arrival at the hospital, Dr. Kirsch assembled a small team to assist with his research — a psychiatric nurse, an anesthesiologist and one orderly.

The patient, Eduard Kross, was kept in a white padded room, lighted by a bank of twelve fluorescent fixtures in the ceiling. The lights were never turned off.

Every twenty-four hours, Kross was brought to a black room, and given an injection, a cocktail of pharmaceuticals comprised of morphine, Prozac and scopolamine. Within minutes he was in a trancelike state, somewhere between sleep and wakefulness, a state they called the dream arcade.

Night after night, Dr. Kirsch and his team brought Edward Kross to the black room, with its sophisticated instruments and recording equipment. From beneath the black room, Luther could not hear much, mostly it sounded like men just talking. Every so often, when Luther was about to doze off in the hot, stuffy confines of the mechanical bay, he heard the screams.

Then, one day, in the fall of 1994, it all stopped. Luther heard rumors, but he believed them to be true by the very nature of the silence in the black room.

Eduard Kross was dead.

That night, from the roof of G10, Luther watched as a pair of men loaded a large body bag into one of the hospital's fleet of patient transfer vans, and left the grounds without turning on the headlights.

Luther had seen this before, many times.

He'd lost count at around a hundred.

1996

Dr. Kirsch found Luther in the Echo Hallway. Kirsch was not a big man—there were many patients, Luther thought at the time, who could easily wrestle him to the ground—but he carried himself with an almost kingly bearing, a worldliness Luther had only encountered in books.

"Träumen Sie?" the doctor asked.

Luther did not understand.

"Do you dream?" the doctor repeated, this time in English.

"No," Luther said. "I do not dream."

The doctor took him by the hand. "Dreams are a magical place. Come with me. I'll show you what I mean."

They walked down a long corridor, through a series of locked doors, then down another hallway, by far the cleanest Luther had ever seen. The floor shone brilliantly, the walls were not scratched and scarred, the lights overhead were dazzlingly white.

They came to a door marked G10/A6. The doctor took out a key, unlocked the door. They stepped into a small dark room. The doctor closed the door behind them. When he turned on the light Luther saw a window in front of him, a window that revealed a room on the other side. In this room sat a man on a wooden chair. The man, who wore a soiled hospital gown, had his mouth open. His head lolled to one side. He had long gray hair and a full beard. Luther could see dried food in the man's whiskers.

The doctor touched a button on the console. "Watch."

Luther walked up to the glass. Within moments the door in the other room opened. Another man walked in, this one old and haggard. He wore a stained green jumpsuit, and moved with a limp.

As Luther observed, the old man took out a pair of very sharp scissors. Luther gasped when he saw the instrument, expecting a pair of orderlies to rush into the room, tussle the old man to the floor, and take the scissors away. Such things were strictly forbidden.

But that didn't happen.

Instead, little by little, the old man began to cut the other man's hair, which tufted out from his raw scalp like weeds on an untended walkway. Every so often the old man would step back to assess his work. Snip here, snip there, then another appraisal.

To Luther's horror and surprise, he did not stop with the man's hair. With the razor sharp shears he suddenly snipped off the tip of one of the man's ears, then quickly went to the other side, snipping that one too. Bright red blood trickled down the sides of the man's face. Luther looked at the doctor, waiting for the man to step in and stop this. But the doctor just watched. Luther turned his attention back to the spectacle.

Before long the old man went to work on the other man's fingertips, not stopping until he had clipped away a small portion of each finger, as well as both thumbs, always retreating a few paces, considering, assessing, evaluating.

Blood began to pool beneath the chair.

"The man with the scissors is dreaming, you see," the doctor said. "He dreams he is a horticulturalist."

"What is that?" Luther asked.

The doctor told him, continued.

"The man with the scissors dreams it is high summer—bright blue sky, warm breezes, a world in full flower—and he is creating a topiary by clipping foliage and twigs from a large perennial, in hopes of creating something fanciful. A peacock, or perhaps a dolphin."

"Why does he keep stepping away?" Luther asked.

"He is looking for symmetry."

The old man moved on to the other man's toes. The seated man's hospital gown was now a deep crimson.

"What about the man in the chair?" Luther asked.

"What about him?"

"Is he dreaming, too?"

"Oh my, yes."

"What is he dreaming about?"

The doctor put a hand on Luther's shoulder. "He is dreaming of winter."

Over the next year Luther saw many shows. Once he saw a man in that small room sit naked in the chair, wearing only a bib, a cloth tied around his neck with what looked like tiny red lobsters printed on it.

In his lap was a metal bowl.

As Luther and Dr. Kirsch watched, the man took a pair of pliers and, one by one, pulled out his teeth, each time dropping them into the bowl with a loud clank.

When the man was finished, toothless and bloodied, an orderly walked into the room, and helped him to the door. Luther never saw that man again.

1997

When the governor of Pennsylvania ordered the hospital closed, and the main buildings were torn down, a lot of the patients were simply released onto the streets of Philadelphia. Some were sent to group homes, some to other long-term care institutions. Most were given fifty dollars and a bus schedule.

For weeks Luther was incapacitated with worry. He did not know what was to become of him. Most of his knowledge of the outside world was to be found in books, and the thought of wandering its dark and dangerous streets filled him with an all but debilitating sense of dread.

But through the grace and kindness of Dr. Godehard Kirsch, Luther was to find a home at the end of the Long Hallway, a massive corridor which began beneath the sub-basement of G10—the only facility left operational after the shuttering of Cold River—and ended almost a mile away, in a warren of rooms fitted like none that Luther had ever seen.

In the first six months of 1997 Luther discovered that the catacombs beneath the hospital were not the only subterranean worlds in Philadelphia.

When it came to the labyrinthine corridors beneath the city, beginning in the mazes under the hospital, Luther's memory was eidetic. In virtual darkness he moved, often following tributaries deep into the sewer system. He learned all the tricks of the underground workers, the virtual timetables for the evening return of homeowners. Beneath the city he learned many things.

But it was in the dream arcade that Luther, with the help of Dr. Kirsch and his associates, would travel the world.

Night after night, in dream after dream, Luther left the confines of G10. In the dream arcade, the recorded reveries of Eduard Olev Kross, Luther was unstoppable. In some of the dreams he was a forger and a thief. In some, a confidence man and an arsonist. In many, when cornered, a taker of lives.

In other dreams—the ones Luther liked best—he searched for a little blond girl named Kaisa. Her beautiful face was the last diorama in the dream arcade, a place to which Luther had begun to visit on his own.

In village after village Luther looked for her, in homes, cafes, train stations, even beneath the hay in barns. He would enter homes in the night, sitting for hours, watching for the first trace of dawn, searching for Kaisa.

He had many close calls, but not once did he have to draw his knife, a beautiful bone-handled blade forged of Russian steel, a present from Dr. Kirsch.

Then, one day, he found the girl.

For weeks he had crept into homes all over the neighborhood, making meticulous entries in his journal. One girl had seemed right at first. But when Luther witnessed a violent tantrum on the playground near her school, he knew she would not do.

The very next night, as always, he put on the old suit, the floppy hat. When he climbed into the city above, he knew that this night would be different. The moon was in a crescent phase, a trimmed fingernail in the black sky, and Luther suddenly felt as if he might be invisible.

He entered the home through the basement, slipped into the small living room, and saw on the mantel a pair of framed pictures, two young girls about four or five years apart. When he saw the younger girl, her fine blond hair held by a thin red ribbon, his heart fluttered.

It was Kaisa.

Over the next three nights Luther returned to the house, listening, waiting, barely able to contain his excitement. On the fourth night, when the house fell silent, he crept up the stairs, and entered the bedroom. When he heard a sound from below—a machine humming to life, perhaps a refrigerator cycling—he stepped into the closet.

When he felt it was safe, he put his hand on the doorknob. Before he could open the door, the door opened for him. It was not the girl for whom he had come. It was the older girl.

For what seemed like an eternity the older girl seemed to be in a trance, staring at him, unmoving. Eventually she retreated, and leaned on the edge of her bed. Luther walked out of the closet, sat down on a small chair, came face to face with the little blond girl. She did not seem to fear him.

"Hello," he said softly. "What is your name?"

"I'm Bean," she said.

"Do you dream?"

The little girl nodded.

"Come," he said. "I'll tuck you in."

Moments later, with both girls beneath the covers, Luther reached out, flipped off the light. He took the small tape recorder from his pocket, put it on the nightstand.

The room was now thick with shadow. Luther sat at the end of the bed. He pressed PLAY. Moments later, the tape began to play.

"Sleep now, little ones," he said. "Sleep."

On his last visit Luther brought with him a bottle of apple juice, poured the girl and her sister a small glass. After they had drank from the cups, he dressed them warmly, led them down the stairs, and into the Long Hallway, at the end of which the doctor waited.

When he brought them back, he knew that the little one — the one called Bean — was the one.

As she drifted off that night Luther tucked the covers around her. She looked up at him, her eyes softly closing.

"Many years from now, on your birthday, I will come back for you," Luther said.

2010

On the night Luther brought Bean back to the doctor, he covered his ears to the screams, and thought of White Rita. He did not know her, of course — they say she bled to death in the Echo Hallway — but he remembered her in the only place he could.

In his dreams.

Months later, when the flowers were put into the ground, when Luther saw the blackened flesh that had been Dr. Kirsch wheeled away, he closed his eyes, and entered the dream arcade.

He never walked out.

February 2013

Luther followed the man from the bodega and took him in an alley behind a block of row houses. In the dream the sledgehammer had been in a barn, a fragrant clapboard structure smelling of damp hay and manure.

In the dream Luther found it on the construction site just a few blocks from the man's house.

"It has been a long time," the man said. He sat in a wooden chair in the center of the field. It had begun to snow.

"Yes," Luther said.

"The doctor is dead, you know."

"I know."

The man hung his head for a moment. At first Luther thought he was going to cry, but instead he began to whisper. Was it a prayer? Perhaps. Luther had heard this before. He had never prayed, would not know whom to pray to, but he never begrudged a person this moment of grace at the very end. There was dignity in all death.

"Why now?" the man finally asked.

"Because the digging machines are here," Luther said. "The digging machines are here and they will unearth all the secrets."

The man dropped his head into his hands, and this time he did begin to cry.

Luther took off his overcoat. The man glanced up, saw the old sackcloth suit, its many bloodstains. He also saw what Luther had in his right hand.

"Do you know me?" Luther asked.

The man nodded. "You are Eduard Kross, of course."

"Yes."

"And I am Toomas Sepp. I always knew that, when this day came, I would be Sepp."

Luther handed the man the railroad spike. Moments later, as snow-flakes glistened his hair, Robert Freitag held the spike to the back of his head.

Luther lifted the sledgehammer high into the air and brought it down with all of his strength. First there was the sound of metal striking metal, iron on iron.

Then there was nothing. Just the silence of sleep, the warm and comforting solace of the womb.

March 2013

It was just after nine p.m., and street traffic was light.

Luther watched lights flicker on, flicker off in the houses on the street, people finishing their dinners, preparing their baths, retiring to their living rooms to watch television, descending to their basements to engage in their hobbies, their perversions, shielded from the streets by cement and glass block.

Luther glanced back at the three-story row house with which he was concerned.

What did he know? He knew the name and profession of the man who lived there. He knew that the man was divorced. He knew that the man had one son, age seven. He knew that on Tuesday nights around seven p.m., the boy would perform one of his chores, that being the taking out of the garbage.

On his many visits to the small park across the street, Luther had observed the boy through his bedroom window on the second floor, had seen the posters on the boy's wall, as well as a bookcase which held a number of action figures.

There were two obstacles.

Luther walked across the street, looked closely at the iron gate that led to the rear of the row house. The gate looked new, a rather gaudy scroll-top portal that appeared to be constructed of cold rolled steel. It seemed to be of the same manufacture as the bars over the front windows, both first and second stories, but not the third. Luther had noticed the first time he paid a visit that, although there were bars on the front windows, there were none on the side windows. Apparently the homeowner, the man with whom Luther had business, surmised that this rather expensive gate was enough to keep intruders from the rear of the property.

Penny wise, Luther thought.

No, the gate was not his obstacle. It had been years since he had encountered a lock mechanism he could not best. There were, however, two other barriers. He could see that there was an alarm system rigged to the gate. If it was not opened and closed with a key, the alarm would trigger. There were also motion detectors at the rear of the property.

Luther knew his way around this.

The other obstacle, the one that would take a little more cunning to overcome, was represented by the two scuffed plastic bowls at the end of the short driveway.

Luther shoved his hands into the pockets of his overcoat. He misted himself into the night, already formulating the medications he would need.

First he would deal with the old woman, then he had a date with a boy who liked a comic book character named the Spectre.

22

The odor was nauseating, a bitter redolence of burned fabric, upholstery ticking, melted plastic, charred wood. It enveloped the entire block.

The flames had reached the south wall of the row house, where firefighters had broken out the windows. Everything was wet and blackened and scorched. The heat, which might have been welcome on a cold and rainy March afternoon, was heavy with acrid smoke.

It was the relentless rain that the PFD captain on scene, a lifer named Mickey Dugan, said might have helped save the entire block.

The cause of the blaze was under investigation. According to the two PPD patrol officers who had secured the scene, front and back, no one came in or out of the premises after detectives Byrne and Balzano left for Priory Park.

Investigators had not yet found any identification on the body found on the creek bank, but both Jessica and Byrne made what would suffice as a positive identification for the time being, pending the woman's brother making it official at the morgue later in the day.

In each hand, beneath the stones, had been a dried, white flower. Both had been collected and sent to the FBI for identification.

They did not find the woman's iPhone. Repeated calls to her number were directed to the woman's voice-mail box. It was not possible to tell if the phone was simply turned off, had its SIM card replaced, or had been destroyed.

*   *   *

By three p.m. police had set up a perimeter around the block of row houses where Joan Delacroix had lived.

Jessica and Byrne stood on the corner, amid the growing crowd. Because this street in Brewerytown was quite narrow, a number of residents on both sides of the street had been evacuated until the blaze had been brought under control.

While they waited to be cleared to reenter Joan Delacroix's house, Jessica and Byrne compared notes. They agreed that from the moment they entered the house—and the victim had called out from the basement—to the moment Byrne descended the steps could not have been more than two minutes.

How had the victim been spirited away, right under their noses, in that amount of time?

Before they could begin to address that question, Jessica looked up to see James Delacroix come around the corner. Jessica wondered if the man had perhaps continued to search the neighborhood in ever-widening circles.

When he saw the police and fire trucks he ran across the street, ducked beneath the yellow crime scene tape, and attempted to enter his sister's house. He was stopped by two young patrol officers.

Byrne stepped forward, took James Delacroix aside.

"What...what happened?" Delacroix asked.

Byrne made eye contact with Jessica, led Delacroix a few houses away. He squared himself in front of the man. "Mr. Delacroix, I'm afraid I have some terrible news for you."

"About Joan?"

"Yes," Byrne said. "I'm sorry to have to inform you that your sister is dead."

Byrne caught the man as he was about to sag to the ground. He got the attention of one of the firefighters.

"Mr. Delacroix," Byrne said, "this man is going to look after you. I'll be back as soon as I can."

Byrne saw the man's eyes begin to roll back into his head. For a moment it looked as if he might be going into shock. He kept a hand on the man's arm until the firefighter met his eye, giving him a look that both Jessica and Byrne knew well, one that said everything was under control

Six detectives from the homicide unit conducted the neighborhood interviews. Many of the people were still on the street, having been prevented from entering their houses. Slowly they were being given permission to do so.

In addition to being the scene of a fire, the area was also the scene of an abduction, a kidnapping that ultimately ended in murder.

While the neighborhood interviews continued, Jessica and Byrne combed the long alleyway that ran behind the row houses and retail establishments on the street.

They saw a man standing at the end of the alley, arms folded, waiting impatiently. A stocky Asian man, he wore a chef's jacket and a look of annoyance.

Byrne introduced himself and Jessica. The man's name was Winston Kuo. He was the owner of the Saigon Garden Restaurant, a small place four doors down from Joan Delacroix's house.

"Is this about the fire?" Kuo asked.

"Yes and no," Byrne said.

The man just nodded.

"Did you know the woman in the third house from the end of the block?"

Kuo thought for a few moments. "Older woman? Caucasian?"

"Yes."

"Not really. I mean, I'd see her from time to time, and we'd nod hello. That sort of thing. I'd see her in the alley when we both were taking out trash."

"Do you remember when the last time you saw her was?"

"A few days, at least. Maybe a week."

"You didn't see her today?"

"No."

Jessica glanced down the street. There were two young busboys huddling in a doorway, trying to keep warm as they waited. "Do those young men work for you?"

Kuo looked over, back. "Yes."

"We'd like to speak to them, if we could."

"That wouldn't be a problem. Unfortunately, they don't speak English."

"Could you ask them if they saw Ms. Delacroix today at all? Especially in the hour or so before the fire started?"

"No problem."

Kuo shouted to the two young men. A few seconds later the busboys came down the street. The looks of apprehension on their faces said that they might be thinking that Jessica and Byrne were from ICE.

Kuo spoke to them in rapid-fire Vietnamese.

The two boys listened, glanced at each other, then back at their boss. They both shook their heads. Kuo asked a second question, and was met with the same response. He dismissed them. Kuo turned back to the detectives.

"They did not see anything. The younger of the two just started yesterday. I don't think he's ever seen Miss...?"

"Delacroix," Byrne said. "Her name was Joan Delacroix."

The tense of Byrne's verb was not lost on Kuo. "Ms. Delacroix. I don't think he knows who she was."

"Have you noticed any comings or goings from Ms. Delacroix's house for the past few days or weeks?" Byrne asked. "Any visitors? Anything unusual?"

Kuo gave it some thought. "I can't say that I have. But I'm usually pretty busy here. Right now I'm the only one on the line."

Byrne took out a card, handed it to the man, made the usual request. Before they left, Kuo pointed to the second floor of the building at the other side of the alley, a former commercial space on the corner.

"You might want to check with Old Tony," Kuo said.

"Old Tony?" Byrne asked. He looked up and saw a silhouette in the window.

"He sees everything."

"You're saying he usually sits up there?"

Kuo nodded. "For a while I thought maybe it was a mannequin or something, you know? Day or night he'd be up there. He never moved. Then one night I saw the ember of a cigar. Trust me, Old Tony doesn't miss much."

The apartment was crowded with furniture, commercial fixtures, paraphernalia. In the corner was a large City of Philadelphia trash can. Next to it were two enormous corkboards. Pinned to the boards were coupons and flyers for everything from pizza to massage parlors to Tai Chi classes. There had to be hundreds.

The tenant of the second-floor corner space — Anthony Giordano — was in his mid-eighties. He was thin but still wiry, had a thick head of unruly white hair, chaotic eyebrows.

Byrne introduced himself and Jessica. They navigated their way to the corner where Old Tony kept neighborhood vigil. Winston Kuo was right. You could see a lot from up here.

"I saw her with this guy," Tony said. "The car was around the corner, but I saw him pull away."

"Did you recognize the man?"

"No," he said. "Sorry. I pretty much only saw the top of his head."

"White guy? Black guy?"

"White."

"What about the car?" Byrne asked. "Have you seen it before?"

"Oh yeah. It's been around here before."

"Can you describe it?"

Tony ran a hand over his stubbled chin. "Well, I've never been too good with make and model. I was never that into cars. Motorcycles were my thing."

"What color was the car?"

"Easy. It was black. Big car. Not new."

"We're talking old-school big here?" Byrne asked. "Olds, Pontiac, Caddy?"

"Caddy I would know."

"Anything distinguishing about it? Any dents, bumper stickers, primer?"

The old man thought for a few moments. "Can't say as I recall."

"Now, Ms. Delacroix, the woman who was with the man, did it seem that she was going with him willingly?"

"You mean like they were friends?"

Byrne nodded.

"I don't think so. He had her by the arm. I thought at first she might have been the guy's mother. You know how some young people treat their parents these days?"

"I do."

"Yeah, well, like that. I wanted to slap him."

Byrne made a few notes, picked up a photograph from the congested bookshelf. It was a picture of a much younger Anthony Giordano in uniform. He was standing between a pair of enormous marble columns. "You're a vet?"

"Yes, sir," Tony said. "I was an MP. Nuremberg."

"At the trials?"

Tony nodded. "Deployed at the Palace of Justice. I got into the Army right at the end of the war. Too young to fight, too old for my ma's house. There were nine of us."

Byrne smiled. "Where were you in that lineup?"

"Dead last. My hand-me-downs were throw-me-downs. Nothing ever fit."

Byrne pointed at the photograph. "What was it like there?"

"Bastards on trial ate better than we did. And we ate pretty good."

Byrne put the photograph back.

"Was your father in the war?" Tony asked.

"Between them," Byrne said. "He served, though."

"Good man."

"He is."

"Still with us?"

"Both feet."

Tony nodded. "Let me ask you something. This guy with the car?"

"What about him?"

"He do something bad to that lady?"

"Yeah," Byrne said. "I'm afraid he did."

Tony nodded. He pointed at the carbine mounted on the wall. To Jessica, it looked to be fully functioning. "Tell you what. If I see the son of a bitch again, can I take him out? I can still draw a bead."

"It would be better if you just gave me a call," Byrne said. He handed the man his business card. "Me or my partner. We'll take it from there."

Tony nodded, considering his options. He smiled at Jessica. "Okay."

"Thank you, sir."

Tony pinned the card on the corkboard, dead center in the mass of offers for gutter cleaning, bathtub resurfacing and unlimited indoor tanning.

When Jessica and Byrne returned to Joan Delacroix's house, PFD was just wrapping up, securing the building. Captain Mickey Dugan noticed the two detectives, stepped forward. He and Byrne had known each other almost thirty years, and there was no need to stand on ceremony.

"You can go in," Dugan said. "First floor only, and then only the north side. We've got it roped off in there. The basement is off-limits."

"Okay," Byrne said.

"Kevin, I'm serious. You walk upstairs and fall through I'm here all fucking night."

As they prepared to enter the house, Byrne took Jessica aside. He spoke softly. "Jess, I think we should—"

Jessica held up a hand, stopping him. She knew what was coming. "I know what you're going to say."

"You do?"

"Of course," she said. "Look, these cases are linked. There's no question about that."

"I know," Byrne said. "But you're SIU now. You have another life. You have school."

"So?"

It was the lamest response possible, Jessica thought, especially to someone who knew her as well as her partner did.

"So you can't put in the time on both cases."

"I'll make up the classes," Jessica said. "I'll find the time."

"And what if you can't?"

Jessica was afraid he would ask this. She'd had her answer locked and loaded, although she was certain it wouldn't come out the way she'd rehearsed it. It did not. "Then I'll just recycle until next semester, Kevin. It's no big deal."

Byrne knew this wasn't true, of course, just as he knew there was no point trying to talk her out of it. It *was* a big deal. It was also her choice.

The conversation, for the moment, was over.

Jessica and Byrne stood near the bottom of the stairs as the CSU officers began taking photographs. There were no bloody footprints, no blood spatter on the stairs, or in the short hallway leading to the back door. When it was dark enough, they would perform a Luminol test, the process by which investigators could detect trace evidence of blood all but invisible to the naked eye.

"Why didn't we hear anything?" Jessica asked.

Byrne didn't answer right away. Perhaps there was no answer to that question. But one thing Jessica knew was that, as soon as this made it to the press, their lives were going to be pure hell. A woman is kidnapped and murdered while two homicide detectives were standing in her living room.

It was a public relations nightmare.

Jessica and Byrne couldn't think about that now. Right now they had to protect this crime scene, and put in motion the investigation.

"Come with me," Byrne said.

Jessica followed Byrne down the short hallway to the living room. They positioned themselves in exactly the same place they were standing when Byrne began calling Joan Delacroix's name.

"We were right here, right?" Byrne asked.

Jessica found her spot on the floor. "Yeah," she said. "Exactly."

Byrne turned his body, blading it toward the hallway that led to the stairs and the kitchen. He was at a forty-five-degree angle to the opening, his left side pointing to the rear of the row house.

"I was facing this way," Byrne said, "right?"

"Right."

"How long would you say it was between the time she yelled 'I'll be right up' and the time I went down the stairs?"

Jessica thought about it. "I think it was about two minutes, max."

Byrne glanced at his watch. He repositioned himself to the approximate place they had been standing when the woman yelled from the basement. Byrne hit a button on his watch. "I'll be right up," he said, echoing the woman. They stood in silence for a full minute, while CSU officers made their way in and out of the house. It was not the ideal atmosphere to attempt to recreate those crucial few minutes, but it would have to do.

Byrne looked at his watch, hit a button.

"He was already down there, Jess. He was fucking down there waiting for her. He was probably down there when we were across the street."

The thought sent a shiver through Jessica. The idea of walking through your house, doing common everyday chores, not knowing that in the shadow, or closet, there was someone hiding, waiting to commit unspeakable violence.

"Let's assume, for the moment, that he *was* down there waiting for her," Jessica said. "During those two minutes he subdues her, threatens to kill her if she doesn't come with him."

"Okay."

"But how does he get away? How does he get her out of the house?"

Byrne pointed to the short hallway leading to the back door, a section that was now cordoned off with yellow crime scene tape. "It's not possible. I would have seen them. The answer is in the basement. It has to be."

Jessica agreed. But they wouldn't be able to go down there until the entire structure was cleared for safety, and that could be days.

"You didn't look away, even for a few seconds?" Jessica asked.

Byrne said nothing.

They would process every square centimeter between the basement steps and the back door. If ever there was a case where the law of transference mattered—the basic premise being that wherever people go, they carry some physical evidence with them, and leave some behind—this was it.

"We didn't get here soon enough," Byrne said.

"Kevin."

"It's our job, Jess. Jesus *Christ,* we were right here."

They stood in the small kitchen, preparing to leave. Before they could button their coats, and prepare for the rain, they both looked at the kitchen table. They saw it at the same time.

There, on the table, was a bowl with a mug upside down in the center. Next to it, on the right, was a tarnished silver spoon.

"Was this here before?" Jessica asked.

"No."

Jessica took out her phone, scrolled through the photographs she had taken of Robert Freitag's small eating area. She found the picture she wanted. It was the same setup. "Look."

"Identical," Byrne said.

"Same spoon."

"Same spoon."

With a gloved hand Jessica picked up the spoon by the tip of the handle. She looked at the inscription. As with the spoon at Robert Freitag's house, it was too worn to read.

"It's definitely silver," Jessica said. "And it definitely is some sort of commemorative."

"This was set up after we left," Byrne said. "This fucker came back. He came back to burn the place down."

Jessica slipped the spoon into a paper evidence bag.

"Let's take a ride."

23

The fourth pawnshop they visited was an old three-ball on Germantown Avenue, near East York Street. The front windows were jammed full of radios, acoustic guitars, speakers, inexpensive watches, even an old instrument that looked like a zither. Just about everything had the word "Sale" on it, as if it would be any other way.

Jessica had visited Mr. Gold Pawn many times when she was young, with her father, who had once been a patrol officer in the district. The original owner—Moises Gold—had always been good for a free water ice.

The shop was now run by the late Moises Gold's sons, twin brothers, Sam and Sanford Gold.

Announced by a bell over the door, Jessica and Byrne entered the shop. To Jessica, it smelled exactly the same as it had when she was ten years old, a combination of glass cleaner, strawberry air freshener and Lemon Pledge, with a top note of bottom-shelf cologne.

Perched behind the counter at the back of the shop was Sammy Gold. Probably in his fifties now, Sammy was shaped like a huge Bosc pear—small head, narrow shoulders, broad chest, corpulent waist. Jessica almost did a double-take when she saw him. Sammy Gold had turned into his father, right down to the black polo shirt, dusted with dandruff, and a hound's-tooth sport jacket. It might have even been the same jacket.

Sammy looked up from his *Daily News.* "Oh my God. As I live and wheeze."

"Sammy," Jessica said. "How are you?"

"One foot in the grave, the other on a banana peel."

His father used to say the same thing twenty-five years ago, Jessica thought. *You go with what works.*

"This is my partner, Kevin Byrne."

The two men shook hands.

"What can I do you out of?" Sammy asked, folding his paper and putting it on the counter.

Jessica took out the evidence bag containing the spoon. "We're trying to track down where this came from."

Sammy reached beneath the counter and unfurled a long black-velvet jewelry roll. Jessica put the spoon on it.

Sammy Gold didn't have to look at it too long.

"Yeah," he said. "I know this spoon."

"You've seen it before?"

"Yeah, but it's been awhile." He pointed to the bottom of the handle, where the engraving was. "See this here? It's a commemorative. We get a lot of them."

Sammy turned around, pulled a long walnut box off the shelf. He placed it on the counter, opened it. Inside were a few dozen spoons of various sizes and finishes. Some gold, some silver.

"Commemoratives are generally not worth that much," Sammy said. "They're more for collectors and completists." He picked up a short round spoon, gold plated. "This one is for Penn House. I think it's dated seventeen seventy-six."

Jessica saw the small sticker on the back: $95.00.

Sammy picked up a second spoon, this one with an oddly shaped bowl that seemed to be two spoons welded together.

"What is this?" Jessica asked.

Sammy smiled. "This is a mustache spoon." He pointed to the lip on the bowl of the spoon. "This here? It was designed to keep your mustache out of the soup."

The rest of the spoons were a variety of different types — coin spoons, spoons with faces engraved on the handles, a few with flowers painted on the bowls.

"Like I said, this stuff ain't worth all that much. I could let you have this whole box for four hundred."

"I think we'll pass on that for now," Jessica said.

Sammy shrugged. *Worth a shot.*

Jessica picked up the spoon they had taken from Joan Delacroix's house. "So you're sure you've had spoons like this one pass through here?"

"Well, not one hundred percent. Like I said, not much money in them. A Rolex I would know. A Fender Strat in a beat."

Jessica pointed to the engraving in the handle. "Do you know where this is from? What it commemorates?"

Sammy reached into a drawer, took out a lighted jeweler's loupe, put it to his right eye, looked closely at the handle of the spoon. "Can't make it out. Sorry." He held up a finger. "Let me ask my brother. He remembers everything."

"I thought he retired," Jessica said.

"So did I."

Sammy took a few steps toward the curtain separating the front of the store from the back. "Sandy!"

A few moments later Sanford Gold came out from the back of the store, a huge, half-eaten hoagie in his hand.

Sanford Gold was the butterfly-wing replica of his brother. Right down to the part in his hair (Sanford left, Sammy right) and the gold pinkie ring on his finger (Sanford left, Sammy right).

"You remember Jessica Giovanni, right?" Sammy asked.

Sanford just stared.

"She's a police officer now. A *detective*."

Sanford stopped chewing, clearly guilty of some sort of misdemeanor.

Sammy held up the spoon. "We've had these in before, haven't we?"

Resigned to dealing with the task at hand, Sandy put his sandwich down on the counter, wiped his hands on his shirt. He pulled up his glasses, scrutinized the spoon.

"Well?" Sammy asked. "We've seen these before, yes?"

Sanford just nodded.

"Do you remember who brought them in?"

"It was that Lenny character," Sanford said.

"Lenny Pintar brought these in?"

"Yeah. The retarded kid."

"Sandy, he's not retarded."

Sanford Gold shrugged, hitched his belt. "So what's the right word now? I can't keep up with the right words anymore. Who the fuck can keep up?" He looked at Jessica. "Sorry."

Jessica nodded.

Sammy thought for a few beats. "Okay, Lenny probably *is* retarded, but you're not supposed to say so."

"Why not?"

Sammy looked at Jessica and Byrne, then back at his brother. "You're just supposed to say he's a little..."

"Challenged," Byrne said.

Sammy snapped his fingers. "Challenged. Thank you."

Jessica took out her notepad. "What can you tell me about this Leonard...?"

"Pintar," Sammy said.

"Can you spell that for me please?"

Sammy did.

"How do you know him?"

Sammy looked at his brother. "How did we first meet him, Sandy?"

As soon as Sammy asked the question, Sandy took another bite of his sandwich. Jessica wanted to handcuff him and body-slam him on the glass. And if that's what she wanted to do, Byrne probably wanted to shoot him. Cooler heads prevailed for the moment.

Sammy turned his attention away from his brother. "He's come in here off and on for years."

"About how long ago did he start coming in?" Jessica asked.

"Maybe fifteen years or so. But he doesn't come in that often."

"Has he pawned a lot of merchandise over the years?"

"No," Sammy said. "It's not like that. He would bring stuff in, usually just junk. I kind of feel for the guy, because he is a little, you know, *challenged,* like you say. He would come in with things, and we'd throw him a couple of bucks. My old man liked him."

"When was the last time you saw him?"

Sammy glanced at his brother once again, then, realizing this was a lost cause, gave it some thought. "Got to be maybe a year now. Easy. About a year."

"Is that when he brought in the spoons?"

"No, got to be longer than that. Maybe a couple of years."

Jessica made the note. "Why do you say he's challenged?"

"Well, it's just the way he acts and talks. If you ever meet him you'll know what I mean. You just kind of know, right?"

"Yeah, I do," Jessica said. She didn't, not exactly, but she needed to move on. "Do you know if Lenny has ever been in jail?"

"You know, now that you mention it, I think he was once. I think he mentioned something about the food being crappy."

"Are we talking county jail or prison?"

"Can't say for sure."

Jessica jotted a few more notes. "Do you have a fax machine?"

At this, Sanford Gold perked up. He swallowed hard, wiped his lips with the back of his hand. "Absolutely," he said. "What do you need? Standalone, all-in-one, color? Inkjet, laser, ribbon?"

"Actually," Jessica said. "I was just—"

"We've got Brother, HP, Panasonic, Samsung—"

Jessica held up a hand, like a traffic cop. "What I meant was, do you have a fax machine, as in a fax machine on which I can receive a fax right now?"

Sanford looked crestfallen. But not for long. He grabbed his sandwich, and disappeared through the curtain into the back room. No sale, no interest.

"What are you gonna do?" Sammy asked. "Can't shoot him."

"Sure you can," Jessica said.

Sammy laughed, reached into his pocket, pulled out an engraved sterling-silver business card case, flipped it open, thumbed out a card. "The fax number is at the bottom."

Jessica took out her phone, called the office, asked for a check on one Leonard Pintar, requesting any results to be faxed to the pawn shop. Within a minute, the fax machine at the back of the shop clicked to life.

Sammy walked to the back of the store, pulled out the two pages. Jessica figured it took every fiber in the man's considerable bulk not to read the fax. He handed the pages to Jessica.

Jessica skimmed the file, handed it to Byrne. As it turned out, Lenny did have a record, but only a minor one. He had been arrested on a disorderly conduct charge two years earlier, but it was determined that he had stopped taking his medications, and engaged in what was probably just a misunderstanding with the rookie patrol officer. He spent less than thirty-six hours in lockup, and was released to the Pennsylvania Department of Welfare. A quick call to the agency revealed that Leonard Pintar was no longer a ward of the commonwealth, and they had no forwarding address. They suggested contacting the Department of Human Services.

"Do you have any idea where we could locate Leonard right now?" Jessica asked.

Sammy thought for a few moments. "Yeah. He works at Reading Terminal Market."

"At one of the counters?" Jessica asked.

"Not really," Sammy said. "From what I understand he kinda stands around and hands out fliers. I think he hangs around the door closest to Filbert. He's got his own style. You'll see."

"Got it."

"By the way, if you ever run into this again, you can just put the spoon in an aluminum pan full of boiling water, add salt, and *voilà*. No tarnish."

"That easy, huh?"

"Yeah. Pan has to be aluminum, though." He handed the spoon to Byrne.

"Good to know," Jessica replied, knowing full well that the knowledge had just passed through her mind like a luge sled. She almost heard it rush by. Chemistry was not her forte. She handed Sammy a card. "If you find out anything, please give me a call."

Sammy took out a leather card case, slipped the card inside. "Sure thing, *Detective.*" He said the last word with a smile, shook his head. "I can't believe how grown up you are."

"Yeah, unfortunately, it's a byproduct of aging."

Sammy laughed. "Don't I know it. Say hi to your dad for me."

"I will," Jessica said. She held up the fax. "And thanks for this."

"On the house."

24

Of all the big box stores, Luther enjoyed Home Depot the most. He loved the massive main corridors, the wide aisles, the high shelves, the colors and textures—plumbing, electrical, lumber, paint, bath, doors and windows—each lane a dazzling assortment of items.

By far, Luther's favorite section was tools. Over the years he had accumulated a wide variety of tools, a chest that would be the envy of not only the homeowner who indulged his significant other in the occasional home remodeling job, but even the serious and dedicated tradesman.

He parked the Toronado at the end of one of the aisles, leaving an empty space on either side. It was one of his foibles, one he had long ago resigned himself to bear. Today he wore a dark blue tradesman's jumpsuit buttoned all the way to the neck, along with a Phillies ball cap. Over the left breast pocket was a white oval, with the name Preston embroidered in red thread.

Upon entering the store he was greeted by an orange-aproned Home Depot employee, a pretty Hispanic girl in her twenties.

Luther smiled, and nodded a greeting.

Today his needs were specific, although just by entering the store he was almost viscerally compelled to browse. But he could not. There was work to do.

Because the store did not provide handled shopping baskets, Luther picked up one of the bright orange buckets, then rethought it. He placed it back inside the others in the stack, returned to the lobby, and retrieved a shopping cart.

Ten minutes later he found himself in the aisle with the painter's supplies, a section with which he was quite familiar. He found what he needed—a large plastic painter's drop cloth—then navigated over to the aisle that offered chains, rope and wire.

Five minutes later he steered his cart to one of the checkout lanes. While a lot of people were taking advantage of the self-serve checkout counters, Luther waited in a long line, behind a man with a dozen sheets of exterior plywood on a trolley.

Luther always paid cash.

He looked at the photograph of the man, the smiling picture he had found in a discarded pamphlet for the doctors' conglomerate at which the man worked. His smile was engaging, bright and exceedingly white.

Before cleaning the bloodied gloves he had used on the old woman, Luther prepared a sandwich, then put away the new supplies.

As he stepped into the main corridor he sensed a presence behind him.

Träumen Sie?

Yes.

What do you see?

Through the fog I see the shape of a man, a heavyset man, with his arms outstretched. We are standing in the Baldone Forest, not far from Riga. It is early spring, and the air is chilly and damp.

Who is this man?

He is a businessman, the owner of a small construction company. His specialty is electrical work. His name is Juris Spalva. His pockets are filled with stones.

How do you know him?

I don't know him. I know of his deeds.

What has he done?

Like the man who killed my sister he is a predator. He often brought young girls to this part of the forest. He would tie their hands with wire, and make them lie down on the mossy ground.

Does the man know why you have brought him here?

Yes. I told him the reason. I showed him a picture of my sister.

What will become of him?

He will stand until his legs no longer support him. Then his flesh will know the cut of the wire.

Träumen Sie?

Yes, Doctor. I dream.

25

Rachel Anne Gray stood in the arched entryway to the kitchen, wondering if it was too late to buy a backhoe and level the house. She glanced at her watch. There was plenty of time. All she had to do was get up a good head of steam, take out one of the load-bearing walls, and: *voilà!*

Instant rubble.

She assessed the fleapit of a kitchen in front of her, still aghast. Three of the cabinet doors were missing, ripped unceremoniously from their hinges. The vinyl flooring had on it a patina of rancid grease, topped with a layer of cat hair. The coffeemaker on the counter contained a few inches of what might have been coffee at one time, but was now dotted with small lily ponds of mold.

In the corner of the living room—which was piled high with dirty clothes, taped moving boxes, and used red Solo cups   was what looked like a small pile of dog shit. *Old* dog shit.

Rachel looked at her watch again. She now had ten minutes. If she was going to do something, she had to get moving.

She unzipped her leather tote bag and almost laughed at the sight of her roll of paper towels, Dustbuster and a can of Pledge. These were her side arms, and usually all she needed to do a quick cleanup of properties she had to show.

They would do her little good in this place.

She reached to the bottom of the bag and found the pair of rubber gloves she kept for emergencies, slipped them on. She then grabbed the roll of paper towels, and crossed the living room. As it turned out, there was more than one pile of dog shit. Some of it had begun to turn white. She took a deep breath, held it, gagged anyway. She tried again, and quickly scooped up the droppings. She all but ran back to the kitchen, opened the cabinet door under the sink.

Of *course* there was no garbage bag. Why would you need a garbage bag when you can just leave your garbage on the floor?

God, she hated renters.

Rachel heard a car door slam out front. The only thing she hated more than renters were buyers who showed up early.

She put the dog crap in one of the drawers, snapped off the rubber gloves, stashed them in her tote bag, then sprinted to the front door and peered through the small window.

The worst. The couple, who were in their mid-fifties, were ambling up the walk—woman out front, man staring up at the gutters (falling off), the roof (missing shingles) and the tuck pointing around the second-floor windows (nonexistent). He already had a scowl on his face.

What they didn't know was that the exterior of the house was its best feature.

Smile, Rachel.

She opened the door, stepped through, onto the (slanted) porch.

"Hi!" she said. "You must be Mr. and Mrs. Gormley. I'm Rachel Gray, Perry-Hayes Realty. *So* nice to meet you."

The woman stepped forward, extended her (limp fish) hand. They shook. The man grunted something unintelligible in Rachel's direction, following it with: "When the hell were those photographs on your website taken?"

Rachel knew she was going to get this question. She'd heard it a lot. Many of the photos her company received were in the house's earlier days, its best days, not unlike those head shots of fading B-actors on IMDb.

"A few years ago, I think," Rachel said. "The house has been on the market for a while, which is why the seller is highly motivated."

"It looks a hell of a lot better online," the man mumbled. "If we knew it was this bad we would've stayed home."

Rachel bit her tongue.

"It needs a little work," she said, stepping to the side, ushering the couple in. Of course, saying this house needed a little work was like saying Joan Rivers once had a nip and tuck.

Rachel closed the door, realizing, not for the first time, that it was much better in situations like this to just stop talking. There was nothing here to sell.

"Holy shit," the man said.

The shit's in the kitchen drawer, Rachel wanted to say. Then they could have a good laugh and move on down the road. Instead she said: "The house is one thousand square feet, three bedrooms, one bath. As you can see, the ceilings are high. Washer and dryer are included."

"Nine-eighty-eight," the man said.

"Excuse me?"

"It's not a thousand square feet. It's nine-eighty-eight. Says so right in your listing."

Rachel just stared for a few seconds. "Yes, of course," she finally said. "My mistake. Let's go upstairs."

She led them up the steps, gazing straight ahead, hoping they would too. The carpeting on the stairs was filthy, cratered with cigarette burns. The handrail was loose. Overhead were water stains from a leak that probably occurred during the Truman administration.

"We have three bedrooms up here, including the master suite," Rachel said. "The other two bedrooms are a Jack and Jill."

Rachel noticed that the woman had taken out a small package of flushable moist towelettes. She couldn't really blame her.

Rachel put her hand on the doorknob to what was laughingly called the master suite, hoping it was at least presentable. She usually did a walk-through with new listings but she had not had time today.

She opened the door, and nearly jumped out of her skin. There, standing in front of her, wearing pajamas, was a ten-year-old boy.

Rachel stepped inside, quickly closed the door behind her.

"Um, hi," Rachel said. "My name is Rachel? I'm with Perry-Hayes Realty?"

Why was she phrasing everything like a question? Maybe it was because this was the middle of the day, in the middle of the week, and this kid was supposed to be in school. Instead, it appeared, he was sleeping on a ratty mattress under a ratty blanket.

Although she had only been a Realtor for three years, she had seen quite a bit. She had once gotten fleas from a North Philly basement condo. This was a first.

"Is your mom here?"

The boy rubbed his eyes. "No."

"Okay. What about your dad?"

The boy yawned. "Uh uh."

"So you're all by yourself?"

He shook his head. "Just my sister."

Jesus Christ, Rachel thought. *There's* another *one?*

Before Rachel could say anything she heard a sound behind her. The door opened. Rachel turned to see an eight-year-old girl, also in pajamas, staring at her from the top of the steps.

Behind her stood the Gormleys, perhaps wondering if these kids came with the house. Maybe they did.

"Hi," Rachel said to the girl. She almost introduced herself, but what the hell would be the point of that?

Before she could corral both kids into one of the bedrooms, Rachel saw Ed Gormley take out a digital camera and start snapping pictures. She wanted to believe he was taking pictures to show his contractor, so that he could get some ballpark estimates on rehabbing the property. This was not possible. In her heart of hearts she knew the only reason he was taking photographs was to show his buddies at the bar what had to be the worst, non-condemned property in Fishtown.

Non-condemned for the moment, Rachel amended.

She turned back to the boy. "Well, we'll just go about our business. It was nice meeting you."

Without a word, the boy walked down the hallway, pushed open the door to the bathroom. Leaving the door open he lifted the lid on the toilet, and proceeded to urinate. Loudly.

Rachel glanced heavenward, looking, hoping, for divine intervention. Maybe a lightning bolt to fry the kid and his sister. And one shot in the ass for Mr. Gormley.

None was forthcoming.

Mercifully, the couple had proceeded down the stairs, into the basement. Rachel had not had the opportunity to visit the basement. She could only imagine. There was probably a foot of water.

Before she could descend the steps she caught a shadow to her left. It was the little girl. She was holding forth an opened flip phone.

"It's for you," the little girl said.

Rachel was stunned. "For me?"

The girl nodded.

Rachel took the phone from the girl. She put it to her ear hoping the phone was a little bit more hygienic than the rest of the house. "This is Rachel Gray."

"What are they taking pictures for?"

Rachel had no idea who she was talking to. It was a woman's voice, but one with which she was not familiar. "I'm sorry?"

"Why are they taking pictures?"

It took a moment to realize what this woman was talking about. "Pictures of the house?"

The woman plowed ahead. "There are pictures on the mother-fuckin' internet. They don't need to take no damn *pictures*."

It suddenly hit her. This was not the owner of the property. This was the mother—such as it might have been—to these two kids. The reason the woman was asking about the pictures was not that she was worried, in any way, that it would hurt the sale of the house. After all, she was a renter. Why would she care? No, no. She was worried that these people, these strangers in her house, might be from children's services and that they were documenting the less than desirable living conditions in this hovel.

Not to mention that her two kids were alone, unsupervised, in the middle of the day. Rachel wanted to mention it. She did not.

Instead, she shifted gears.

"Ah, okay. I see what you're saying. My clients are just taking a few snapshots of the interior to get an idea of some of the work that might need to be done if and when they purchase the property."

"They don't need any more pictures," the woman said. "Tell them to look at the pictures on the internet. Put Charisse back on."

Who the hell is Charisse? Rachel thought.

Of course. Charisse was the little girl. She handed the phone back to her. As Rachel turned to continue down the steps she heard the little girl say "Uh huh" about ten times.

Rachel took a deep breath at the bottom of the stairs, thinking about how she would begin to close. If she sold this one, she would rocket into the GPAR Hall of Fame on the first ballot.

In the end it didn't matter.

The Gormleys were already on the front walk making their way to the car. Rachel could tell by their body language that they were gone for good.

Who could blame them?

Five minutes later, as Rachel walked to her car, she glanced at the window on the second floor. The little boy was watching her, his big empty eyes staring out like a caged puppy.

26

Leonard Pintar looked enough like his faxed photograph for a positive identification, but the intervening years had been hard, it seemed. He was of above average height, thin almost to the point of gaunt. Jessica pegged him at about six feet tall, 135 pounds.

When they stepped inside the Reading Terminal Market they noticed him right away.

He's got his own style, Sammy Gold had said.

This was an understatement.

Leonard Pintar wore a lavender French cuff shirt, gray work pants and black patent leather loafers — the kind with the gold chain across the upper. The chain was missing on his left foot. It had been replaced with string. His hair was fashioned in an old-school pompadour, and behind one ear was a non-filter cigarette.

Jessica got the man's attention. "How you doing?" she asked.

The man looked over. "I'm aces!" He handed her a flyer. Jessica took it from him.

"Are you Leonard Pintar?" she asked.

"The one and only. Except for my daddy. And his daddy. But I go by Lenny."

"Nice to meet you, Lenny." Jessica opened her ID wallet.

Lenny looked at the badge and ID. He balled a fist, shook it at the ceiling, then put his hands in his pockets. He took a deep breath, blew it out quickly. "Okay. I'm ready."

"You're not in any trouble," Jessica said, not really sure if that was the truth or not. "We just need to ask you a few questions."

"No math, okay?"

"Excuse me?"

"No math questions. Or questions about chemicals."

Jessica glanced at her partner. Byrne gave her a look she knew well, the one that said: *He's* your *friend. You began the interview, you finish it.* Jessica looked back at Lenny, committed to seeing this through.

"Understood," Jessica said. "May I ask where you live, Lenny?"

"I live with Mrs. Gilberto. Mrs. Gilberto makes great Salisbury steak. You should come by."

"I love Salisbury steak," Jessica said. "Is this a group home?"

Lenny nodded.

"Can you tell me how long you've lived there?"

"Now, see, that's math already."

"You're right," Jessica said. "I forgot." She knew she could get this information from DHS. "Would you say it was a long time?"

"Long time."

"And where did you live before that?"

Lenny again looked at the ceiling, this time doing a calculation of some sort. "I think I was up to Norristown then."

Wow, Jessica thought. *A straight answer. More or less.* Usually, her inclination would be to ask where the person lived in Norristown, a community about twenty-five miles northwest of Philadelphia in Montgomery County, the boyhood home of David Rittenhouse Porter, former governor of Pennsylvania.

But Jessica had the distinct feeling Lenny Pintar was talking about Norristown State Hospital. Norristown was a long-term adult psychiatric facility run by the Pennsylvania Department of Welfare.

"Ah, okay," Jessica said. "You mean *Norristown.* Up there on Sterigere Street?"

Lenny's face lit up. "Yeah! You been?"

It occurred to Jessica that he might be asking if she had been a patient at Norristown. Sometimes, as in this moment, she felt as if she might be a candidate. "I have a cousin who works there."

Lenny snapped his fingers. "You must mean Margaret. You look just like her."

"I get that all the time," Jessica said. "What about before that? Where did you live before that?"

"Easy peasy. The Big Place."

Jessica waited for more. More was not forthcoming. "Does the Big Place have another name?"

Lenny smiled. "Don't need one. That place was so big they had to bring in them machines."

"Machines?"

Lenny began to nod his head furiously. "Yeah. *Oh,* yeah. Every night, right after supper, they brought in them fog machines. Christ dipped in *chocolate,* they was big. Big as a damn dump truck."

Jessica looked at Byrne. Byrne broke into a big smile. Lenny laughed, wagged a finger at him.

"You knew I was messing with you, right?" Lenny said. "Just then. She didn't know, but you did. You knew."

"I knew," Byrne said.

"You are good, buddy boy-o. Senior class. Full-page ad."

"The fog machines," Byrne said. "The Big Chief in *One Flew Over the Cuckoo's Nest*."

Jessica figured Byrne said this more for her benefit than Lenny's.

"It's an old nut house joke," Lenny added as an aside to Jessica. "All the nuts like that one. The ones who get it, anyway."

"A classic," Byrne said.

"Score one for the big man. The Big *Chief*."

Lenny put up a hand for a high-five. Not surprisingly, to Jessica, Byrne slapped a palm with the man. Byrne knew how and when to ease a conversation into an interrogation, and they weren't quite there yet. The good news was that Lenny dropped his hand, and didn't attempt to high-five Jessica. She wasn't ready to touch him.

What the high-five *did* mean was that Byrne had just gotten the ball. It was his interview now.

"The reason we're here today is that we visited a place called Mr. Gold Pawn over on Germantown," Byrne said. Are you familiar with that place, Lenny?"

"Yeah. That place is beautiful."

"The man who runs the shop says you've come in there from time to time, is that correct?"

Lenny nodded.

Byrne reached into his pocket, took out the silver spoon they had taken from Joan Delacroix's house. "I need to know about these spoons, Lenny."

"Yeah. Okay. The spoons. Knife. Fork. Spoon." He made drawing gestures in the air, perhaps aligning the utensils in his mind.

"Are these from the Big Place?" Byrne asked.

"Oh yeah. One for everybody."

"You mean spoons just like this? With this stamp on the handle?"

Lenny squinted, looked at the spoon. "No, no, no. The ones we had was ones with something else on the handle. Those ones? The ones you got? Those was for company."

Byrne looked at the man, waiting. Nothing. "What was written on the spoons you had, Lenny?"

"Property of the Commonwealth of Pennsylvania," he said with grave import. "They shoulda stamped that on *us*. Back of the neck. Like the shirts at Walmart."

"And the spoons were the same?"

"No. The ones we had was different steel. These was the good ones. Had silver in 'em. Most of these got swiped."

"Stolen by the patients?"

Lenny closed his eyes again. He remained silent.

"We don't care about anything that was taken from the Big Place," Byrne said.

Lenny opened his eyes. "Is the statue up?"

"Yes," Byrne said. "Just last week, in fact. The *statue* of limitations is up. You're in the clear."

Lenny looked relieved. "I think more got stolen by the doctors," he said. "Lots of times the spoon part, the big part, was tore off."

Byrne pointed to the bowl of the spoon. "You mean this part?"

"Yeah. The old-timers used to bend them until they broke. They said them handles was good to use as keys. Said if you jiggled 'em long enough some of the doors would open. I never did, though."

"Why not?" Byrne asked.

Lenny shrugged. "Hell, the stuff on my side of the door was scary enough. No need to see what was on the outside." He leaned in, as if to share a secret, and whispered: "They say he *bit* 'em off. The big part."

"Who bit them off?"

Lenny looked behind himself, over both Byrne's and Jessica's shoulders.

"They called him Null," he said softly.

"You mean like null?" Byrne asked. "As in null and void?"

"I never heard about nobody named Boyd."

"Okay," Byrne said. "So tell me about this guy Null."

"There was, how shall I say, rumors about him. Super*cilious* rumors."

"Of what nature were these rumors?" Byrne asked.

Jessica almost smiled. Byrne was getting into Lenny's rhythm. She'd never met anyone better than her partner when it came to this.

"Well, they say, in the Big Place, Null would sneak around with a busted-off spoon. They say he could get in and out of your room."

"He would use it like a skeleton key."

"Ex*actly*, Big Chief. Lots of skeletons there. Especially in the closets."

"I see. And this Null, did he have a name?"

"I don't know anything about that. But everybody's got a real name, I guess."

"True enough. How did you come to hear about this guy?"

Lenny looked at the floor for a few moments, then leaned forward and whispered: "They say he was a man who committed murder."

For Jessica—and her partner, she was certain—all sound in the Reading Terminal Market ceased on that word.

"He committed murder?" Byrne asked.

"Yeah. Of all those crazies up to the Big Place—and believe me, I met them all up close and personal, they all smelled like old vacuum cleaners—there weren't too many who committed murder."

"Okay," Byrne said. "I understand."

"Most of us was, as they say, just a little bit behind on our mental rent. Or maybe it was all a dream. I'm not really sure. They were all about dreaming in the Big Place."

"Dreaming?"

Lenny made a zipping motion over his lips. "You're gonna have to ask Leo about that."

"Who is Leo?" Byrne asked.

"Leo," he repeated, as if he were mentioning someone known worldwide, like Cher or Madonna.

"Leo is his name. The man who wrote the big book. About dreams. You should talk to him. He talked to me but I don't think my name is in it. I saw a copy once, at that big store by city hall. I looked in the back."

"The back? The back of the store?"

"The back of the *book*. That long list of stuff. It's alphabeticalized."

"The index."

"Right. No Leonard P. Pintar. My daddy was Leonard E. He wasn't there either."

"Do you know Leo's last name?" Byrne asked.

Lenny buried his head in his hands. For a moment, Jessica thought he was about to start crying. After a long uncomfortable silence he looked up and said, simply: "No."

27

Rachel Gray had not taken the traditional path to her real estate license.

When she was in high school she carried enough credits so that she did not have to attend every day, and began a work-study program when she was sixteen. By the time she got to Drexel University—

where she attended on a five-year, co-op plan, a plan that allowed her to achieve a bachelor's degree and work at the same time—she found she could sell anything. As part of her co-op she got a job selling high-end women's fashion at seventeen, and became one of the youngest key holders at a woman's clothing retailer at the King of Prussia Mall.

That was the month she moved out of the hell on earth that was her home life.

In her final six months of co-op she landed a position with a chic women's clothing store near Rittenhouse Square. While she didn't get along particularly well with the store's owner, a woman who felt threatened by Rachel, she did get along with the owner's husband, who had a number of real estate ventures working at any given time around the city.

The man offered to send Rachel to real estate school.

At just twenty-one, Rachel thought the idea of selling real estate was the craziest thing she'd ever heard. Who buys real estate?

In short order, she accumulated the sixty hours needed to take the test for her real estate agent's license. She passed the test on her first go, and within a month she was off on her first sale, which she closed within days.

Armed with that one sale, she marched into the main office of Prudential Roach at 530 Market Street, and was promptly hired.

After two years in the trenches at Prudential, Rachel networked her way over to a new, upstart independent realtor, started by two women who had been in Rachel's shoes about twenty years earlier.

Of the thirty or so agents employed by the company, only a handful came into the office every day. In this age of the smartphone, it was possible to be a Realtor, a broker, even a manager, without putting in any face time, but Rachel noticed early on that the highest producers were the ones who showed up every morning.

At the moment, in the world of the Philly condo, it was a buyer's market. Granted, the commissions were not what they were ten years ago, but Rachel, and every other ambitious Realtor in the city, had every intention of making it up in volume.

Rachel had a dozen condo showings this week alone. Twelve that were on the books, that is.

She had other appointments that were not.

Rachel sat at a table at Marathon on Market Street with her friend Denise Sterling. Denise, who was just a few months older than Rachel, was a home stager. Home staging was a boutique profession of stylists brought in by either brokers or sellers to decorate or "stage" a home in the hopes of turning hesitant looky-loos into love-struck buyers.

"How was your weekend?" Denise asked.

"There was a weekend?"

Denise smiled. "Yeah. That's the thing that starts Friday afternoon and doesn't end until Monday morning around nine."

"Oh, yeah," Rachel said. "I did a half-dozen walk-throughs in Bella Vista."

"Sounds exciting. Anything for me?"

"Maybe. What did you get up to?"

"I met this guy at Blurr on Saturday night." Blurr was the nightspot *du jour* in Old City. "Why do men still think silk sheets are sexy? It's so *Penthouse*. Ugh."

"How would you know about his sheets?"

"I'm a home stager. It's what I do."

"Slut."

Denise smiled. "I prefer consort."

Rachel laughed, sipped her coffee. She told Denise her story about the house in Fishtown.

"There were really two kids there?" Denise asked.

"Two that I saw."

"So, what you're saying is there were no casually deployed Tiffany bags or Jacobsen Egg Chairs?"

Rachel laughed. One of the tricks home stagers used was to bring in their own furniture and décor. Denise and her partner Arnaud maintained a small warehouse in Port Richmond from which, at short notice, they could deploy sofas, dining-room sets, artwork, area rugs, even linens, or anything else that might reverse the invasion of poorly thought-out design decisions.

"No, but I'm pretty sure there were *scrambled* eggs on the kitchen floor," Rachel said.

As they finished their coffee Denise glanced at the calendar app on Rachel's phone. "Uh oh."

Rachel looked up. "What?"

Denise pointed to Rachel's four o'clock the next day. "Mrs. Backfire again?"

Mrs. Backfire was a term they'd come up with for a woman named Gloria Vincenzi.

"Yeah," Rachel said. "What are you gonna do?"

"Um, you could say no?"

Rachel shook her head. "I just can't. Not yet."

One of the great challenges of selling real estate in a city like Philadelphia, one that a lot of people who were not in the business might not imagine, was signage. Not the creation of the sign, or the materials out of which it was made, but simply where to hang it.

More accurately: *how* to hang it.

The easiest ones were the row houses that had a railing. The ones that did not meant you had to drill into the brick, many times using an anchor. Rachel had become quite proficient in the art of drilling into stone, even to the point of discussing carbide drill bits with the friendly gentleman at Home Depot. In addition to her Windex, rubber gloves, paper towels and disinfectant, she often walked around with a power drill. As well as a spare battery, one that she kept on a charger in her car.

And while there were certain challenges indigenous to all Realtors in Philadelphia, or any major city, Rachel Gray had her own set of trials—some might see them as advantages—that most others did not.

Rachel was four-feet eleven inches tall.

Early on in her career she learned that one of the toughest aspects to being a businesswoman under five feet tall was that some buyers did not take her seriously, a fact that made her work twice as hard as almost every other agent at the agency.

The first perception was that she was too young. She'd actually had a buyer who asked if she needed to clear her offer with somebody older at the agency. She had one client who actually patted her on the head. He nearly retrieved a bloody stump.

Rachel knew all the tricks: wearing vertical striped suits, finding just the right heels for work, choosing V-necks and three-quarter sleeves, always wearing monochromatic outfits. She'd recently gotten rid of a lot of the length to her hair, opting for a boyish clip—shorter on top, with the sides combed down and back. It was also the lightest color she'd ever gone with, a medium blond with lighter blond balayage highlights.

In the end, despite the head-patters and the oh-so-hysterical Munchkin jokes, she was consistently in the top three salespeople at Perry-Hayes. Her motto?

If your feet touch the ground, you're tall enough.

Her two o'clock showing, Justin and Paula Bader, were ten minutes late. While Rachel often used this time for a few last-minute touches, it was unnecessary today. This property—ably and creatively staged by Denise Sterling of Sterling Interiors—was perfect. There was soft rock playing on the stereo, a table full of place settings from Crate & Barrel on the dining-room table, even a trio of huge pillar candles alight on the dresser in the master bedroom.

At ten after two Rachel heard a car door slam. She walked to the front door. She assessed the Baders as they came up the walk. He was tall, looked to be about forty-five, wore casual slacks, cowboy boots, and one of those dark blue boiled-wool sweaters with the quilted shooting patch on the shoulder. The woman was almost as tall, late thirties, Bottega Veneta pleated slacks, matching shawl collar jacket, white blouse. She carried what looked like an Anya Hindmarch satchel, although from this distance it could be a knockoff.

Rachel glanced at the car at the curb. It was a new Audi A8.

The Hindmarch was real.

Rachel smoothed her face, gave her cheeks a quick pinch. Showtime. She opened the door. "Hi! I'm Rachel Gray."

The man was on the porch first. He towered over her.

"Well, aren't you the cutest itty-bitty thing?" he said.

Yeah, like your dick, pal.

"I get that all the time." Rachel smiled. "Please come in."

At home, four hours later, Rachel studied the huge map on the wall in her kitchen. Of the ninety-five dots on the map, sixty were in red, the rest were green. In the past three years more than seventy-five percent of the homes in this area had gone up for sale, and Rachel had visited them all. Gaining entry, without any paperwork involved, had taken some doing. On the wall next to the map were a series of photographs, taped together to form a crude panorama. On each photograph was a legend chronicling precise dimensions, elevations and distances.

She took one of the pictures down, placed it on the table. She dialed the number.

"USS, this is Bancroft."

Bancroft Tyson was an old friend from real estate school, and one of the prettiest men Rachel had ever met. In her line of work she ran across her share of handsome men, men who carried themselves well but weren't all that good-looking, as well as men who oozed sex appeal based on some physical trait or ability. Bancroft was just pretty. And, somehow, he wasn't gay. Rachel would kill for his lips and lashes.

"Hey there," Rachel said.

"My favorite dirt merchant!"

Bancroft was the only person Rachel would let get away with calling her that.

He worked for a company called USS—United Showing Service. The company acted as a clearinghouse for Realtors to gain access to properties. All the major brokerages in the Philadelphia area subscribed to USS. If you wanted to show a property that was listed with another agency, you called USS, and they portioned out a time for you, as well as supplied you with the combination to the lockbox on the door, the box that contained the key.

By using USS, you were guaranteed that there would be no one else showing a property at the same time.

They made their small talk, but soon got around to the reason for the call.

Bancroft lowered his voice. "I can only do that one on Linden tonight. There's no one scheduled until tomorrow morning at nine."

"Who's listing?" Rachel asked.

Bancroft told her. It was the biggest broker in Philly. When this was the case, unlike a listing with a mom and pop agency, there was little chance of someone showing up unexpectedly.

Except for the owner. That was always a danger.

Bancroft gave her the information she needed.

"Thanks, honey," Rachel said. "I owe you."

"Be careful," Bancroft whispered.

Always, Rachel thought.

28

The dog was an English Mastiff, somewhere in the range of 160 pounds, most of it muscle.

Luther had no interest in getting an accurate reading.

After he had thrown the tainted meat over the fence, the dog had taken it — a full pound of fresh beef brisket, laced with sodium pentobarbital — into her mouth and all but swallowed it whole. If Luther's calculations were correct, it would not take more than twenty minutes. He would have preferred to inject the dog with the drug, thereby assuring its effectiveness, but he was not about to risk getting that close.

If the dog had been older, or trained as an attack or guard dog, she would not have gone anywhere near the food. Luther had once been pursued along the Emajõgi River by a Russian bounty hunter who had, in his posse, a pair of young Alsatians. No amount of trickery with poisoned or drugged meat threw them off the trail. Luther was only saved by lashing spring rains, and his ability to hold his breath for great periods of time while crossing the Emajõgi.

On this day, the Philadelphia rain had relented for the moment. The street shimmered beneath the street lamps. Luther sat at the bus-stop bench in front of the row house, glanced at his watch.

It was time.

He took the comic book from his messenger bag, placed it carefully, faceup, just yards from the gate. A few minutes later he heard a noise coming from the end of the driveway.

The boy was taking out the trash, right on schedule.

Out of the corner of his eye Luther saw the boy preceded by the dog to the gate. The boy unlocked the gate, struggled with the two large Hefty bags. Luther saw the dog stop at the sidewalk line. He had been right. They did have an electronic fence.

"Mister?"

Luther closed his eyes for a moment. The dream had begun.

He took the earbuds from his ears, looked around. Seconds later his gaze fell upon the boy.

"I'm sorry," he said. "Did you say something to me?"

The boy pointed to the comic book on the sidewalk. It was a copy of *The Spectre* #10, still in its plastic sleeve. It was a somewhat rare edition, but only in Fine condition, and by no means precious. Luther had purchased it at a comic book emporium in New Jersey for $28.50. He'd gone to New Jersey just to be on the safe side. He did not want any blowback in case the proprietor of a Philadelphia store knew the boy. The Spectre was not the most famous of the DC characters.

"Is that yours?" the boy asked.

Luther made a show of following where the boy was pointing. He regarded the comic book on the ground. "Oh, *man,*" he said. He made an even bigger show of looking into his messenger bag, which was unzipped. "It must have fallen out. Thanks, buddy."

The boy just stared. "You like the Spectre?"

Luther picked up the comic. He did not put it into his bag, nor did he approach the boy. He simply turned to address him. "He's okay, I guess."

The boy rolled his eyes. "*Okay?* Seriously?"

Luther shrugged. "I'm more of a Marvel guy myself."

"Dude."

"I'm not sure about Captain America yet," the boy said. "I don't even know what his superpower is supposed to be. The movie was okay, but that's just because of Hayley Atwell."

Luther smiled. "I am *so* telling your father you said that."

"Tell him. He likes her, too."

The boy stood with the gate open, half in and half out of the property. The dog sat at his side, every so often raising her nose into the air, in Luther's general direction. Luther surmised it was a remnant of the beef brisket that lingered.

"Okay. She's hot," Luther said. As he spoke to the boy he kept his eye on the four windows that overlooked the breezeway between the row houses. For the moment, there was no movement, no shadows. "I just think that, on the whole, Marvel is the way to go."

"Sorry," the boy said. "DC rules."

"You really think so?"

"Uh, *yeah?* And if it was just Superman and Batman it would be enough."

Luther held up *The Spectre.* "I just bought three of these."

The boy looked stunned. "You have *three* of those?"

"I do. One for my son and one for my nephew. They're both about your age."

"Who is the other one for?" the boy asked.

Luther looked at the windows, down the street, back at the boy. "Okay. I'm busted. The other one is for me. Don't tell anybody."

The boy laughed. "I thought you were a Marvel guy."

"Yeah, well, the Spectre is pretty cool."

The boy glanced back down the driveway for a moment, then turned his attention back to Luther. "Would you consider trading one of them?"

Luther struck a pose. "I might," he said. "Depends on what the other man had to trade."

Before the boy could answer Luther saw the curtains move in one of the second-floor windows. He prepared himself to leave, and come back another day. He could see that the dog was still fully alert, and he would never make it past her down the driveway.

A moment later the curtains were stilled. Luther turned his attention back to the boy.

"Well," the boy began, "I might be able to part with *Spiderman* 344."

"Interesting," Luther said. "344."

"It's *only* the issue where they introduce Carnage."

"Now, see, I don't know about that," Luther said. "Carnage is tight, but I think I'd be losing money." He held up the Spectre issue. "Not to mention that I would have to go back to the store and buy another one of these to replace this one."

"Well, *I* think it's a good trade," the boy said. "And I trade all the time."

The boy reached down and patted the dog's head. As a negotiation tactic, it was not bad, Luther thought. Dealing from a position of strength.

Luther waited the appropriate amount of time before responding to the boy, and closing the deal.

"You drive a hard bargain, young man."

The boy grinned. The dog wagged its tail, perhaps sensing another treat. Luther noticed a tremble in the dog's front legs.

"So we have a deal?" the boy asked.

"We do," Luther said. He took the comic book out of his bag and handed it through the gate. The dog tried to sniff it. "So when do I get my merchandise?"

The boy turned, looked at the patio behind his house, then up at the windows. "I can get it for you now. But I can't let you inside the house. You have to stay in the back."

"That's okay," Luther said. "I understand. I'll wait here. It's cool."

At the word *cool* the boy stopped, turned. He looked up and down the street. "You don't have to stay out here." He glanced at the night sky. "It's starting to rain again. You can come back. The patio is covered."

Before stepping on the property, Luther asked: "Is your dog friendly?"

The boy smiled. "Who, *Dolly?*"

"Dolly," Luther said. "Is she friendly?"

"Oh yeah," the boy said. "She's just a baby. Besides, if you're with me you're okay."

The boy pushed open the gates fully. Luther stepped through. As he followed the boy down the driveway he slipped his hand into his overcoat pocket, through the inside flap, and caressed the handle of his knife, his senses on full alert. If the dog intuited danger, and moved on him, Luther would roll to the ground and try to cut her throat, hoping that the drug had slowed her.

A few steps later Luther saw the dog's back legs wobble.

The patio behind the house was surrounded on three sides by a seven-foot-high fence, intertwined with ivy and dormant clematis. There was a wrought-iron table and four chairs, as well as a large barbecue grill covered with plastic, still tied down for the season.

Luther stole a glance at all the windows at the rear of the house. He saw nothing moving.

"I'll be right out," the boy said.

"So, that was the Spiderman Death of Gwen Stacy issue and the framed Wolverine poster, right?"

The boy giggled, shook his head. He pulled open the sliding glass door, stepped inside the house, closed it behind him.

Less than a minute later, with the dog unconscious, Luther followed.

29

Byrne stared at a map of Northeast Philadelphia. Priory Park was circled in red. The park was situated in an area of the city that, because of the easy access to the I-95, had grown to include a number of industrial and commercial parks that ringed the southern end of the park.

Byrne looked at the houses to the north of the park. Was there a connection? He wondered what, if any, canvassing John Garcia had done after Robert Freitag's body had been found in the field. Byrne had driven the streets at that side of the park, getting out a few times, looking for a vantage point. There was none.

Even with the dearth of leaves there had been a month ago, it was impossible to see through the trees to the field. Being able to see the creek, where Joan Delacroix was found, was another story. There were a half-dozen areas where, if someone was jogging or walking a dog at the right time, a clear line of sight was available.

He looked at the crime scene photographs of Joan Delacroix, at the way her body was posed, feet together, arms straight out to the sides. Why had the killer placed the large rocks on her hands? Why had he put the woman's shoes on the wrong feet?

What did the white flowers mean?

Glancing back at the map, Byrne tried to discern a pattern in the spots where both bodies were dumped. No, he amended. They were not *dumped*. They were *placed*. He'd had quite a lot of experience with bodies in parks, and mostly they had been simply left. Some were buried.

These victims were left in the open for a reason.

Robert Freitag had been deliberately carried to the center of the field, sat upright in a chair, and killed with a railroad spike. Byrne had encountered almost every type of murder weapon in his time. Never this one.

Joan Delacroix, as far as they could conclusively determine, was carried to that spot on the bank of the creek. They had found depressions in the earth near to where the large stones were located. She had been killed by blunt-force trauma, possible with one strike each from the large stones.

Footwear impressions had been found next to the holes, but because of the rain CSU could not get an accurate read on the tread pattern. What they did have, however, was not incompatible with the footwear impressions collected from the Robert Freitag scene.

Just to say he did it, Byrne again tried calling Joan Delacroix's iPhone. As expected, as had happened for each of his previous dozen calls, it went straight to voice mail.

On the way home Byrne stopped at the Barnes & Noble on Rittenhouse Square. While there he picked up an *iPhone for Dummies* book, then stopped into the Cosi on Walnut Street. By the time he was done eating he felt he had a fairly good handle on how to handle a FaceTime call on his phone.

He got home with just a few minutes to spare.

He knew how to operate the phone, but the question now was where to set it up. He wanted the background to not be too distracting. He first set it up on the dining-room table, turned it on, got a preview of what it would look like. Not bad, he thought, but he could see through the doorway behind him, the messy bedroom, the unmade bed. Plus the lighting made him look like he hadn't slept or shaved in days, which wasn't far from the truth.

He tried the kitchen, and with the overhead light off, and the phone propped on the pass through to the dining room, coupled with the soft light from the table lamp on the counter, it looked pretty good. Or as good as it was going to look.

A few moments later his phone rang, and Byrne felt a twitch in his heart. He hadn't seen his daughter in a few months, and at first, when her video image appeared on his iPhone screen, she looked to him like a young woman who looked like Colleen.

But it was her.

She smiled her mother's smile, signed hello. Byrne signed back.

Colleen, who had been deaf since birth, the result of a condition called Mondini Dysplasia, was attending Gallaudet University, the country's first and most preeminent college for deaf and hard of hearing undergraduate students. Since she moved from Philadelphia, Byrne had only managed to see her every few months or so, and his heart ached over it.

There was music in the background. It seemed a little loud to Byrne—or would have been if he were in the same room with his daughter—but obviously this was not a distraction to Colleen. They had often joked about how one of the benefits to deafness was not having to put up with music you hated, or loudmouthed jerks. Sometimes Byrne envied her. Especially about the jerks.

"How is school?" Byrne signed. It was a standard question. Colleen was a straight-A student.

"Good," she said. "I'm thinking about a second major."

Byrne thought about how she got her smarts from her mother. A *second* major. He often thought about whether or not he could have handled one at her age.

"Sounds great."

"By the way, I'll be in tomorrow."

This was a surprise. "Tomorrow?" Byrne signed. "I thought you were coming in two weeks."

Colleen smiled. "Don't you want to see your beautiful daughter?"

"Of course. That was *happy*. A *happy* question."

"I'm done with my classes and I don't have my midterms for a week. I thought I'd come up."

"That's great. We'll go to dinner somewhere nice."

"You don't have to do that."

"Says who?"

On-screen Byrne saw someone walk in front of the camera, sign something to Colleen. It was way too fast for Byrne to pick up. Colleen responded, then pointed at her iPhone. The boy—who looked about seventeen—signed a *sorry* to the camera, then bolted.

"My ride is here," Colleen said.

"What's going on?"

"We're going to the movies. A Fellini double bill. *La Strada* and *Amarcord.*"

Colleen had to fingerspell Fellini, which Byrne didn't quite get at first. But he knew the film titles, which were both subtitled. Even though Colleen did pretty well lip reading non-subtitled films, she had gravitated to foreign and silent films since she was a young teenager.

"Okay," Byrne said. "Have fun."

"So, I'll see you tomorrow?"

"Can't wait."

As she signed this, Byrne thought he saw something.

Was that a ring? On her *ring* finger?

"What's that?" Byrne signed. He pointed to Colleen's left hand. Which, from her perspective, would have been backwards.

"Got to go," Colleen signed. "Love you."

Before Byrne could respond, the screen went black. Byrne sat still for what had to be a full minute, trying to catch his breath.

Was his daughter *engaged?* Was that why she was coming into Philly two weeks early? Was it because she wanted to make an announcement?

Detective Kevin Byrne suddenly felt nauseous.

30

The man sat on one of the dining-room chairs. Although he was in his fifties, his hair had only a few touches of gray around the temples. Luther wondered if he colored it. Although his recollection of the man was clouded by time, by dreams, he recalled the man's vanity. Luther decided that if he were to go and look in the medicine cabinet in the bathroom off the master suite, he would certainly find a box labeled *Just for Men*.

The man, unfortunately for him, would not be able to lead the way. In addition to the duct tape over his mouth, there was duct tape around the ankle of each foot, binding him to the legs of the chair. There was also duct tape around his hands in the back.

The man's name was Edward Richmond.

Dr. Edward Royce Richmond.

"It has been years since you and I have shared a room," Luther said. "I daresay that the dynamic has changed. Has it not?"

The man's eyes shifted left, right.

"I know you cannot answer. I posed the question just for effect."

Luther crossed the room to the fireplace. There, arrayed on the mantelpiece, were a number of family photographs. One of them showed the man in a dark tuxedo with his arm around an attractive young woman. Luther surmised it was his wife.

"She is quite beautiful. It seems a tragedy the two of you could not work it out."

The man shifted his weight in the chair, pulsing at his restraints.

Luther put the photograph back on the mantelpiece, picked up another. This one was of the boy as an infant, the type of inexpensive photo studio shot sold to young families through direct mail. The frame was cheap and gaudy. Five ceramic balloons spelled *Timmy*.

"Timmy," Luther said. "That is the boy's name." He did not pose this as a question, but rather made a statement. "I don't think the diminutive fits his personality and demeanor. I don't think it will serve him in school and later in life. I should think Timothy more appropriate."

At the mention of his son's name the man began to sweat even more profusely.

Luther walked back across the room, stood directly in front of the man. He then sat on the edge of the coffee table, looked into his captive's eyes. "I already have some of what I've come for. Do you know what I'm talking about?"

The man shook his head violently side to side. Luther nodded. "I have the remnants, or at least some of them, of our time together. I found the newsletters, some of the photographs, and an interesting document that was folded and placed into the same large envelope as your last will and testament. Would you like me to read it to you?"

The man screamed, but the sound was muffled by the duct tape over his mouth.

Luther reached into his pocket, took out the document, unfolded it.

"To whom it may concern," he began. *"Let this document serve as my confession. The things that I did, the research in which I took part during the years 1992 to 1996, I did of my own free will. To the families and descendants of those I harmed, I ask forgiveness. I believed, at the time, what we were doing was in the interest of science. I know now that I was wrong, and if there is a God, and I stand before him now, I will answer for my sins."*

Luther paused for a moment, then folded the document, and slipped it back into his pocket.

"Science," Luther said. He knew that he needn't say more. He looked down, sniffed the air. The man had wet himself. This was to be expected. Luther was certain that this man—this fully diminished man sitting before him, this powerless man who had stood before many others as Luther stood before him now—had witnessed such a degrading display many times.

"And so to business," Luther said.

Luther took off his overcoat and draped it over the chair. He reached into his back pocket and removed the black felt hat. He put it on his head. When the man saw his clothing, the many bloodstains, he began to cry. His tears ran across the duct tape in thin rivers.

"Now, I am going to ask you one question. I will ask you this question only one time. Nod your head if you understand me."

With tears streaking his face, the man nodded.

"Good. Before I ask this question, you should know that your son is in the upstairs bathroom. I know you are curious about him, and his well-being. I assure you he is fine. For the moment."

At hearing this, the man tried desperately to stand up. He rocked side to side so violently that he tipped the chair over, crashing to the floor. Luther allowed the man to spend himself. He then reached over and lifted the man to the upright position. When the man had calmed somewhat, Luther continued.

"As I was saying, Timothy is in the upstairs bathroom. He is bound in much the same manner as you." Luther reached out and held the man by his shoulders. "The only difference is that the boy is in the bathtub. I have done this to facilitate the draining of his blood."

The man screamed loud and long and hard, the veins protruding in his neck and on his forehead. Once again, when the strength of his instinctive reaction diminished, Luther continued.

"I want you to know that it need not come to that. As a man of science, I'm sure you know that not all outcomes are certain."

Luther leaned very close to the man.

"Now, to return to the matter at hand. I will ask you this question, and you will give me a truthful answer. The question regards the existence in this home, or elsewhere, of anything that ties you to the experiments conducted during the years nineteen ninety-two to nineteen ninety-six at Cold River. I am talking about anything, and everything, no matter how small or peripheral. You will tell me where it is, and I will judge its relevance."

Luther once again sat on the edge of the coffee table. He looked directly into the man's eyes, which were now a bright crimson, filled with tears.

"I will remove the tape from your mouth," Luther said. "You will not scream, nor raise your voice in any manner. When I remove the tape I will ask you the question, and you will give me a truthful answer. Do you understand this?"

The man nodded his head slowly.

Luther reached out and gently removed the duct tape. As soon as he had done this the man gasped for air, sucking down great gulps. He began to cough, his shoulders shaking.

When he settled down, Luther stood up, towering over him. "Do you have the material I seek?"

The man took a few more deep breaths, gathering himself. "Look, you don't understand. That was a long time ago. I'm sorry for what happened. But you don't have to do this. I have some money. Not a lot, but it's yours."

Luther waited for a moment, then reached into his bag, removed the roll of duct tape. He put another piece over the man's mouth, drew his bone-handled knife, and ran up the stairs.

When Luther descended the steps he thought, for a moment, that the man was dead. His head was slumped forward and his skin was pallid.

But when Luther reached the bottom tread, it groaned beneath his weight, and the man sat upright. He had, it seemed, fainted for just a moment.

Luther crossed the living room, his knife in hand. Making certain that the man kept his eyes on the blade, Luther took a cloud-white handkerchief from his pocket, wiped off the blood.

"Your son is not dead. Not yet. I am now going to offer you a courtesy I rarely extend. I'm going to give you the opportunity to answer my question." Luther sat back on his heels, the knife now at his side. "Look at me, Dr. Richmond."

The man slowly focused his eyes on Luther.

"I will now remove the duct tape. You will have five seconds to tell me where the documents or photographs I am looking for are located. If you do not, I will bring your son down here one piece at a time."

Luther removed the tape. Quickly this time. The man did not hesitate to tell him what he wanted to know.

"In my safe," he said.

"Where is it?"

The man told him. Without being asked, he also told him the combination.

The photographs took Luther back. He recalled some of the people in them; others, not. He flipped through them, glanced once at each. When he was done, he put them all in his bag, and knelt before Dr. Edward Richmond.

"Have you told me everything?" Luther asked.

The man nodded.

"Good. I'm afraid that time has run out for you, Dr. Richmond, but if I find out that you are lying to me, and the authorities learn the truth behind Cold River, I will revisit your son. It may not be soon, but it will happen one day. He will awaken in his bed, and I will be there."

Luther zipped shut his bag, took out his knife.

"It is time to go, Juris Spalva."

When Edward Royce Richmond heard the name of the Latvian businessman, it was clear that he remembered the dream—the steel garrote, the forest floor slashed with blood, the body ravaged by animals.

It was then that Dr. Richmond began to cry in earnest.

Ten minutes later, it was not Luther who opened the trunk of the car in the closed garage. Luther was dreaming. It was Eduard Kross who slammed shut the trunk lid.

He had one stop to make before heading to Priory Park.

31

Jessica dreamed of warm sand, cool water. She was three years old, standing on the beach in Wildwood. She had a red plastic bucket in one hand, and was carefully shoveling small shells into the bucket with the other.

Nearby, her brother Michael was throwing a Frisbee with one of his friends. Her mother and father were sitting on a big blue beach towel. As always, her father was listening to a baseball game on his transistor radio while her mother had her nose stuck in a book, every few seconds looking up to make sure her little girl wasn't being washed away to Europe.

Jessica felt the sun on her face, felt the water tickling her little toes. She heard the seagulls, and tasted the saltwater taffy lingering on her tongue.

She scooped some of the sand into her plastic shovel. But when she reached over to put the shells in her bucket, something was wrong.

It wasn't shells in the pail.

It was dried white flowers.

Suddenly, there was noise behind her, a sound of metal on metal. It seemed to echo, as if she were now in a cave.

Then there was the sound of footfalls.

Jessica sat up, disoriented, her heart racing. She turned to see Vincent, Sophie and Carlos standing behind her.

As it turned out, she wasn't down the shore. She was on the couch in her living room.

Jessica took a few moments, tried to calm herself. She rubbed the nap from her eyes, glanced at her watch. She wasn't wearing a watch.

"Was I snoring?" she asked.

Vincent shrugged. "Not so you'd notice."

"What does that mean?"

"It means not more than usual."

"What are you saying?" Jessica asked. "You're saying I *snore?*"

"No, honey. I was joking." Vincent nudged Carlos. Carlos giggled.

Sophie pointed at the television. "Who's winning, Mom?"

Apparently it was some sort of sporting event. "I don't know."

Sophie sat on the arm of the couch. "You don't know who's winning the game?"

Jessica reached around, hugged her daughter. "Sweetie, I don't even know who's *playing.*" Jessica glanced back at the TV. It was the Sixers. "The basketball team is winning."

It was Sophie's turn to giggle.

"How was practice?" Jessica asked.

Sophie had recently lobbied to take up a musical instrument. At first she had wanted a cello, but the idea of scratchy string music around the house for a few years had been too much of a gamble. Not to mention the challenge of carting around an instrument that was as big as her daughter. After much discussion, they arrived at the flute. Sophie Balzano took to it surprisingly quickly.

"It was good. We did duets. With a piano."

"That sounds great, honey." Jessica silently berated herself for missing this mini-milestone. There had been too many of late.

Vincent leaned over, kissed Jessica on the top of her head. "Did you eat?"

Jessica had to think about it. "I'm Italian, Vince. There's a pretty good chance I did."

"Oh, that's too bad." Vincent held up two big white plastic bags. He smiled.

"Chickie's and Pete's?" Jessica asked.

Her husband nodded.

"Maybe just a little."

An hour later Jessica found herself at the dining-room table, three of her textbooks open in front of her.

The last time she had formally studied a subject was when she'd gotten her undergraduate degree in Criminal Justice. She had always been a good student, all through grade school and high school, a quick study with most subjects.

Having grown up the daughter of a police officer, she knew that most of the skills she would need on the street would be taught by the older, more experienced cops in her squad, as well as by the mere performance of her duty. A classroom and a textbook could teach you things like methods of research in sociology and the basic tenets of victimology, but when it came time to take a six-foot-tall 250-pound man whacked out on PCP to the ground in a rainstorm, it helped to have on-the-job training.

Life plus lumps equals wisdom.

But now, in her second year of law school, she found one thing lacking that used to come to her so easily. The power to concentrate.

Her mind kept straying to the cases.

Sophie glanced up from her math homework, caught Jessica staring at her.

"What, Mom?"

"Nothing."

"Mom."

Busted. "I don't know. This is just…nice, you know? You and I sitting here, both doing our homework." Now *there* was a sentence Jessica thought she would never utter.

"What are you working on?" Sophie asked.

Jessica glanced at her workbook. "Well, right now I'm studying the difference between partnerships, limited partnerships and limited liability partnerships."

Sophie smiled. "We did that last year," she said. "You need any help?"

"I might."

Sophie put down her pencil. "I'm going to get some chocolate milk," she said. "Do you want some?"

"No," Jessica said. "I'm okay."

Sophie slid off her chair, walked into the kitchen. She soon returned with a large glass of chocolate milk and a coaster. Jessica noticed a few cookie crumbs on the front of her daughter's sweater. She decided to give the kid a break on the after-dessert snacks.

Sophie sat down, knitted her fingers. This was a serious Sophie Balzano, all of a sudden. Jessica wondered what was coming.

"Mom?"

Jessica put her finger on the workbook page. She'd read the same line four times now. "Yes, sweetie?"

"Can I buy a CD?"

Jessica zoned. Her eleven-year-old daughter wanted to buy a certificate of deposit? "A CD?"

Sophie nodded. "I have my own money."

Ah, Jessica thought. *Music.* "What CD, honey?"

"Adele."

Jessica knew the name, but couldn't place the music. Was it G? PG? PG-13? R? NC-17? "Which one?"

Sophie rolled her eyes. "I think she only has two, Mom."

"I know. Her first album was..."

Another eye roll. "It was called *19*?"

"Like I didn't know that, too," Jessica said. "Tell you what, why don't you save your money and I'll see if it's at the library? I can look it up from right here on the computer."

Sophie gave Jessica the fish eye. "You mean like rip the disc? Is that even legal?"

At this crucial moment in child-rearing, and law enforcement, Jessica's cell phone rang. Saved by the ringtone. Jessica held up a finger, picked up her phone.

It was Byrne.

Jessica answered. "Hey."

"There's another body."

Jessica's heart sank. It couldn't be in the park. The park was covered. She asked anyway. "In Priory Park?"

"Yeah," Byrne replied. "In Priory Park."

"I thought the park was under surveillance."

"It was. There were four cars on duty."

Jessica decided not to ask the obvious question for the moment. "Are we going in?"

"Yeah," Byrne said. "Boss wants us there. Can Vince watch the kids?"

"Yeah. He's home."

"I'll be at your house in five minutes."

As Jessica walked up the stairs to get ready to leave the house she put her phone on speaker. She placed it on the dresser. "Do we know what happened?"

"I don't have all the details yet. A body was found DOA in the northwest part of the park. Near that old chapel."

Jessica slipped on her jeans, pulled a PPD hooded sweatshirt over her head. She took the lockbox from the shelf in her closet, unlocked it, slipped her service weapon into her holster. "Do we have an ID on the victim?"

"We do," Byrne said. "We also have something else we didn't have before."

"What's that?"

"We've got a suspect in custody."

32

The path a detective takes to a gold badge in the homicide division of the Philadelphia Police Department is often nearly identical to the path taken by other detectives. Every detective, of course, begins their career as a patrol officer. At some point, usually after two or three years on the street, you ask yourself why you are doing this job, and whether you want to make a career out of it.

There are a number of reasons to enter the police academy. Some people join after a tour in the Armed Forces, finding the idea of the structure, the command strata and life in a paramilitary organization appealing. Some join out of a sense of inferiority or superiority, believing a badge and a weapon will nourish or overcome these character flaws. Some join because they really want to help people.

But after a few years of last-out shifts—the tour that usually runs from eleven p.m. to seven a.m.—and dealing with belligerent drunks, drugged-out zombies, crying children, strong-arm robbers and the scourge of domestic violence that seems to escalate with every passing year, there comes a moment when a decision needs to be made. Those who decide to pack it in, acknowledging that police work was not for them after all, retire from the force in their twenties, and move on to

other jobs, other challenges, other certainly more financially reward-
ing careers.

Some of those who decide to stay set their sights on one crime.
Homicide.

For many in law enforcement there was no higher calling than the
work of the homicide detective.

In almost every instance, retiring from the homicide unit meant retiring from the life. Rare was the case where a homicide detective moved
over to another squad. Rarer still was the homicide detective who
retired, then came back to the force.

In all of Jessica's experience she had run across this once. Detective
John Shepherd had worked his way to the homicide division the hard
way. He came up at a time when there were few black detectives in the
squad. John Shepherd neither asked for nor received any quarter. Of
his many abilities as a detective, his work "in the room" was unparal-
leled. When detectives had a suspect in an interview room, a suspect
who was shutting down, or about to call for a lawyer, detectives
brought in John Shepherd.

Shepherd had retired a few years earlier, had bounced around in a
few private security gigs, and landed a nice job as head of hotel security at the Sheraton Society Hill. But the challenge of stolen luggage,
push-in artists and jammed room safes proved to be inadequate for
him. Four months earlier he had come back to the squad and asked for
his old job back. The homicide unit, with four open slots, was lucky to
get him.

Now in his fifties, his hair mostly silver, he cut just as wide a path,
perhaps even wider, than he had almost twenty years earlier.

Arriving at Priory Park, Jessica and Byrne found Shepherd standing
behind a sector car on Chancel Lane, talking to a patrol officer.
Because they worked different shifts, neither Jessica nor Byrne had
run into Shepherd since his return.

"Welcome back, John," Jessica said. They hugged. "We've missed you."

"Thanks, Jess." He gestured to the flashing lights, the CSU van. "I see that things haven't changed that much."

"Are you back on day work?"

"I am," Shepherd said.

Shepherd and Byrne shook hands. "Good to see you, Johnny."

"You losing weight?" Shepherd asked.

Byrne smiled. "I'll find it again." He pointed at the field. "What do we have?"

"We have a DOA on the other side of the park. Male white, fifties. Looks like he may have been strangled. ME's up there now."

"Who found him?" Byrne asked.

Shepherd pointed at the young officer. "P/O Kenneth Weldon," Shepherd said. He got the young man's attention, beckoned him over.

The officer was clearly shaken. He was short, no more than the minimum height for the department, and no more than twenty-one years old. Officer Weldon nodded to the three detectives.

"Tell us what happened," Shepherd said.

The officer pointed in the general direction of his post. "I was parked at the northwest end of the park, in the parking lot near the boarded-up chapel. I heard the call go out on the radio that there was an individual walking through the park, heading south through the trees from the bottom of Ashlar Road."

"What did you do?"

"I took the call," Weldon said. "Our orders were to detain anyone in the park after dark. I hit the lights, got back onto the avenue, drove down here to Chancel, then east. When I got here I met up with Dash."

"Dash?"

"Sorry, sir. Officer Dasher. Unit 1814."

"What did you observe?"

"When I got out of my vehicle I saw an individual, a white male. He was carrying something large on his shoulders."

"Where was he?"

Weldon pointed to an area in the middle of the field, about twenty yards away. "Right about there."

Jessica looked in the direction. Even with the headlights of four cars and the CSU van, it was pitch black. The area was not far from the spot at which Robert Freitag had been found.

"What did you do?" Shepherd asked.

"I ordered him to drop whatever he was carrying and get down on the ground."

"Did the individual comply?"

"Yes, sir," Weldon said. "Without incident."

"And you're saying he was observed coming through the trees from that direction?" Shepherd pointed to the northeast end of the park. It was the end opposite from where the new body had been found.

"Yes, sir."

Shepherd took it all in. "Thank you, Officer," he said. "I'd like you to deploy at the eastern end of Chancel Lane for now. Redirect any nonessential traffic."

"Yes, sir."

Jessica could see the relief in the young officer's eyes. Even in a city like Philadelphia it was possible to spend an entire career on the streets without encountering a dead body. This kid was already a veteran.

The three detectives walked over to the idling sector car, unit 1814. John Shepherd nodded to the officer standing near the trunk, P/O D. Dasher. Dasher walked over to the rear passenger door, opened it. A few seconds later, the occupant got out.

To say the least, the suspect was not what Jessica had expected.

The kid was pale and drawn, no more than seventeen. His hair was dyed a raven black, cut into a modified Justin Bieber sweep, more than a few weeks since a shampoo, and he had what appeared to be a dozen silver rings in his right ear.

In the harsh light thrown by the headlights of the police car, Jessica could see the kid was on something. His eyes were glazed.

Shepherd approached him, produced his ID.

Jessica noticed immediately that the kid was trying to posture himself as a hard case, but she had the feeling that this façade would begin to dissolve in short order. A lot of people think they can sit in an interview room or be interviewed at a crime scene and throw down attitude, a belief certainly fostered by a few decades of TV cop shows. Whenever Jessica watched shows like *Law & Order,* and saw the soccer mom or the kid who delivered groceries or the guy who works at Baby Gap—all of whom were hauled in on suspicion of murder, no less—giving detectives a hard time, she had to laugh.

"Just so you know, I'm the good cop, she's the great cop," Shepherd said, pointing at Jessica. "If you and I don't strike up a deep and meaningful relationship, we'll send in the bad cop."

"Where's the bad cop?" the kid asked, with slightly less attitude than just a few seconds earlier.

Shepherd pointed to Byrne, who was leaning against the CSU van, arms crossed.

Shepherd took a step back from the kid, giving him a little room. He picked up a wallet from the hood of the patrol car, flipped it open, glanced at the license, the kid, back. "Dustin David Green," he said. "Do you still live at this address? On Tasker?"

"Not really."

Shepherd poked through the wallet, found nothing of interest. He tossed it back onto the hood of the car. He stepped in.

"Now, you see, we're off to a bad start. A *very* bad start. I asked you a simple question, one that required a simple yes or no answer. In fact, it was the simplest question I'm going to ask you all night. And I can see that we're going to be together *all* night."

The kid rocked side to side a little. "Okay, what I meant was, I *used* to live there. Now I kind of stay with friends."

"Better," Shepherd said. "Not nearly good enough, but better. Before we're done I'm going to need all their names and addresses."

Shepherd backed up, continued.

"Now, tell me how you came to be in this place, at this time."

The kid shrugged. "What do you want to know?"

Shepherd took a deep breath, exhaled slowly. He ran a hand over his chin. "Okay, let me see if I can lay this out for you so you'll understand."

The kid wobbled. Shepherd steadied him.

"This is now officially a homicide investigation," Shepherd said. "There was a man killed here tonight. Do you understand me so far?"

The kid went even paler. "Somebody was killed?"

"Yes, Dustin. Somebody was killed."

"For real?"

"Yes, for real. Not like in *Modern Warfare 3,* or *Left 4 Dead*. For real."

The kid just stared.

"So, until I say differently, you are our number one suspect. If I say so, you will never go home again. Ever. Think about it. You go from here, to the station, to a courtroom, then to prison. Forever. And trust me, you are not going to do well in prison. You'll be selling your ass for Nicorette within two days."

Shepherd's version of possible scenarios wouldn't happen exactly the way he described, but Dustin Green didn't seem to know that.

"I don't know anything about anyone getting killed," the kid said.

"Walk me through it, Dustin," Shepherd said. "Nice and slow, so even I can understand."

The kid looked around, over one shoulder, then the other, as if his story might be on the way, being delivered to him like Chinese take-out. When he could no longer stall, he began. "All I know is, this guy said he'd give me five hundred bucks to drive his car up here. That's it. I don't know what else I can tell you."

"Where did this happen?"

"Old City. On Second."

"Five hundred dollars and what else?"

The kid went squirrelly. "Just the five."

Shepherd took a moment, then walked over to the sector car. He picked up a baggie off the hood, a twisted sandwich bag containing a few blue pills. He held it up to the light. "This was part of the payment, too, wasn't it?"

"Those aren't mine, man."

"I see," Shepherd said. "So, you're saying that someone put these in your front pants pocket?"

"I was just holding them for someone."

"Who?"

"My cousin."

"What's your cousin's name?"

"Huh?"

Shepherd turned to look at Jessica. "Isn't it amazing how they always go deaf on that question?"

It was true. That question caused hearing problems in just about everyone who spoke to the police. The world was full of no-name cousins.

John Shepherd closed the distance between himself and Dustin Green. He towered over the kid by five or six inches. Playtime was clearly over.

"Let's go," Shepherd said. "We're going to book you for murder."

"Wait."

"Turn around and put your hands behind your back."

"Wait!"

Shepherd backed off, glanced at his watch. "You have one minute to tell me the entire story. Begin now."

The kid started talking.

"Okay, okay, okay. This guy, he gave me the money and the beans, and he told me to drive his car up here. I was supposed to park near that chapel, just off the avenue. He also told me to walk all the way over to the other side of the park, then come down this street here."

"Chancel Lane."

"Is that what it is?"

"Why did this guy ask you to do this?"

"I have no idea. Five *hundred*, man. I didn't ask."

"It didn't sound a little strange to you?"

The kid wavered again. "I don't know. I guess."

Shepherd pointed to the big plastic garbage bag on the ground behind the sector car. "What about the bag?"

"He told me to carry that bag and leave it in the middle of the field. That's it. I swear to God."

"Little early in the conversation for God," Shepherd said. "We're going to go over this story many more times. *Many* more. You might want to save God for later." Shepherd held up the baggie. "What are these pills?"

"They're supposed to be some new kind of X."

"So, you decided you would pop some X, and then go to work?"

The kid went squirrelly again. This time, Jessica could see that he had begun to sweat. A lot. "No. This guy said if I did this job right there were more jobs on the horizon. I wasn't going to screw this up by getting high before the job was done. This guy expressly told me not to take the beans until I delivered the car."

"So you popped the pills after you got to the park."

The kid just nodded.

"How many?"

He held up two fingers, like a peace sign.

Shepherd took the information in. "So who is this guy?"

"Just some guy, man."

"You don't know his name?"

The kid shook his head.

"Where do you know him from?"

Another shrug. "I just see him around. We all just see him around."

"Who is *we?*"

"Just us. The kids I hang around with on the street."

"These are kids you go to school with?"

The kid almost laughed. "Just street kids, man. We see this guy around sometimes. Older guy, but cool. Sometimes he lets us do jobs for him."

"You've done jobs for him before?"

"Not me. But I know people who have."

"What's his angle?"

Now the kid got very interested in his own shoes. He shuffled in place, licked his lips, continued to perspire. "I have no idea, man. He never tried anything with me, or any other of the kids I know."

"What does this guy look like?" Shepherd asked. "Is he black, white, Hispanic?"

"White guy, kind of thin."

"How old?"

Yet another shrug. "I have no idea, man. Thirty? Forty? How old are *you?*"

Shepherd let the kid slide on that one. When you're seventeen, the whole adult world is forty.

"Can you describe him to a sketch artist?"

"Yeah, no problem. I can even draw him for you. I'm pretty good."

Before John Shepherd could ask another question the kid swayed again, this time losing his balance. Jessica was beginning to doubt that those pills were ecstasy. Whatever they were, they were starting to kick in. Shepherd, of course, noticed this, too. He eased the kid over to the sector car, leaned him against the hood. He got down to business. "Tell me about the car."

At this the kid lit up. "Fucking beautiful, man." He suddenly realized what he said in front of a homicide detective. "I mean, it was hot."

"I need make and model, Dustin."

The kid looked at the sky for a moment. "I can't tell you that. It was old school. *Grandpa* old, like a classic. *Dukes of Hazzard* classic. But in perfect shape."

"What color was it?"

"Black."

Jessica glanced at Byrne. It was just what Old Tony Giordano had said about the car that was used to abduct Joan Delacroix.

"Did the car have a bench seat? Buckets?"

The kid stared. He didn't know the difference.

"Did he tell you what was in that big bag?" Shepherd asked.

The kid's eyes were starting to fog. Jessica had to wonder how much more conversation—specifically detailed conversation—they were going to get from Dustin David Green.

Shepherd got the attention of one of the EMTs, beckoned him over.

"He said he took two of these," Shepherd said to the paramedic. "He says they're X, but I don't think so. Check them out, okay?" The paramedic nodded as Shepherd handed him the bag of pills.

Shepherd then walked over to P/O Dasher. He told him that, when the EMT had finished with Dustin Green, he was to take Green to the Roundhouse, and sit on him until he got there.

Shepherd returned to where Jessica and Byrne waited.

"What's in the big bag?" Byrne asked.

"Shredded paper," Shepherd said. "Looks like it was picked up from an office Dumpster. CSU is going to try to piece some of it together, see if we can get a lead on the source."

"So the kid was a diversion," Jessica said.

"Looks like it."

"Where's the victim?" Byrne asked.

"About twenty yards into the trees from the chapel parking lot."

"So it's right near where Weldon was parked when he got the call."

Shepherd nodded.

Jessica considered this. This was a true nightmare for any young officer. Even a veteran cop. Weldon was drawn off his post by a diversionary tactic, only to find out that a murder was committed within what would have been his clear line of vision.

"What about this black car?" Jessica asked. "The car the kid drove up here?"

"Long gone," Shepherd said. "I've got units securing that lot now. I was hoping we could get some tire impressions, but then we got this damn rain."

Jessica had hardly noticed. It seemed it would never end.

It was now evident that the compulsion that drove this madman to commit these crimes in Priory Park would not be denied.

Shepherd pulled out onto the avenue, heading north. In a few minutes they were at the north end of the park. They pulled off, into the parking lot of the old stone chapel. There were half a dozen departmental cars, as well as a CSU van.

"You say we have an ID on the victim?" Byrne asked.

Shepherd nodded. "We do. We got a positive from running his vehicle." He pointed to one of the vehicles in the lot, a new Chrysler 300. As a matter of procedure they would now have the car towed to a police garage, where, away from the elements, they would process the entire vehicle. The victim's car was its own crime scene.

"I figure the killer drove the victim up here in the 300, and when the sector car took the call, he walked the victim into the woods, killed him, then took off in his own car."

"The mysterious black car," Jessica said.

Shepherd nodded. "When Officer Weldon got back up here he found the Chrysler where you see it right there." Shepherd put his laptop on the dash, hit a few keys. Soon a photo ID came up on the screen.

"The victim is one Edward R. Richmond, MD, late of Spruce Street."

Jessica glanced at her partner. A doctor, a nurse and a man who worked in the pharmaceutical industry.

"Detectives went to the victim's residence, found the doors wide open."

"Was there anyone at the house?"

Shepherd nodded. "A seven-year-old boy. The victim's son."

"Where was he?"

Shepherd consulted his notes. "He was in the upstairs bathroom. He was bound and gagged with duct tape."

"What's his status?"

"Some bruises, a few small cuts, probably in shock."

"Do we know if he can describe our subject?" Jessica asked.

"No idea. He's on the way to the hospital. I put a call in to the ER at Jefferson. They'll give us a call, if and when."

They sat in the car for a few minutes, watching CSU officers walk into and out of the clearing. Soon they saw the medical examiner's investigator with his photographer in tow. The investigator nodded at Shepherd. The detectives were cleared to begin their investigation.

"Ready?" Shepherd asked.

Jessica desperately wanted to say, *No thanks.* "Let's do it."

"There are umbrellas in the back."

When Jessica opened her door, the first thing she heard was the low rumble of the generator that CSU had set up for their portable lighting. She grabbed an umbrella and began to make her way through the trees, drawn to the ethereal glow of the halogen lamps.

When she stepped into the clearing she saw the victim for the first time. The scene was horrifying. Edward Richmond's body was suspended between two trees, arms out to his side, a wire holding him up. The wire wrapped around his neck, cutting deep into his throat, spiraling around each arm, then looped up to the lowest branches of the trees. He wore a white dress shirt and dark slacks. His feet were bound together with wire. The long shadow cast on the floor of the forest made him look like a scarecrow.

At his feet, splashed with blood, were a ring of white flowers.

"Detective Shepherd?" came the voice through Shepherd's two-way. It sounded like one of the EMTs on the other side of the park.

202 • *Richard Montanari*

Shepherd keyed his rover. "Yeah."

"Are you still on scene?"

"I am," Shepherd said. "What's up?"

"You'd better get back here."

33

Rachel parked across the street. The house was a four-bedroom, two-and-a-half-bathroom stone front with hardwood floors and a sunporch. It was overpriced for the street, but that was not Rachel's concern at the moment.

She got out of her car, took her phone out of her pocket, pretended to make a call. It was a great way to scope a neighborhood without just standing around looking. Not that anyone would mistake her for a burglar.

She was dressed all in black—stretch pants, full zip hoodie, tech stretch gloves. She had even taken a black Magic Marker to the reflective strips on her running shoes, having noticed one night that she could probably be seen from a block away.

Finding the street deserted, she walked up to the door and, using her small LED flashlight, found the lockbox. In a few seconds she entered the combination she had gotten from Bancroft, retrieved the key, and slipped it into the lock. She clicked off her flashlight, looked up and down the street. Deserted. She couldn't be certain that she wasn't being observed from the houses across the street, but it was a chance she always took. It was a chance she *had* to take.

She stepped inside, closed the door behind her.

She headed to the basement.

She launched the compass app on her phone, found her bearings, then took out her portable electric screwdriver, and removed the vent for the cold-air return. She pulled herself into the crawl space, pleased to find that most of it was poured concrete. There was only about two feet of clearance, but at Rachel's size it was enough. She put her flashlight in her mouth and began to crawl. At the far end she saw a dim light.

She let herself down, into the plenum, walked about fifty feet north, which, according to her calculations, brought her just behind the corner row house. She pulled herself up into the crawl space, but this time she was not so lucky. The crawl space was packed earth, not concrete. It was damp and moldy.

She reached into her pocket, pulled out a small face mask, put it on over her nose and mouth. When she reached the end of the crawl space she stopped, listened for activity. Hearing none, she dropped down onto the basement floor.

From upstairs she could hear the faint sound of a television program drifting down, a sitcom of some sort. She glanced at her watch, then took out her notebook. If her averages were right, and they had yet to be proven inaccurate, the television would be turned off within twenty minutes.

Rachel Gray sat on the floor, beneath the stairs, and waited for silence.

34

It was after two a.m. when Jessica and Byrne left the park. The body of Dr. Edward Richmond had been removed from the scene and transported to the morgue on University Avenue. There would be an autopsy at nine-thirty a.m.

Jessica and Byrne would be back at the Roundhouse in just a few hours for a task force meeting.

They learned at just after one o'clock that Dustin Green had become cyanotic on the way to the hospital. En route his condition worsened and, according to what Jessica learned from John Shepherd before they left the park, Green began to exhibit symptoms of a condition called hypoxia, a complete lack of oxygen in his lungs.

Dustin Green died at 1:07 a.m.

A toxicology report would be rushed through channels. If the kid was telling the truth, then the man who had hired him to drive the car for five hundred dollars and pills had murdered him to prevent his speaking to investigators. The narcotics unit would be copied in and most likely put a pair of detectives on the task force to try to track down the pills.

There were now four bodies on this madman.

When Jessica and Byrne arrived at a small residential area west of Priory Park known as the Cloisters, Jessica was sure they had gone the wrong way. She kept it to herself for the moment. Because they had learned that parts of I-95 were closed due to high water, they decided to take Roosevelt Boulevard back to the city. What they got was a wrong turn.

Jessica glanced at her watch. It was too late to play lost. She tapped the navigation screen in the dashboard. "Let's see, what is this thing, again?"

"I don't need a map," Byrne said. "I know where we are."

Byrne pulled into a driveway, turned around. He hit the gas, a little too hard, the way you do when you realize you just went six blocks in the wrong direction, and you want to make up for lost time.

"We need to get detailed work histories on these people," Byrne said. "A doctor, a nurse and a man who worked in medical sales. At some point their pasts link up. Either in school or at a job."

Jessica made a few notes.

"You know," Byrne added, "I think we should check out the neighbor—"

Jessica saw the shadow first, then the shape. It was less than twenty feet away. She screamed: *"Kevin!"*

Byrne slammed on the brakes. The Taurus fishtailed as it hurtled forward.

There, in the middle of the street, in the middle of the *night,* stood a two-year-old girl.

They were going to run her over.

35

Luther sat in the main corridor, the wide catacomb below G10. The Long Hallway was almost a mile in length, and at the far end, the end at which Luther had lived for more than three years—the silent place—he could see pale yellow light. As a boy he would run from one end of the corridor to the other, hiding in the alcoves and niches, watching as they transferred patients between buildings, covering his ears to the ranting and raving of the mad citizens of the hospital.

The echoes never fully ceased.

The dead doctor stood before him, bathed in shadow.

"You have disappointed me," he said.

Luther could not see the doctor, but he had seen his charred body after the fire. It was better this way. "I know," he replied. His own voice sounded young, like a child's.

The visage of the doctor shimmered, his white coat a chimera in the gloom. "You know what you have to do."

When Luther returned from the park he'd found the main door open. It was a mistake, the biggest he'd ever made.

But that wasn't the worst of Luther's problems. Not by a long shot.

You know what you have to do.

Luther rose, walked slowly toward the light, just as the final dream began to unspool in his mind.

No, Luther thought. *This is not like the dream.*

This is not like the dream at all.

36

The little girl sat on the wrought-iron bench in the middle of the small turnabout at the end of the street. She had fine blond hair, blue eyes, pale, nearly translucent skin. She wore a pink Care Bears hoodie, denim pants. On her feet were what appeared to be brand-new Baby Reeboks, feet that barely made it to the edge of the bench. She carried a small pink purse with a gold-colored plastic shoulder strap. On the zipper was clipped a charm of some sort.

When Byrne had slammed on the brakes, the girl had not jumped back or, for that matter, reacted in any way to the car barreling toward her. Byrne had stopped well short, backed up, pulled to the curb, leaving the car running and the headlights on.

Jessica had picked up the girl and carried her to the bench. When Jessica did this the girl had not fought her or resisted in any way, nor had she cried out in pain. That was a good thing. But neither had the girl uttered a single word.

That was *not* such a good thing.

Jessica knelt in front of the bench. "Are you okay, sweetie?" she asked.

The little girl looked over at Byrne, then at her hands. She did not respond.

"What's your name?"

The girl remained silent. In the distance, probably on the avenue a few blocks away, the sound of an ambulance siren rose into the night. The girl did not look up, did not react.

"My name's Jessica." She gestured at Byrne. "This is my friend, Kevin."

Nothing. For a moment, Jessica wasn't sure the little girl had heard her. Her stare was so distant, so sad, so . . . what?

Wise, Jessica thought. The girl couldn't have been three, yet her eyes mirrored a lifetime of trial.

"Are you hurt?" Jessica asked. "Does anything hurt?"

The girl did not answer.

Jessica did a quick inventory of the girl's face, hands, arms, legs. Nothing visible. No bruises, no lacerations, no blood, no rips or tears in her clothing. But that didn't mean she wasn't hurt.

Jessica stood up, turned a slow, full 360. Only one of the houses in the immediate vicinity had a light on, and that was a dim amber glow on the third floor of a brick row house, a candelabra bulb in the window. Probably a night-light of some sort, she thought. Other than that, the dozen or so houses around them were dark, their tenants surely fast asleep. There was not even the flickering blue light of a TV on any of the closed and shuttered windows.

Jessica crouched back down. "Can you point at your house for me? I can take you back to your mom."

Nothing.

Jessica pointed over her left shoulder. "Is it this house?"

Silence.

Jessica pointed over her right shoulder. "This one?"

Zip.

In her time on the police force Jessica had interviewed thousands of people. Most of them had been citizens with nothing to add to the case she was investigating, the conversations being of the forensic interview variety—a non-leading dialogue. Some had been material witnesses, some had been collateral witnesses, and quite a number had been witnesses who turned into suspects. She was usually quite good at finding the tell—the involuntary behavior or gesture or mannerism that gives information to the questioner—knowing that all but the most hardened criminal could not hide it.

When she'd asked the little girl about her house Jessica watched the girl's eyes carefully. The girl did not cast a glance right or left, nor up at any of the nearby houses, most of which were what Philly natives called trinities—tall, three-story row homes.

How was this possible? Jessica wondered. *Did someone just drop this little girl off in the middle of an intersection, in the middle of the night, like some unwanted pet?*

Jessica glanced at the small plastic purse, which was now in the little girl's lap. It was oval in shape, a faux-alligator material. The tiny charm hanging off the zipper appeared to be a heart.

"Is it okay if I look in your purse?" Jessica asked.

At the word *purse* the girl looked up, turned her head, made eye contact with Byrne. Jessica suddenly understood. The girl wanted to talk to *him*. This was the third or fourth time she'd glanced over.

Jessica stood up, took a few steps back. Byrne walked forward, knelt down, put his hands on the bench, on either side of the girl. After a few long moments the little girl looked up, directly into Byrne's eyes. When she did this, Byrne smiled.

Although Jessica would think about this moment many times over the next few weeks—and would not be comfortable swearing to it in a court of law—she thought she saw the little girl blush.

"This is a *very* pretty purse," Byrne said.

Nothing. The girl shifted on the bench. She crossed her feet.

"My daughter had a purse just like this when she was your age."

The girl lifted a forefinger, dropped it. It was a reaction to Byrne's conversation, his nearness. This was good.

"Now, let's see. What color *is* this?" Byrne asked, angling the purse into the cone of yellow light thrown from the street lamp. "Is this red?"

The girl was too sharp for such a trick, it seemed. She remained silent.

While Byrne plied his Irish charm on the little girl, Jessica walked back to the car, got on her phone, and contacted the commander of the PPD communications unit. She soon learned that no one had called in a missing child in the past few hours—or all day, in fact. Rare for Philadelphia. Jessica then called her own supervisor and put in a request to broaden the request to the five-county area, which included Bucks, Chester, Montgomery and Delaware counties. It didn't make a lot of sense that this child might have gotten here in the middle of the night from another county, but it wouldn't be the craziest thing she'd ever encountered in her time on the force. Not even close.

As she waited on the phone, Jessica glanced over at Byrne and the little girl. They were now sitting next to each other, hands folded in their laps, staring straight ahead, as if waiting for a bus. Jessica noticed that the girl had moved a few inches closer to the big man next to her.

Jessica's supervisor soon came back on the line and told her that the alert had gone out.

"Okay, Sarge," Jessica said. "Thanks."

She clicked off, walked back over to the bench, sat down next to the girl.

"Is it okay if Jessica looks inside your purse?" Byrne asked the girl.

Even though the girl appeared to be warming to Kevin Byrne, Byrne probably figured that certain rules still apply—this being the one about girls and purses. The girl didn't react at all, so Jessica leaned in and gently removed the purse from her lap.

"Kevin is right," Jessica said. "This is *very* pretty. It's a lot prettier than my purse."

She carefully unzipped the handbag. There was only one thing inside, a half sandwich of some sort, sealed in a plastic sandwich bag. There was nothing else—no pictures, no ID card in case the girl ever got lost. Holding the sandwich bag by the edges—if for no other reason than it was a long ingrained habit—Jessica put it back in the purse, zipped it shut.

"We're going to take you to look for your house now," Byrne said. It appeared that, for the moment, he had decided not to phrase things like a question. It was an old trick with children. If you made things a statement, it was easier to get them to agree. Even if the response was silence.

Both Jessica and Byrne stood up. A few seconds later the little girl slid off the bench. They all walked over to the idling car. Byrne opened the rear passenger door. The little girl put the shoulder strap of her purse over her shoulder, climbed in. Byrne gently clicked the harness around the little girl, closed the door, then slipped into the front passenger seat. They probably should have called the Special Victims Unit, requesting a child's car seat, but it was late.

"Jess," Byrne said.

"What?"

"Hang on."

Jessica looked at her partner. "What is it?"

Byrne chucked a thumb over his shoulder. "She can't see."

Jessica angled the rearview mirror. It was true. The little girl couldn't see out of the car, so she would not be able to point out her house.

Byrne unbuckled his seat belt, opened the door, walked to the rear of the car. A few seconds later he got back in, and pulled the little girl onto his lap. Even though it broke a handful of traffic laws in the city of Philadelphia—probably the Commonwealth of Pennsylvania, as well—Byrne did his best to strap them both in with his shoulder harness.

"Everybody ready?" Jessica asked.

"Ready," Byrne said.

As expected, the smallest member of their entourage said not a word.

Twenty minutes later, having driven slowly up and down every street in a four-block radius, they returned to the spot where they had first encountered the girl.

How far would a girl this age roam? Jessica wondered. *Two blocks? Three?* Jessica recalled when her own daughter Sophie had been a toddler. Sophie had wandered from their tiny front yard in Lexington Park and made it nearly to the corner before Jessica broke all land speed records to get there and retrieve her. Jessica knew that Sophie would never cross a street at that age, but there was still plenty of danger to be found on sidewalks and driveways.

This little girl had not only crossed the street, she was standing in the middle of an intersection. How long had she been there? Had people seen her and driven on? Jessica didn't want to think about that right now.

Jessica looked at the girl. She was resting her head on Byrne's shoulder, lost in the twilight before sleep. Her eyes were open, but Jessica could tell she was not far from drifting off.

Jessica glanced at Byrne. It was a silent communiqué that said they had pretty much run out of options. If the little girl wasn't going to offer any information—and it appeared now that she would not—there wasn't much they could do at this hour.

Five minutes later they headed to Children's Hospital.

37

Jessica's first cousin Angela was a registered nurse, working nights at Children's Hospital. On the way into the city Jessica had called Angela, telling her about the little girl they had found. Angela had agreed to meet them at the emergency room intake.

"She's fine," Angela said, taking off her latex gloves and popping them into a waste receptacle. "No bruises, no trauma. Externally, anyway."

They stood in the ER waiting room, all but empty at this hour.

The question had to be asked, as little as Jessica wanted to ask it. "No sexual assault?"

"No," Angela said. "Nothing like that. Thank God."

"How old would you say she is?" Byrne asked. "Two?"

Angela looked through the glass, back. The little girl was sitting on the examining table, her hands folded piously in her lap.

"A little older," Angela said. "Two and a half. Give or take."

"And she didn't say anything?" Jessica asked.

Angela shook her head. "Not a word."

For a moment Jessica considered that the girl might not speak English, but even if that were the case she would have made a sound of some sort. Wouldn't she? Children her age were rarely quiet for long.

"So, she responded to you?" Jessica asked. "I mean, she seemed to understand what you were saying?"

"*Oh,* yeah. I asked her to open her mouth and say *ah* and she did. I asked her to sit back a little bit on the table and she scooted. Very responsive. Right now I'd have to say she's my patient of the day. Hands down the most adorable."

It was true. Even in the unforgiving glare of the fluorescent lights she looked like a little angel.

"Do you think she—"

"But I will say this," Angela said, interrupting Jessica. "Every time I asked her to do something she looked out here first."

"Out here?" Jessica asked. "At us?"

"Not at both of you. Just Kevin," Angela said. She gave Byrne a playful punch on the shoulder. Ever since Angela had met Kevin Byrne she'd had a major crush on him. "Looks like you have a little buddy."

Jessica glanced back in the examining room. Angela was right. The little girl was sitting on the paper-covered examining table, staring at Byrne with her big blue eyes.

"She'll be okay in there for a few minutes?" Byrne asked.

"Oh, yeah," Angela said.

Jessica and Byrne walked down the hallway, to the vending area.

"What do you want to do?" Byrne asked.

Jessica considered their options. She checked her watch. It was 4:10 in the morning. If it had been much earlier—as in yesterday—and they were off the clock, they might have driven back to the area and done a door-to-door. There was no way they could do that now. In just a few hours this would be a job for the divisional detectives in the Northeast. It certainly wasn't a case for Homicide.

On the record, they'd found a missing child—a child no one appeared to know or care was missing—and they'd followed procedure. More or less. The little girl seemed to be fine. They'd taken her to a hospital, had her checked out.

No dead body, no homicide. There was only one thing they could do.

They would have to take the little girl to DHS, the Department of Human Services.

On the way to DHS, they stopped at an all-night carryout. Jessica pulled the car to the curb, put it in park.

"Want something?" Byrne asked.

"I'm good," she said.

Byrne unsnapped his seat belt, lifted the little girl effortlessly from his knee, placed her gently on the seat. "I'll be right back."

While Byrne went into the store the little girl watched him. Jessica wanted desperately to connect with the girl, but she remained silent. Part of it was due to her fatigue; the rest came from her belief that anything she said right now might serve to weaken the bond that her partner had begun to build with the girl.

Five minutes later Byrne came out with a big bag. He got in the car, reached in the bag, handed Jessica a diet decaf Snapple. He knew her too well. "I'm good" meant: *Get me something that doesn't trash my diet or circadian rhythms any more than they already are.*

In the intake room at DHS, Jessica watched as Byrne walked the little girl over to the DHS worker. With the appropriate forms signed, it was time to leave. Before turning to the door, Byrne reached into the shopping bag and removed the small plush rabbit he'd bought at the bodega at some ridiculous markup.

At first the girl did not respond, but after a few moments she took the toy. Byrne then took out his camera, took a few close-ups of the girl. This would be sent to the detectives at the Special Victims Unit. If that turned up nothing, the picture would be sent to all the TV stations.

Byrne put his camera away, stood up. Even though Jessica had worked with Byrne for years, she often forgot how big he really was. Jessica was five-eight in stocking feet, but presented herself taller, especially on the job.

Now, looking at her partner, he looked so much bigger than the little girl. Like a giant. Byrne kissed a forefinger, touched the girl on top of her head, turned and walked out to the parking lot.

The little girl, now hand in hand with the DHS worker, didn't take her eyes off him. Outside, Byrne stood next to Jessica. They both waved. Instead of waving back, the little girl lifted a hand to her face, extended a tiny forefinger, and placed it to her lips.

Ten minutes later, in the parking lot at the Roundhouse, each by their own car, they stood, each to their own thoughts. The discovery of the little girl had interrupted their train of investigative thought regarding the horrific scene they had encountered in the park. They would be back to that soon enough.

The sky was still black. Jessica was thankful for that. She hated going to sleep at dawn.

Jessica broke the silence. "What is the maximum number of hours a person can be awake and still function?"

"Human or cop?"

"Cop."

"Forty-eight."

"Damn," Jessica said. She wasn't even close. She opened her car door, hesitated. "You and I both know we're going to follow up on this," she said, pointing in the general direction of the Department of Human Services at 15th and Arch.

"Yeah," Byrne said.

"So, when we talk about her tomorrow, we have to call her something, right?"

Byrne nodded.

"I mean, something other than 'The Little Girl We Found in the Middle of the Street.'"

"True."

Jessica continued, as if this were an opening statement. It reminded her that she had homework. At her age. "And I refuse to call her Jane Doe."

Byrne opened the door to his car, hesitated for a moment. He reached into the shopping bag, pulled out the little pink purse.

Jessica smiled. "I'm not sure that's a good look for you."

"You haven't seen my new Easter outfit yet."

"So, how did you get her to give it up?"

"I made her a swap for the stuffed bunny," Byrne said. "She was a pushover."

"Sweet-talker."

"It's a gift."

"So you saw that, right? When we left? She put a finger to her lips like she was telling us to be quiet."

"Yeah," Byrne said. "I saw it."

"Any idea what that was all about?"

"Not a clue."

Jessica took a deep breath of cold night air, trying to will herself awake. It didn't help. She took out her keys. "Let me guess," she said. "You're not going straight home, are you? You're going to make a stop at Eighth and Poplar."

Byrne laughed. "I thought I'd swing by the lab and drop this off. It's on the way."

It was technically true. Jessica slipped into her car.

"What was the name of the street where we found the little girl?" Byrne asked.

Jessica thought about it. She tried to visualize the encounter. Then she remembered. She'd taken a picture of the girl standing in the intersection. It was an old habit—at least as old as camera cell phones on the job—and a few years earlier she had gotten into the habit of taking establishing shots at crime scenes. She fished the phone out of her jeans pocket, navigated to the photo folder. She soon found the picture she was looking for, a photograph of the girl standing in the middle of the street, looking tiny, and precious, and lost. Jessica's heart flickered at the sight.

"Got it." She tapped the screen, enlarging the photo, and swiped to the top. "The intersection was Abbot Road and Violet Drive."

Byrne slid into his car, thought for a moment, turned and said: "Let's call her Violet."

38

As she approached the row house on Callowhill, Rachel noticed from across the street that her sign—one she had put up with great care just a few days earlier—had been defaced with some unrecognizable gang graffiti.

Assholes, she thought.

She opened her trunk, took out her drill, turned the Phillips head bit into the chuck. She hit the button. Of course, the battery was low. A few minutes later, new battery in place, she took down the Perry-Hayes sign with a small picture of Rachel Gray in the corner (Denise called it actual size, ha ha), and put up the new one. It was quick enough work, but one she had done too often in recent days.

By the time she put the old sign in the trunk of her car, she saw the woman heading up the street.

"Hi, Gloria," Rachel said.

"Hi," the woman replied.

Because Rachel had a background in women's fashion, she was very attuned to a potential buyer's wardrobe. Most of the time she could pinpoint every aspect of an outfit: designer, price point, shoes, bag, accessories, jewelry. Sometimes she even played a game with it. When a woman who was particularly well turned out had her back to Rachel, she would close her eyes and sniff. If she detected a fragrance, she would compliment the woman on it, asking the label. Nine times out of ten she was right.

With Gloria, sadly, it was another game Rachel played, one for which she rebuked herself every time. Gloria Vincenzi had two or three outfits that she mixed and matched. Rachel had noticed the seams coming apart on the woman's jacket a few months earlier, and now noticed that the seam had begun to separate even further. It broke her heart.

"When Frank and I were first married we lived in a house not much smaller than this. It was over on Fitzwater Street. Do you know Fitzwater?"

"Yes," Rachel said. "I have a property on Fitzwater. Where was your house?"

Right near the corner of Fitzwater and Fourth.

"Right near the corner of Fitzwater and Fourth," the woman said.

Next door to the dry cleaner's.

"Next door to the dry cleaner's," Gloria added.

Frank Vincenzi, Rachel thought.

After Rachel had shown Gloria Vincenzi fifteen or so properties — houses with a more than three-hundred-thousand-dollar spread in asking prices, a range no home buyer in the history of realty ever spanned — Rachel did a little digging.

The reason Rachel had never met Gloria's husband, Frank, a man about whom she knew a great deal, even down to his taste in instant mashed potatoes—Hungry Jack—was that there *was* no Frank Vincenzi. Frank Vincenzi passed away from pancreatic cancer in 2001.

Gloria Vincenzi was still looking for their first little house.

As Rachel locked the front door, Gloria said what she always said, and that was: "Well, I guess we'll keep looking. I'll call you."

Rachel did not know how much longer she would do this. But for now it was all right.

She understood.

She was looking for something herself.

When Rachel returned to the office there was a note on her desk from her boss. Diana wanted to see her.

Rachel got a cup of coffee, walked down the hallway to her boss's corner office, knocked on her door.

Diana Perry was the co-owner of the company, in addition to being a broker and an agent.

"Come on in," she said.

Diana was always well-dressed. Although she saved her pricier outfits for the monthly staff meetings, awards banquets, and the like, she was always stylish in the office. Diana had to be in her early forties, but she presented herself much younger.

"Mr. and Mrs. Bader stopped in this morning."

The Baders were the amazon couple, the cowboy and the Saks model. Rachel tried to read her boss's face. Diana Perry, like all the best brokers, revealed nothing.

"They made an offer on the property you showed. Full price. Cash."

Yes.

Rachel tried to contain her joy. "You know, I had a feeling about them," she said. It wasn't true. She had long ago given up on those sorts of hunches. "Did we call the seller?"

"We did. Paperwork is underway. Not bad for twenty minutes' work."

It was true. Outside of drug dealing, there were few ways to make more money in less time than selling real estate.

Diana got up, walked around her desk, closed the door to her office. She sat on the chair next to Rachel's.

"First off, congratulations. Good work."

"Thanks."

Diana took a few moments. "I got an interesting call yesterday."

"A new listing?" Rachel asked.

"Yes and no."

Diana Perry, although in possession of a good sense of humor, was not one to play games. Especially when it came to the agency.

"I don't understand," Rachel said.

Diana tapped her pen a few times on the desk. "It was about your house. We have an offer."

At first Rachel thought she misunderstood. "My house?"

Diana nodded.

"But my house isn't for sale."

"That's what I told them."

Rachel was one of the few people she knew in her age group to own a house. She had paid off the house with her first big commission, a multiunit sale in the Piazza, a condo complex built on the site of the old Schmidt's Brewery.

Diana continued. "I just thought that maybe it was..."

Time, Rachel thought. That's what Diana wanted to say. But she's too nice to say it. "Time?"

"That. I'm sorry. It's none of my business."

"It's okay," Rachel said.

"They mentioned a number, though. I think you should know that."

"A nice number?"

"A *very* nice number. You think about it, and let me know if you want to hear it."

"Okay," Rachel said. "I will."

She got up from the chair in a sort of a fugue state, afloat on her great sale—and the nice check it would bring—but also on the concept of actually selling her house. It had never occurred to her that she might do it, or at least not until she was older. Then again, she didn't want to turn into a Gloria Vincenzi.

She thought about it all through dinner, a quickly forgotten meal at the Chinese restaurant around the corner from her house.

When she got home she put on the TV just for the sound. At about ten o'clock she flipped it off, went upstairs to the bathroom. She brushed her teeth, washed her face, moisturized. She stood for a moment considering her reflection. She had not known many of her relatives, indeed she did not even know what mix of nationalities and heritage she was. She had fair skin and hair, with eyes a deeper blue than most. Was she Irish? Scots? Or perhaps she was something farther north than that. Nordic or Baltic, perhaps.

She flipped off the light, walked out of the bathroom, down the hall. She anticipated the slight creak of floorboards near the top of the steps, as she always did.

She glanced at the white bar of light beneath the door at the end of the hall. She did not touch the knob, nor turn it and enter. She never did. She wondered if she ever would.

It was about your house. We have an offer.

Rachel had many times wondered how she might react to such news. She thought about the number of properties she had sold over the last few years, how the news of a good offer to the sellers changed their lives. Properties, especially homes, changed hands many times in the lives of the brick and mortar and wood.

She walked down the stairs and entered the kitchen, made herself a cup of chamomile tea.

As she put away the tea she noticed that there was only one other cup in the cabinet. When had she packed all the others away? On what day had she resigned herself to this all but solitary existence, even to the point of packing away dishes and cups and saucers and bowls and platters?

She got dressed, walked out the front door, stood on the sidewalk. The street was dark and quiet.

She looked at the solitary light burning in the upstairs window. She always thought she saw shadows move on the blinds, but she never had.

She never would. She knew that, but it never stopped her.

We have an offer.

Maybe Diana's right, Rachel thought.

Maybe it is *time.*

39

In the hours since Dr. Edward Richmond's body had been found, a task force was formed, fully funded for all the overtime that would most likely be needed to investigate the four murders — Robert Freitag, Joan Delacroix, Edward Richmond and Dustin Green.

There were now eight detectives assigned to the task force. Calls had been made from high on high to all the science divisions involved in the cases — fingerprint, DNA, criminalistics, document — which were also authorized overtime.

The FBI had sent over their initial findings on the flowers found at all three murder sites. The white flower left in the hands of both Robert Freitag and Joan Delacroix, as well as placed in a circle at the feet of Edward Richmond, was called *anaphalis margaritacea,* more commonly known as Pearly Everlasting. It was a perennial flower indigenous to many areas of North America and, according to the FBI report, had been dried and finished using an over-the-counter hair spray. Any forensic possibilities beyond this were negated by the rain, which helped to as good as completely deteriorate the integrity of the evidence.

As to the little girl, two detectives from the Special Victims Unit had canvassed the area where Violet was found, and had spoken to all but a handful of the people who lived in the immediate area, showing a picture of the girl, with no results.

As a result, or despite a result, a picture of Violet had been broadcast on all the local television stations, and published in both the *Inquirer* and the *Daily News*. So far, no one had called DHS claiming to be a member of the little girl's family.

Jessica knew that if no one came forward, Violet would be placed in emergency foster care by day's end.

At just before noon John Shepherd walked into the duty room. He looked as if he hadn't slept. Many times that was the case with a new homicide, certainly one discovered late in the afternoon or evening of the previous day.

"Sorry about that kid," Byrne said.

Shepherd sat down on the edge of a desk. "Not as sorry as I am," he said. "Didn't get anything out of him before he coded. No description of our boy. Except for white and thirty or forty."

"I take it that wasn't just ecstasy he was on," Jessica said.

Shepherd shook his head. "Turns out the pills he had—the pills he said he got from the guy whose car he drove up to the park—were laced with potassium cyanide."

"Cyanide?" Jessica said. "I haven't heard of that in a while."

"Tox isn't complete yet. It might have been a cocktail."

"So our guy got the kid to drive his car to the park, knowing the kid would take the tainted pills, and not be able to roll on him if he was caught."

"Looks like it," Shepherd said. "He had to bank on the kid actually doing the job, not coding in the black car before he made it up to the park."

"How could he depend on that?" Jessica asked.

"Good question. Two ways, the way I see it. One, the kid hoped to do another job for the guy in the future. Or two, the guy scared the shit out of him."

And with good reason, Jessica thought.

"How's the boy doing?" Byrne asked. "The victim's son."

"He's stable," Shepherd said. "I'm hoping to talk to him today."

"What about the place setting on Richmond's table?"

Shepherd took out his phone, scrolled through the pictures. He stopped at one, tapped it to enlarge it, showed it to the other two detectives.

There, on the dining-room table of the victim's house, was a large soup bowl with a mug turned upside down on it. Next to it, on a folded linen napkin, was a silver spoon.

Anthony Giordano looked significantly better than he had when they'd first met him sitting watch in his second-story window over-looking the alleyway behind Joan Delacroix's house. He had trimmed his beard and even gotten his unruly eyebrows in check. Jessica wondered if he had used the Best Cuts coupon on his corkboard.

"Thanks for coming in," Byrne said. "How did you get here?"

"Took the bus."

"We'll get you a ride back."

Tony gestured at Jessica, who was standing across the room, talking to John Shepherd. "She Italian?"

Byrne smiled. "She is."

Tony glanced back at Jessica. "Man, if I was fifty years younger."

"Did I mention she's married to a cop?"

Tony looked surprised. "She's married?"

Byrne nodded.

"She's not wearing a ring."

"It's a whole new world, my friend."

Byrne pulled out a chair for the man. Tony sat down.

"What I'd like to do is go through some possibilities to try to identify the car you saw the other day."

"You mean pictures?"

"Yes," Byrne said. "We don't have the pictures here, though. They're
on the internet."

"I hope you can find them. I don't know the first damn thing
about it."

"Not a problem."

Byrne sat down in front of the terminal, navigated to a site they
sometimes used to ID cars. The site was divided by decades, starting
with the 1930s.

"Where do you want to start?" Byrne asked.

Tony thought for a few moments. "I'm thinking the sixties," he said.
"That's when everything went to hell, and I stopped paying attention.
I don't think it was any older than that."

"Okay," Byrne said. "So you think it was a big car, right? A full-size
sedan?"

"Yeah."

They began to scroll through the database of full-size sedans from
the 1960s: DeSotos, Imperials, Newports, New Yorkers, Galaxies,
Lincoln Continentals. Among them, Tony did not recognize any that
looked like the car he had seen.

They moved on to the 1970s, this time scrolling past Eldorados,
Impalas, Mercury Marquis, Monte Carlos. They were just about to
move on to the 1980s when Tony sat up a little straighter in his chair.

"That's it," he said. "That's the one."

Anthony Giordano was pointing at a 1977 Oldsmobile Toronado.

"How sure are you that this is the car?" Byrne asked.

"Not one hundred percent. Like I say, I usually only saw it from behind when it was parked on the street. Do you think we can find a shot of just the rear end, taken from above?"

"It's the internet. We can find anything." A few moments later, on Flickr, they found an overhead shot.

"That sure as hell looks like it," Tony said.

"Good deal," Byrne said. He hit a few keys, and began to print off some copies. While they were printing, Tony said: "Funny thing about cars. There's that eight- or ten- or twelve-year period in your life— from, maybe, twelve to twenty years old, for boys, anyway—when you know every make and model, every change in the grill, every fender skirt, every fin, every taillight."

"What decade was yours?" Byrne asked.

"The forties."

Byrne nodded. "What was your dream machine?"

"Easy," Tony said. "It was a nineteen forty-one Buick Club Coupe. Three-speed manual on the column, Fireball straight eight."

"What color?"

"Powder blue."

"Sweet."

The two men stood up. "We really appreciate you coming in," Byrne said, helping the old man with his coat.

"Happy to help," Tony said. "Got me out of the house."

"If you see that car show up again, you call me."

"Will do." He glanced across the room at Jessica, who was working at a computer terminal.

"She's married, huh?"

"I'm afraid so."

"The good ones always are."

"Truer words," Byrne said. "Come on. I'll walk you down."

*   *   *

By the time Byrne got back to the duty room, Hell Rohmer was sitting on one of the desks. He wore a knee-length leather duster and a black porkpie hat. In his hands was a large brown envelope.

"I come bearing gifts," he said.

"Gifts are good," Byrne said. He got Jessica's attention.

"About those Polaroids," Hell began. "I managed to get only one of the pictures off the cardboard backing. The reason for that is as follows: the longer any kind of adhesive sits, the more it integrates with the fibers on both surfaces, making it essentially one surface."

"I always tell Kevin that," Jessica said. "Now maybe he'll believe me."

Hell smiled. "But first to this one." He held up one of the Polaroids—the one taken of the man sitting at the long table with dishes on it. Jessica saw where Hell might be going with this, and she found that her heart had begun to race.

Hell pointed at the dishes and silverware on the table.

"I had this section enlarged," he said. "It took a little pixel manipulation, but after a few half-steps, I got it up to eight hundred percent." He reached into the envelope, extracted a nine-by-twelve enlargement. He put it on the table. "There's an engraving on the handle. It reads DVSH. It stands for—"

"Delaware Valley State Hospital," Byrne said. "Cold River."

The Delaware Valley State Hospital was euphemistically called Cold River because of its close proximity to the Delaware River. Over the almost one hundred years of its operation, many patients had wandered off the grounds, only to end up in the Delaware. The ones who didn't drown or die of hypothermia had only one travel tip for fellow inmates upon their return to the institution: stay out of the water.

When Jessica was small—she imagined it was this way for half the kids who grew up in Philadelphia—her father would threaten her with the place.

"Clean your room or I'm going to send you to Cold River," he would say. Cold River was the boogeyman place. It had been closed for a long time.

"This is what Lenny Pintar was referring to," Jessica said. "The Big Place."

She picked up the enlargement. The engraving on the spoon was clear, because when this photograph was taken the etching was new.

"These are our spoons," she said.

"Yes, they are," Byrne replied.

Hell looked up. "You have these spoons?"

"Long story," Jessica said.

Hell got back to business. "Okay. About separating the photographs from the mounting cardboard. The good news is that, if you can get the two surfaces apart, the surface that originally held the adhesive becomes a virtual fingerprint tablet. Like a built-in Super Glue chamber."

The Super Glue method of retrieving fingerprints, known as *cyano-acrylate fuming,* was a process where items suspected of containing latent fingerprints were put in a sealed chamber with hot water, a heating element, and a small amount of Super Glue. It was a fairly uncomplicated way of obtaining prints from a nonporous surface, but also carried the danger of overprocessing, and losing the specimen forever. Jessica had seen it happen more than once. Many times, you only had one shot in the Super Glue chamber.

Hell retrieved a final item from his envelope with a grand gesture. It was an enlargement of what looked to be a thumbprint.

"This was on the back of this photograph?" Jessica asked.

"It was," Hell said. "And because I always wanted to grow up and be a detective, I took the initiative." At this he took a document from the inside pocket of his coat. "Cue the *CSI* theme music, please."

"Hell."

"Right." He handed the printout to Jessica. "The gentleman whose prints were on the back of that rather unpleasant Polaroid lives in North Philly. His name is Lucius Winter."

Jessica sat down in front of a computer terminal. She ran a PCIC check on Lucius Winter. Moments later she had results.

Lucius Winter was a small-time criminal, twice convicted of misdemeanor assault, once tried and subsequently acquitted of armed robbery. The address was his last-known.

Jessica held up the Polaroid of the naked man sitting on the table next to the photograph on the computer screen. There was no doubt. The man in the photograph was Lucius Winter.

Byrne stepped forward, hit a key on the keyboard, scrolling down. "Jess."

Jessica looked at the screen. She saw the stats. Her pulse spiked. Lucius Winter was a white male, six feet, 165, brown and brown. But none of those details leapt off the screen.

Lucius Winter owned a black 1977 Oldsmobile Toronado.

40

The target house was a dilapidated building on Fifth Street, near Diamond Avenue. They sat in an unmarked van three doors east, on the opposite side of the street.

The process of obtaining a warrant was as maddeningly slow as it was necessary. While the team deployed, Jessica stayed behind, typed out the affidavit of probable cause, then faxed it over to the district attorney's office, where it had to be vetted by an ADA. Sometimes the process needed to involve the U.S. Attorney's office.

Once the affidavit was checked for anything that might cause the case to be jettisoned if it ever came to that, the ADA had to take it to a judge. Taking it to the right — and available — judge was always tricky. Once a judge signed it, the actual warrant need not be physically taken to the scene.

Until they got the warrant, all they could do was observe and wait. They could pursue an individual, but they could not enter the premises. Cars came and went. Pedestrians walked up and down the street. None of them was Lucius Winter.

Byrne tried the man's number again. The phone just rang. No voice mail, no answering machine.

They waited.

Byrne got the call at just after three p.m. They had their warrant.

The back door of the unmarked van opened, and two SWAT officers exited the vehicle, crossed the road. They wore full urban tactical gear and carried SIG 556 rifles. They flanked the front door of the target house as one of the detectives from North, in body armor, brought a Stinger battering ram up the steps.

Byrne drew his weapon, deployed to the left of the door, John Shepherd to the right. Byrne counted down a silent three.

The detective drew back the Stinger, smashed it into the door, just above the lock. The door splintered off the jamb and crashed to the floor.

"Philadelphia Police! Search warrant!" one of the SWAT officers yelled as they breached the door.

Byrne and John Shepherd were next to enter.

In the dim light Byrne saw the layout of the small row house. A living room to the right, stairs left, hallway ahead leading to a kitchen. It was a typical layout, no more than ten feet wide.

"First floor *clear!*" one of the SWAT officers yelled. One of them went upstairs; the other, down.

The only furniture in the front room was two tables, both in front of the windows. On each table was a lamp, no shade. The lamps were plugged into old-school timers, then into the wall sockets. Each lamp had in it what was probably a 25 or 40 watt bulb.

"Basement clear!" came the shout from the lower level.

"Second floor clear!"

The house was empty. Byrne and Shepherd holstered their weapons, took a few moments to decelerate. Byrne walked over to one of the lamps, carefully put his hand over the bulb. It was warm. He checked the timer. The lamp was programmed to turn on at three in the afternoon, and off at three in the morning.

While John Shepherd headed upstairs, Byrne went into the kitchen. Like the front room, the kitchen was devoid of any furniture. There was a thick layer of dust on all the countertops and appliances. Byrne touched the burners on the stove. Stone cold. He opened the refrigerator. It was empty, unplugged.

A quick check of the cabinets showed nothing but shredded shelf paper and mouse droppings. Byrne turned to see Shepherd coming down the steps.

"Anything upstairs?" Byrne asked.

Shepherd shook his head. "There's a bed frame in one of the bedrooms, no mattress. Nothing in the closets."

The two men assessed what they had found here, which amounted to nothing. It was clear that no one lived in this house, but the timers on the lamps were there to give the impression that someone did.

"I'm going to check the basement," Byrne said.

"Okay," Shepherd replied. "I'll call this in."

Byrne walked down the narrow stairs. The basement layout mirrored the house above, long and narrow. There was an alcove for the furnace, which looked to be 1950s vintage. There were thick cobwebs in the open ceiling. Byrne ran his Maglite beam around the space. Dust, more shredded paper and droppings, an old card table folded against one of the walls.

No signs of life.

Byrne was just about to head back upstairs when something caught his eye on the basement wall that faced the street. Or, more accurately, something did not catch his eye.

He crossed the room, put his ear to the wall. He took a step back. This made no sense. He went back upstairs, out onto the sidewalk. He was right. The glass block windows at the level of the sidewalk had bars over them.

Byrne went back inside, stepped off the distance from the front door to the back door. He went downstairs and repeated the exercise. According to his rough calculation there was about three feet—a full stride for him—missing.

Byrne took out his phone and made the call.

"Tell me about this place," Byrne said. "Who lives here?"

Someone had called the building's landlord, a stout Ukrainian woman who had shown up with a snarling, one-eyed Rottweiler and a bad attitude. John Shepherd explained to the woman the wisdom of keeping the dog a good distance from the men with guns. She tied the dog to a railing three doors down, then returned.

"Mr. Winter lives here," she said.

"Describe him."

The woman shrugged. "I haven't seen him in a while. Long time."

"He probably looks the same. What did he look like when you last saw him?"

"White man. Ordinary. Little too skinny."

"How does he pay you?" Byrne asked.

"I get check every three months."

"A personal check?"

She thought about it. "No. Money order."

"Do you make copies?"

"Who does copies? I deposit."

"How often does Mr. Winter come and go?"

"I never see him. He pays rent. Quiet. No problems."

"No red flags there?"

"What flags?" the woman asked.

"Christ."

The woman pointed at the splintered jamb. "Who's paying for this?"

"I'll get you a money order," Byrne said. "We'll let you know if we need anything else."

The three dozen or so dogs under the command of the K-9 Unit of the Philadelphia Police Department were all male, all German shepherds. The dogs were trained in three disciplines — the detection of narcotics, cadavers or explosives. The cadaver dogs were sensitive to any and all human scents, not just those of the deceased.

At just after four p.m., Sergeant Bryant Paulson arrived with Papa, a seven-year-old shepherd who got his name first for having an unusual amount of gray hair on his snout, even as a puppy, and then had it bronzed due to his rather prodigious ability to sire large litters.

Papa was the best cadaver dog in the department. He wasn't in the cellar more than five seconds before he sat down in front of the brick wall that faced the street, alerting his partner, Sergeant Paulson.

Byrne had been right. There were windows on the outside, but not the inside. The basement wall was false.

And there was something human behind it.

An hour later, two officers with CSU began work on the wall. The work was slow, because they were not there for the express purpose of demolition. After determining that the cement block wall was not load bearing, they began with a saw with a silicon carbide blade at the bottom joint of the top row of block. They then cut both vertical joints, tapping out the dried mortar as they went. After removing the top row of block, they made quick work of the rest, which was simply a matter of using cold chisels to tap out the mortar between the blocks.

When they removed the fifth course, and saw the first bone in the wall, Byrne knew who it was.

They had just met the shadowy Mr. Lucius Winter.

41

Luther watched the police from the rooftop of the building across the street.

He had parked the Toronado—the first car he had ever driven, out one night with Lucius—in another part of the city. He now knew he could never drive it again. When the time was right he would burn it.

He had one other vehicle, a nondescript ten-year-old van. Like Lucius, the man who first owned the van had once been a patient at Cold River. Luther had buried him in a landfill in New Jersey three years earlier, and had stored the van in a garage he rented in Bridesburg.

Now he would need it.

He climbed down the fire escape, cut through an alley, began to walk down 4th Street, his hands shoved deeply into the pocket of his overcoat. He felt the comfort and heft of the bone-handled knife in its sheath. He tapped the side of the knife, thinking, thinking. He stood at 4th and Diamond, waiting for the light to change. He looked to his left, and saw a horse-drawn cart with wooden wheels, clattering along on the cobblestones. The man driving the rig was wizened, ancient. His corncob pipe billowed gray smoke.

Luther blinked, and knew that it was not a horse-drawn cart at all, but rather a delivery truck. Painted on its side was a young man and a young woman, their brilliant white teeth glowing in the gray winter light.

Luther hurried across the street, picked up his pace, the sound of the doctor's voice echoing in his head.

You know what you have to do.

42

"D on't make me take that phone away from you," Colleen Siobhan Byrne signed. "I've been working out. I can do it."

Byrne smiled. She was right. She looked like she could take him in a fair fight.

"Sorry," Byrne said. "I was supposed to get a call by seven o'clock."

The call was coming from the ME's office, a preliminary report on the human remains found in the false wall. The truth was Byrne was still winding down from the raid on Lucius Winter's house.

The two detectives assigned to the case had determined the specifics in short order. After interviewing neighbors, they learned that occasionally there were voices and the sound of a radio coming from the property, but never loud enough to warrant a complaint.

As far as family was concerned, detectives were able to locate the man's brother, who told them that after Lucius had done his two stretches in prison, he was all but disowned.

In addition to his time spent in prison, Lucius Winter had once been an inpatient at the Delaware Valley State Hospital.

While the murder of Lucius Winter was being investigated by the SIU of the homicide unit, the connection to the current spate of murders was undeniable. The crime scene unit would be working every inch of the man's house well into the night.

Byrne turned off his phone. "I'm all yours," he said.

"I'm the luckiest girl in Philly," Colleen signed.

The waiter brought their salads, and with them what was probably his fifth smile for Colleen Byrne. The kid was about twenty, good-looking. Colleen vamped appropriately. Byrne always got better service when he dined with his daughter.

"I don't know," Colleen said when they were midway through their entrees. "I'm thinking about changing my major."

Colleen had talked about being a teacher for as long as Byrne could remember. Starting as early as junior high school she had tutored other kids, often inner-city hearing-impaired kids to whom deafness was an even greater obstacle. Quite often, an insurmountable one.

"Why would you want to do that?" Byrne asked. "You've always wanted to go into teaching. I thought that was a done deal."

Another pause. "I'm not sure I'm cut out for it, Dad."

"What are you talking about? You're great with kids. You're great with adults."

Colleen shrugged. "I don't think I have the patience."

If there was one thing his daughter had it was patience. It was one of the many qualities she had inherited from her mother. She certainly didn't get it from him.

"Of course you do, honey," Byrne said.

"I'm thinking about switching over to business administration."

Byrne just nodded. It was one of those moments as a parent that you just had to flow with the conversation. Although, anything that made his daughter happy would make him happy, too, he'd always had his mind and heart set on his daughter becoming a teacher.

Maybe that was just because he always figured that was what Colleen wanted to do.

They lingered over coffee, neither wanting the dinner to end. Byrne told Colleen about Violet.

"How old is she again?"

"Maybe two and a half."

"And she was in the middle of the street?"

Byrne nodded. "Just standing there."

"Was she okay?"

"As far as we could tell," Byrne said. "At least, physically. We took her to Children's Hospital to see Jessica's cousin Angela. The little girl wasn't hurt. No cuts, no bruises."

"Are you sure she isn't deaf?"

"She isn't. When Angela examined her, she said the little girl understood everything she said, responded to her requests. She can hear. She just doesn't talk."

Byrne pulled up in front of his ex-wife's house, where Colleen stayed when she was back in the city. He pulled to the curb, put the car in park. They sat for a while, watched the people scurry along the sidewalks in the rain.

Colleen butterflied a hand, getting Byrne's attention. He looked over. She had covertly placed a silver band on the ring finger of her right hand.

"It's a friendship ring. I'm not engaged, okay?" she signed.

The word was a fresh arrow. Byrne imagined it would be for a while, followed by the rest of the quiver—proposal, consideration, marriage, pregnant, *grandpa*. For as small a target as the human heart might be, there was always room for another barb.

"Okay," Byrne said. "I just saw the ring on your finger. Freaked me out a little. It was on your right hand, but it was the left side of the screen. Some detective I am."

"You know you'd be the first person I would tell."

"Even before your mother?"

Colleen smiled. "I have two hands," she signed. "I'd find a way to tell you both at the same time."

"Fair enough."

Colleen unsnapped her umbrella. "Keep me posted on that little girl, okay?"

"I will," Byrne said.

"Text me if something happens."

"Okay."

Colleen thought for a few moments. "Someone has to come forward. She's somebody's little girl."

At that moment Byrne knew that his daughter was not going to be a businesswoman.

Colleen leaned over and gave him a hug and a kiss. She opened her door, got out of the car, closed the door. Byrne rolled down the passenger-side window.

"So, lunch on Friday?" he asked.

"Sure," Colleen signed. "I'll come by the Roundhouse around two."

"I love you, sweetie."

"Love you too, Dad."

As he watched Colleen walk up the steps, and into his ex-wife's house, her words resonated.

She's somebody's little girl.

As Byrne sat at a red light at 10th Street, he picked up the little pink purse. He thought about the process of how it came to be in his hand, at this moment, the journey it had taken. It was designed, manufactured, distributed, put on the shelf in a store, purchased, and given to the little girl.

Who gave it to her? Who made the half-sandwich?

In the streetlight coming through the window he looked at the little charm hanging off the zipper, and suddenly felt his chest tighten.

He pulled over to the curb, the understanding a thunderclap in his mind. He turned the locket over, saw the engraving on the back:

PPD 3445

He recalled the words as if he'd heard them yesterday.

If you're ever in trouble, just present this to any detective in Philadelphia. They will take care of you.

It was right there.

It was right in front of him the whole time.

How had he missed it?

43

The drive north was a slog. Rain plus snow plus slush.

He stopped at a diner on Route 611 near Tannersville, a twenty-four-hour spoon. It looked clean and inviting.

As long as the coffee was strong, he would have no complaints.

She poured him a cup without even asking. He must have had the look. He hadn't been able to take his mind off the locket since leaving Philadelphia. Somehow he had a menu in his hands.

"What can I get you, hon?"

Byrne looked up. The waitress was in her late thirties, dark haired, pretty. He did a quick sweep. No wedding ring. Her laminated name-tag read NICA.

Monica? Veronica? If she smiled, he'd ask.

Byrne slipped the laminated menu back into the holder. "Pancakes and sausage."

"Links or patties?"

Her accent was pure eastern Pennsylvania. Byrne wondered if she'd ever been out of Monroe County.

"What would you recommend?"

Nica looked out the window for a moment. The fog was rolling across Route 611. In this gray light Byrne thought he read a little pain beneath her sunny demeanor. She looked back.

"Me? I'd take the patties."

"And why is that?"

"Because I see how they're made."

She smiled. Byrne asked.

"So, Nica is short for Monica or Veronica?"

"Actually, it's short for Dominica."

"Very pretty."

"Thanks..."

Byrne soon realized she was waiting for something. Then it hit him. *Man* he was getting rusty. "Kevin."

"Kevin," she said. "It suits you."

"Thank God," Byrne said. "I'm way too old to answer to anything else."

She smiled again. "My husband was a Trooper, you know. Troop N, Hazelton."

Byrne nodded. He decided not to ask Nica how she knew he was on the job. He'd given up thinking he looked like anything other than a cop years ago.

"Your husband's retired?"

A dark moment passed. Byrne understood. He'd asked the wrong question. Too late now. *Damn.*

"No," she said. "Walt died. In '09."

Byrne hadn't expected this. Nica looked way too young to be a widow.

Before he could stop himself he said, "I'm sorry." He'd always wondered why people said such things to total strangers. He imagined it was, as was the case with him, something instilled by parents. He continued, knowing he was digging a hole, but for some reason could not seem to stop himself. "Did it happen on the job?"

Nica shook her head. "No," she said. "It was the cancer."

The cancer. It was one of the many reasons Byrne wanted to move to a small town one day. Things like cancer were still given proper weight.

"Top your cup?" she asked.

"Please."

Byrne wolfed down his food in record time. Part of it was that he had not eaten since his dinner with Colleen. The other was that he saw that the weather was turning, and he had to get on the road.

Nica came back with the coffeepot. Byrne declined a refill.

"Good pancakes," he said.

She tossed a hip, pulled her pad out of her pocket, tore off his check, slipped it delicately onto the counter in front of him. She lowered her voice to a whisper.

"At my house they come with blueberries."

Byrne smiled. He loved straightforward women. "I love blueberries."

After paying his check, Byrne turned at the door, waved.

"You be careful on the road," she said. "Stop back sometime."

Byrne walked into the coming storm. He flicked a glance at the name of the diner, the blue and yellow sign at the road.

He'd remember.

Byrne traveled another hour north, his mind a deadfall of questions. As pretty as the waitress was, and as much as it was nice to be flirted with, by the time he reached the exit his mind had returned to the reason for the trip, and the darkness that compelled him.

He pulled off, entered the parking lot for the campground.

Ten minutes later, as he found himself on the winding trail, it began to snow.

He was not prepared for the cold. He was underdressed. With his leather-soled shoes, every step into the forest was a challenge. More than a few times he had to hang onto a tree limb to keep from falling.

Byrne looked at the hand-drawn map again, already yellowed with age. Somehow it had gotten dark in the past twenty minutes. He pulled out his mini Maglite, shined it on the paper. Snow fell on the page, and when he tried to wipe it off he smeared the crude drawing.

"Shit."

Byrne turned 360, saw nothing but darkness. The smart thing would be to head back down, find a motel for the night, try again tomorrow.

That's when he saw the light on the other side of the field, perhaps a half-mile away. It was dim, but it was there. He started toward the light.

He was halfway across the field when he saw someone coming toward him. Byrne's hand instinctively went to the weapon in his holster. He stepped behind a tree, his heart racing. What had he gotten himself into? He wasn't in the city anymore. He was way out of his element.

But there was nothing he could do now. He steadied himself, stepped back into the field, into the open.

In front of him, no more than ten yards away, stood a man with a very big crossbow in his hands. Byrne lifted his flashlight, shined it on the man. What he saw made the breath catch in his throat. The man in front of him looked bad, almost craven—long hair and beard, sunken cheeks, red-rimmed eyes. Byrne had not seen him in a while, and what he saw now broke his heart. At one time Ray Torrance had been a mountain.

"My God," Torrance said. *"You."*

Byrne held up the charm he'd found on Violet's purse. The first time he'd seen it was when Ray Torrance had shown it to him three years earlier, and told him the words he'd said to the teenage girl.

If you're ever in trouble, just present this to any detective in Philadelphia. They will take care of you.

On the back of the locket was Ray's badge number:

PPD 3445

From time to time, over the past three years, Byrne had thought about the locket, about Ray Torrance. He wondered what had become of both. He'd wondered if he'd ever see either of them again.

He never expected it to be with a two-year-old-girl.

"I found it," Byrne said.

On the trip from Philadelphia, Byrne had considered what Ray Torrance might say or do when he told him. When Ray fell to his knees and began to scream, Byrne realized that the locket was connected to a darkness more profound than he knew.

All Kevin Byrne could do at that moment, on a frigid mountain trail in Pennsylvania, was help his friend to his feet, and begin the long walk back.

THREE

44

Word had floated through the Roundhouse, and the department, that Detective Raymond Torrance was back in town.

Torrance had worked in a number of different squads and districts over his more than two decades on the force, had made a lot of friends. A few enemies, too, of course. It came with the territory. It was virtually impossible to do twenty years or more as a detective and not step on other cops' cases, not ruffle feathers, not ride forensic and science teams a little hard. It all depended on your style, and your closure rate. Detectives who closed cases got a lot more leeway.

Then there were the people you put in jail. They did not remember you fondly.

The fliers were put on bulletin boards at every district in the city. The party would be held at Finnigan's Wake.

Jessica watched the man work his way around the duty room. She had seen Ray Torrance around at events back in his day, but had not known him. She *had* heard the legend. When it came to the Special Victims Unit, Ray Torrance's name was spoken in whispers.

Jessica also knew that he had been injured badly on the job a few years ago, but did not know the details. Byrne told her what he knew about the incident, which wasn't very much.

"Who was the teenage girl?" Jessica asked.

"I don't know. All I know is Ray gave her a heart locket, and told her to show it to any detective in Philly if she ever needed help."

"Did you know about it?"

Byrne nodded. "He told me about it when he was in the hospital."

Jessica looked across the room, saw Ray Torrance sharing a moment with Dana Westbrook.

And then it hit her.

"Oh my God, Kevin. The locket was—"

"Yeah," Byrne said. "The little charm attached to Violet's purse."

Before Jessica could say another word she looked up to see Ray Torrance slipping on his overcoat, shaking hands with the other detectives. He was getting ready to leave.

Jessica glanced at her watch. She had to leave as well. If she was lucky, she would get about five hours of sleep this night. She had an early-morning class.

Ray Torrance walked over to where Jessica and Byrne were standing. He gestured to the less than elegant décor that was the homicide unit.

"Some things never change," he said.

"Not the good stuff," Byrne replied.

Torrance turned to Jessica. It looked like he was about to say something, but remained silent.

For some strange reason, at that moment, Jessica wanted to hug him—he looked so pained, so lost—but she stopped herself, even though his sad eyes brought out every maternal instinct within her. She extended her hand.

"It's great to see you," Jessica said.

"The pleasure is mine," Torrance replied. They shook hands. Ray Torrance's hand was calloused, but his grip was warm and gentle.

"Hope to see you again soon," Jessica said.

Torrance smiled. "I'll be around."

The next day they spent the morning and early afternoon on the phones, trying to track down personnel who had worked at Cold River, without any luck. By two o'clock they had called every hospital in Philadelphia, Bucks, Delaware and Montgomery counties. Although the offices for the administrators were for the most part forthcoming, they were told that, to the best of their knowledge, there were no doctors or nurses on staff who were at one time employed by the Delaware Valley State Hospital.

It seemed unlikely, but Cold River's reputation, such as it was, might have made for less than full disclosure on application forms.

What had gone on there? Jessica wondered.

Jessica looked at the legal pad on Byrne's desk. All but two of the hospitals had been crossed out.

"I knew the place had problems, but I didn't think it was this bad," Jessica said. "Nobody worked there?"

Byrne just stared at his computer screen.

At two o'clock Colleen walked into the duty room. She sat at one of the empty desks. Byrne got her attention.

"I've got two more calls to make and then we can go," he signed. "You okay?"

Colleen smiled. "I'm fine."

Jessica made her next call, to a small clinic in Chester County. She was soon routed to the person who handled HR, Human Resources, for the facility. As she had been told for most of the day, no one currently employed, or recently employed, had once worked at the Delaware Valley State Hospital.

She was just about to make the final call on her list when she looked over to see Byrne with his hand in the air, trying to get her attention. She and Colleen walked over to where Byrne was sitting.

"Yes," Byrne said into the phone. "That would be great." Byrne gave a thumbs-up. "We'll be up in about an hour. Who should we ask for?" Byrne scribbled a name on his notebook. He underlined it three times. "That would be fine. Thanks very much."

Byrne hung up.

"You found someone who worked at Cold River?" Jessica asked.

"Yes," Byrne said. "I talked to a woman in HR at this place called Sunnyvale. She said that there was a woman in her facility who once was one of the administrators at Cold River."

"What is Sunnyvale?"

"It's a nursing home in Montgomery County. She said this woman — Miriam Gale — was a director of personnel at Cold River for a long time, right up until they closed the main hospital. The woman I spoke to said Miriam is ninety-one."

"Will this woman talk to us?"

"She said that Miriam would not have a problem talking to us, but *we* might have a problem talking to *her.*"

"I don't understand."

Byrne glanced at Colleen, back at Jessica. "Miriam Gale is deaf."

Jessica took this in. They would need an interpreter. "Does anyone at Sunnyvale sign?"

"I didn't get that far. I figured we'd go up there and wing it. If we have to, we can write out the questions on paper."

Jessica could see that Byrne was doing his best not to look at his daughter. Colleen thumped a hand on the desk, got his attention. She signed: "Well?"

"Well what?" Byrne replied.

"*Hello?* Deaf person here."

"I don't know what you're talking about."

"Let me help."

Byrne took a few moments. "That's okay, honey," he said. "I can sign pretty well, you know. I can handle this."

Colleen brought her hand to her mouth. She was trying to keep the laugh inside.

"What?"

Colleen waved the question away. "Nothing."

Byrne looked at Jessica, then back at his daughter. "I can't ask you to do this, Colleen."

"Dad."

"I would have to clear it with the boss, and I just don't think she'd—"

"I'll ask," Jessica said. She slid off the desk, crossed the duty room. On the way, she and Colleen did a quick, covert fist bump.

45

The Sunnyvale Center was a long-term, nonprofit nursing home funded, in part, by the taxpayers of Montgomery County. The 360-bed facility provided sub-acute and skilled care to its residents.

On the way to the nursing home Jessica had written a number of questions on a notebook page, and Colleen had typed them into her MacBook Air. The plan was—that is, if everything was cleared by not only the administrators and caregivers of the facility, but the woman herself—that Colleen would ask the woman questions in American Sign Language, then type the woman's answers into the laptop so that Jessica and Byrne could read them.

When they met the chief administrator, they were given the expected caveats—those being that Miriam Gale was ninety-one, was on a host of medications, and could only answer their questions for a short period of time.

Having cleared that hurdle, Jessica, Byrne and Colleen were led down a broad corridor to the woman's room. Before they entered, Colleen took Jessica and Byrne to the side.

"I think I should go in first," Colleen signed.

"Why?" Byrne asked.

Colleen thought for a moment. "You can be kind of a scary guy, sometimes," she said. "I hope that doesn't come as a shock."

Byrne looked at Jessica, back at Colleen. For a moment it looked like he was going to argue the point. In the end he just made the sign for: "Okay."

A few minutes later Colleen walked out of the woman's room.

"How did it go?" Byrne asked.

"She's really sweet. I asked her about her deafness. There's a big difference between someone who was born deaf, like me, and someone who became deaf later in life."

"What did she tell you?"

"She said she'd always had some degree of hearing loss, even as a child, but when she contracted meningitis in her late forties she became deaf."

"Does she know why we want to talk to her?"

"Not all of it. I don't *know* all of it. I just told her that you are with the police, and that she can help. I told her that you just wanted to know a little bit about Cold River."

"Thanks, honey," Byrne said. "Good work." He looked at Jessica. "Ready?"

Jessica nodded.

They entered the room.

The space was a two-bed room with a highly polished floor, cream-colored walls, and a pair of healthy plants on the windowsill. The floral print of the drapes matched the bedspreads, and a pair of bright Mylar balloons were attached to both tray tables.

Miriam Gale sat in a wheelchair by the window, a green and white afghan over her legs. Her hair was cloud white, pulled back into a long braid that curled around one narrow shoulder. At the bottom was a turquoise clip.

Colleen got the woman's attention.

One at a time Colleen finger-spelled "Jessica" and "Kevin." There was no real need for either detective to produce ID. Jessica thought about shaking the woman's hand, but she didn't know if she should. The woman looked frail. Instead, Jessica just waved.

Miriam Gale smiled.

Colleen put her laptop on one of the tray tables, opened it. She sat down in front of Miriam, adjusted the table so that Jessica and Byrne could see the screen.

When Colleen was set, she looked at her father. Byrne nodded. It was time to begin. Colleen glanced at the laptop screen, signed the first question.

"What years did you work at Cold River?"

The woman began to sign slowly, carefully crafting each word.

"I started in nineteen fifty-three. I worked there until just before they closed the main hospital for good."

"When was that?"

The old woman thought for a moment. "It was nineteen ninety-two."

"How did you come to be employed at Cold River?" Colleen signed.

"It was right after the Korean War. My husband Andrew was wounded at Pork Chop Hill. He was in Company K. When he came back his doctor admitted him to Cold River. Now, keep in mind, this was long before they called it Post Traumatic Stress Syndrome. Back then they just called it shell shock. Did you know that?"

Colleen shook her head.

"That's what they called it back then. When I went to visit Andrew I learned they needed nurse's assistants and orderlies."

"This was in nineteen fifty-three?" Colleen asked.

"Yes. It was September of nineteen fifty-three."

As the woman signed her responses, Colleen typed them on the laptop. Jessica was more than impressed with the young woman's typing skills. Any mistakes she made—and there were few—were instantly corrected.

"By the time I got there, it was already overcrowded, of course. There was a relatively new kitchen and dietary building, but the patient-to-staff ratio was terrible, something like sixty to four. Still, we made do. Cold River was like a self-contained little city."

Every so often, as Miriam signed, she would stop to massage her hands. Jessica imagined that the woman must be in some pain to do what she was doing. Without being asked another question, she continued.

"The newest addition to the hospital after I had been there for a while was N3. This was called the Active Therapy Building. Personnel and staff were excited about this, because it represented a step forward in patient care, as opposed to the mere warehousing of the mentally ill."

"Did you work in N3?"

"Oh, yes. Now, there was that big pharmaceutical company based in Camden back then. They were working on this new wonder drug similar to Thorazine. In those days the hospital had upwards of two thousand patients who were wards of the state. I'm sad to say that many of these men—and they were mostly men—were eager to volunteer as test subjects, having no idea what they were getting into."

The woman stopped for a moment, massaged her hands, continued.

"Although we were not privy to the numbers, the rumors were that dozens, perhaps hundreds, of patients died from sickness related to pharmaceutical testing."

The woman thought for a few moments, then raised her hands to continue signing. Jessica noticed from the corner of her eye that Colleen had stopped typing. When she looked a little more closely, she noticed that Colleen's hands had begun to tremble. Jessica got Byrne's attention.

Byrne raised a finger, getting the woman's attention. He crossed the room, knelt down in front of his daughter. With his back to the old woman he spoke very carefully, so that Colleen could follow him.

"Are you okay?" he asked.

Colleen nodded. Jessica wasn't so sure.

"Do you want to stop?"

At this, Colleen took a deep breath, exhaled. She shook her head. *I'm fine,* she mouthed silently.

Byrne took a few more moments, scrutinizing his daughter's eyes. Jessica could see that Byrne was having second thoughts about allowing this to happen. She glanced at Miriam. The woman was sitting with her hands in her lap, looking out the window. In the powdery late winter light Jessica could see the young woman who had gone to work at the Delaware Valley State Hospital sixty years earlier.

Byrne stood up, reached out, touched the woman on her shoulder. She looked up at him. Byrne signed: "Would you like to continue?"

After a moment the woman smiled at Byrne. She took his hands in hers, and formed the proper ASL sign for the word *continue.*

Byrne smiled, repeated the question, this time signing properly. The woman nodded. Byrne crossed the room, stood again by the door. Colleen looked over. Byrne nodded.

Colleen glanced at the laptop screen. She seemed a bit lost. The old woman got her attention, and continued.

"By the time I was promoted to be the assistant to one of the administrators, I had already lost all my hearing, but I learned to lip read pretty well as a child, and I took to ASL rather quickly. At that time there were almost 6,500 patients at Cold River, in fifty-eight buildings."

Miriam reached out to her tray, took the plastic cup in both hands. Jessica wanted to sprint across the room and get it for her, but she could see the pride the woman took in doing it herself. When she had taken a few sips, she continued.

"At that time a lot of prefab housing was built to the west of the hospital, and a lot of the staff bought them. Some of them went for as little as four thousand dollars. Imagine."

Colleen smiled, signed: "A good sofa costs four thousand dollars today."

"It does?"

The woman looked at Jessica, winked.

"After that I worked my way up in administration. Andrew died in nineteen seventy-eight. We had no children. Work was my life. Eventually the governor ordered Cold River to be closed in phases. That was the beginning of the end." She took another sip of water. "Cold River was bad in the later years. We all knew how bad it was."

"What do you mean?" Colleen asked.

"You have to understand. The nineteen seventies and eighties were a time of great strides in the research, development and administration of revolutionary new medications. Thorazine was on the way out. Prozac was being developed."

Colleen pointed to the next question on the laptop, looked at her father. Byrne nodded.

"Did you ever hear of a patient called Null?"

The woman looked confused for a moment. She turned to look at Colleen, who finger-spelled the word null. Although the woman did not immediately respond, Jessica could see that the name meant something to her.

"You hear all sorts of things in an institution the size of Cold River. At its height, on any given day, there were more than seven thousand human beings in those buildings, and people will talk. Add to the mix the fact that a large percentage of those people—and by no means do I mean this to be constrained to patients only—were given to hallucinations, and you begin to doubt a great deal of what you hear."

She paused again, massaged her hands. Jessica sensed that they were coming to the end of the interview.

"There were a lot of well-known doctors, both clinicians and researchers, who passed through Cold River over the years. There was one man who caused quite a stir when he arrived. His name was Dr. Godehard Kirsch. They even built that new building for him. G10. It stayed open after the hospital closed. He died in a fire there."

"When did Dr. Kirsch come to Cold River?"

The old woman looked out the window for a few moments, perhaps gathering her thoughts. The rain looked to be turning to snow.

"I think it was nineteen ninety-one or 'ninety-two. I was only in G10 twice, mind you," she signed. "And that was only the first floor. The basement was sealed off from the rest of the staff and personnel."

"What sort of work did Dr. Kirsch do?"

"I never met the man, nor knew anybody who did. I never saw any of the documents that they produced, but his work was said to be in the area of dream engineering."

Byrne stepped forward, typed a new question. Colleen signed what Byrne wrote.

"Who did you mean when you say 'documents that they produced'? Who is they?"

"Dr. Kirsch assembled a small team. I believe there was an anesthesiologist, a psychiatric nurse and one orderly. They had a funny name. I don't know if the name was official, but it was what they were known as throughout the rest of the facility."

"What were they called?"

The old woman looked right at Jessica when she answered. "They were called *Die Traumkaufleute*." She finger-spelled the foreign words.

Colleen did her best to type this. When she was finished, she asked: "Do you know what that means?"

The old woman nodded. "I only know this because my mother's family was German. The name means 'The Dream Merchants.'"

Byrne typed a final question. Colleen asked it.

"What happened to the indigent patients who died at Cold River?"

The woman took a long pause. For a moment, Jessica thought she might not answer. Finally, she signed: "I can't say for sure, but we heard that many of them were buried in a field across Chancel Lane. In a place called Priory Park."

Before they left, Colleen showed the woman a list of names. Robert Freitag, Joan Delacroix, Edward Richmond, Leonard Pintar, Lucius Winter. One by one the woman shook her head. She did not know any of them.

Colleen hugged the old woman, then turned away quickly. Jessica could see the tears in her eyes. She left the room first.

As a nurse's assistant took Miriam Gale's blood pressure and temperature, Jessica looked at the small bookcase in the corner of the room.

"Kevin."

Byrne looked over. There, on the woman's shelf, were a handful of books. One of them was titled *Nightworld* by a man named Martin Léopold. She opened the book, turned to the back flap.

There was no photograph, but rather a short bio.

The author lives in Philadelphia.

"Martin Léopold," Jessica said. "Do you think he's the Leo your friend Lenny Pintar was talking about?"

"He could very well be."

While Byrne brought the car around, Jessica lingered in the doorway, watching Miriam Gale sit by the window. Every so often she would massage her hands.

Before she turned away, the woman raised her hands, signed something. Jessica wondered for whom it was meant.

Rachel sat in the hallway on the second floor. She could all but hear the sound of her sister's footsteps running down the hall, for her sister had never walked anywhere. She was always so full of energy.

Rachel stood up, took a deep breath, braced herself.

She opened the door for the first time in almost three years. In the past three years the only people to enter this room were the cleaning ladies, and they had dusted and replaced the lightbulbs as needed.

There was no furniture in the room, nothing on the walls. The only indication that two little girls ever occupied the space were the notches on the casing of the closet, notches showing slow, steady growth, although Rachel had eventually topped out at just under five feet.

Rachel sat on the floor in the corner, near the window. She recalled the time she and her sister had thought the shadow thrown by the large pin oak tree next to the house had been the claws of a giant lobster, and after that they would never eat lobster again, or crab for that matter.

Rachel held her sister's picture in hand, a photo taken of her in the days before she disappeared, her hands on her hips, her face fashioned into a diva pout, a look Rachel remembered well.

What am I doing? Rachel thought. *All these years of looking at other houses, of crawling through crawl spaces, of walking through subterranean corridors and catacombs and sewers. Years of trying to relive the twilight walk they took, to find the raggedy man, to find the man in the white coat.*

Had it all been a dream?

"Oh, Bean," she said through the tears. "What happened to you?"

After the party, Byrne and Ray Torrance sat in a quiet corner on the second floor of Finnigan's Wake. Below them, on Spring Garden Street, the traffic crawled through the freezing rain, which the weatherman promised would become snow.

"I don't know the whole story, Ray," Byrne said. "I can't make a move before I know the story."

Torrance put the locket down, took a few moments, began.

"We had this case up in the Northeast. Series of break-ins."

Breaking and Entering was not in the purview of SVU. There had to be more. "What year are we talking?"

"I think it was around 'ninety-seven," Torrance said. "Boogeyman stuff where a guy was coming into these houses in the middle of the night, going upstairs or whatever, and sitting in the bedrooms of these little girls."

"All girls?"

Torrance nodded. "Yeah. All girls. They were all five or six years old. All blond."

"No assaults?"

"No, believe it or not. That's just it. This guy is just sitting in their rooms. No sexual contact, no contact at all. The only reason SVU got involved at all was the ages of the girls.

"But there was one case where the guy came back a number of times. It was the first time he did that, as far as we could tell. So we get a call from the chief's office to shut this guy down. I caught the case, set up a time with this girl's family, and I went up and talked to her."

Torrance called for another drink.

"So I go up there, and I meet the girl. A little doll. Her name was Marielle. Marielle Gray. Her nickname was Bean. I went up, talked to her, but I didn't get much. The girl had an older sister, but the mother wouldn't let me talk to her."

"Why?"

Torrance shrugged. "The mother was a boozer. I guess she couldn't deal with it. And that was it. There were no more reports after that."

"What spooked the guy?"

"No idea," Torrance said. "But you know and I know that these guys don't just stop."

Torrance's drink came. He took a sip.

"So, fast forward about ten years. I'm working this case, a runaway. Twelve-year-old boy. I'm down on South making a few inquiries, kicking the curbs. I look up and I see her standing across the street."

"The girl," Byrne said. "Marielle."

Torrance nodded. "I'm not sure how I knew it was her. I was thirty feet away, it was night, and it had been ten years. There was just something about her. I knew."

"What happened?"

Torrance hesitated, sipped his drink. "She saw me, and I guess she knew, too. I imagine I hadn't changed that much in those years. A little heavier, I suppose. A little slower. But she went from being this little kid to a young woman."

Byrne just listened.

"I tried to get across South but it was a Friday night and there was a lot of traffic. A lot of people. By the time I got to the other side of the street, she was gone. When I got back to the office that night I went through my files, got the mother's phone number, called, even though it was late."

"Did you talk to the mother?"

Torrance shook his head. "That number belonged to someone else at that point. The guy—this very pissed-off guy who I awakened at one in the morning—told me that he'd had the number almost five years." Torrance drained his glass, rattled the cubes, calling for another. He looked at Byrne. Byrne shook his head.

"When I saw her that night I knew she was on the game. I *knew* it, and I didn't react fast enough."

"What did you do?" Byrne asked.

Torrance shrugged. "What *could* I do? I shook the bushes for a few weeks, bugged-out my confidential informants. I didn't have a picture of her, so basically I was looking for a fifteen-year-old blond girl. That describes half the runaways in Philly."

The waitress brought Torrance his drink. He knocked back half of it in one gulp. Byrne had never seen Ray Torrance hit it this hard. But Byrne knew that this was a confessional.

"So six months later I see her again. In Old City. She looked hard, Kevin. She'd put on weight. I could see that the streets were making her old before her time."

Byrne knew all too well what he meant. He'd seen it himself many times. And it happened a lot more quickly than people realized.

"This time she didn't see me. She was standing in the doorway waiting for someone. She had shopping bags in her hands, so I knew someone was paying for her clothes. I pulled my hat down low and crossed the street. I was standing in front of her before she could make a move."

"Is this when you gave her the locket?"

Torrance nodded. "Yeah. I had picked it up at this little place near Eighteenth and Walnut. It was right after the first time I had seen her on South. I didn't know if I would ever see her again, but I hoped, you know?"

"What did she say?"

"At first she made a move to run away. I blocked her in. She struggled with me for a few seconds, but I told her that I just wanted to talk. Nothing more. Just talk. After a little while she settled down."

Torrance took another sip of his drink, continued. "I had rehearsed the speech I was going to give her for weeks, maybe months. Hell, I'd probably been thinking about it for ten *years*. But when I opened my mouth nothing came out. It all sort of vacated my brain when I looked into her eyes. Her young/old eyes. In that second I saw that little girl sitting at her dinette table. I knew that whatever I said wasn't going to make any difference. Not at that moment. I just reached into my pocket, and pulled out the locket."

"What did she do?"

"At first she didn't want to take it. I had considered this, of course. I had a speech for that eventuality, too."

Byrne saw Ray's eyes begin to mist. He looked away for a few seconds, giving the man time. Torrance continued.

"Standing in that alley, with my hands wrapped around her hand, knowing that she had the locket, I felt better. Not good, but better. There was now a link between us, and the possibility that she would get out of the life someday. I had given her a portal, something I'd rarely been able to do in my whole time in SVU."

Torrance drained his glass again, called for another. When he did this he met Byrne's eyes, and saw in them the concern.

"I'm okay, Kevin."

Byrne said nothing.

"I was just about to give it one more shot, trying to talk her in, when I looked into her eyes and saw the fear. She was looking over my left shoulder when she drew her hand away from mine. The alley was pretty dark, but there was a light at the mouth of the alley, in a doorway that led to the kitchen of a hoagie shack. It cast a shadow on the wall. Before I could turn around I saw the shadow getting larger and I knew someone was coming down the alley. Fast.

"The next thing I knew, my lower back caught fire. I was down on the ground. I tried to wrestle my weapon out of my holster but I suddenly felt as if I had no arms. I looked up and saw Marielle with her hands at her mouth. She was white as a sheet."

The waitress brought Torrance his drink. This time, he didn't pick it up. He just stared into the amber liquid.

"Right before I blacked out I looked back at the brick wall at the end of the alley, and saw the shadow of the man who cut me. All I remember was the hat."

"The hat?"

Torrance nodded. "Yeah. The silhouette of a floppy hat."

Byrne didn't have to ask about the next hours, days and weeks of Ray Torrance's life. By eleven o'clock on the night Ray Torrance was attacked every police officer in the city of Philadelphia was aware of what had happened to one of their own.

In the end, there were no arrests. All trace of Ray Torrance's attacker, and the girl, were gone.

Byrne and a dozen detectives went to visit the man in the hospital a few days after the incident. That's when Torrance told them about the locket, and what to do if they ever found it.

Three weeks later Ray Torrance left the hospital, and the police force. As far as Byrne knew, no one in the PPD had spoken to the man until Byrne found him on the mountain. Years earlier Ray had given him a map to his cabin in the Poconos.

"Do you have any idea what happened to Marielle?" Byrne asked.

Torrance shook his head.

"She might be alive," Byrne said, before he could stop himself. He knew how it must have sounded to Ray. It sounded exactly as it would sound if someone tried to hand him the same line.

"No she isn't," Torrance said. "She's dead. You know it, I know it."

"What can I do for you, Ray?" Byrne asked. As the words left his lips he realized how inadequate they sounded, as well as how limited the scope would be.

"I need in on this, Kevin."

And there it was.

"I don't know what I can do," Byrne said. "Back in the day, when you and I were coming up, it was a lot easier to fly under the radar. Now, not so much."

"I know I'm not on the job anymore. Look at me. The job wouldn't even *have* me anymore. I just want to be in the loop, you know? I've got to know what happened."

"Right now it's just a found child case," Byrne said. "This locket doesn't tie her to any open investigation."

"My attempted murder case doesn't count?"

"Don't go there, man."

"You're right," Torrance said. "I'm sorry."

There was nothing to be sorry about. Byrne would probably have said the same thing.

Torrance got up, stood in front of the large window that overlooked the Benjamin Franklin Bridge in the distance. He didn't speak for a long time, but when he did he said the three words that Byrne knew were buried deep in his heart.

"I killed her."

When Torrance turned back, Byrne saw the pain in his friend's eyes. He didn't know what to do. The only thing he could do, at this moment, was to sit there and listen. To just be there. And for that, he had all the time in the world.

Byrne and Torrance stood outside Finnigan's Wake, near the short steps on 3rd Street. Torrance was smoking.

Since the smoking ban had gone into effect in most Philadelphia bars and nightclubs (the rule had something to do with what percentage of your income was derived from alcohol, no one understood it) small designated areas had sprung up just outside the entrances to watering holes—from small corner taverns in Grays Ferry to the poshest hotel bars in Center City. On any given night—whether it was ninety degrees with a hundred percent humidity or ten below zero with a wind chill factor of minus forty—you would find tiny clusters of smokers, attached to the building like gargoyles, enshrouded in gray smoke.

"She seems good," Torrance said.

"Jessica?"

Torrance nodded.

"I don't know what I'd do without her," Byrne said. "She makes me look a lot better than I am. Best partner I've ever had. Best partner you *could* have."

They were joined by two more smokers. They edged down the sidewalk.

"Unfortunately, I'm going to find out soon what it's like not to work with her," Byrne went on.

"Why is that?" Torrance asked. "She's retiring?"

Byrne nodded.

"She's a *kid*."

"She's going to law school."

"Uh oh."

"Trust me. She's going to land on the right side."

Torrance flicked his cigarette butt into the street.

The voice came from behind them.

"You know, you can be arrested for that."

Byrne and Torrance both turned to see two women in their mid-twenties descending the steps. One redhead, one blonde. At this time of the night, in this light, they both looked off-the-chart gorgeous.

"Is that right?" Torrance said.

"Yeah," the blonde said. "Don't make me pat you down."

The two young women laughed, walked down 3rd Street. Byrne and Torrance watched.

"One of life's great ironies," Torrance said.

"You mean how, when you're twenty-two, you have no idea how to talk to women. And once you're over forty you're too old to do anything about it?"

"That's the one."

Torrance waited awhile, shot his final arrow. "Look, I realize there's only so much you can do on this," he said. "Just copy me in on everything. Okay?"

"Yeah," Byrne said, hoping the decision would not come back to haunt him. "Okay." He buttoned his coat to the top, wrapped his scarf tighter. "By the way, I have news for you." He pointed down the street. "Those two women you just talked to?"

"What about them?"

Byrne gave his response the proper weight. "They're both cops."

Torrance looked punched. *"What?"*

Byrne nodded. "Yep. Both rookies out of the Twenty-third."

Torrance glanced up the street at the two young women, who were getting into a car at the corner of Green and 3rd, just beyond the sprinting capabilities of men of a certain age. He looked back at Byrne. "Unbelievable."

"No argument there."

Byrne checked his watch. He had to be in court in the morning to testify in a case he had closed almost three years earlier. "We should go."

Torrance nodded, hooked a thumb over his shoulder. "I'm gonna run back in and say goodbye."

"Take your time."

When Torrance left, Byrne looked down Spring Garden Street. It was clear and cold, and the neon and traffic lights reflected off the street. He wondered if it would ever be spring.

When Ray Torrance didn't return, Byrne walked up the steps, back into the bar. He got the barmaid's attention.

"Did Ray come back in?"

"He left."

Byrne went upstairs, and down to the Quiet Man's Pub. The place was all but deserted.

Ray Torrance was nowhere to be found.

It was well after three a.m. by the time Byrne put his head down on the pillow. Within minutes he was awakened by someone pounding on his door. In the dusk of half-sleep it sounded like a shotgun blast. His first instinct was to take his service weapon with him to the door, but he'd had far too much to drink.

He opened the door to see two young patrol officers in the hallway. In between them was a barely coherent Ray Torrance.

His face was streaked with blood.

"Are you Detective Byrne?" one of the officers asked.

"Yeah," Byrne said. "What happened to him?"

"Not sure," the officer said. "But you should see the other guy."

"Is the other guy pressing charges?"

"No, sir."

Byrne stepped into the hall. He got hold of Torrance, hooked a meaty arm around his neck.

"Thanks, guys," he said. "What house do you work out of?"

"Sixth."

"I'll remember."

"Have a good night, sir."

Night, Byrne thought as he lugged Ray Torrance inside and closed the door. Young officers on last-out always called it night, even at four in the morning.

Had he ever been their age?

Ray Torrance sat on the couch. Byrne sat on the chair. The man's face had begun to swell.

"Christ, Ray. What did you do?"

Torrance shrugged. "I have some stuff in storage. There was a little misunderstanding with the owner about hours of operation."

Byrne pointed at the cut on Torrance's forehead. "You want to get that looked at?"

Torrance gave him a look, the old Irish flatfoot look. Byrne went into the kitchen and got the Irish first aid kit — a bottle of Bushmills, ice, and a paper towel. Torrance used all three.

After a few silent minutes Torrance reached into his bag, took out a large rectangle of paper. On it was scribbled a number of words and numbers, connected by a series of arrows. As Torrance began to unfold the paper, Byrne could see that the edges of the creases were soiled with time and use. Whatever this was, it had been folded and unfolded many times.

When Torrance turned it over, and smoothed it out on the coffee table, Byrne saw that it was a map, specifically a city map of a small section of Northeast Philadelphia. Marked on the map were dozens and dozens of red Xs. Before Torrance could say a word Byrne realized what he was looking at.

"These are the break-ins you were talking about," Byrne said. "These are the places your boogeyman hit."

Torrance didn't answer right away. He just brought a hand to his mouth and stared at the map. A few moments later he nodded and said, "Yeah."

When they had been in the bar, and Torrance had told him that there had been a number of break-ins, Byrne figured he meant five or six. If each X on this map was a separate case, he now knew there were more than three dozen.

"The first one was up here," Torrance said, tapping an index finger on Grant Avenue. "The last one, Marielle's house, was down here." He tapped the lower left of the map.

Byrne scanned the grid, felt a small spike in his pulse. "They're all around Priory Park."

Torrance reached for the bottle of Bushmills, tipped a few more inches into his glass. Byrne knew that his friend was probably six sheets to the wind by now, but he didn't stop him. Ray wasn't going anywhere else tonight.

Dozens of break-ins surrounding Priory Park, more than fifteen years earlier, and now the bodies of three homicide victims, four counting Dustin Green. What was the connection?

Because Ray Torrance was not officially involved in any investigation, Byrne kept these questions to himself.

Torrance stared at the map for a few more moments, then reached back into his bag. He pulled out an old VHS tape, glanced up at Byrne.

"Please tell me you still have a player."

Byrne rummaged through his hall closet, hauled out his VHS machine, brought it into the living room. He searched a few drawers, found the RCA cables, hooked it up. He flipped on the TV. Torrance handed him the tape.

"You're sure you want me to see this?" Byrne asked.

"Kev."

Byrne held up a hand. He'd asked. It was all he could do. He slipped in the tape, hit PLAY.

The video was a high-angle shot of what looked to be a vinyl dinette set. On the right side of the frame was an empty chair. Behind the chair, on the floor, was a pair of royal blue laundry baskets.

After a few moments a little girl slides onto the chair. She wears a pair of magenta pants and a floral long-sleeved T-shirt. Her face is partially obscured by the swag light fixture. She looks to be about four years old.

In the background is the sound of a Saturday-morning cartoon show on television.

The girl knits her fingers, waits.

From offscreen:

"My name is Ray."

The little girl looks down at her hands. She remains silent.

"What's your name?" Ray asks.

The girl looks up, to her right. From off camera: "It's okay." A woman's voice. Byrne assumes it is the girl's mother. The girl looks at Ray.

"Marielle," she says.

"Marielle. That's a *very* pretty name."

"Thank you."

"I heard that they call you Bean."

Marielle nods.

"That's a funny name. How did you get that name?"

Another shrug. Another look off camera. She looks back at Ray. "It's because I like string beans."

"You like string beans?"

Marielle nods.

"I like string beans, too!" Ray says. "Especially with mashed potatoes. Do you like mashed potatoes?"

The little girl nods again. "With butter."

"Got to have butter," Ray says. "Now, Bean, do you know who I am?"

"Yes. A p'liceman."

"That's right. Do you know why I'm here?"

Marielle nods again.

"Why am I here?"

"The man in the closet."

"There was a man in your closet?"

"Yes."

"Do you know his name?"

Marielle shrugs.

"It's okay," Ray says. "I see people all the time and I don't know their names."

Marielle shifts her weight on the chair.

"Now, this man, did he come out of the closet and into your room?"

Marielle nods.

"What did he do?"

"He told stories."

"Stories? What kind of stories?"

Another shrug.

"Were they scary stories?"

"No," she says. "They were sleep stories."

"Sleep stories?"

The little girl nods again.

"You mean stories like when you're sleeping?"

"Yes."

"How many times did he come to visit you?"

Marielle thinks for a few moments, then holds up both hands, all fingers out.

"Ten times?"

Marielle shrugs.

"Did you ever go anywhere with the man?"

"Yes."

"Where did you go?"

"He took me and Tuff for a walk. To meet the other man."

"What other man?"

Marielle looked at her hands again. When she didn't answer, Ray continued.

"This man," Ray says. "The man who was in the closet. Can you tell me what he looks like?"

"I made a picture of him."

"May I see it?"

Marielle slides off the chair. She soon returns with a piece of white construction paper. When she turns it over there is a stick figure drawing of a man.

"This is the man?"

Marielle nods.

"He looks like a scarecrow," Ray says.

Instead of answering, the little girl just folds her hands in her lap, and remains silent.

When Byrne came back from the kitchen, two steaming mugs of decaf in hand, Ray Torrance was fast asleep on the couch. He had rewound the tape to an instant when Marielle's face was in profile, her scarecrow drawing in hand. The tape showed both the little girl and the drawing in freeze frame.

As Byrne put the mugs down on the coffee table, Ray Torrance mumbled something in his sleep.

"PWD, man."

"What?" Byrne asked.

Torrance remained silent, his eyes still closed. He turned onto his side.

"What did you say, Ray?" Byrne asked. "I didn't hear." It sounded like *PPD.* Philadelphia Police Department. Maybe Ray was reliving the case in his dream.

Nothing. The man was out cold.

Byrne took the remote out of Torrance's hand. He then got a blanket out of the hall closet, tucked it around his old friend, and turned off the television.

49

The surveillance on Priory Park was no longer covert. There were patrol cars at either end of Chancel Lane, as well as two SWAT officers deployed on the roof of the old stone chapel at the northwest end of the park.

At the eastern end there were three cars in short rotation watching the entrances from the avenues.

In addition, because Priory Park was a state park, the PPD requested assistance from park rangers. There were four rangers on foot patrol.

At nine-thirty a.m. Byrne got a call from the desk sergeant. He picked up the phone, punched the button. "This is Detective Byrne." He listened for a few seconds, glanced at Jessica. "Okay, bring him up."

"What's going on?" Jessica asked.

Byrne hung up the phone. "James Delacroix is downstairs. He wants to talk to us."

It had been just a few days since they first met James Delacroix. Somehow, in that short period of time he had become a different man, someone Jessica might have passed on the street without recognition. Grief, and the shock of a loved one's sudden, violent death, had a way of making a person smaller. His jacket hung loosely around his shoulders.

Byrne crossed the room to meet Delacroix at the doorway. He extended his hand. "Mr. Delacroix," he said. They shook hands. "How are you holding up?"

Instead of answering the question—after all, what answer would be truthful at a time like this—the man just lifted his shoulders slightly, dropped them.

"Come on over here," Byrne said. "I'll get you a chair."

The man seemed to float across the duty room, as if he had no weight or substance at all. Byrne found an empty chair, rolled it over to one of the desks. Delacroix sat down. Jessica sat across from him.

"Can I get you something?" Jessica asked. "Coffee, soda?"

After a few seconds Delacroix looked up. "No," he said. "I'm fine, thank you."

Byrne sat down. Both he and Jessica waited a few moments for the conversation to begin. Soon it became clear that the two detectives had to initiate this encounter.

"What can we do for you?" Byrne asked.

Delacroix leaned forward, steepled his fingers. "My sister and I were born twelve years apart," he said. "She was very protective of me when I was small. But by the time she reached her late teens, and began college, everything changed, of course. She had her own life, her own friends, her future to think about."

Jessica had seen this many times. Whatever reason had drawn Delacroix to the station needed to be prefaced by history. It probably had nothing to do with why he was there, but in these first days and weeks of grieving, when the whole world seemed to be moving on, it was necessary.

"We shared a pair of safe deposit boxes," he said. "One each. I told her I didn't need one; she insisted that I did. And although we each had access to the other, we had an understanding, an unspoken understanding, that whatever we had in our boxes was sacred. Important papers, such as our wills, any deeds or titles to automobiles or property, was always clearly labeled. These are things to which, if and when the need arose, we would have legitimate access."

At this Delacroix stopped for a moment. Jessica could see his eyes beginning to well with tears. Clearly, the need had arisen to address his sister's property. Jessica got up, crossed the duty room, and came back with a small roll of paper towels. As she handed the roll to Delacroix, she reminded and scolded herself about the fact that there were no boxes of Kleenex tissues anywhere. God knew enough people cried in this room. James Delacroix tore off a few of the towels, folded them, dabbed at his eyes. He nodded a thank-you. Jessica sat down again.

Somewhat composed, he continued. "We always said that there would be one envelope in our boxes that was not to be opened until after our deaths. I went to the bank today, and took out the contents of my sister's safe deposit box."

Delacroix turned the flap on his messenger bag, reached inside. Jessica found that she was holding her breath. She had no idea what he was going to take out of the bag. It turned out to be a cassette tape. A seemingly ordinary, inherently benign cassette tape. James Delacroix put the tape down on the desk. Through the clear plastic cover Jessica could see that there was something written on the label.

"The only thing in the envelope in Joan's safe-deposit box was this tape. This tape and a small note." Once again he reached into his bag. This time he pulled out a small piece of notepaper. He unfolded it. For a moment it appeared that he would read it aloud. His hands began to shake. Jessica reached out to take the man's hands in hers.

"Would you like me to read it for you?" she asked.

The man just nodded. Jessica took the note from him. The paper was a quality linen, buff in color. At the top, printed in deep burgundy ink, was JOAN CATHERINE DELACROIX. Jessica scanned the two lines that were hand printed on the paper. It was not what she expected. She looked up, at Delacroix.

"Do you want me to read this out loud?" she asked.

The man dabbed at his eyes again. "Yes. Please."

Jessica cleared her throat.

"My dear brother, if I have come to an untimely end, please take this to the police. To whom it may concern, if my brother James has preceded me in death, please destroy this without listening to it."

A silence fell between them. Byrne spoke first. He pointed at the note.

"Mr. Delacroix, do you recognize this as your sister's handwriting?"

"Yes," he said. "That's Joan's writing."

"Do you have any idea why she would have written something like this?"

Delacroix thought for a few moments. It was clear he had already spent some time on this question. "No," he said. "My sister helped people. She wouldn't harm anyone. She didn't have enemies."

"Why do you think she may have feared or anticipated an untimely death?"

Something seemed to dawn on the man. "Wait. This is why they tried to burn down her *house,* isn't it? They were trying to destroy this *tape.*"

James Delacroix broke down crying. Jessica handed the note to Byrne. She once again took James Delacroix's hands in hers.

"Have you listened to this tape?" Jessica asked.

"No, I...I didn't..." he began. "I didn't have the courage. To be perfectly honest, I'm not sure I want to know what's on it. Part of me does, but a greater part wants to remember my sister as she was. If there is something on this tape that helps you find the person who did this to her, that will be enough for me. I don't need to know the details."

Jessica reached into her coat pocket, retrieved a pair of latex gloves, snapped them on. She picked up the cassette tape box by its edges, opened it. She shook the tape onto the desk, then turned the tape so both she and Byrne could see what was written on the label. It was a name:

Eduard Kross

Jessica looked at the other side. The label was blank.

"Mr. Delacroix," Jessica said, "do you recognize this name? This Eduard Kross?"

Delacroix glanced at the tape, at the label, as if seeing it for the first time. He shook his head. "No."

"We know this is a terrible time for you," Jessica said. "With your permission, we're going to listen to this. It certainly appears that this is what your sister wanted. Do we have your permission to listen to this recording?"

"Yes," he said. "You have my permission. What I mean is, it's okay."

Jessica glanced at Byrne. He had questions.

"Just to make sure you understand," Byrne began. "Once we listen to this tape, it becomes part of the investigation. Part of the official record. That cannot be undone. Do you understand what I mean by this?"

The finality of what Byrne said took a moment to sink in. Once it did, Delacroix nodded again. "I understand."

"Good," Byrne said. "And there may be things on this tape that lead us in certain directions, down certain paths that we are bound by duty to follow. While we hope that these avenues of investigation are in your sister's best interest—*your* best interest—we can't guarantee that. Do you understand this as well?"

It appeared that Delacroix might suddenly be feeling that bringing this tape to the police might not have been such a great idea. It was too late for that now.

"I do."

"Okay," Byrne said. He took out his notebook. "Just a couple more questions. Are you up for it?"

"Sure."

"We know that your sister was employed as an RN," Byrne said. "Can you tell us about her work history?"

James Delacroix regrouped, began. "Well, she graduated at the top of her class at Penn State. She worked as a registered nurse at Jefferson. But after a while she went back to school and became a psychiatric nurse."

"Do you know where she worked then?"

"She moved to California, and I know she worked at Cedars-Sinai," Delacroix said. "You should know that by the time she got out of nursing school I was just starting junior high school, and a whole new set of personality and lifestyle conflicts came between us. Our parents died within just a few years of each other, and for maybe five years after that we kept in pretty close touch." Delacroix blotted a tear on his cheek.

"So your sister worked as a nurse her entire professional life?"

Delacroix nodded. "Yes. But there was one stretch of time when we didn't talk at all. It was not for lack of effort on my part, however. I sent her cards and letters, but they all came back *Return to Sender.*"

"How long of a period of time was this?" Byrne asked.

"I don't know. Maybe four years or so. Less."

"And you don't know where your sister worked during this time?"

"No," he said. "I didn't even know where she was living during those years. When we got back in touch there were many other things to talk about, and I didn't ask."

"Do you recall when this was?" Byrne asked.

He is going to say 1992 to 1996, Jessica thought. *The same missing years from Robert Freitag's resume.*

"I think it was right around nineteen ninety-two," Delacroix said. "From nineteen ninety-two to 'ninety-six."

"Is it possible your sister worked at the Delaware Valley State Hospital during those years?"

"You mean Cold River?"

"Yes."

"It's possible, I suppose. I don't know."

"There's only one more thing I need to ask for right now," Byrne said. "It may happen that there will be things on this recording that we don't understand, things that, as a family member, you may be uniquely qualified to explain. Will you be willing to talk to us again on this matter?"

James Delacroix took a deep breath, released it slowly. In doing this, Jessica saw a measure of resolve returning. He seemed a little bigger. "Absolutely, Detective. I want you to find the man who did this terrible thing."

"We will do our very best, Mr. Delacroix," Byrne said. "I give you my word."

James Delacroix stood up on legs steadier than those with which he'd entered the room. They all shook hands. Byrne took the opportunity to propose something Jessica knew needed to be done.

Holding Delacroix's right hand in his own, Byrne pointed to the cassette tape on the desk with his left. "I take it that, when you removed that tape from the safe deposit box, you were not wearing gloves."

Delacroix shook his head. "No. I wasn't."

Byrne released the man's hand. They began to walk toward the door. "What we'd like to do, if you don't mind, is to get a set of your fingerprints while you're down here. That way, when we process the tape and the box for fingerprints, we can eliminate yours."

"I understand," Delacroix said. "Where do you want me to go?"

"I'll walk you down there," Byrne said. "It will only take a few minutes."

Jessica watched the two men leave the duty room, and disappear around the corner, heading to the ID unit. She turned and walked back to her desk. She glanced at the tape, reading again the label through the clear plastic box.

Who is Eduard Kross? She picked up the note, reread it.

An untimely end.

What did Joan Delacroix know about the grotesque and bloody act that ended her life?

Perhaps that answer was on this tape.

They huddled in a corner of the duty room. Byrne spoke softly. "We've got Robert Freitag in medical sales, we've got Joan Delacroix as a nurse, we've got Dr. Richmond. All three of our victims had a tidy little meal set up in their kitchens, each with a spoon from Cold River."

Both detectives had the same thought. Jessica voiced it.

"Do you think these people were that research group Miriam talked about? This *Die Traumkaufleute?*"

"It's possible. And this Dr. Kirsch died in a fire. Remind me to check the obituary archives in the *Inquirer.*"

While Jessica made the note, Byrne held up the cassette.

"Have you ever wanted to listen to anything more than this?" he asked.

"Maybe *Blind Man's Zoo* when it came out in nineteen eighty-nine."

"What's *Blind Man's Zoo?*"

"It was a 10,000 Maniacs album."

"Really?" Byrne asked. "10,000 Maniacs?"

"Hey," Jessica said. She snatched the tape from his hand. "The Maniacs *rocked.*"

*   *   *

The Audio Visual Unit of the PPD was located in the Roundhouse basement. Among its many duties was the supply and maintenance of A/V equipment and support material—cameras, televisions, recording devices, collateral audio and video gear. In addition, the unit analyzed surveillance audio and video evidence for every unit in the department, as well as keeping an official record of every public event in which the mayor or police department was involved.

Now forty, the commander of the unit, Sergeant Mateo Fuentes, was a true denizen of the dark confines of the basement, and suffered fools not at all, especially when it came to his time and equipment. Fuentes had helped set up and create the Video Monitoring Unit, which monitored police cameras throughout the city. The unit's value had proven to be immeasurable over the past few years.

Jessica and Byrne found him in the editing bay, working on a recording of the mayor's recent speech.

"When are you going to Hollywood?" Byrne asked.

Mateo stopped the recording, turned in his chair. "When they bring Billy Wilder back from the dead. Everything after him sucked."

Byrne smiled. "You'll get no argument from me."

Jessica held up the audiocassette. "We'd like to listen to this tape."

"I live to serve."

Jessica handed Mateo the cassette. Mateo scrutinized it. "Old-*school*," he said. "I haven't seen C-90s in a long time." He held up the tape. "Has this been processed?"

"It has," Byrne said.

Mateo took the tape from its box. "Well, it looks like it's still in good shape." He glanced at Byrne. "What are we listening for?"

"Don't really know," Byrne said. "We haven't listened to it yet."

"Okay then." Mateo sat a little straighter in his chair. "So it might be the covertly obtained animal ruttings of a sitting Philadelphia councilperson in some one-star motel down the shore?"

Byrne looked at Jessica, back at Mateo. "It's certainly possible," he said. "But I doubt it."

"One lives in hope. What's the job?"

Byrne told Mateo about the murder of Joan Delacroix, as well as the note that accompanied the tape. Accordingly, Mateo took his role in the investigation a lot more seriously now.

"And that's what the note said?" Mateo asked. *"In the event of my death?"*

"In the event of my *untimely* death," Byrne corrected. "We sent the document over to Hell Rohmer to see if he can lift anything from it."

Mateo absorbed the details of the note for a moment. He glanced up at the two detectives. "Do you want to listen to this now?"

"If we could," Byrne said.

Mateo put down the tape, opened a desk drawer, retrieved a ball-point pen. At first, Jessica thought he was going to begin making out a form, a receipt for the evidence. Instead, he inserted the ballpoint cap in the left-hand spool, tightening the slackened tape.

"I can't tell you how many times people have managed to ruin the tape by not tightening the leader."

Jessica knew that Mateo was pretty much talking to himself at this point. He opened the larger drawer in the file cabinet to his left, took out a Panasonic tape player, probably as old-school as the C-90 tape. Mateo plugged it in, opened the top, slipped in the cassette tape, and clicked it shut.

He hit REWIND, making sure the tape would roll from its start.

"Shall we?" Mateo asked.

"By all means," Byrne said.

Mateo hit PLAY. A few seconds later the recording engaged. At first it was just a low hiss. Then, a click. Although Jessica was no expert at any of this, she could tell just by the difference in sound that the acoustics had changed. Moments later, someone began speaking.

It was a man with a deep voice, speaking another language.

"Träumen Sie?"

As the recording continued, it became clear that whatever this was, it was all in a foreign tongue.

"Do you know what language this is?" Byrne asked Mateo.

Mateo held up a forefinger. He adjusted the volume on the tape player. A few seconds later he stopped the tape, rewound it, reached behind to one of the shelves next to his desk, retrieved an audio cable, plugged it into the side of the tape deck then into the back of one of the laptops on the desk. When the tape was fully rewound, he hit FAST-FORWARD for just a few seconds, stopped it again. He then opened a program on the laptop, clicked one of the controls, and started the tape again.

"Träumen Sie?"

Mateo adjusted some of the meters in his audio program. Both Jessica and Byrne listened for a full minute, understanding and comprehending nothing. Jessica was just about to say something when there was a break in the audio, and another man began to speak. He, too, was speaking in a foreign language.

Great, Jessica thought. Their murder victim had a Berlitz tape, wrapped in a cryptic note about her death.

"Do you know what language this is?" Byrne repeated. Before Mateo could respond a voice came from behind them.

"It's German."

Both Jessica and Byrne turned to see Josh Bontrager standing at the back of the room.

"German?" Byrne asked.

"Yeah."

"I didn't know you spoke German," Jessica said.

Bontrager crossed the room, sat on a stool. "I don't, really. But if you grow up around Pennsylvania Dutch, you hear enough of it."

"Okay, I'll bite," Jessica said. "I always thought Pennsylvania Dutch was, well, Dutch."

"Lots of people do," Bontrager said. "I'm certainly no expert on this, but I'm pretty sure that it comes from Deutsche. Hence, the German."

"So, the Amish and the Mennonites speak German?" Jessica asked.

"Not really. The Amish and the Mennonites are religious faiths. Pennsylvania Dutch is a language of sorts. It's kind of a smash-up between English and German. Believe it or not, I think there may be a little Yiddish involved. Don't quote me on that, though."

Jessica pointed at the paused recorder. "Do you know what these guys are saying?"

"Gosh, no," Bontrager said. "I just know a couple of words and phrases. Stuff like *schnickelfritz* and *wonnernaus*. When we were kids *schrecklich* was a big one."

"What does that mean?"

"I think it means scary," Bontrager said. "It gets pretty dark in Berks County at night."

"Do you know anyone who might be able to help us with this?" Jessica asked.

Bontrager thought for a few moments. "Well, ever since I left the church, there aren't a lot of people in Bechtelsville who are too crazy about me. My family is cool, but that's about it. Let me make a few calls. I'll find someone."

Bontrager stepped out of the room, his phone already in hand.

"So, *schrecklich* means scary?" Jessica asked.

"Apparently."

"And that's where Shrek gets his name?"

Byrne laughed. "I think you've been hanging around little kids too much."

"Tell me about it."

Byrne turned to Mateo, got his attention. Mateo took off his headphones.

"Is there a way to clean up the sound on these recordings?" Byrne asked.

Mateo just stared.

"Okay, dumb question. What about putting all of this on a single disc, or making it an MP3?"

Mateo pointed at his screen, at the progress bars, and the digital readout of audio levels. It was already in the works.

Byrne just nodded. For a guy so knowledgeable about all things audio, Mateo Fuentes was able to communicate a great deal without a single word.

"Call me," Byrne whispered.

On the way back upstairs they saw Josh Bontrager on the phone. He held up a finger, finished his conversation, clicked off.

"I've got someone who can translate your recording," Bontrager said.

"That was fast," Jessica said.

"It's the goatee."

Bontrager took out his notebook, scribbled in it, tore off the page and handed it to Jessica. "Her name is Elizabeth Troyer. She's in the language department at Villanova."

"Does she know we'll be contacting her?" Byrne asked.

"I just talked to her. I told her one of you will be there this afternoon."

An hour later Byrne talked to the woman, who said she would be happy to help. He had a copy of the cassette sent over by what would have been a messenger if the PPD had any kind of budget. Instead, Byrne gave it to a detective who had business in Radnor Township.

50

Rachel had been a sophomore at college when she got the frantic call from her mother about Marielle running away. By then, her mother had slipped into raging alcoholism, and told Rachel that she was going to put all of Marielle's belongings on the curb for trash pickup.

Rachel raced back home to find that she was too late. When she walked into her old room, a room she shared for many years with her sister, a room that held all her memories of childhood, everything was gone.

Rachel found her mother sitting in the kitchen that day, a half-empty bottle of bottom-shelf whiskey on the table. They argued for what seemed like an hour, her mother all but incoherent.

It would be their final fight.

Two hours later her mother—with a blood alcohol content of 0.16—flipped her car on the westbound lane of the Vine Street Expressway, right near the turnoff onto I-76.

She was pronounced dead on the scene.

For years Rachel wondered if her mother was coming to see her. It was the route her mother always took when she came to Drexel University.

Rachel had spoken to her boss earlier in the day, and Diana told her that the offer on the house was for $350,000, which was at least $75,000 more than for any other house on the block.

The sale, of course, was contingent on an inspection.

Rachel stood in the doorway to Bean's room. She wondered if the new owners had children, and if two new little girls would grow up in this space.

She would find out soon.

The buyer would be there in twenty-four hours.

51

Named for St. Thomas of Villanova, and located in Radnor Township, northwest of Philadelphia, Villanova University was the oldest Catholic university in Pennsylvania.

Byrne met the woman Josh Bontrager had contacted, Elizabeth Troyer, in her small office near the language lab in Mendel Hall.

In her mid-thirties, Elizabeth Troyer was an Associate Professor of English.

"We appreciate you taking the time," Byrne said.

"I'm happy to help, but I'm afraid I cannot say it has been a pleasure."

"Why is that?"

She picked up the notebook, held it for a moment. She did not open it. "As you requested, I did listen to this tape. Not all of it, mind you, but a fair sampling. I am not a linguist, nor an audiologist by any stretch of the imagination, but I can tell you that there are two distinct voices on these tapes."

"Only two?"

"Yes," she said. "It seems the recordings were made in a small room of sorts. There is no echo."

"Can you tell anything about who is speaking?"

"Not much, I'm afraid. I can tell you that it is two men. I can also tell you that one of the men, the one asking the questions, seems to be quite educated. His grammar, syntax, vocabulary, all point to a university-level education."

"What about where they are from?"

"The man who is asking questions is indeed speaking German. The other man is not so easy to pin down. I believe it is one of the Uralic languages."

The look on Byrne's face must have conveyed a question. Before he could ask it, she answered.

"The Uralic languages are a family of about three dozen tongues, mostly called Finno-Ugric today. The name derives from people who lived in or near the Ural Mountains. A number of languages are loosely associated with the Uralics—Hungarian, Finnish, others."

"And you're saying that the other speaker on this recording, the one not speaking German, is speaking one of these languages?"

"Yes, I believe so," she said. "Although I think it is more Finnic. Balto Finnic, perhaps."

She stopped the recording, rewound it to the beginning. She then reached into a drawer in her desk, took out a pair of headphones, plugged it into her tape player. "Do you have a few moments?"

"Absolutely," Byrne said.

She rose from her desk, walked across the room to the bookcase. She ran her finger along the spines of the books on the top shelf, stopped, and removed one of the volumes. She stepped back to her desk, put the headphones back on, and started the recording.

Byrne could no longer hear it.

On the other hand, hearing it the first few times had not helped. Once again, as he had many times before, he promised himself that as soon as he had some free time he would try to learn a foreign language.

The woman closed her eyes as she was listening. After a minute or so she restarted the recording, played it again. She stopped it one more time, flipped through the book on her lap. She came to a page, read for a few moments, then restarted the recording. A minute later she took the headphones off. She hit the eject button, took out the tape, and handed it to Byrne.

"It's Estonian."

"Estonian?"

"Yes. One of the men is speaking German, the other is speaking Estonian. I am sure of it."

Byrne made a few notes. "What about context?"

"You want to know what they're talking about?"

"Whatever you can tell me would be of great help."

At this, the woman sat down in one of the chairs by the window. She reached into her bag and took out a small silver case. She opened the case, extracted a small white pill, placed it on her tongue. She poured herself a half glass of water, drank it. Whatever she was about to say, it appeared it was going to have some negative effect on her.

When she reached into her bag, and took out a pack of cigarettes, Byrne realized it was going to be worse than that.

"Do you mind?" she asked, holding up the pack.

"Not at all," Byrne said. It wasn't entirely true, but this was her patch.

The woman tapped a pair of cigarettes halfway out of the pack, offered one to Byrne. He shook his head. She then opened the window, extracted a lighter from her purse, lit the cigarette, drew deeply, and blew the smoke out the window.

"I could probably lose tenure over this," she said, holding up her cigarette. "Sometimes I think it would be worth it."

Although Byrne had never been much of a smoker, he was always amazed at the effect a cigarette could have on someone. Along with the smoke, it appeared, the woman had released at least some of the anxiety she anticipated in relating the details of what she heard on the recording.

Ritual now complete, the woman opened her notebook.

"As I stated, I only listened to portions of the tape, but I heard more than enough to understand the structure of these conversations, if not their exact nature. Once again, I can only understand half of it, and not even close to every word at that."

"I understand."

"What I determined from the German speaker was something— how shall I put this? something *disturbing.*"

"Disturbing? How so?"

"I'm not exactly sure," she said. "You said this was, in some way, related to an investigation? A homicide investigation?"

"Yes."

She nodded. "I don't want to mislead you about something that really amounts to what is probably no more than a feeling on my part. As I said I am not fluent in German. I am conversational, but not fluent."

"Okay."

"I do feel confident in telling you that the German speaker in this recording seems to be coercing thoughts from the other person."

Coercing, Byrne thought. "Are you saying that this might be a tape recording of some type of interrogation?"

She was silent for a moment. "Maybe coercing is the wrong word." The woman took another hit on her cigarette. She then reached in the drawer of her desk, took out a small travel ashtray. She carefully butted the cigarette into the ashtray enclosed with swivel top. She opened the window more fully. Byrne had to admit the fresh air helped.

"Maybe I'm completely wrong about this," she said. "There are as many nuances in German as there are in English. There are a number of instructors here at the university who can give you a precise translation of this material."

The woman was retreating. Byrne said nothing.

"I'm afraid we don't have anyone here at the university who speaks or teaches Estonian or any of the Finno-Baltic languages. There isn't that much call for it. At least at a college this size."

"I understand."

"I am, however, a member of one or two national and international organizations. I could send out a few feelers. I'm sure I could find someone in very short order who could help you with the translation of the Estonian side of this conversation."

Byrne thought about it. He considered the woman's statement that the questions being asked in German were "disturbing." There was now no doubt that this recording was evidentiary in a homicide, perhaps a series of homicides. He'd had some reluctance about even bringing it to the university, and now that he knew that the tone, if not the context, of what was being said on the tape was dark in nature, it would probably not be the best thing to bring more people into the fold.

"That's very kind of you," Byrne said. "I'm not sure where this recording fits into the investigation just yet. And I think you can understand the need for confidentiality here."

"Of course."

"So I'll let you know whether or not we need you to contact any of your colleagues."

The woman looked a little relieved. "Do let me know, then. I'd be more than happy to help."

"Did you make a copy of this?"

"No."

Byrne glanced at his notepad. "I'm wondering about the first thing said on the tape," he said. "After the date and time. That *Träumen*…"

"It's a German expression. *Träumen Sie.*"

"Do you know what that means?"

"I do. I believe it was phrased as a question. It translates as 'Do you dream?'"

"'Do you dream?'" Byrne repeated.

"Yes."

Byrne stood up. The woman followed suit. They shook hands. "Thanks so much for your time and your help. It's much appreciated."

"Any time."

"And if you could keep this to yourself, it would probably be best for the time being."

"Okay," she said. "On one condition."

"And what is that?"

"You don't tell anybody about the smoking."

Byrne smiled. "Trust me. Nobody is better at keeping secrets than the police."

The woman returned the smile. She opened the door to her office. "Even under oath?"

"Especially under oath."

Byrne sat in the parking lot. He watched the students scurry across campus in the freezing rain, wondering if he was ever that young. When he was their age he was already a police officer. He wondered about their choices, his choices.

His mind soon returned the recording.

Träumen Sie, he thought.

Do you dream?

He considered the book in Robert Freitag's house, and its inscription: *Perchance to dream.*

They were all about dreaming in the Big Place, Lenny Pintar had said.

Die Traumkaufleute.

The Dream Merchants.

Byrne looked at the clock, saw that it was after one a.m., hit the speed-dial number before he could stop himself. Jessica answered in two rings.

"Hey."

"Were you sleeping?" Byrne asked.

"I don't sleep," Jessica said. "I work, I study, and I make sandwiches without crust."

"What were you doing just now?"

"Okay, I nodded off. What's up?"

Byrne told her about his visit to Villanova.

"That's what she said? Disturbing?"

"Yeah. Her word."

Jessica was silent for a moment. "What do you think she meant?"

"She didn't want to say too much, probably thinking it would be misleading without context. She's probably right. She said she thinks it sounds like a Q and A, and the questioner, the one speaking German, is coercing answers out of the other speaker."

"Do we know what language that is?"

"Estonian."

"Wow. Okay. What's our next step with this?"

Byrne told her that the woman offered to track down someone who could translate the Estonian part of the recording.

"I think we should take her up on it," Jessica said.

"Yeah. You're probably right."

"Oh, by the way, I checked the obituary on Dr. Kirsch. Kirsch died in a fire in the basement of G10, along with two administrators from the hospital."

"Does it sound like Kirsch might have been involved in nefarious activities?"

Jessica laughed. "Are you sure you don't want to go to law school?"

"Maybe I will. It's got to be easier than this."

"I'll read the obit again tomorrow when I'm not cross-eyed with exhaustion."

"Okay," Byrne said. "See you in the morning."

"It is morning."

"See you later."

Byrne poured himself another few inches of Bushmills. He walked over to the dining-room table, took the cassette tape out of his bag. He turned off the music he was listening to—Rory Gallagher's *Irish Tour '74*—then opened the cassette deck. Before he inserted the tape he took out his pen and made sure he took up the slack on the left side of the reel, Mateo Fuentes's stern brow in his mind's eye. He popped in the cassette, pressed PLAY, turned off the lights, sat in the chair by the window. As he did this it occurred to him that he might be turning into Old Tony Giordano.

There were probably worse fates.

After a few seconds the recording started. After the time stamp, he heard the question again, the one he now knew meant: "Do you dream?"

Byrne closed his eyes. He tried to imagine the room in which this recording was made. There were clearly two men, one more or less interviewing the other.

Were they sitting in chairs, facing each other? And, if so, what kind of chairs? Were they comfortable, upholstered chairs? Were they utilitarian, folding metal chairs? Byrne tried to listen for some kind of echo, some audible reflection of sound off metal. He heard none.

He took a sip of the Bushmills, put his feet up on the windowsill. Was this recording made at Cold River? Was this part of the secretive research Miriam Gale had alluded to?

When the second man began to speak, Byrne—

—*is on a long road, unpaved, winding through green hills, the near distance dotted with farmhouses, idyllic, the sound of footsteps on hardpan, now accented with the sound of rain pelting through tall trees, the smell of—*

—sackcloth and wet straw.

At three a.m. Byrne surrendered to his insomnia. He got out of bed, walked over to the bathroom, all but drowned himself in cold water. He glanced out the bathroom window. The street was quiet, still. He walked back into the living room, eyed the bottle of Bushmills. It eyed him back. There was only an inch left. Was there anything sadder? Maybe. But not at the moment.

He resigned himself to the fact that it was in fact today, not last night, not anymore. He put some coffee on and tried to will himself alert.

Fifteen minutes later, a pot of strong coffee at his side, he sat down at his dining-room table, opened his laptop. It took about twenty seconds for him to dump the last inch of whiskey into his cup, justifying it, as always, that he was Irish, and now his coffee was, too.

The only thing he knew about Estonia was that it was a Baltic country, along with Lithuania and Latvia. It was not as if he was scholarly about Germany, not by any means, but Estonia was a blank slate.

Within minutes he learned the basics. Estonia was approximately the size of Vermont and New Hampshire combined, with a population of about 1.3 million people. The capital was Tallinn, a seaport on the Gulf of Finland, about fifty miles south of Helsinki. Their form of government was a parliamentary democracy, but it had not always been so.

From the early seventeen hundreds to the First World War, Estonia was ruled by the Russians. In 1917 Estonia declared its independence, and by 1920 Russia recognized it as a sovereign state. Unfortunately, for the people of Estonia, that independence was short-lived. The Second World War ushered in the darkest time in Estonia's history. Between 1939 and 1945, as a result of both the Nazi and the Soviet occupations the country lost 180,000 citizens.

Those dark days—years of oppression, starvation and brutality— continued for decades. In the late 1980s, with the onset of Glasnost, controls on the freedom of expression were eased, and the singing of banned songs caught fire through Estonia, resulting in what was known as "the singing revolution."

In 1991 the Soviets once again recognized Estonia as a sovereign nation. Three years later the last of the Soviet troops left the country.

Byrne did an image search for Estonia. From what he found the capital city of Tallinn was beautiful. It looked to be from another time, a beautifully preserved and restored medieval city. The people seemed to have kind faces; the streets were clean and not covered in litter and graffiti.

In the course of his online searches he had a brainstorm. It might've been a Bushmills storm, but nonetheless he navigated to a web page for the administrative offices for the city of Tallinn. He clicked around for a while, and found the page for the municipal police department. He located the contact email address, opened his email program.

He rationalized what he was about to do this way: If, as the woman at Villanova had told him, the context of that which was being discussed in the audio recording was "disturbing," then it probably wouldn't make the best sense to have a citizen — or, more accurately, someone who was not in law enforcement — do the translation.

God knew the world had big ears these days.

Byrne composed a brief email query to a man named Peeter Tamm, listed as the media relations officer for the city of Tallinn municipal police department, requesting help in the translation of the recording. He didn't know if he was following the correct PPD protocol when it came to things like this, because he had never before encountered a thing like this.

Before he could stop himself, he hit SEND, and heard the email begin its journey across the Atlantic.

52

The evidence from the four homicides—Robert Freitag, Joan Delacroix, Edward Richmond and Dustin Green—was posted on a giant white board in the duty room. Arrows made what few connections there were.

The autopsy of Edward Richmond concluded that the man had died from asphyxiation due to strangulation. The murder weapon was, presumptively, the steel wire with which he had been propped between the trees in Priory Park, a wire that had crushed the man's trachea. The angle of the wound indicated that the strangulation had occurred when the man's body weight pulled him down. The time of death was very accurately pinpointed at 9:30 p.m., literally minutes after P/O Weldon got the call and was drawn off his post.

To put it mildly, morale was not high on the first floor of the Roundhouse as it related to these cases.

With the FBI now involved, doors previously unavailable to the PPD were being breached with ease. A search of IRS records for Edward Richmond, Joan Delacroix and Robert Freitag showed that each had been in the employ of the Delaware Valley State Hospital between the years of 1992 and 1996.

Jessica and Byrne sat at one of the desks, the crime scene photos spread out before them.

"This all goes back to this building," Byrne said. "This G10."

"So there were dream experiments being conducted in G10. What kind of dream experiments?"

"I have no idea. I've got a call in to Martin Léopold's publisher. Waiting to hear back if he'll talk to us."

"In the meantime, I'm going to see if there's a copy of that book in the library."

Before Jessica could reach one of the computer terminals, Byrne's iPhone rang. He looked at it.

"Wow," he said. "I'm getting a call from Estonia."

"From Estonia?"

Byrne looked a little sheepish. He quickly explained sending the email to the Tallinn Municipal Police Department. "Okay. It seemed like a good idea at the time."

"It looks like it might have paid off."

"See if Mateo is free," Byrne said. While Jessica called the A/V Unit, Byrne answered the call, launched the FaceTime app, positioned his iPhone on one of the dividers between the desks. He tapped the appropriate icons.

On-screen was a medium shot of a man sitting in an office chair.

Peeter Tamm looked to be in his late forties—blond hair, green eyes, a trim mustache. He wore a dark vest sweater, crisp white shirt and striped tie. The background was a pair of file cabinets and the corner of a white board. From everything Byrne could see, law enforcement in Estonia was about as glamorous as it was in the United States.

"Hello," Tamm said. "Is that Detective Byrne?"

"Yes," Byrne replied. "Do I call you detective?"

The man smiled. "Peeter will be fine."

"Please call me Kevin."

"Kevin it is. I must admit, I don't get a lot of communication from the States. I was both surprised and pleased to get your email."

"Well, we could use a little help."

Tamm nodded. "Perhaps you can tell me exactly what you are looking for, and I will tell you how we can help."

Byrne gave the man very broad details on the cases, and the existence of the tape recording. Peeter Tamm listened intently.

"I don't imagine you run across too many cases that have an Estonian connection," Tamm said.

"This is a first."

"It is a little different here. Shall I explain?"

Wow, Jessica thought. A super-polite cop. Maybe she would move to Estonia.

"Please," Byrne said.

"In Estonia, the police authority prefectures were recently merged with Border Guard Board—similar in some ways to your Homeland Security—to form one authority called PBGB. The Central Police office is in Tallinn, but serious crimes such as homicides are investigated in other prefectures in other regions of the country."

"What about your forensic investigations?" Byrne asked. "How is that handled?"

"This is done by the Estonian Forensic Science Institute, which is administered by the Ministry of Justice. The biggest facility is here in Tallinn, but there are regional labs in Tartu, Kohtla-Järve and Pärnu."

"What about language translation services?"

"Oh, yes. As you might imagine, there are a lot of languages spoken here."

Jessica noticed that the man spoke almost unaccented English.

"In your email you mentioned the name Eduard Kross," Tamm said.

"Yes," Byrne said. "The name came up in connection with the current homicide investigation. It's written on the label of the audio recording we have."

"I must confess that I had not heard that name in a while. The name Eduard Kross, while not known to younger Estonians, conjures something of the beast to those of us who are older."

"How so?"

Tamm took a few moments. "I imagine the name and legend of Eduard Kross is similar to that of Great Britain's Jack the Ripper, although far less has been written about Kross. Almost nothing, really."

"He was a killer?"

"Yes," Tamm said. "But it seems there is a lot more folklore connected to his name than documented fact."

"What is the folklore?"

"Over a period of maybe thirty years or so, they say he moved through the forests and mountains of all three Baltic nations. In that time he committed a number of crimes—arson, forgery, robbery."

"And murder."

"Yes," Tamm said. "Legend has it that he murdered more than one hundred people."

"And he was never caught?"

"Oh, yes. I'm not clear on when, but it was during the Soviet period. Perhaps the early nineteen eighties."

"What happened to him?"

"It's my understanding that he went to a gulag, where he died shortly thereafter. Again, this is all speculation, the stuff of campfire fable."

"And why did he commit all these crimes?"

"This is even more vague. But they say his father was a respected dentist. When his father informed a high-ranking officer in the German army that he would lose all of his teeth, the officer had Kross's mother and father and sister killed. It is said that Eduard hid and escaped."

Byrne made a series of notes. "Well, this is very helpful," he said.

"Not at all. Is there anything else we can do?"

Byrne explained about the tape, and how they could use a translation.

"We would be happy to do this," Tamm said. "We have some of the best translators in the world here. Send along the file when you are ready."

"We're ready now."

Tamm gave Byrne an email address. At a nearby terminal, Mateo Fuentes sent the compressed audio file. Within seconds, Tamm looked back at the screen.

"The file has arrived," Tamm said. "When the translation is complete, how would you like me to send it?"

"Fax will be fine," Byrne said. "Or if you'd like to scan it and attach it to an email that would be good, too."

"A .pdf file would probably be best."

"Great," Byrne said. "By the way, have you ever been to the United States?"

"I have. Many years ago, I took my honeymoon in Miami Beach."

"Miami is nice."

"You should come to Tallinn someday. It is a beautiful city. And there are a few advantages to working for the police here."

"Such as?"

"Our police cars are made by BMW."

Byrne looked out the window, at the parking lot behind the Roundhouse, at the line of ice-shrouded departmental sedans. Most were Ford Taurus. He looked back at the screen. "Are you guys hiring?"

Tamm smiled. "I will be in touch shortly," he said. "Be safe."

"Thanks," Byrne said. "You too."

The conversation with the Estonian detective put a spring into the step of the investigation. It felt like progress. While they waited for a response, Ray Torrance showed up in the duty room.

To Jessica, Ray Torrance looked a lot better. He had shaven, and had gotten some color back, despite the bandage on his forehead. He asked about the investigation. Byrne explained about making contact with the Estonian police officer.

"What a world," Torrance said. "I remember when we were coming up, SVU was located in that old police horse stable. Now you pick up the phone and call Estonia."

Before the war horses could get too deeply into the old days, Jessica looked up to see Josh Bontrager crossing the duty room. Fast.

"How did it go at Villanova?" Bontrager asked Byrne.

"Good," Byrne said. "She was very helpful. Thanks for contacting her."

"No charge."

"Josh, do you know Ray Torrance?" Byrne asked.

Bontrager put his documents down on the desk. "Never had the honor," he said.

"Josh Bontrager, Ray Torrance." The two men shook hands.

"I've heard a lot about you," Bontrager said.

"There are two sides to everything," Torrance said with a smile. "I hope I get the chance to defend myself."

Bontrager laughed. "It's really great to meet you."

"And you."

"Josh is working a bad one," Byrne said.

"Funny you should mention," Bontrager said. He made a motion to open the binder on the desk, stopped himself. Jessica saw him steal a glance at Byrne. It was a look she knew well. Byrne gave a slight, almost imperceptible nod of his chin. It was not lost on any of the detectives in this corner of the room, including Ray Torrance. What Josh's look meant was a question, and that question was: *Can I speak freely in front of this man?*

Byrne's nod meant *yes.*

Josh Bontrager opened the binder on the desk.

"We're getting labs back on my DOA. Also, we finally got an ID. His name was Ezequiel 'Cheque' Marquez, eighteen years old, late of Ludlow."

"Was he banging?" Byrne asked.

Bontrager shook his head. "Not officially. He was a fringe player. A couple of misdemeanor assaults, some stuff as a juvenile. Nothing felony grade." He opened one of the envelopes. "It took a while to toss that room where he was killed, but we did find these."

Bontrager pulled a photograph out of the envelope. It was a close-up of a box of cigars, a four-pack of Dutch Masters coronas. The box was unopened.

"So these belonged to Marquez?" Byrne asked.

"Yeah," Bontrager said. "His fingerprints are all over it."

"What about reefer?" Jessica asked. Dutch Masters coronas, along with El Productos and White Owls, were the cigars of choice when it came to rolling blunts.

"Didn't find any." Bontrager pulled another photograph out, this one a picture of the back of the box of cigars. In the upper left-hand corner was a pricing sticker. The sticker only showed the cost of the item. "There are six stores within walking distance of the crime scene that sell these. We canvassed all of them, and the only one that has a sticker like this was the City Fresh Market on Oxford."

"So you're thinking Marquez bought the cigars there on that day?"

"I can do better than that. Turns out the market has had a number of robberies in the last few years. They have a really good security system, and they dump their hard drives once a month."

Bontrager pulled a USB flash drive out of his pocket, sat down at one of the computer terminals, and slipped the drive into an open USB port. Within a few seconds there was an image on the screen. It was a high-angle shot of the checkout line at the Super Fresh. In the upper right-hand corner was a date and time code.

After a few seconds a young man enters the frame on the right. He is second in line behind a woman carrying a sleeping infant.

"This is your victim?" Byrne asked, tapping the screen.

"Yeah," Bontrager said. "That's Cheque Marquez."

On-screen, the woman with the infant pays for her purchases, and leaves the store. Marquez steps forward. He drops a bill on the conveyor belt, and the cashier rings up the cigars. Marquez shoves the change into his right front pocket, the cigars in his left back pocket.

The line moves up. Next in line is a teenage girl with a box of baby formula.

"Now watch this," Bontrager said.

Instead of leaving the store, Marquez walks over to the Red Box machine, leans against it. He picks up one of the coupon books, leafs through it. There wasn't one detective watching the video who thought the young man had any interest in coupons. This was a stall, a case.

The camera angle cuts to a shot from above the front doors to the market, pointing to the area where Marquez was standing. Again, it is obvious he is waiting for someone, or something.

The camera then cuts to the parking lot for about ten seconds, then back to the original angle, over the checkout line. In line now is an older woman, with a tall man in a raincoat behind her. The woman takes her time paying. It looks like she is scrutinizing the LCD monitor for discrepancies. She eventually swipes her card, signs, and takes her bags.

She steps forward. The tall man steps up.

The camera again cuts to the front door angle. Marquez is watching the woman as she puts down her bags, buttons her coat. When she picks up her bags, she drops her credit card to the floor. She doesn't notice, just keeps on walking.

Marquez sees the card. He puts his foot on top of it.

In the instant before the woman leaves the store, she looks up at the camera.

As Jessica felt the floor pull away beneath her, Bontrager stopped the recording.

"That's Joan Delacroix," Jessica said.

"Yes, it is," Bontrager replied.

"Wait," Jessica said. "Your victim and our victim are in the same place at the same *time?*"

"Yes," Bontrager said. "And it gets better."

Bontrager hit PLAY. The recording continued. On it, Joan Delacroix continued out of the store with her bags, without turning around. A few seconds later, inside the store, Marquez bent down and picked up the credit card.

Bontrager again paused the recording.

"Was this credit card on him when he was found?" Byrne asked.

"No," Bontrager said. "It was nowhere to be found at the crime scene, either."

Jessica looked over at Byrne, then at Ray Torrance. She was hoping for a brainstorm from one of the two men. They were both seemingly mesmerized by the image on the screen.

"Does the ME have a time of death on Marquez?" Jessica asked.

Bontrager flipped through his notes, found the medical examiner's estimate.

"That's twenty-four hours before the woman was killed," Jessica said. "It kind of rules out Marquez for Joan Delacroix's murder."

"It does," Bontrager said. "Question: when Joan Delacroix was found at Priory Park, was her purse found at the crime scene?"

Jessica shook her head. "No. Her purse was at her house. It's in evidence now."

"Do you have a list of the contents?"

"We do," Jessica said. She crossed the room, retrieved the binder for Joan Delacroix. She then flicked through the documents, found the one she was looking for. "In addition to her driver's license, a Macy's charge card and a hundred and seventeen dollars in cash, she also had an Edward Jones issue MasterCard."

Bontrager reached into the envelope, pulled out a photocopy of a receipt. It was from the City Fresh Market, with a time code of exactly the moment Joan Delacroix paid for her purchases on that day. The card she used was an Edward Jones issue MasterCard, with a matching number to the one found in her wallet.

"Well, this is just getting better and better, isn't it?" Jessica said. "If Marquez lifted this woman's card, how the hell did it find its way back in her purse?"

"Maybe he followed her out of the store, and gave it back to her," Torrance said.

Bontrager restarted the recording. The camera angle cut to the parking lot view. On-screen they saw Joan Delacroix leaving the store. She walked off-frame to the left. A few moments later, Marquez walked out of the store, and all but ran off-frame to the right, in the opposite direction.

"Now you can see why I am no longer a detective," Torrance said.

Bontrager again hit PAUSE. "I wish I had some answers here, but I'm about as lost with this as you are. That said, remember what I said about curiouser and curiouser?"

Jessica couldn't imagine what was coming.

"I was just down at the lab getting some of the preliminary tests from the Marquez job," Bontrager said. "I was talking to the tech in the blood lab, and he asked me if I would bring over a couple of documents from the Delacroix case. It turns out the woman's blood type was AB negative. As you know, that's extremely rare."

It was true. Less than 1 percent of the population of the United States was AB negative.

"The tech told me he runs across AB negative maybe once a year, or once every two years," Bontrager said. "He's telling me this because he ran across AB negative from two different cases in one day."

Bontrager reached into the envelope, and pulled out a pair of documents that detailed two different blood tests.

"It turns out the other instance of AB negative blood was found on another one of your cases," Bontrager said.

"You mean, other than Joan Delacroix?" Jessica asked.

"Yes. There was trace evidence of blood on the inside of that sand-wich bag."

"What sandwich bag?"

"The sandwich bag in that little girl's purse."

"Violet?" Jessica asked. "There was blood on the bag in her purse?"

"Yes," Bontrager said. "And it's not just that the blood on that bag is AB negative. It's a dead solid match. The blood in the little girl's purse belonged to Joan Delacroix."

In all the time Jessica had been a homicide detective she had never quite had as many bombshells dropped on a case as those that had just happened here. She looked up at her partner, then at Ray Torrance.

Byrne was staring at the documents on the desk.

Ray Torrance was staring at Kevin Byrne.

53

The foster care home was a double row house in the Francisville section of North Philadelphia.

Byrne and Ray Torrance were met at the door by a woman in her early forties. She had about her an unflappable air, a woman who spent her days corralling small children—being climbed upon, drooled upon, defied and defiled by people no more than two feet tall.

There was now an official connection between the little girl and an ongoing homicide investigation. It was for this reason, and many others—not the least of which was that Violet did not need a longer parade of adults coming in and out of her life—that Byrne decided to keep Ray Torrance in the background.

Torrance voiced no objections.

*   *   *

There were four children in the front room. Violet was wearing a purple sweatshirt and matching sweatpants. Okay, not an exact match. It was the kind of match made at Walmart when you were trying to buy a birthday gift for someone named Violet.

Violet was at one of the small tables, by herself, working on a castle made of blocks.

According to the woman who ran the home, Violet had yet to say a word. She said the little girl responded to instructions, and slept through the night, but had yet to answer a question.

When Violet saw Byrne there was a moment of hesitation. Byrne watched her carefully as she spotted him, looked away, then got up, walked across the room, and put her arms out. Byrne picked her up, and she wrapped her arms around his neck.

He walked her back to the table.

"What are we building?" Byrne asked.

No answer. He put the little girl down, and she went immediately back to her task. At first it looked like Violet was going for a pyramid shape, but when she stacked the blocks too high, they all fell over.

Still no reaction. No anger, no frustration, no joy. As Byrne watched her gather together the blocks for another try, he marveled at how pale she was. Her skin was almost paper white; her hair was nearly white blond. Someone, it seemed, had found a barrette for her, a clip to keep the hair from falling into her face. The barrette, in the shape of a five-petal flower was, of course, a shade of purple.

Byrne watched her for a while, woefully unprepared to talk to the little girl. He simply didn't know what to ask her. He knew she had been seen by a child psychologist, to whom the girl had not uttered a word. If a behavioral therapist couldn't get anything out of her, what chance did a big dumb cop have?

Apparently, none.

When it came time to leave, Byrne gave Violet another hug.

She stood next to the table, watching him as he crossed the room. But when Byrne turned around to wave goodbye to her, he saw that her attention had been drawn away from him. She was looking at the television.

Violet stood in front of the screen. She looked over at Byrne for a moment, then back at the TV. She put her tiny hand on the screen.

The movie playing was *The Wizard of Oz*. The scene was the one where Judy Garland comes around the bend on the yellow brick road, and meets Ray Bolger for the first time.

It was the scarecrow.

Violet was trying to touch the scarecrow.

They stood on the sidewalk in front of the row house. When it began to rain again they stepped under the awning of the bakery next door. The aromas of fresh bread and pastries were maddening. Byrne had not eaten all day.

"This is a bit of a reach, Ray."

"Come on, Kevin. You saw that sketch that Marielle made. She said the man looked like a scarecrow."

"All due respect, *you* said it was a scarecrow. She didn't correct you on that."

"You're saying there's no connection?"

Byrne considered what Torrance was saying. He wanted to shoot it down. He had no ammunition.

"One night," Torrance said. "Give me one night on the streets. If I don't make the link, I'll go back to my cabin."

"I don't want that, Ray. Nobody wants that."

"Look, I won't insult you by asking if you have a case or two you can't shake. Christ, I know for a fact you do. You don't get to pick and choose which ones get to you."

Byrne looked at his old friend. His posture was stooped, he was leaning forward. He didn't want to reduce this once great cop to begging. He put a hand on the man's shoulder.

"One night," Byrne said.

Ray Torrance smiled.

"But first we have to get some of this bread."

It had been a while since Byrne had done this kind of street work. He never cared for it. It mostly amounted to drinking coffee, trying to stay not only awake but alert and on point, playing bathroom tag team with your partner, and getting home at dawn with nothing to show for it. Once in a while you got lucky, and the person for whom you were looking made the mistake of going where they should have known not to go, and you had them.

That was rare.

There were a few places in Philadelphia to find street kids. If you were a runaway you came in through the bus terminal on Filbert, or the majestic, cavernous 30th Street train station. These were your points of entry.

But the place you hung out, once you got here, was South Street. Especially after dark. You could hang out at the malls during the day, right up until closing time, but after that you headed to South.

Both Byrne and Torrance dressed down as much as possible. Byrne wore his leather coat, jeans, his comfortable black boots. He didn't know how much running might be involved this night. None, he hoped. Torrance was between wardrobes, as it were. He borrowed one of Byrne's old navy pea coats, and a pair of dark gray corduroys. They were about the same size, and the ensemble, even as dated as it might've been, suited him.

They began the search near the bottom of South Street, in front of Downey's. After an hour or so they split up for a while, Torrance staying in touch via a burner cell phone Byrne had bought for him.

When they reconvened, at ten o'clock, they had talked to maybe three dozen teenagers. They'd learned nothing. The temptation to slip into one of the many bars on South was great, but they decided to give it until midnight.

The girls couldn't have been more than fifteen or sixteen. They both stood with their cell phones in hand, glancing at them every few seconds, as if the answers to all life's problems could be found on a four-inch LCD display.

Maybe they could, Byrne thought. He'd looked everywhere else, and so far came up empty.

"You guys are cops, right?" one of the girls asked.

"I'm not a cop," Torrance said.

It was technically true. Ray was an ex-cop. Byrne had not produced a badge or ID.

Torrance took the photograph out of his pocket. "I'm trying to find this girl," he said. "She's not in any trouble or anything. And you won't be in any trouble if you help us."

It was a high school photograph of Marielle Gray, one taken just a few weeks before she ran away from home. Ray Torrance had gotten it out of a yearbook he had purchased online.

One of the girls, the taller one, took the picture from Torrance and looked at it closely. When she was done she handed it to the other girl who did likewise.

"I like her earrings," the short one said. "Do you know where she got them?"

Byrne heard Ray Torrance take a deep breath, exhale. "No," he said. "I think they were a gift. Does she look familiar to you?"

The girl handed the photograph back, shook her head. "No," the girl said. "Sorry."

Torrance reached into his coat pocket, took out a coupon for a pizza place on South, courtesy of an old friend, a former detective from

Major Case who had recently opened a parlor. Torrance had been handing them out all night.

Torrance then pulled out a pencil, put the coupon on top of a newspaper box, scribbled his cell phone number on the back. "If you think of anything, like where you may have seen this girl, or who she might have hung out with, give me a call." He handed the coupon to the taller girl. "If not, this is good for a free slice."

The other girl looked hurt. Ray Torrance reached into his pocket, pulled out a second coupon, handed it to her. "One for you, too."

Both girls smiled.

"Just one other thing," Torrance said. He reached into his inner pocket, took out a picture of Dustin Green. "Do you know him?"

The girls looked at each other, then at the ground.

"You *do* know him," Torrance added.

"Yeah," the taller girl said. "We know Dusty. I heard he died. Is that, like, true?"

There was no reason to lie. The kid's death was probably in the paper. "Yeah," Byrne said. "He did."

"He said there was a guy he used to do things for," Torrance said. "An older guy."

"I know who you mean," the taller girl said.

"You do?"

"I think so. This guy would show up now and then. Always has money. Drives this really cool old car."

"A black car?" Byrne asked.

"Yeah."

"This guy, the guy with the black car," Torrance said, "could you describe him to a sketch artist?"

"No problem."

"Do you know his name?"

"Sure," the girl said. "His name is Luther."

54

Jessica stood over the printer, the fatigue a grand piano on her shoulders. She had soldiered through two morning classes, and still managed to get to the Roundhouse by ten a.m.

The transcripts of the recorded tape, sent by the detective in Estonia, had arrived in Byrne's email box at seven a.m. Jessica was making copies for all eight detectives on the task force.

The man the two street kids called Luther was a cipher. There was no record of him in any police database. There were plenty of men named Luther in the system, but none of them looked like the sketch made from the girls' description.

A copy of the sketch was in every sector car in the city of Philadelphia.

They had processed the MasterCard found in Joan Delacroix's purse, and found no trace evidence of blood or fingerprints. The card had been wiped clean with a bleach solution. There was only one plausible explanation, and that was that whoever had killed Cheque Marquez, had also killed Joan Delacroix.

The direct line between the two homicides had yet to be drawn.

Eight detectives, along with Sergeant Dana Westbrook and the captain of the homicide unit crowded into Westbrook's office. Each had a copy of the transcript—fifty-five pages in all—in hand.

Kevin Byrne stood at the front of the room.

He began to read:

January 12, 2:15 p.m.
Building G10
Subject: Eduard Kross
Träumen Sie?

Yes, I dream.

Where are you?

I am in Riisipere. A small village in Nissi County. Near the center of town. I have been walking for days. I smell of the road.

What is the year?

It is the spring of 1964.

What do you see?

I see a small town square, cut into quadrants. At the center is a crumbling bandstand. The structure is early Stalinist era, terrible construction, already falling down. Not enough sand for the mortar. To the right is a café. In front are four tables. No umbrellas. It is too early in the season.

Who is seated at the tables?

An elderly couple. The man wears a blue flannel coat with rips at the elbow. The woman is heavy. She seems to have no shape beneath her coat. Her hair is dyed an uncommon shade of red, far too young for her years. They are thick-waisted, thick-witted. Peasants. The man drinks a mug of ale. The woman just stares.

Who else is seated at the tables?

No one.

Can you see inside the café?

Yes. I can see a young woman. She is cleaning off one of the tables near the door.

She works at the café?

Yes.

Will you go inside?

I will.

Tell me what you see.

I enter the café. To the left is a bar, five or six stools. Another old man sits at the far end. In front of him is a small shot glass, filled to the brim. He stares at it, does not look up when I enter.

Do you sit down?

Yes. I sit at one of the tables, farthest from the door, farthest from the light.

What do you smell?

Cabbage, beets, fatty beef. Beneath it all is the stink of the provinces, cheap vodka, the sweat of the fields.

What of the young woman?

She is now standing next to my table, her right hand on her hip, waiting. She wears a much laundered dress with a soiled apron tied around her waist. She is very beautiful. Her eyes are ice gray, Slavic. Her lips are the color of coral.

Do you speak with her?

Yes. I order my food. A beef stew. Without a word, the young woman walks across the café, through the swinging doors, into the kitchen. A swirl of steam greets her. Soon she returns with my stew. The bowl is chipped and cracked. I notice she wears a ring on her left hand, a simple silver band, tarnished. I finish my stew, leaving the gristle on the table as a gratuity.

What do you do then?

I place a few coins, in the correct amount, on the bar top, and walk into the early evening air. I cross the square, and step onto the bandstand. I roll a cigarette, smoke it.

Are you alone?

I am.

What do you feel?

I feel the beast stir within me.

Can you describe the feeling?

No more than I could describe my own birth.

What do you do now?

I sit in the bandstand until it is full dark. Soon, the lights are extinguished in the café, the only illumination now are the gas lamps on the quadrant. The young woman exits the building, slips a padlock through a hasp. She pulls a scarf tightly around her throat and begins to walk north, into the darkness.

Do you follow?

Yes.

Where does she take you?

Through the forest. She seems to know the way, walking along a beaten path. We soon come to a clearing, then a gravel lane that runs parallel to the tracks. This is the line that leads to Tartu. We follow it for a full kilometer.

What do you see?

In the distance I see lights.

A farmhouse?

No. It is a small house, near the railroad tracks. I watch her enter. When it is safe, I walk up to the house, peer in the window.

What do you see?

I see her preparing dinner — peeling brown carrots. She is the station master's wife. I do not mean either of them harm. I just want to rob them. But the man sees me peering in the window. He picks up a rifle and puts it to my head. His name is Toomas Sepp.

What happens then?

He marches me to the stable, makes me lie down in the barn, in a pile of fresh manure. He says that this is where I belong. He freely insults my mother. He does not see the steel neck yoke on the floor, beneath the wet hay. I am able to subdue him with it.

What do you do then?

I tie the woman up in the stable. When I come out, I reenter the house, remove one of the wooden chairs, then take the chair to the center of the small field next to the barn.

Where is the man?

He is tied to the bumper of an old car. With a hammer in hand, I untie the man, and lead him to the chair. Along the way, I pick up an old spike laying next to the tracks. When he is seated I tell him to voice a prayer, if he knows one.

Does he pray?

Yes. I tell the man that if he gives his life, I will spare his wife.

Does he agree to this?

Yes. Sitting in the middle of the field, he holds the spike to the back of his head. I lift the hammer and bring it down with all my strength.

Träumen Sie?

Yes, Doctor. I dream.

For a long time, no one in the room said a word. What Byrne had just read was an account of Robert Freitag's murder, committed nearly fifty years earlier, halfway around the world. The circumstances were not the same, but the act was identical.

Over the next ten minutes or so they all read the rest of the transcripts in silence.

In 1966 Eduard Kross bludgeoned to death a woman named Etti Koppel, and left her body on the banks of the Narva River, large stones on her hands. He'd dressed her in the dark, placing her shoes on the wrong feet.

In 1970 he killed a Latvian businessman named Juris Spalva by suspending him between two trees with a steel wire wrapped around his neck.

In 1977 he killed a thief named Jaak Männik by cutting out his eyes.

Robert Freitag was Toomas Sepp.

Joan Delacroix was Etti Koppel.

Edward Richmond was Juris Spalva.

Ezequiel Marquez was Jaak Männik.

"As far as I know, this has never been published anywhere. No books or articles," Byrne said. "According to Peeter Tamm these murders are considered ancient history in Estonia. I asked him to look and see if he could find any books written on this Eduard Kross. He said he searched the libraries and the bookstores, and found none."

Dana Westbrook looked at the transcript for a few long moments. "Sorry to be such a dunce, but where is Estonia again?"

Byrne reached in the folder, produced a printout he had made from Google Maps.

"Tamm told me that a lot of the records — police records, birth and death certificates, marriage licenses, and the like — from the years of Soviet occupation were destroyed."

"So we're thinking that someone — this Luther — is basing these murders on this tape?" Westbrook asked.

"It's possible."

Westbrook held up the transcript. "What *is* this, though? He calls him 'Doctor' at the end of each session. Is this a therapy session with a psychiatrist?"

"I don't think so," Byrne said. "I think the voice on that tape is Eduard Kross himself, and I think he was dreaming when it was recorded. I think these are recollections from his life."

"How did our subject get hold of this?"

"I think he was a patient at Cold River when Joan Delacroix worked there," Byrne said. "I think he was a subject of this *Die Traumkaufleute* group. I think they created this monster, and now he is visiting this violence on them."

"But why now?" Westbrook asked. "It's been years. The place is shut down."

Byrne thought for a few moments. He looked out the window. The rain was pouring down in torrents. There was a flood advisory for the city in effect. He looked back at everyone in the room, and said: "I don't know."

A few minutes later, Jessica's cell phone rang. She stepped out of the office, took the call. When she stepped back in, everyone was gathering their belongings. She got Byrne's attention.

"I just heard from Martin Léopold's publishing house. They said they spoke to him, and that he would be delighted to talk to us."

"Delighted?"

"His word."

"That may be a first."

55

Torresdale was a neighborhood in the far northeast section of the city, bounded by the Delaware River to the east, Holmesburg to the south, and Bensalem in Bucks County. Long before there was a Main Line, this area of the city was considered the poshest address in Philadelphia. Torresdale was still home to Holy Family University.

The house was a large Edwardian mansion on a slight rise, one of the last surviving riverfront estates, just a few doors down from historic Glen Foerd. On the front grounds were a lily pond, a rose garden and a huge weeping hemlock. To the right, along the banks of the Delaware, was a boathouse, which looked to be in the process of restoration.

When Jessica and Byrne turned into the driveway, Jessica was struck by the meticulous care of the grounds. There was a landscaper pruning the hedges that bordered the path down to the river.

"I think we're underdressed," Jessica said.

Byrne put the car in park, cut the engine. "A badge is the best accessory," he said.

The woman who answered the door was in her sixties. She wore a high-collared black dress, buttoned to her throat, closed with a beautiful cameo brooch. Her fingers were long and delicate, her face powdered and smooth.

"May I help you?" she asked.

Jessica held up her ID. "My name is Jessica Balzano, this is my partner Detective Byrne."

The woman looked dumbstruck for a few moments.

"The police?" she finally asked, a slight tremble in her voice.

"Yes, ma'am," Jessica said. "Please don't be alarmed. Nothing's wrong."

The woman remained silent.

"Does Martin Léopold live here?" Jessica asked.

The woman brought a hand to her throat, fingered the brooch. "Yes."

"Is he in?"

Another hesitation. "I...of course. Yes."

"We'd just like a word with him," Jessica said. "If he's available."

After another pause, the woman opened the door fully. "May I take your coats?"

"That won't be necessary," Byrne said. "We won't be that long."

The foyer was octagonal in shape, with raised panel walls, and gleaming white quarry tile. Jessica noticed there wasn't a speck of dust anywhere.

The woman gestured toward a room off the foyer.

"Please wait in here."

The library was imposing. Three walls held polished mahogany bookshelves, floor to ceiling. There was a fire in the fireplace. A pair of dogs, young Weimaraners, circled and sniffed both Jessica and Byrne, then went back to their station beneath the table, their dark chocolate eyes shifting back and forth, their wagging tails betraying their excitement.

While Byrne perused the titles of the books on the shelves, Jessica scanned the rest of the room. There were oil paintings on the walls — one huge canvas was of an imposing man with a white beard, dressed in a late-twentieth-century naval officer's uniform. Another painting was of a beautiful valley with a church steeple in the distance.

The floors were lustrous hardwood. There was a stunning Sarouk rug. The house was clearly built at a time when the railroad men made their fortunes.

A few moments later Jessica heard the sound of hard soles on the quarry tile of the foyer.

"Detectives."

Both Jessica and Byrne turned to the sound of the voice.

The man entering the room was possibly in his seventies, but his posture was perfect, his eyes bright and clear. He wore a dark gray cardigan, black slacks, soft loafers. His hair was a gleaming silver, fluffy, as if just washed. He crossed the room to Jessica first, extending a hand.

"I am Martin Léopold."

Jessica took his hand. It was soft and smelled of a very expensive emollient. For a moment she thought the man was going to kiss her hand. He was that elegant.

"Jessica Balzano, Philly PD," she said. "Thank you for seeing us."

"You are most welcome." He turned to Byrne. "Martin Léopold."

As Byrne introduced himself, the two men shook hands.

The woman stood in the opening to the foyer, looking a little relieved now that Léopold was in the room and apparently the world was not coming to an end. At least for the moment.

Still, she seemed stuck in space.

"It's all right, Astrid," Léopold said to the woman.

He turned to his two guests. "May I offer you something? Coffee? Tea?"

Both Jessica and Byrne held up a hand. "We're fine, thanks," Jessica said.

"The coffee is a Fazenda Santa Ines," Léopold said. "A yellow bourbon. Astrid makes a beautiful cup. Might you reconsider?"

Jessica looked at Byrne, back. "That would be lovely."

Lovely? Who the hell says *lovely?* This place, this man, was having an effect on her.

Astrid waited a few more seconds. Léopold dismissed her with a nod. She closed the French doors, but Jessica could see the woman's silhouette behind the frosted glass. After a few more moments she padded off.

Before they got down to business Jessica made a quick scan of the wall of photographs opposite the fireplace. The pictures were of Martin Léopold, in this very room, posing with three former mayors of Philadelphia, the sitting governor and various luminaries from the world of Philadelphia art, medicine and industry.

Léopold turned back to his guests.

"And how may I assist the Philadelphia Police Department?" he asked.

"It's our understanding that you wrote a book about dream therapy," Byrne said.

"Yes," Léopold said. "A few years ago. More than that, now."

"Can you explain what dream therapy is?"

Léopold thought for a moment. "Briefly stated, dream therapy is employed by behavioral therapists in an attempt to understand a patient's psychology by recording and analyzing the patient's dreams."

"How available is this therapy?" Byrne asked.

"The interpretation of dreams goes back to the Egyptians and the Greeks, although I will say that most of the interest in it over the years has been shamanistic, used in the creation of prophecy."

"Are you saying the field is not taken seriously?"

"Oh, it most certainly is. There have been great strides in the last one hundred years, especially in the area of lucid dreaming."

"What is lucid dreaming?" Byrne asked.

"Lucid dreaming is where the subject *knows* that he or she is dreaming."

Jessica made a few notes. "What can you tell us about the research that was being done at the Delaware Valley State Hospital?"

Léopold took a few moments before responding. "I believe you are referring to a man named Godehard Kirsch."

"Yes," Jessica said.

Léopold walked over to the fireplace, stoked the logs. He replaced the stoker in the rack, then reached into the pocket of his cardigan, took from it a leather tobacco pouch. He held up his pipe, an expensive-looking Calabash. "Do you mind?"

"Not at all," Byrne said.

"It is my last remaining vice," Léopold said. "Although, at my age, it is one of the few in which I can still participate." He sat in a tall wing-back chair, next to the fireplace, motioned to Jessica and Byrne to sit down. "Please."

Jessica picked a leather chair. Byrne sat on the couch. Martin Léopold began the pipe smoker's ritual—cleaning, filling, tamping. A few moments later Astrid brought the coffee, served it. *Léopold was right,* Jessica thought. It was delicious.

"You ask about Godehard Kirsch," Léopold finally said.

"Yes," Byrne said.

"Alas, I don't know much. Kirsch was a bit of an enigma. He was an East German, so much of what he published—specifically his early work—did not make it out of the country, of course."

"And he worked in this field of dream therapy?"

"Yes. It is my understanding that he came to this country as some sort of brain trust exchange. I believe it was in the early nineteen nineties."

"This is when he came to Cold River?"

"Yes."

Jessica checked her notes. This was in sync with what they had learned from Miriam Gale.

"Did you ever meet the man?" Byrne asked.

"I did. Just once, and then for only a few moments. I found him quite courteous and engaging. As much as I would have loved to chat with him for hours, I was there to talk to some of his patients."

"Do the names Leonard Pintar or Lucius Winter ring a bell?"

Léopold thought for a moment. "No. Sorry."

"What about a man named Luther?"

"Again, I don't recall these names. Bear in mind, this was a long time ago, and I did not have unfettered access to patients there. Far from it. The interviews I was able to conduct were very controlled. There were always two staff members present, usually a therapist and an orderly."

"How many patients did you interview at Cold River?" Byrne asked.

"I would say no more than a few dozen. I was there in the waning days of the facility. Even though they knew I was writing, if not a scholarly work, one based on research, they saw me as a journalist of sorts. I was not trusted, to say the least."

"Were you allowed to ask questions about the dream research?"

Léopold nodded. "I was. But just in the very general sense."

"May I ask which field you are in?"

"I have degrees in both psychology and neurology." He crossed his legs, puffed the pipe, which seemed to have gone out.

"But all of this is ancient history in the field. The research being conducted now in this field is quite exciting. Recently, neuroscientists at MIT successfully engineered the content of dreams by replaying certain audio cues that correlated to the previous day's events."

"This was done with human subjects?" Byrne asked.

Léopold smiled. "No," he said. "This was done with rats. The research centers on the hippocampus, and the way that portion of the brain encodes those things we have experienced into memory. This has fascinated researchers for a hundred years. Perhaps more."

"So you're saying that the research being conducted at Cold River was in this area?"

"I can't say for sure. Keep in mind this is more than twenty years ago. If there was any research with human patients in this area, it would certainly not have been publicized. These experiments at MIT are less than a year old. Nobody really cares about rats, you see. But their dreams..."

Jessica checked her notes. "Mr. Léopold, we won't keep you much longer. Just a few more questions."

"Of course."

"When you were at Cold River, did you hear of a patient called Null?"

"Null? As in zero?"

"Zero?"

"Yes, null is the German word for zero. To answer your question, there was talk of a patient around whom the secretive research centered. I imagine a doctor of German extraction may have called him Null, or Patient Zero."

Jessica made the note. "One last question. Do you know what happened to Dr. Kirsch?"

"Dr. Kirsch perished in a fire at Cold River. I am told that almost all of his research went up in flames that day. Pity, on both counts."

Jessica looked at Byrne. He had no questions.

They all got to their feet.

When they reached the front door, Léopold paused. "One moment."

Léopold walked slowly back into the library. A few moments later he returned, a large book in hand. He handed it to Byrne. Jessica saw the title. *Nightworld*.

"This is your book," Byrne said.

Léopold nodded. "Pages 515 and 516 concern Godehard Kirsch," he said. "I would have written more but, alas, there simply was not enough data."

"I really appreciate this," Byrne said. "I'll take good care of it, and get it back to you as soon as possible."

Léopold held up both hands. "Consider it a gift. If it in any way helps with your investigation, I will be most pleased."

"Thank you, sir."

Léopold smiled. "Perhaps you can return here one day when you have more time. I would love to discuss with you the hostile mind."

"I would be honored." Before Byrne stepped onto the porch he asked one final question. "Does the term *Die Traumkaufleute* mean anything to you?"

"*Die Traumkaufleute?* The Dream Merchants?"

"Yes, do you recall ever hearing it before?"

"No," Léopold said. "But I think I now have a title if I ever write a sequel to my book."

They rode back to the Roundhouse in silence, both absorbing what they had learned from Martin Léopold. Byrne's theory of where Luther had found his blueprint for these murders was looking better and better.

What it did not provide, however, was what was going to happen next.

Rachel had changed her outfit four times already, and still wasn't satisfied. She hadn't quite gotten it through her head that this wasn't a showing. This was *her* house. *Bean's* house.

The buyer was due within the hour.

She had thought about calling in Denise to do a little staging, but decided against it. What would be the point? The buyer had offered $75,000 more than the house was worth. There was no way, or point, to try to improve on that.

Earlier in the day she made a ritual of burning all the maps she had collected, all the data and diagrams on the houses in her neighborhood, the dossiers she had compiled on everyone who had moved into the neighborhood over the past few years, trying to find someone who might have been the tall man in ragged clothes, trying to locate the path they had taken that night.

That episode in her life, when the raggedy man had come to visit, and where he brought her and Marielle, was part of her past.

The fact that she might never know what happened to her sister was a reality with which she would have to one day come to terms. Selling this house, and all the ghosts it contained, was the first step.

Rachel looked out the window for the hundredth time. It occurred to her that she should have gotten some other agent from the office to handle this showing. It was too late for that.

She thought about having a glass of wine to calm her nerves a little, then ruled that out.

Instead, she paced the living-room rug in front of the picture window, until it occurred to her that this is exactly what her mother used to do when she was drinking.

Rachel sat down, and waited.

57

Luther crouched in the hallway underneath the lobby of what had once been G10. The voices of everyone who had ever passed through these corridors echoed in his mind. Hubert Tilton lying wasted in his bed. White Rita lying dead at the end, her trail of afterbirth glimmering under the flickering lights.

Luther began to run, past and present now one continuum, the lights of the dream arcade blistering by, the eyes of a thousand dead watching, judging.

You know what you have to do.

He crawled through the crawl space, barely fitting his body beneath the bridging overhead, rending new seams in the tattered suit.

Luther thought for a moment of stopping, of spending the rest of his time here, wasting away in this tight space like old Hubert Tilton, his bones found by some future contractor.

Tap, tap, tap.

The digging machines were close.

Luther looked up, his energy all but spent, saw the dim light coming from the vent. At one time he would have taken the time to carefully remove the vent from the block. Instead, he positioned his body, found purchase in the compacted earth, and kicked out the aluminum grate with one thrust.

He dropped into the room, reached into his pocket, took out the sealed bag, the bag containing the cloth. Even through the plastic he could smell the ether.

A few minutes later he made his way slowly up the steps.

Träumen Sie?

    Yes.

Where are you?

    Hotel Telegraaf.

What is the year?

    1980. I am here to see someone.

Who?

    A woman from my past. She is the widow of the man who killed
    my mother and father. The man who killed Kaisa. Frau Abendrof.

What will become of her?

    I will take her to my home, and keep her until she dies.

You will take her to the black room?

    Yes.

Luther opened his eyes. He was standing in the middle of a room.

He looked to his right, saw a woman standing near, just as she had many years ago.

The woman turned around, surprised.

Luther stepped forward, rag in hand, and said: "Hello, Tuff."

58

Jessica made her notes about the visit with Martin Léopold. She wasn't sure that they had learned anything new, but she noticed that the three binders were starting to bulge with documents. She had already used up two full notebooks on the Robert Freitag case alone.

Ray Torrance had been useful in the investigation. Byrne had recounted how the two men had gotten the information about the man named Luther—which was what they now called the man they were hunting—the night before. Torrance was by no means an official presence, he did not have a badge, but everyone, brass on down to patrol officers, respected his presence.

The plan, at least for the moment, was for Jessica, Byrne and Ray Torrance to get a bite to eat, and then come back to the Roundhouse to plug all this information into the picture.

The picture shattered at just before nine p.m.

It was Byrne's iPhone ringing. They looked at the incoming call.

It was from Joan Delacroix. It was a call from the grave.

"Get Mateo up here," Byrne yelled.

A few seconds later Byrne answered his phone. In an instant, a man's face appeared on the screen.

It was the face of a killer.

FOUR

59

In her time as a homicide detective, one thing that Jessica Balzano had learned was that you could not judge a suspect by his appearance.

The man on the screen, the man responsible for at least four homicides, was ordinary in every way. He looked to be in his late thirties. He had dark hair, dark eyes. He was clean shaven.

In the duty room, off to the sides, out of range of the cell phone's camera lens, stood Dana Westbrook, Josh Bontrager, Maria Caruso, John Shepherd, Mateo Fuentes and Ray Torrance.

"Your name is Luther?" Byrne asked.

"No," the man said. "Luther is asleep."

"I see. Who are you, then?"

"My name is Eduard Kross."

He is fully gone, Jessica thought. *He has become the madman in his dreams.*

"How do we meet, Mr. Kross?" Byrne asked.

Luther stared into the camera. "We will meet soon. There is something you must do for me first."

"I'll do what I can," Byrne said. "But I need to know what it is before I commit."

"I want the little girl."

A stunned silence filled the room.

"I'm not sure I know what you mean," Byrne said.

"The little girl. She got away from me by mistake. I left the doors unlocked, she climbed out of her bed and simply walked up the stairs of an old SEPTA maintenance shed, and into the night. You know how the little ones are."

"Sure," Byrne said. "You have to watch them every minute."

"I want you to bring the girl to the Priory Park Station. I want you to put her at the bottom of the steps at the street level, then I want you to walk away. You will come alone. I want her there in exactly one hour."

Jessica glanced at the wall clock. The station was less than a thousand feet from the eastern edge of Priory Park. Even if they would consider such a thing—which they never would—it could hardly happen.

"Please look at your watch, Detective."

Byrne did.

"What time do you have?" Luther asked.

"It is 9:01."

"Very well." On-screen Luther reset his watch. "We now have precisely the same time, so there can be no miscalculations. I detest them. Do you?"

"Yes," Byrne said.

"You—and you alone—will bring her to the station. I will be watching."

Jessica looked at the wall behind the man. It was gray, a bit scarred, probably painted concrete block. It was as nondescript a marker as you could imagine. He could have been anywhere in the city.

But if he was going to be at the rendezvous point within an hour, Jessica thought, he could only be so far away. Jessica heard rustling on the other side of the duty room. Maria Caruso was pinning a large map on the wall.

"Sixty minutes is not a lot of time," Byrne said.

"If it is something you want to do, it can be done."

"I know my bosses, and this is not something they *ever* do. I'm not optimistic about this."

Luther stepped away from the camera. A few moments later he returned.

"I've known many police over the years, Detective. Most, I would say, were honorable men. Some were driven by power, the kind of power that allowed them, through the authority of the badge, to exert superiority over other men. Many were driven by a sense of duty. I believe you are one of the latter."

Byrne said nothing. Everyone in the room was waiting for the shoe to drop. Madmen like Luther did not make demands without an "or else" attached.

On-screen Luther held up what looked to be a thick sheaf of computer printouts, old-style pages with the holes on the sides, printed on a dot matrix printer. He riffled the paper.

"Do you know what I have here, Detective?"

Byrne removed his suit coat, draped it over the back of the chair. "No," he said. "I do not."

"This is a printout of the names and addresses of more than twelve hundred former employees of Cold River. The list was printed in the administration offices at the hospital in nineteen ninety-two. That said, being more than twenty years ago, one has to assume that some of these people are dead. I think there is no question of that. You and I both know the tragic inevitability of death. Would you agree with me on this point?"

"Yes," Byrne said.

Luther thumbed the pages again. "I think it also safe to assume that some of them moved away from Philadelphia. Again, a surety. Agreed?"

"Agreed."

"So, let us be generous in our estimations. Let us say that half the people on this list have either died or moved away from the city in the past twenty years. That would leave six hundred people."

Byrne waited a few seconds before responding. "I'm not sure what your point is, Mr. Kross. I need some help here."

"Forgive me. I think you'll agree that it is quite likely that these six hundred people have family—wives, husbands, sons, daughters, all of them now sitting comfortably and safely in their homes, their futures bright and assured, partly because of the good work, the vigilance, of the Philadelphia Police Department."

Jessica noticed that the entire time this man had been speaking he had not once raised his voice, or showed any stress at all.

"I digress," Luther continued. "Here is my proposal to you, Detective. You now have less than sixty minutes to deliver the girl to me. She is rightly mine, not yours. If you do not deliver the child to me, I will begin to work my way down this list."

Byrne said nothing.

Jessica saw Dana Westbrook step to the far end of the duty room. She picked up a phone, punched in a number. She would begin to scramble the necessary personnel.

"I know exactly where to begin," Luther said. "I have already visited many of their homes in anticipation of a stalemate such as this. Granted, I did not think the stakes would be quite this high, but we find ourselves on opposite sides of this chasm, and now we must deal with the space between us."

Jessica glanced at Byrne. She saw the muscles in his neck cording tightly. She knew that he wanted to jump through the screen and take this guy down. She also knew that he was a detective with more than two decades' experience. Negotiation was part of the job.

"Mr. Kross, as I'm sure you can appreciate, you've put me in a difficult position. My job, a job I've had for a very long time, is about saving lives, about preventing the sort of thing you're talking about."

"I understand. Do you think I'm bluffing?"

"No, I do not. But the scenario with which I have been presented is delicate. I'm only a police officer. The decisions about things like this are made way above my pay grade."

Luther looked directly into the lens. "Perhaps I afforded you too much credit," he said. "For a time I thought you a worthy adversary. I was tracked for thirty years through the Estonian and Latvian countryside without success."

My God, Jessica thought. *This man truly believes he is Eduard Kross. Whatever walls existed in his mind between himself and his engineered dreams had crumbled. His speech had even begun to affect a Baltic accent.*

"Let us see who is first on my list." He lifted the ream of computer printouts, glanced at the first page. "Lillian White. Aged seventy-one years."

Out of the corner of her eye, Jessica saw Josh Bontrager sit down at a computer terminal. He tapped a few keys. He was looking for a Lillian White.

"She worked at Cold River for nearly fourteen years. She was an administrative assistant. I remember her. She always smelled of ointment and spearmint candy. None of the latter was ever offered to me."

Byrne just listened. Jessica glanced at Josh Bontrager. He shook his head. He did not have Lillian White's address yet. He continued tapping keys on the keyboard.

Luther stood up, leaned against the wall behind him. He crossed his arms. "Lillian Georgette White. I assume this woman is unknown to you, Detective. I mean, personally. Am I correct?"

With this new information, that being the woman's middle name, Josh Bontrager found her address. He hit the print key on the keyboard, then sprinted from the duty room. From the hallway, out of Luther's earshot, Bontrager would send out the call. Sector cars would be en route to the address within seconds.

"Yes," Byrne said. "She is unknown to me."

"But not, I predict, for long. If you are as efficient as I believe you to be, I am certain that, armed with this woman's full name, you have determined her address. Do you think you can get there in time to save her life?"

Byrne hesitated, buying a few seconds. "I don't know. Maybe yes, maybe no. On the other hand, there doesn't have to be the need to do so. Why don't we meet somewhere and discuss it?"

"Time is such an intangible *précis*. What is a moment to you may be an eternity to someone else."

Jessica glanced at the door to the duty room. Josh Bontrager gave her the signal that sector cars had been dispatched. Jessica wrote a note to that effect and put it on the desk in front of Byrne.

"Why would you bring harm to this woman?" Byrne asked. "Was she in some manner responsible for what happened to you at Cold River?"

"No," Luther said. "But she is *your* game piece, not mine."

Game, Jessica thought. *This man thinks this is all a game.*

"I fear you will not make it to her home in time, Detective."

Byrne cleared his throat. Another stall. "Why is that?"

"Because I am already there."

At this the man turned the camera. On-screen now was a thin, white-haired woman, sitting in an upholstered dining-room chair. There was duct tape around her chest. Both her arms were taped to the arms of a chair.

Next to her, on a TV tray, was a pair of poultry shears.

Luther stepped behind the woman. "Have you ever seen a horticulturalist at work?"

"Wait," Byrne said.

"Give me the girl, Detective."

Without a word Luther picked up the shears, placed the blades around the thumb of the woman's left hand, and snapped them shut.

The woman screamed. A thick spray of blood burst forward, dotting the lens in crimson.

Luther held the woman by her hair until her body went limp. He wiped the shears on her dress.

"Nine more fingers, ten toes," he said. "Perhaps she will be a dolphin."

He walked up to his camera, looked directly into the lens from just a few inches away. His face filled the screen.

"Life is a ladder of regret, Detective. Up one rung for the things you have done. Down two for the things you have not."

"Mr. Kross," Byrne began. "Don't—"

"The thing you did not do is agree to give me what I want. Down two rungs, Detective Byrne."

Luther glanced at his watch. "If you are thinking about contacting the media and having them broadcast a warning to all former personnel of the Delaware Valley State Hospital, I would advise against it." He held up the list of names. "Hundreds of people, all in different locations. I will begin to visit them one by one if I see or hear even one mention of this in the media."

Luther looked at his cell phone camera, tapped a few buttons. Seconds later, on the screen, there was what looked to be a live web cam shot of a young woman sitting on the floor, a petite young woman with blond hair clipped into a boyish cut. Her eyes were closed, but she appeared to be breathing. Jessica saw no blood or injuries.

"Look at her, and tell me what you see."

"I see an innocent person," Byrne replied.

"Very well. Know this, Detective. If you don't give me what I ask, this young woman will be the last to die tonight, and you will watch every second of her agony."

"Wait," Byrne said. "You don't have to do this."

Luther looked at his watch. "You now have forty-four minutes. We will meet soon."

"*Wait.*"

"You know what you have to do."

When the screen went black, everyone in the room looked at Mateo.

He had been standing behind Byrne, next to Ray Torrance, out of camera range. In his hand was a small HD camcorder. He had recorded the exchange.

"Did we get a capture?" Westbrook asked.

"Yes," Mateo said. "Crude, but we've got it."

"Get a freeze-frame of his face, and get it out to every district."

Jessica glanced at Byrne, then at the clock.

Forty-two minutes.

60

The eight detectives crowded around a huge map of Philadelphia, posted on the wall in the duty room. Dana Westbrook put four push-pins around the area that included the Priory Park Station. Around them she pulled a length of string, and cordoned off the area.

"We're going to deploy here, here and here," Westbrook said, indicating the northern, eastern, and western ends of the station. "Is anyone familiar with the station up there?"

No one answered.

Westbrook turned to Maria Caruso. "Get someone from SEPTA down here. Tell them to bring maps showing any access tunnels, as well as all the tracks leading to and from that platform."

Maria Caruso rolled her chair over to a desk, got on the phone.

"I think I need to go in alone," Byrne said. "I don't think there's any doubt that he's going to carry out these threats."

Westbrook thought about this. "Obviously we're not going to give him the girl," she said. "But we've got to make him think we are going to."

"I'm not sure how we're going to do that," Byrne said. "I think he's a little too smart for any tricks."

"If Luther calls again, can we track him?" Westbrook asked.

"If he calls using Joan Delacroix's iPhone, we can locate him with the Find My iPhone app."

Westbrook looks at Mateo. "Are we set up to do that here?"

"We can do it from any computer terminal, but we need to know the Apple ID and password."

"Do we have that?" Westbrook asked.

Jessica shook her head. "James Delacroix is the only one who has it. I'll call him." Jessica walked across the duty room, took out her phone. She scrolled down to James Delacroix's number, called him. She got his voice mail, left a message, stating only that it was very important that he give her a call back. She clicked off, waited a few moments, tried again. She got the same result.

Jessica crossed the duty room. "No answer," she said.

"If we don't get that information, is there a way to pinpoint his location?" Westbrook asked.

"We might be able to," Jessica said. "If he stays on for a while, I think we can track him."

Westbrook thought for a few moments.

"Jess, I want you to get over to RCFL," Westbrook said. "They are a lot better equipped to handle things like this than we are here."

The Regional Computer Forensic Lab was near Villanova University.

"I'll get on the phone and talk to the commander of the unit," Westbrook said. "I'll see if we can scramble their best tracker. In the meantime, keep trying James Delacroix's number."

"I think Kevin should have my iPhone and his, plus a TracFone," Jessica said. "If Kevin takes my iPhone we'll be able to track him through GPS. If our guy calls Kevin again, he can talk to him on his phone."

"Write down all these numbers before you leave," Westbrook said. She turned to all her detectives. "Are we clear on our assignments here?"

Everyone nodded.

"We're going to have SWAT deployed at four vantage points. Jessica, you're at the computer lab. Josh, you will be point man here. Maria, I need you to monitor radio. There's going to be a lot of chatter in the next hour or so. I need you to hear everything I don't."

Westbrook turned to John Shepherd. "John, I think you should get down to the little girl's foster home. We don't know what this guy knows, or what he might find out. Go pick up the girl, and bring her here."

"Got it."

Once again Byrne went through his notes. He scribbled the address of the emergency foster home on a blank page, tore it off, handed it to John Shepherd. Shepherd grabbed it, and left the duty room.

Westbrook looked at her detectives.

"We don't negotiate," Westbrook said. "We take this man down, and we come back safe."

As Jessica grabbed her coat, and one of the two-way radios from the charging rack, she glanced at the clock over the door leading out of the duty room. It was 9:22. If they were to take this killer at his word, someone was going to die in thirty-eight minutes.

Byrne put on a Kevlar vest. As he was pulling the Velcro tabs tight he thought about Luther's victims. Robert Freitag, Joan Delacroix, Edward Richmond. They were three of the four people who made up the Dream Merchants, a research group that had implanted evil from one man to another.

When the leader of the group died in that fire, and the man who now calls himself Eduard Kross had been loosed into the world, Byrne wondered if Godehard Kirsch's dying thoughts had reconciled what he had done with what was to come.

Had he known? Was Luther the first? Have there been other patients along the way who did not have the potential, or were not as receptive as Luther?

And why now?

Life is a ladder of regret.

As Byrne checked the action on his Glock 17 and replaced it in his holster, it came to him. The answer was in that dusty shoebox in the ceiling of Robert Freitag's row house. That's what that page from the *Inquirer* was all about. The only article that mattered was the one about the condominium construction in the Northeast.

It was on the site where Cold River once stood.

They were going to dig up the bodies.

Luther, or whatever his name really was, was getting rid of people who knew the secrets buried in that park. And that meant not only the people who were members of the research team—*Die Traumkaufleute*—but perhaps any other members of the administration staff at Cold River.

Byrne didn't want to do it, but there really was no choice.

He ran back to the duty room, found Dana Westbrook, proposed his plan. After a few long moments, she agreed to run it by the brass.

On the way down to the parking lot behind the Roundhouse, Byrne sent the text message.

61

Rachel awoke in darkness. Her head pounded.

She had not had the dream in years, the dream of walking through tunnels, hand in hand with the man in raggedy clothes. There was a time in her life, a time when she dreamed about nothing else. In each of those dreams she had tried to see the man's face, but every time she looked at him, his face was blank—no eyes, no mouth. Just his soft voice, speaking a language she did not understand.

Her head milled, her eyes throbbed.

She was sitting on the floor. She felt around. The floor was concrete, cold, pitted.

Beyond this, she dared not move, not yet. She could tell by her breathing that she was in a small room, a *very* small room.

"Marielle," she said, softly, just to get a gauge on the echo. There was none. She slowly lifted her right hand, touched something soft. She closed her hand around it. It was a forgiving material, maybe wool. A coat.

She was in a closet.

As her eyes adjusted to the darkness, she saw that there was a line of dim light coming from under the door. To her right were a few pairs of shoes, small shoes, lined up against the wall. She could not see colors, but she could see that two pairs of the shoes were sneakers; two were hard soled.

On one of the hooks above she could barely make out a few shapes. One of the things hanging from a hook looked like a terry-cloth bathrobe.

Another hook had something shiny hanging from it. Rachel reached out, touched it. It was a rain slicker.

No, Rachel thought. *It can't be.*

She then heard sounds coming from the room beyond the door, the faint sounds of a television, an old show that she used to watch when she was small.

Rachel slowly reached up, found the doorknob, turned it to the right. It was not locked. She stood, opened the door slowly, and stepped into the room.

The room was white, brightly lighted, and it took a few moments for her dark-adapted eyes to adjust. To the right she saw a white dresser and a hope chest. She saw two single beds, both aligned along the far wall, the low headboards meeting at a single nightstand. On the nightstand was a lamp, a few small knickknacks in the shape of turtles. There was also a book.

The tears began to well in Rachel's eyes before she crossed the room to the nightstand. She picked up the book. It was *Goodnight, Moon* by Margaret Wise Brown.

It wasn't possible, but it was all here. All of it.

She was in her bedroom, the one in which she and Marielle had grown up. It was their room, right down to the last detail.

The faint noise of the television continued. After a few moments Rachel heard something else, the sound of a voice coming from behind her.

"Once upon a time there were two little girls named Tuff and Bean," came the voice, a voice Rachel knew well, a voice she had not heard in many years.

It was her mother.

62

Byrne stood on the upper level of the platform at the Priory Park Station. The rain fell in torrents, rolling off the roof of the shelter in waves. Because of the storm, SEPTA had suspended service. What street traffic there was crawled along.

The train platform, on both levels, was deserted.

From his vantage point on the upper level, Byrne had a visual on the drop-off point, that being the bottom of the steps on the street level. Every few seconds he checked to make sure all his devices were on, and online. Luckily, they all showed almost fully charged batteries.

On the way to the train station Byrne was told that a patrol car from the 3rd District had taken Colleen up to Sunnyvale to meet with Miriam Gale. Because of the urgency of the moment, and the possibility of blowback if something went terribly wrong with the operation—and there was a good chance that might happen—Dana Westbrook had to run the idea of bringing a civilian into the operation a few rungs up the chain of command. A call had first gone out to the department's handful of connections who spoke ASL. None were immediately available.

The one thing in favor of the plan to enlist Colleen Byrne was that she had a connection—albeit brief—with the old woman.

As Byrne huddled against the wall in the train station, he checked his watch.

It was 9:50.

63

The Regional Computer Forensic Lab was a state-of-the-art facility in Radnor, Pennsylvania. Funded by the FBI, its purview was to support state and local enforcement with the examination of digital evidence—computers, GPS devices, cell phones, PDAs, video.

A good deal of the work done at the lab was extracting deleted data from computer hard drives, as well as data on cell phones.

Instead of driving herself in a department car, and taking the chance of getting caught in traffic, Jessica rode in a sector car, lights and siren all the way. They took the Schuylkill Expressway north, having to slow down a few times due to flooding.

Jessica was met at the door by the deputy director of the lab, Lt. Christopher Gavin. Gavin whisked her through the night security station.

"Have you been briefed?" Jessica asked on the way.

"I have," Gavin said. "I just got off the phone with Sergeant Westbrook. This guy sounds like a piece of work."

Jessica had worked with Chris Gavin in her rookie year in the 6th District, and then again when she was working with the Auto Theft Unit.

Gavin began his career as a radar man in the Navy, then became a patrol officer, making his bones in the tough Richard Allen projects in the 1980s when Philly was burning due to the crack wars. He rapidly advanced to Sergeant and, in the late 1990s, when the need arose, started the computer unit, then housed in the basement of the 1st District headquarters. In 2006, when federal funding came through, he established the RCFL. Since that time his lab had been instrumental in the investigation and prosecution of every aspect of computer crime.

"How's your father?" Gavin asked.

"He's good," Jessica said. "Thanks for asking."

They walked into the computer lab at ten minutes to ten. The room was large and dimly lighted, with a dozen workstations. At this hour there were only three analysts at work.

"What do you know about the process?" Gavin asked.

"Not much. We've used it a few times, but that was back in the stone age."

"You mean like three years ago?"

Jessica smiled. "Something like that," she said. "Back when cell phones were tracked by triangulation."

The process of triangulating the location of a cell phone was based on signal strength and, as the name implied, three cell towers. While accuracy with triangulation was accurate—sometimes within a few hundred feet—GPS tracking could often pinpoint a signal with extreme precision.

"We still do some triangulation," Gavin said. "But you're right. Almost everything is GPS now. Most smartphones have it built in."

"What do we need for this to work?"

"There is only one must, and that is that the cell phone must be turned on. If the cell phone is turned off, or the battery is removed, we're sunk."

Jessica related the details of tracking Joan Delacroix's cell phone to Priory Park.

"This is good," Gavin said. "Are you sure your subject is using that phone now?"

"Yes. My partner entered the woman's contact information on his phone, and when our guy called earlier it came up. It's the same phone."

"Also good. Keep in mind, if he swaps out the SIM card, he's gone."

"We wouldn't be able to track it if he does that?"

"No," Gavin said. He sat down at a computer terminal, one with a thirty-inch HD monitor. Jessica pulled up a chair next to him.

"What is the Apple ID?" Gavin asked.

"For my phone?"

"The other user," Gavin said. "The subject."

"I don't know it," Jessica said. "When we initially tracked her phone to Priory Park, it was entered by the victim's brother. I put in two calls to him, but he hasn't called back."

"Well, we're going to need it to track the phone."

Jessica took out her notepad, frantically flipped the pages. She found what she was looking for. James Delacroix's phone number. She called it, but within four rings she got his voice mail.

"Mr. Delacroix, this is Jessica Balzano again. I need you to call me immediately."

Jessica left all pertinent phone numbers, starting with the phone number to the direct line on the desk at which she was sitting.

"What can we do while we're waiting?" Jessica asked.

"We can set up tracking on both your iPhone and Detective Byrne's iPhone."

Jessica wrote down the information in her notebook, handed it to Gavin. He keyed in the information. Jessica was amazed at the speed of his typing. Within a minute there was a split screen on the LCD monitor in front of them. Gavin typed a few more entries. Now there were identical street maps on both sides of the screen. A few more keystrokes brought the images closer, showing maybe a five-block area on each side. A small blue icon was positioned in the same place on both maps.

Gavin tapped the screen on the left. "This is Detective Byrne's position, tracking your iPhone." He tapped the screen on the right. "This is his iPhone. As long as he keeps them both on, we'll be able to track his movements. If, for some reason, the two devices begin to move in different directions, we'll be able to see where they're going."

Jessica called James Delacroix's phone again. Once more she got his voice mail. They couldn't wait any longer. She called the Comm Unit, gave them Delacroix's address, and instructions to send a sector car there.

Gavin stood up. "Want some coffee? It's fresh."

Jessica thought about it. Her nerves were completely jangled already. But now was no time to go on the wagon. "Yeah," she said. "That would be good."

As Chris Gavin walked across the computer lab Jessica turned her attention back to the screen.

64

The downpour was relentless.

From his vantage point above street level, Byrne could see a SEPTA van a few blocks away. He knew that the workers were attaching plywood covers to the sidewalk ventilation grates to prevent flooding belowground.

At 9:55 Byrne's phone buzzed. He looked at it. It was a FaceTime call from Colleen. He did not know if he was standing in enough light for his daughter to see him. One more step out of the shelter and he would be soaked.

He answered the call, held the phone up at arm's length. He then realized that he could not sign with one hand. He looked around the shelter. There was a newspaper case for an independent paper, a sleazy tabloid called *The Report*.

Finally good for something, Byrne thought. He walked over to the newspaper case, put the phone down on top of it, leaned it against the handle.

He looked at the screen. Colleen was warm and dry. At that moment she again looked like his little girl. It was a mistake to have brought her into this, he thought. Too late for that.

"Hi, Dad," Colleen signed.

"Are you at Sunnyvale?"

Colleen nodded. "I am. Somebody called the administrator while I was on my way up here. It's all set. They're waking up Miriam now."

"Do you know what you need to ask her?"

"I think so," Colleen signed. "We want to know if she remembers the names of any of the people who worked in administration at Cold River in the last few years it was open."

We, Kevin thought. It suddenly occurred to him that he might just have put his daughter in harm's way. "Are there officers there with you?"

Colleen smiled. She picked up her phone, and angled the camera down the hallway. There stood two rather large young patrol officers. Colleen brought the camera back around to herself.

"I'm fine, Dad. Eddie and Rich know who you are. They're going to take care of me."

Eddie and Rich. His daughter had a way of getting to know everyone in about two minutes. "Okay."

"Is there anything else you want me to ask Miriam?"

Byrne thought for a few moments. "Ask her first about the names of any administration staff who were specifically involved in G10. We need those names first, if she has them. First and last names, middle names or initials will help."

Colleen nodded in understanding. "If she remembers the names, how do I get them to you?"

"Just text them to me, and I'll get them over to dispatch. Make sure that we start with G10 personnel, and work from there. If she happens to know whether any of these people still live in Philadelphia, it would be really helpful."

Colleen looked offscreen for a moment. Byrne heard someone speaking to her from down the hallway. Colleen must have picked up the meaning of what was being said to her. She nodded, held up a finger, meaning she would be right along.

"They just told me that Miriam is awake and alert. She's sitting up in bed, waiting for me."

"Okay, honey," Byrne said. He almost said *be careful,* but she was probably in one of the safest places in the tri-county area this evening. Especially with Eddie and Rich on the case.

"Text me if and when you get something."

"I will," Colleen signed. "I love you."

"I love you, too," Byrne replied.

But his screen had already gone black.

If Luther could be trusted to follow through with both his threats and his promises, he had to be within ten minutes or so of the drop-off point—if, indeed, he did not have accomplices, and that was a big if. There were more than a dozen detectives deployed in a broad circle of the area surrounding the train platform. In addition, sector cars patrolling the area were on a high alert to take a call at a split-second's notice.

Add to this the imminence of the full force of the storm bearing down on the city, and there was a good chance that all of this would go wrong, and more people would die.

As the wind buffeted the shelter with cold rain, Byrne stared at his phone, willing it to make the sound that signaled a new text message had arrived.

The phone remained silent.

The anticipation was maddening.

Byrne wondered if Jessica had made it to the computer lab yet, and if they had tracking set up on his devices.

He stepped back into the shadows, took out his cell phone, one that belonged to the homicide unit, an untraceable TracFone. He speed-dialed Jessica.

"I'm here," she said.

"Do you have me on-screen?"

"We do. Everyone is in position," Jessica said. "All on standby."

"Do we have a fix on our subject?"

"No," Jessica said. "We don't have the phone's Apple ID. Without that, we can't track him."

"So we have no idea where he is right now?"

"No," Jessica said. "We've got a sector car en route to James Delacroix's house. Should be there any second."

"And if we don't find him we're flying blind?"

Jessica didn't like to tell anyone in the field that they were a target, especially her partner. "Unfortunately, yes."

Byrne heard a landline ring in the background where Jessica was. Jessica answered. "Yeah, Sarge."

It was their boss, Dana Westbrook. Byrne heard Jessica say *okay* a few times. He knew his partner well. She was not happy.

Jessica got back on the line with Byrne. "We've got a problem, Kevin."

"What's wrong?"

"Sector car went to James Delacroix's house. They knocked, rang the bell. Nothing. They went around back, looked in the window. They saw blood on the floor. The patrol officers then took down Delacroix's door and found him in the basement."

"What happened?"

"Hard to tell. But they said he was in a pool of blood."

Byrne gripped the phone tight enough to break it. "What's his status?"

"They found a pulse. EMS is on the way, but they're stretched pretty thin tonight, and half the main arteries are flooded."

Byrne hated to ask the question that needed to be asked. "What about the information we need?"

"They did a quick walk through. They did not find his laptop. They said the charging cable was on the floor in the dining room."

"That's where he used it when we were there."

"Yeah."

"What's our next step?"

"There's only one. We're going to need to get a warrant to track Joan Delacroix's phone."

"Is it in the works?"

"Maria Caruso is typing it up now. We've Paul DiCarlo at the DA's office standing by, and a judge on his way to the office. As soon as his pen hits the paper Chris will be on the line with Delacroix's carrier."

Jessica glanced at the clock every ten seconds. It had never once worked to make the process speed up, but she couldn't help herself. When she took her eyes off the clock she looked at the large LCD monitor, at the two identical maps, at the icons at the center of each.

She knew that Byrne was not out there alone—there were a dozen armed personnel within a block or so—but you could not tell that by looking at the maps.

On the maps he looked completely isolated.

When the desk phone rang at 9:59 Jessica nearly jumped.

"Balzano."

"We've got it," Westbrook said.

Within a minute they had the GPS coordinates for Joan Delacroix's phone. A few seconds later they saw a second icon show up on both sides of the map. A red icon.

It was Luther. Jessica got Byrne on his TracFone.

"Kevin. We've got the warrant."

"Do you have a fix on our subject?"

"We do. He's a block away. He's moving east on Chancel Lane."

"Does anyone have a visual?"

Jessica checked with tactical. "No," she said. "Not yet."

The red icon moved closer and closer to the green icon in the center of the screen.

"Subject is closer," Jessica said. "A hundred yards."

"Still on Chancel?"

"On Chancel."

"I can't see anything."

On-screen the icon's progress slowed. For a moment it appeared to be sidetracking north. Jessica again checked with tactical, both on the ground and on the rooftops. No one had yet made visual contact.

Suddenly the icon began to move. Fast. It was on a course directly to Byrne's position.

"Kevin, he's on the move again. He's heading right toward you."

No response.

"Kevin."

Nothing but static.

The red icon on the screen disappeared. Jessica turned to Chris Gavin.

"What happened?" she asked.

"He must have turned the phone off," Gavin said. "We lost him."

65

Luther stood on the roof of a shuttered fabric store, just a block from the Priory Park Station. The only movement was the river of water rushing down Chancel Lane.

He looked at his watch. It was ten o'clock.

He had turned off the phone less than a block away, knowing that every second it was on they could see him, could track his movements.

Luther scanned the train platform at the end of the street, saw the figure standing on the upper level, a dark blue gouache against the darker backdrop of the shelter. He saw no smaller figure standing with the man.

Perhaps the girl was behind him. Perhaps she was in the stairwell leading down to the lower level of the platform. Luther wanted to believe these things, but he did not.

They had betrayed him. They believed he would not make good on his promise.

They would see who he was. If they did not know the legend of Eduard Kross by now, they would very soon.

When he reached the portal at State Road he did not bother to open the door with his keys. Instead, he pulled back and rammed his fist through the glass.

He entered the dusty space, ran down the steps into the basement. He could hear the rain pelting the roof, the drip of water through the holes in the ceiling.

He pulled the vent off the wall, and shimmied through.

Träumen Sie?

Yes, I dream.

Where are you?

I am in Tartu. Near the university. It is night.

What is the year?

It is the autumn of 1957. There are heavy rains. The streets are flooded.

Where are you going?

I am going to the home of a streetcar conductor.

Why will you do this?

I am going to visit him because he humiliated me. I did not have the full fare for a ride of just a few blocks, but instead of showing me off the streetcar, he felt the need to ridicule me. To ridicule my clothing. He called me *kerjus*.

A beggar.

Yes.

What will you do when you see him?

I will teach him the grace of civility.

How will this lesson be taught?

My blade is keen. I think he will understand.

Will you leave his children orphans?

No. His children will not be orphans.

And why is this?

I will also teach them a lesson.

Five minutes later Luther stood across the street from the row house. Through the downpour he saw the shadows flicker across the window shades. The conductor, it seemed, was at home. When he saw the small figures silhouetted against the window shade, he knew that the man's children were home as well.

66

At 10:05 Byrne's rover crackled. He took it out of his pocket.

"Byrne."

"Kevin, it's John Shepherd."

"What's up, John?"

"Who's on channel?" Shepherd asked.

"Jessica, Chris Gavin, everyone at HQ."

"Okay," Shepherd said. "We've got issues."

For a terrible moment Byrne's mind flashed on Colleen.

"What's going on, John?" Westbrook asked.

"I'm down at the foster home now. I just talked to the woman who runs it. The little girl isn't here."

"What do you mean?" Byrne asked. "She *has* to be there."

"She isn't. About ten minutes before I arrived, the woman said a detective from the PPD was here. She said the man told her the little girl might be in some danger, and he wanted to take her into custody."

"Did you send someone, Dana?" Byrne asked.

"No," Westbrook said. "It didn't come from this office."

"This detective," Byrne said. "He showed her a badge?"

"Yeah," Shepherd said. "She said she didn't look closely at the picture ID, and he didn't offer."

For a few long moments there was no chatter on the line.

"What did this detective look like?" Westbrook asked.

"Hang on," Shepherd said.

As Byrne and everyone else on the line waited, John Shepherd asked the woman who ran the foster home the question. In the background they heard the woman give her answer. Byrne felt his heart sink. He reached into his pocket for his ID wallet. It wasn't there. He checked all his other pockets.

Gone.

By the time Shepherd got back on radio Byrne—and every other person on the channel—knew what had happened.

"It's Ray Torrance," Shepherd said.

"It's Ray," Byrne echoed. "You say he got there about ten minutes before you did?"

"Yeah," Shepherd said. "I got caught in a flood on Arch. I had to go around. The whole city is inundated."

"We've got to put an APB out on Ray and Violet," Jessica said.

"Do we know what he's driving?" Shepherd asked.

Byrne felt for his personal keys, even though he knew it was an exercise in futility. "Yeah," he said. "He's driving my car."

"Okay. Do you know your license plate number?" Jessica asked.

Christ. He didn't. He told Jessica as much. Providing he survived the night, he would have plenty of time to beat himself up about it later. Some cop.

"I'll get it," Jessica said. "Hang on."

While Byrne waited he tried to pinpoint just when it was that Ray Torrance was able to lift his ID. It had to have happened when Byrne was taking the FaceTime call from Luther. He'd had his suit coat over the back of the chair. Ray had been standing next to him.

Byrne heard Jessica hitting computer keys. He then heard her dialing yet another number. She put out an all points bulletin and a BOLO—a Be On the Lookout—for Byrne's car. It was something Byrne thought he would never hear.

A few moments later Jessica got back on channel. "Okay. The alerts are out," she said. "Just to confirm, Ray is armed, right?"

Byrne recalled that Ray Torrance had gone to his storage locker the night he showed him the videotape. He'd probably had a weapon there. Maybe more than one. "Yes," Byrne said. "He is."

"I figured as much," Jessica said. "I put it in the alert."

"I don't want him taken down hard," Byrne said.

"We understand," Westbrook said. "None of us do."

When John Shepherd clicked off, Byrne put the rover back in his pocket. He looked down Chancel Lane. The water ran down the thoroughfare in broad streams. Nothing else moved.

67

Luther stood just outside the bathroom window. The window shade was up a few inches, and he could see into the brightly lit room. Before long someone entered. It was a girl of eight or nine years old. She wore flannel pajamas in a floral print. She stood at the sink for a few moments, making funny faces in the mirror, then reached over, picked up a toothbrush, put a small amount of toothpaste on the brush, and began cleaning her teeth.

Luther thought of Marielle, of the nights he had taken her by the hand and watched as she did just this very thing.

At 10:10 Byrne's phone buzzed. It was a text message from Colleen. The message contained three names. The first two included middle names, followed by MD. The third entry was just a first and last name.

There were no addresses.

Byrne wiped the face of the phone. His hands were trembling in the cold. He forwarded the text messages to Jessica.

*   *   *

The text came across the screen at the computer lab at 10:12 p.m. Jessica saw the names.

"I'll take the first two," Jessica said to Chris Gavin.

They began to search the police database.

The first name on the list, Elijah D. Ditmar, MD, was listed to a residence on South 47th Street, near Chester Avenue, in the Squirrel Hill section of West Philadelphia.

No, Jessica thought. *Too far.* If Luther needed to get back to the drop-off point by eleven o'clock, or whenever he was going to set as the next deadline, he would never make it, not even if the weather was good.

And the weather was anything but. Twice in the past few minutes the lights in the lab had flickered.

"The third name on the list is a bust," Gavin said. "The block where the house used to be was torn down three years ago. There's a Rite Aid and a Subway there now."

"I have a hit on the second name. Ronald B. Lewison, MD. He lives at 3223 Ralston Street. That's less than four blocks from the drop-off point."

"It has to be where he is headed," Gavin said. "If he isn't already there."

Jessica got on the phone to dispatch. They would send everybody and their mother to the location. She then scrolled down to the phone number listed on the screen.

She dialed the number. It went directly to voice mail.

Someone was on the line.

Luther leaned very close to the window, the image of the young girl becoming Marielle, becoming his beloved sister, Kaisa, taken from him all those years ago.

He took out the old woman's phone.

* * *

"Jess."

Jessica turned to Chris Gavin. He was pointing at the large LCD monitor. The map had shifted. The red icon was back on-screen. But it was no longer close to the green icon, Byrne's position. It was four blocks away.

"It's the Lewison house," Jessica said. "He's there."

Luther called the detective. In a few seconds the man answered.

"I saw you," Luther said. "You were alone."

"Let's talk about this," the detective said. "Let's work this out."

"You let me down."

"We don't have the girl."

"I don't believe you," Luther said. "I told you, in very specific detail, where to bring the girl, and when. I also told you what would be the consequences should you fail to follow my instructions. Now you will see in *scarlet* detail what I meant."

"You don't understand—"

"No, sir, I'm afraid it is *you* who does not understand. All bodies that fall tonight will be on your conscience. For—"

"—example," the man said. Byrne could hardly see the man's face in the darkness. From time to time the right side of his face was illuminated with a bright yellow light, but it was not enough to give Byrne any kind of context of place. He could have been anywhere.

On-screen, the image began to shake. In an instant a new image appeared. At first it was so bright that it overexposed the screen. But in a few seconds, Byrne could see that he was looking in the window at a room of some sort. From time to time raindrops washed across the lens, transforming the image into a shimmering watercolor.

When the lens cleared Byrne's heart fluttered. He was looking at a little girl brushing her teeth.

The image again shook as Luther's face came back into focus.

"The little girl—the little girl who is mine—I want her to be this girl's age one day."

Byrne's TracFone buzzed. He scrambled to get it out of his pocket and silenced before Luther could hear.

"I want you to make a promise, Detective," Luther said.

"I'll do what I can," Byrne replied, not having any idea what was coming. He had to keep the man talking. He wiped the TracFone on his coat. He glanced down. He'd made it worse.

"I want you to make a promise," Luther repeated. "Not to me, or even to yourself, but rather to the people in this house. I want you to promise them that no harm will come to them, that you will do everything in your power to give me what I want, what is rightfully mine."

"Yes," Byrne said. "I can make that promise."

"I want you to say it aloud."

Byrne got the TracFone clean, saw the message: *We have sub fixed. Cars en rte. Keep hm talking.*

Luther waited for the detective to respond.

"I just heard from the commander of my unit," the detective said. "We know where the girl is. We have her."

"Where is she?"

"There was a mix-up," the detective said. "The officer who was supposed to pick up the little girl and bring her down here went to the wrong place. He's on his way here right now."

Liar, Luther thought.

"The streetcar conductor showed me the same incivility," Luther said. "He thought there would be no consequence. For him it was merely a moment that came and went. But I remember. I remember it all."

"Wait," the detective said. "What you're talking about—the conductor and his family—that didn't happen to you. It happened to someone else. These are not your memories."

The detective's words were obscured by the staccato rhythms of the rain on the roof of the row house gutters overhead.

Luther once again turned the cell phone camera to the window. The girl was now standing in front of the window, drying her hands on a towel. This time she was making funny faces in the night-blackened window.

"Can you see, Detective?"

"Don't," came the faraway voice from the phone's speaker.

Luther was now face to face with the little girl, inches away. Through the window he heard a phone ring. It was an older phone, a landline.

"I'll get it!" the little girl yelled. She put the towel back on the rack beneath the window, and turned toward the bathroom door.

Before she could take a step, Eduard Kross punched his fist through the glass, grabbed the girl by her hair, and pulled her into the storm.

68

Rachel sat with the tape recorder in her lap. She had found it under the bed. Bean's bed.

She had listened to her mother's voice reading a fairy tale three times through. She knew that her mother had recorded it for her and Bean one afternoon when she was sober, knowing that by nine or ten o'clock, on any given night, she would be too drunk to do it.

Rachel hated her mother for drinking, for dying in a car crash, but she loved her for doing this.

She stood up, put the recorder on the bed, looked again at the room. She now knew what had happened. It all came flooding back, all the nights the raggedy man had come to their house, their room. He had been watching years later when her mother threw out everything in Bean's room. Her mother had put everything on the tree lawn and the raggedy man had come in the night and taken it, making a room for Bean in these catacombs.

Rachel walked to the door, grabbed the knob. As expected, it was locked. She glanced above the door, at the web cam in the steel mesh cage. She looked around the room, searching for options.

She walked over to the hope chest, opened it. It was too much to have asked for the contents to still be inside. It was empty. The same was true with the small drawer in the desk.

There were no windows in this room, just the one door, and the cold-air return in the wall to the left of the door, near the floor.

Rachel glanced again at the web cam. There was no red or green light on the camera, so she had no idea if she was being watched. But she soon realized that there was something she could do about it.

The light switch next to the door had no on-off switch; it was just a blank faceplate. Rachel walked back to the desk, opened the top. There was a half-mortise lock built into the desk, but the key was long gone, probably before Rachel's mother and father even bought it. But Rachel recalled how every time she let the hinged top of the desk fall—scaring Bean half out of her wits—the escutcheon would fall off.

Rachel closed her eyes, hoped against hope.

She let the top fall, and sure enough the thin metal escutcheon fell to the floor. She stole another glance at the web cam, then kicked the metal strip toward the door.

Two minutes later she had the two screws in the blank switch plate out, and the wires separated.

The room went dark.

While the switch plate had come off with relative ease, the screws holding the cold-air return were a different story. They had been painted over so many times that finding the slot in the screws, in the dark, had proven to be all but impossible. For a few terrifying seconds Rachel thought the worst, that the screws were Phillips head, which would have put an end to her plan.

But, slowly, she had managed to find the slots in the screws, and gently turn them to the left. Before long she had them all out. She ran the escutcheon along the top and the sides of the grill, digging out years of dry paint. Every so often she tried to pull the grate from the wall, without success.

Finally, using the thin metal strip as a lever, she began to pull the grill from the wall. When she thought it was out far enough, she worked her fingernails behind it on both sides, and pulled with all her strength.

The grate came free.

She put her ear to the wall, listened. She heard nothing.

Rachel looked through the opening into the next room, hoping that the heat ducts had long ago been removed, and there would be passage. There was. The room on the other side was dark, but she had to take the chance.

She took off her jacket and shoes, removed her belt. She shoved them all through the opening. She then put her arms through the hole in the wall, and began to squeeze herself through.

Five minutes later Rachel found herself on the other side of the wall. It was one of the first times in her life she was glad she was barely five feet tall.

The room was pitch black. Rachel felt her way up the wall, over to the same wall where the door was in the room she had just left. Within seconds she found a light switch. She flipped it on.

This room was large, much larger than the room she had just been in. There was a queen-size bed, a refrigerator, a kitchenette. There was a television on a stand, a bookshelf with books and DVDs.

He lives here, Rachel thought. *This is where the raggedy man lives.*

She turned to the door that led to the hallway. There was no key in the lock, just a hasp with an open padlock hanging from it. She quickly put on her shoes, her jacket, her belt, took a deep breath, trying to prepare herself for whatever was on the other side of this door.

They didn't call her Tuff for nothing, right?

Rachel Anne Gray opened the door, and found she wasn't prepared, not by a long shot. There was someone standing in the hallway, just a few feet away.

"Hi," the person said.

It was her little sister.

It was Bean.

69

The image had gone black for a few seconds. Byrne heard what sounded like breaking glass, then the image on the screen seemed to spin out of control.

Then he heard the scream.

Byrne ran down the steps of the train platform. When he reached street level the water was over his shoes. He tried to orient himself. He raised Jessica on his TracFone.

"He's got her," Byrne yelled into the phone.

"Who?" Jessica said. "He's got *who?*"

"The girl. At the Lewison house. Where the *fuck* are the sector cars?"

"They'll be on scene within a minute."

Byrne looked at his watch. The location was almost four blocks away. He could never make it there in time.

"Stay on channel," Byrne said.

He ran across the platform, upended a trash can, dumped the garbage onto the ground. He dug through the discarded fast food trash, cans, newspapers. He found a handful of paper napkins, discarded the wet ones. He pulled the iPhone out of his pocket, cleared the screen.

It was dark, but Luther was still on the line. There was an image of a street lamp. Rain drove across the illuminated area. The street was flooded, deserted.

Luther turned the camera to his own face. His eyes were manic, possessed.

"Do you dream, Detective?"

Byrne knew he had to keep the man on the line. "Yes, Mr. Kross. All the time."

"When you dream, are you always the hero? The white knight?"

"No," Byrne said. "I am not."

The camera moved. In the stuttering image Byrne saw the girl who had been brushing her teeth. She was propped against the base of a street lamp. She was not moving. The image returned to Luther's face. He now wore a floppy black hat, soaked with rain.

"I fear in this dream you will be vanquished," he said.

Luther turned the camera around, again showing the girl. Byrne could not tell if she was dead or alive. From the left side of the frame he saw the blade of a knife, a long, bone-handled knife.

No, Byrne thought. *Don't.*

Luther pulled the hair from the right side of the girl's neck. He lay the long blade up against the skin at the base of her throat.

"This is your nightmare, Detective. For the rest of your life."

"Drop the weapon! Get down on the ground!"

For a moment Byrne did not know where the shout came from. He soon realized it came from Luther's phone.

Officers from the 8th District were on scene.

The image on-screen tumbled, went black.

The last thing Byrne heard coming through the small speaker on his phone was the sound of gunfire.

70

Jessica got the call from the commander of the 8th District, Sergeant Cullen Sweeney. She reached Byrne on his iPhone.

"Is he in custody?" Byrne asked.

"No," Jessica said. "He's gone. The officer who fired his weapon said he thinks he may have hit him, but he can't be sure. He said if there was any blood on the sidewalk it was instantly washed away."

"How did they lose him?"

"It's dark and it's raining. They just lost him. They said he was there one second, and in the next second he was gone."

"What about the girl?" Byrne asked.

"EMS is checking her now."

"He didn't cut her?"

"No," Jessica said. "He didn't."

Byrne was silent a few moments. "What about tracking the subject?"

"We don't have him. He must have turned off the phone, or threw it away."

"He didn't throw it away," Byrne said.

"How do you know?"

"Because he's not done yet."

Jessica glanced at the map on the computer monitor. "We've got a perimeter set up. Five blocks in all directions. If he's hit, he can't be moving that fast. We'll get him."

Byrne put the phone in his pocket. He glanced into the train tunnel, at the swallowing darkness.

He closed his eyes, thought about the last call from Luther, the video image of the cell phone camera panning across the street. Something had been out of place, but he could not put his finger on it.

Then he saw it in his mind's eye. Behind the girl, the sewer grate had been taken off, and was propped next to the curb.

They said he was there one second, and in the next second he was gone.

Byrne thought about the night Ray Torrance had slept on his couch. After they had watched the videotape of the little girl called Bean, Ray had passed out. As he slept he had mumbled something, something Byrne had not quite understood.

Ray did not say *PPD*. He'd said *PWD*.

Philadelphia Water Department.

Detective Ray Torrance had suspected that whoever was breaking into all those homes was using the miles of interconnecting sewers and catacombs beneath the city.

Byrne knew where the madman had gone.

71

At first Rachel thought she was hallucinating. Her little sister stood in the doorway to the room. She wore a small pink rain slicker.

"My *God*," Rachel said. "Bean."

Rachel slowly fell to her knees. She put out her arms.

The girl stepped into the room. She hugged Rachel. It was no hallucination, no dream. She was real, and she was just like Rachel remembered her when she was a toddler, the same clear blue eyes, the same fine blond hair.

Rachel pulled back just as a shadow fell across the doorway. She looked up.

Behind the girl was a man. A big man. He wore a long dark coat. He was not the raggedy man, but someone else, someone who walked the very edge of Rachel's memory, a memory that had been lost to her dreams for years.

Then she remembered. It had been sixteen years, and his face was lined and drawn, but she remembered his eyes. His kind, sad eyes.

He walked across the room, sat on the edge of the bed. Bean took a few steps, put her tiny hand in the man's hand.

"My name is Ray," the man said. He pulled the little girl onto his knee. "And this is your niece."

72

Träumen Sie?

I see them.

Whom do you see?

My mother and father. They are facedown on the floor of the cellar. There are bright scarlet pools of blood around them.

Where are you?

I am in the crawl space. I ran here to hide when I heard the soldiers at the door. I saw Major Abendrof bring my parents down here. He put a gun to their heads and shot them.

What do you see now?

I see Kaisa, my sister. She is standing against the far wall. She is crying. She is singing.

What does she sing?

She sings Põdramaja. It is a nursery rhyme about an evil hunter knocking on the door of a rabbit's house in the forest. She sings this when she is afraid. The major stands before her with his weapon in his hand.

Will you reach her in time?

I don't know.

Träumen Sie?

No, Doctor. I do not dream.

73

Byrne stood at the mouth of the tunnel. He took out his Trac-Fone, dialed Ray Torrance's number, the throwaway phone he had bought for him. He didn't expect a response, but Ray answered.

"Where are you, Ray?"

A long pause. Byrne could hear the sound of rushing water in the background.

"I'm where I should have been three years ago. *Sixteen* years ago."

"You knew this guy lived underground. PWD. You knew it."

"I didn't know it, Kevin. But I've had a lot of sleepless nights to think about it. It's the only thing that made sense."

"Why did you bring the little girl into all this?"

"You heard him," Torrance said. "If he didn't see the girl, he wasn't going to deal. It had to be done. She's with me now. She's safe."

"You put her in harm's way."

"She'll be fine. When this is over, I'm going to take her somewhere safe. I should have done it for Marielle three years ago, and I didn't. This is my chance to make it right."

"Let me help," Byrne said. His voice had taken on a pleading tone. He knew that Torrance heard right through it.

"Walk away, Kevin," Torrance said. "This is my play."

"Ray, you can't—"

"I love you, brother."

Then the phone went dead.

Byrne tried calling again, but it went to the generic voice mail. He took out his iPhone, plugged in the earbuds with the inline microphone. He called Jessica.

"I'm going to look for Ray," Byrne said.

"Let me get someone down there with you. I'll come."

"There's no time."

Byrne turned off the phone, drew his weapon, and stepped into the blackness of the tunnel.

The water in the runoff was over a foot deep. For a while Byrne tried to walk the edges, but it was useless. He had to walk the middle of the sewer pipe to have any chance of maintaining balance.

His small Maglite was of little use in the utter blackness of the channel.

After a few hundred yards he came to a corridor that met the main tunnel at a T-junction. Byrne could see dome lights in the distance. Trying to preserve his bearings he walked down the narrow hallway. Every so often he came to doors, many cut crudely into the brick. Most had no hardware.

A hundred feet or so from the main tunnel he found a door, slightly ajar. He shouldered it open, shone his flashlight. Inside the huge room, piled floor to ceiling, was furniture, clothing, lamps, toys. A few feet farther into the tunnel he found more doors. Room after room were filled with discarded items, possibly collected for decades, all had the smell of decay and mold. One room was a small, makeshift surgery. There were long brown streaks of dried blood on the floor.

The water in the runoff was now up to Byrne's shins, and rising fast. He soon came to an opening, a spacious two-level junction with sanitary sewers above, and a storm sewer below. There were a pair of dim lights in mesh cages overhead. Byrne checked his phones. There was no signal where he was. He looked behind him, back to where he had come from.

This was a mistake. He had to get backup.

When he turned back he saw a trio of shadows growing on the wall. He spun around, his weapon raised.

It was Ray Torrance. He stood on the other side of the opening. With him was Violet, and a young woman, the young woman in the room they had seen on Luther's phone. Torrance took a step back. He did not have a weapon in hand.

"Take them out of here," Torrance said.

"I will," Byrne replied. "You're coming with us."

Torrance shook his head. "No. I can't do that."

"What are you talking about, Ray? It's over. We've got officers at every outlet from this section. He can't get out. It's over."

"It's not over. You don't know."

Byrne edged closer. "Then tell me. Let's get up on the street, we'll dry off, grab a bottle or two, and you'll tell me."

"You know, and I know, that's not going to happen," Torrance said. "I took your badge. I stole your car."

"You *borrowed* my car, Ray. And when I lost my ID you found it. Clean hands. Over."

"Then I showed it to the woman at the foster home. Come on, Kevin. I kidnapped the girl."

"Let me talk to the DA," Byrne said. "You know I can be convincing. Old Irish soft-shoe."

Torrance shook his head. "You go on ahead. I'm going to stay here and finish this thing. It started sixteen years ago, and I finish it tonight."

"Ray, I can't—"

"He cut me, Kevin. In that filthy fucking alley. I pissed blood for a month. It ends here. It ends now."

As Torrance stepped back, a shadow darted across the wall overhead. Before anyone could react, Luther dropped from the spill-off tunnel near the ceiling. He landed just behind Violet. Byrne heard the bone snap in one of his arms.

Luther's shirt was drenched with blood. Even in the dim yellow light Byrne saw the wound in his shoulder. He had been hit with a round.

In his right hand was the bone-handled knife.

Luther pulled Violet closer to him, looked down at her. "Bean."

"No," the young woman said. Byrne could now see that she was a little older than he originally thought. "*I'm* Bean."

Luther looked confused, as though he had never seen the young woman before. "But you—"

"Yes," the young woman said. "I've grown up."

Luther loosened his grip on Violet's shoulder.

"I said I'd come back for you," Luther said. "Why didn't you wait?"

"You're here now." She reached out a hand. "Come with me. We'll go back."

The sound started as a low-level hum. It was more a sensation than a sound. The cobblestones beneath their feet seemed to vibrate.

"Go back?" Luther asked.

"Yes," the young woman said. "We'll be a family."

The sound got louder. The solitary bulb in the cage housing flickered.

Luther dropped his hand slightly. The knife was now just a few inches from Violet's cheek. "To Tallinn?"

The young woman took a few steps toward Luther and Violet. "Yes," she said. "To Tallinn."

Luther looked at the young woman. He dropped his hand further, began to tap the blade on his thigh.

It was all Ray Torrance needed.

He lunged at the man with full force. As he did, Luther brought down the knife, slicing Torrance from his right shoulder to his left hip. Torrance shrieked as blood splattered against the wall.

Torrance locked Luther in a bear hug as the man continued to slash at his back, the blade plunging deep into his flesh.

"Go!" Torrance yelled.

Rachel grabbed Violet by the hand. They trudged through the rising water toward Byrne.

Torrance had the man in a death grip. He began to move him toward the edge of the high wall over the storm sewer.

Below them the water raged.

As they neared the brink, Ray Torrance locked eyes with Byrne. It was a look Byrne had seen before. He'd known a few people who had suffered years from a terminal illness. It was the look of acceptance.

Torrance closed his eyes, fell backward, bringing Luther with him, just as the water roared through the storm sewer beneath them. The noise was deafening. It filled the cavernous opening with thunder.

Moments later, as the sound of the rushing underground river echoed off the stone walls, the two men were gone.

74

In the aftermath of the storm, which had spanned from New Jersey to central Ohio, the Commonwealth of Pennsylvania put the amount of damages to roads, buildings and infrastructure at close to three hundred million dollars, with most of the damage occurring in the eastern part of the state.

The marine unit of the Philadelphia Police Department was kept very busy in the days after the storm. The Delaware River was a major shipping channel, and while crews worked to clear debris from the river, passages needed to be kept open.

In the end, it was the Coast Guard that found the body of an unidentified male in his late thirties or early forties near the Baxter Water Treatment Plant. About two hundred yards south they found the body of Raymond Torrance, a retired detective with the PPD.

Despite their wounds, autopsies concluded that both men had died as a result of drowning.

75

The first day of spring in Philadelphia was always a mystery. There had been years when the city was pummeled with five inches of snow, high winds and icy rain. There were also years when the sun shone brightly and skies were scrubbed blue. This year March 21 was one of the latter. By eight a.m. the temperature was already sixty degrees.

The story of the man named Luther, and his murderous rampage, was still being unraveled. The *Inquirer* ran a series of articles about Cold River, focusing partly on the new construction that had been temporarily halted while the parks and forests nearby were examined for more remains.

The Philadelphia Police Department, along with the FBI, were using methane probes, and other sophisticated devices, to help determine where, if any, other bodies had been buried. The process promised to take weeks, if not months.

In the meantime, the newspapers ran grainy, black-and-white photographs of the deplorable conditions that existed at the hospital.

While investigators believed that the full story of what happened during the last days of the Delaware Valley State Hospital might never be known, little by little people were coming forward, both hospital personnel and former patients alike.

The PPD turned the audio recordings of Eduard Kross's dreams over to the FBI's behavioral science unit, in the hope of divining meaning from them, and perhaps applying their findings to unsolved homicides that had occurred in and around Philadelphia County over the last twenty years.

Both James Delacroix and Edward Richmond's son Timothy were treated for their wounds, and released from the hospital.

The funeral was attended by police officers from as far away as Chicago.

Ray Torrance was buried next to his parents in Holy Cross Cemetery in Lansdowne.

Jessica had not known the man well, but she could not stop the tears. It was such a waste. She thought of the torment Ray Torrance had lived with for years, and it broke her heart. As she stood watching the casket lowered into the earth, Byrne put his arm around her. They both had seen this too many times in their time on the force.

As the first flower was dropped on the casket, Jessica glanced at her father. Peter Giovanni, in full dress blues, was stoic, as always. But Jessica knew that each time this happened, each time the bagpipes played, it took a little more from him.

It took something from them all.

76

Two days after Ray Torrance's service, as Jessica was just finishing up her reports, preparing to leave the office, her phone rang.

"Balzano, Homicide."

"Detective Balzano, this is Jane Wickstrom with DHS."

Jessica didn't recognize the name. Perhaps sensing her confusion, the woman continued.

"I work with Pat Mazzello. I'm her supervisor. We met at the Survivor's Benefit last year."

Jessica sort of recalled the woman. Blond, fifties, a little chatty. "Yes, of course. How are you?"

"Very well, thanks. Do you have a minute?"

"Sure. What can I do for you?"

"I have some good news about Violet."

The name Violet had stuck, it seemed. Jessica had heard that the little girl had begun to respond to it.

"What's the news?" Jessica asked.

"I found a really good program that deals with children, young children who have been through some recent trauma."

"Well, Violet certainly qualifies."

"I spoke to the director of the program and she told me that they have an immediate opening. They're located in upstate New York, and the program is an intensive, twenty-one-day residential program."

"That sounds great," Jessica said. "How soon will the process start?"

"That's why I was calling," Jane said. "I'll be flying out with Violet later tonight."

"Tonight?"

"Yes, sometimes the wheels turn really quickly. I think you'd agree, this little girl has been through enough, and the sooner she can go through the process, the sooner she can get back to Philadelphia and into a stable home environment."

Jessica knew that Violet's biological aunt, Rachel Gray, the young woman Luther had kidnapped, was in the process of petitioning the court for custody. "How can I help?"

"Well, right now, Violet is at DHS. Seeing as she knows both you and Detective Byrne, I was hoping one of you could pick her up and bring her to my house. There's plenty of time, the flight doesn't leave till nine o'clock. I don't live that far from the airport."

Jessica glanced at her watch. She was hoping for a bubble bath, dinner, half a bottle of Pinot Grigio, windowpane-rattling sex, and ten hours of uninterrupted sleep. In precisely that order. But the job goes on.

"Sure," Jessica said. "I can pick her up. Where are you located?"

Jane Wickstrom gave her an address.

"Do I need to pick up anything for Violet?" Jessica asked. "Things she might need on the flight?"

"Thanks, but I'm just about to run to the store. No need for you to stop."

"Okay then," Jessica said. "I should be at DHS in about ten minutes. Give us another thirty, and we'll be there."

*   *   *

When Jessica arrived at the Department of Human Services, it was all but deserted. She signed in and took the elevator to the intake room.

The little girl was sitting in a chair in the waiting room. When Jessica walked into the room Violet looked up and smiled.

This was a good thing.

On the way to Jane Wickstrom's house Jessica made a few attempts at conversation. Most of the time, the little girl just responded with a nod or shake of the head. By the time they got off I-95, Violet was humming a song, a song that was vaguely familiar to Jessica, but one she could not immediately put her finger on.

She pulled over in front of the row house, parked the car.

"Are you ready?"

Violet looked out the window, then back at Jessica. It suddenly occurred to Jessica that the little girl didn't understand the question. Ready for *what?*

"We're going to go see Jane," Jessica said. "Do you remember Jane?"

Violet looked down at her hands. She remained silent. Jessica wondered just how to explain who Jane was. It'd been a long time since she'd talked to someone as young as Violet.

"Jane is the nice lady with blond hair. Pretty blond hair like yours. She's really nice."

Violet looked out the window again. After a few moments Jessica got out of the car, opened the rear passenger door, unlatched the belt on Violet's car seat.

Without being prompted Violet stepped out of the car. She walked to the sidewalk, waited. Jessica took the little girl by the hand and together they walked up the sidewalk.

Jessica was just about to ring the doorbell when she saw the Post-it note:

Det. Balzano. Ran out to the store. Make yourself at home. BRB!

Jessica opened the door, stepped into the house. A few seconds later she turned to see Violet still standing by the door. She looked so small.

"You can come in, honey. It's okay."

Violet took a few tentative steps into the living room. She glanced around at the bookshelves, at the magazines on the coffee table, at the pictures on the wall. Jessica followed her gaze. One of the framed photographs on the living-room wall was of Jane and what appeared to be her sister, along with her sister's children. The kids in the photograph looked to be about eight, five and three. They were standing on a beach somewhere, possibly down the shore. Violet seemed transfixed.

Jessica glanced at her watch. If the flight was at nine o'clock, and they allowed ninety minutes or so for the check-in, and all the other crap you had to put up with to fly these days, and they were about ten minutes from the airport, it was time to leave.

"Are you thirsty, sweetie?" Jessica asked.

Violet said nothing.

"Why don't I see if Jane has some juice?" Jessica pointed to the big wingback chair next to the fireplace. "You can sit here, okay?" Without a word Violet crossed the room and climbed onto the chair.

"I'll be right back," Jessica added.

Jessica walked down the short hallway toward the kitchen. She opened the refrigerator and found that there was apple juice, orange juice and grape juice. She didn't expect an answer, but she thought she might give it a try. Perhaps if she wasn't in the same room with the little girl, the little girl might answer.

"Violet? Do you want apple juice or grape juice?"

Jessica closed her eyes, waited. Nothing.

Ah, well, Jessica thought. *Worth a shot.* She decided to just take two of the bottles into the living room, along with a cup.

She crossed the kitchen, opened one of the glass-front cabinet doors next to the sink, took out a small juice glass. When she closed the cabinet door she saw the reflection behind her, and felt the barrel of a gun touch the back of her head.

7 7

Byrne finished filling out the reports by seven o'clock. If there was a less glamorous aspect to what he did for a living than filling out the seemingly endless paperwork, he couldn't imagine what it would be. Maybe a stakeout in high summer after a full Mexican meal.

He went through each of the forms one last time, dotting every *i,* crossing every *t,* ticking every box. He checked the dates, addresses, names, police codes, checking for inaccuracies. There were none. Somehow, as fatigued as he was, there were no mistakes.

He signed his name in the appropriate places, clicked his pen, stood up, crossed the duty room, and put the reports on his boss's desk.

As he slipped on his coat, he checked his cell phone. He had a text message from Jessica, sent about thirty minutes earlier. Byrne scanned the message. Jessica said she was on her way to pick up Violet, and take her to Jane Wickstrom's house—whoever that was—and from there they were taking the little girl to the airport to fly to New York to enroll Violet in a treatment program.

Byrne put that day's *Inquirer* and his iPhone into his shoulder bag, and was just about to zip it up when he heard the tone that signaled he had new email.

No more, Byrne thought. *I'm done for the day. Hell, I'm done for the week. Maybe the month. I'm off duty. There's a burger and a Guinness waiting for me somewhere in this city.*

Ah, who the hell was he kidding?

He sat back down, took his iPhone from the bag. He tapped the mail program, marveling at how quickly he had taken to the Mac interface. The program opened, and Byrne saw that the email he'd just received was from Peeter Tamm. The subject line read: *Eduard Kross Redux.*

Byrne tapped on the email icon. He began to read.

Kevin,

I trust you are well. As a man of 46 years (somehow) I am still amazed at the depth and breadth of this thing called the internet. Even though the people of Estonia were among the first to pioneer its use, I was a latecomer to the concept and practice. I say this to you because as easily as I can read the *Eesti Ekspress,* I am able to read your hometown newspaper. I read with great interest, greater concern, and no small measure of sadness, the details—or, at least those interpreted and reported by your print media—of the case about which you first approached my department.

It appears that it all came to a tragic, if not foreseen, ending. I was sorry to read of Detective Raymond Torrance's death.

The other reason for this missive is the attached file. Not unexpectedly, as a result of our inquiries into the infamous Eduard Kross, people's memories were awakened. While much, if not most, of his past life and terrible deeds remain unknown, he was not the complete cipher we had thought. There does indeed exist a photograph of Eduard Kross as a boy of 17 or so, perhaps the last image of him until he was captured at a limestone quarry in northeastern Estonia.

I apologize for the poor quality of the attached JPEG. The photograph was sent to me via facsimile from a man in Lithuania. It is a copy of a copy, if you will.

I hope that this will not be the last of our communiqué. Having shuffled paper for the last few years, I must admit being a detective again, even for just a few days, was most gratifying. I hope I was of some help.

With my very best wishes, and hopes for our new friendship,
Nägemist!
Peeter

Byrne tapped the icon for the attached photograph. A moment later it appeared on the screen. The photo was of a young man in a dusty four-button suit, the sleeves of which exposed the dirty cuffs of his shirt. His dark hair was hastily and inexpertly cut. He stood on a country road. Behind him was the corner of a dilapidated building, as well as the rear bumper of a truck.

In all, the boy in the picture looked ordinary in every way. Except for his eyes. There was no light in his eyes.

Byrne was just about to leave when the phone vibrated in his hand. He was getting a call. He had intended to make a video call to Colleen later in the evening, but now was just as good a time as any. Even better. He needed to talk with someone who loved him.

He tapped the icon. It was not Colleen. For some reason, he was getting a call from Peeter Tamm. He propped the iPhone on his desk, answered the phone.

Tamm was dressed much the same as he had been in their last call, but this time he was wearing a maroon tie.

"Peeter," Byrne said.

"Hello, Kevin. *Tervist* from Tallinn."

"Greetings from Philly."

"I fear you have probably had enough of me. My wife says to anyone who will listen that a little bit of Peeter Tamm goes a long way."

"Not at all," Byrne said. "I was just reading your email."

"I know that it is the end of your workday there, so I won't keep you too long. There is something that I forgot to include in my email to you."

"Not a problem. What's up?"

"As I said, your inquiry into Eduard Kross reignited the detective in me. Today I spoke with the young lady who translated the audio file you sent to me, the text of Eduard Kross's mad dreams."

"She did a great job for us," Byrne said. "The next time you see her, please pass along thanks from all of us at the PPD."

"I will." Tamm stood up for a moment, leaned out of the frame. When he sat back down he had in his hands a small pile of documents. "I have something here regarding the recording that I think you'll find as fascinating as I have."

"What do you have?"

"I don't know how well you can see this, or if you have any experience with these things." Tamm reached over to a desk lamp, angled it toward himself. He then held up one of the pieces of paper, positioning it in the beam of the lamp. The image was a little blurry at first, as the camera racked its focus. Byrne soon recognized that the document was some sort of printout of a pattern, not unlike that produced by a lie detector machine.

"After the recording was translated, I took it over to our audio lab," Tamm said. "We employ the same technicians and analysts used by our central government. They are very good. The graph you are looking at is a voiceprint of the German speaker on the recording."

Byrne was sure that Tamm was trying to hold the document steady. Nonetheless it shook in front of the camera.

"I don't know too much about this," Byrne said.

"Nor do I," Tamm replied. "Please bear with me for a moment, though."

"Sure."

Tamm then picked up a second document. He held this up to the camera. "This is a voiceprint of the second speaker. The Estonian speaker on the recording."

Byrne tried to focus.

"Well, Peeter, from here they look far too similar for me to make any kind of judgment about them." Byrne often went through moments like this when dealing with latent prints in the ID Unit. They all looked the same.

"These two voiceprints are not similar," Tamm said.

"Ah, okay," Byrne replied. "They look similar to me."

"What I mean is, they are not similar. They are identical."

Byrne was certain he had misunderstood what Peeter Tamm said.

"I'm not sure I heard you correctly," Byrne said. "Could you say again?"

"The voices on the recording," Tamm said. "The analyst in our audio lab did an analysis of the recording and determined that both speakers in the recording are the same."

"Wait, are you saying that both of the men in that recording—the one speaking German, and the one speaking Estonian—are the same *person?*"

"Yes," Tamm said. "Our analyst in the audio lab is very good, inarguably one of the best in Estonia. He says there is no doubt in his mind but they are the same person. The man asking the questions in German and the man responding in Estonian is the same man."

Byrne almost got to his feet. He then remembered that he was on a video call. He thanked Peeter Tamm for his time and effort. Tamm, a fellow detective, recognized the urgency, and signed off.

Byrne again looked at the JPEG photograph of Eduard Kross. And saw it. The *eyes*. He had seen them before.

Twice.

78

Unlike the first time he had visited the house, Byrne saw no vehicles in front, no activity on the grounds. This time there were burlap cloths over all the hedges, and the construction materials were gone from the partially renovated boathouse.

Byrne slowly worked his way around the perimeter of the building. He glanced through the kitchen window. The table and chairs had been removed. Beyond the kitchen he saw white sheets over the massive dining-room table.

He continued around the structure, looking in all the windows. Empty.

Byrne then walked down the path at the rear of the property, to the small carriage house. The door was ajar. He raised his weapon, toed open the door.

There, in the small kitchen, he saw Jessica sitting at a table. Behind her stood a man with a gun to her head. Byrne recognized the man as the gardener who was clipping the hedges the first time they had visited Martin Léopold's house.

Byrne had no choice.

He put his weapon on the floor, and his hands above his head.

They sat on the floor in the wine cellar, back to back, their handcuffs circling a steel stanchion support. The man they had seen working on the hedges the first time they visited sat on the narrow steps, a Colt Defender in his hand. Both Jessica and Byrne's service weapons were on a table across the room, magazines removed.

Before long Jessica heard the muffled sounds of police cars arriving, the faint clamor of a dozen or so detectives and patrol officers fanning out. Byrne had called for backup on the way to Torresdale, but because they had been led to the wine cellar by way of a hidden door, concealed behind a bookcase off the study, Jessica knew it was unlikely they would be found.

Whoever was upstairs in the house would tell the officers that Byrne had come and gone, and would let them search the premises. Jessica surmised that Byrne's car was probably already at the bottom of the Delaware.

After about twenty minutes Jessica heard the cars pull away.

Sometime later the door at the top of the stairs opened, and Jessica saw a pair of highly polished shoes descend. The man who was their captor had cut his hair short, dyed it a deep mahogany. He wore a dark suit and overcoat.

Martin Léopold was the real Eduard Kross.

"The years between our first and second independence was a terrible time," Kross said. "Imagine a city like Helsinki—a free city—being just fifty miles away. I fancy it was much like the prisoners in your Alcatraz and San Francisco."

"Two hundred years, then freedom," Byrne said.

"Yes," Kross said. "From Peter the Great until the First World War, then independence until Hitler. By the nineteen nineties the civic archives were in shambles. Birth records, death records, marriage records. To switch an identity, especially on a long passage such as mine, was not all that difficult. The staff at Cold River accepted it without question."

"You impersonated Godehard Kirsch?"

"I *became* Dr. Kirsch."

"And Kirsch was thought to be you. To be Eduard Kross."

Kross smiled. "Lithium, in higher doses, is quite debilitating. From the time I overpowered him, to the moment of his death, he never spoke another word."

"So, at Cold River, you recorded yourself?" Byrne asked.

"Yes," Kross said. "We built a small recording studio with quite expensive acoustics. I was the only one allowed in the room. Except, of course, for our subject."

"The real Dr. Kirsch."

Kross nodded. "For a while. After him there were many. If Cold River had anything, it had no shortage of test subjects."

"Who are all buried in Priory Park."

"Not all," Kross said. He buttoned his coat, slipped a homburg on his head.

"Who was it that died in the fire?" Jessica asked.

Kross shrugged. "It was of little consequence. All that mattered was that the two administrators—the only people at Cold River who could identify me as Godehard Kirsch—also perished in the blaze. That day I became Martin Léopold."

"What about Luther?"

"Ah, Luther. He was the perfect subject. A blank slate, if you will."

"You implanted your own dreams?" Byrne asked.

"A bit simplistic, Detective."

"And the little girl," Byrne said. "She's your daughter, isn't she?" Byrne glanced around the room, nodded toward a door cut into the stone wall on the other side. "You were raising her down here. This place leads to the catacombs."

Kross said nothing.

"Why Marielle Gray?" Byrne asked. "Why did you select her?"

For a few moments Kross was silent. He then reached into his coat pocket, pulled out a pair of photographs. He crossed the room, held them in front of the two detectives. One photograph was quite old, sepia-toned, creased. The other was newer. Both were pictures of girls around the age of five. The resemblance between the two was uncanny.

"That is your sister," Byrne said, nodding at the old photograph. "The one the Tallinn detective told us was murdered."

"Yes," Kross said. "Kaisa."

"What happened to Marielle?"

Kross did not answer. He didn't have to. Jessica saw the tell. It was a momentary flick from the man's cold eyes, but it was there, a glance at the white flower in his coat lapel, the same flower found at the crime scenes.

Jessica did not know how much time had passed after Kross left. More than once she found herself being jarred awake. There were no windows in the wine cellar, but Jessica calculated they had been down there more than five hours. Her arms and legs were numb.

The man sitting on the steps watched them in silence, weapon in hand. When his cell phone vibrated, he glanced at the text message, then stood up, holstered his weapon, walked up the steps, and through the door.

Before long Jessica heard a car take off, the sound of the engine growing fainter and fainter.

Twenty minutes later Byrne managed to work the phone from his pocket.

79

The manhunt for Martin Léopold—the man they now knew to be a serial killer named Eduard Olev Kross—included personnel on the state, city, county and federal levels.

Homeland Security was also alerted. In the six or so hours it was conceivable that Kross had made it to Canada. If he had been able to mask his real identity in the U.S. for more than two decades, there was a good chance that he had credentials that might get him across the border without too much trouble.

As of ten days later, no one answering Kross's description, or Violet's, had left the country through any international port.

They had simply vanished.

As to files—personal records, medical records, even utility bills—all that was left in the Torresdale mansion was a pile of ashes in the massive fireplace in the great room.

Forensic accountants for the FBI, in examining the dozens of accounts closed in the weeks before Kross's departure, speculated that Kross had slowly drained Godehard Kirsch's Swiss accounts for more than twenty years.

Jane Wickstrom, the DHS worker at whose house Jessica had gone to drop off Violet, was found bound and gagged in the basement of her row house. She had made a full recovery. Investigators believe it was Eduard Kross's housekeeper, Astrid, who made the call to Jessica.

80

When he first saw her in the catacombs he'd thought she was a teenager. Now she looked her age. Still a young woman, but no child.

The U-Haul truck idled a few yards away.

"Where are you headed?" Byrne asked.

"Center City," Rachel said. "It's time. There are only ghosts here."

She took a few seconds, glanced back at her house. Byrne knew that she'd recently sold it for just under market value. The offer she'd gotten — the call to her agency — had come from Luther, at the behest of Eduard Kross. When Rachel dropped the price, on the open market, she received an offer in days.

"It was not knowing, you know?" she said. "That was the hardest part."

It did not take the FBI investigators long to determine where the Pearly Everlasting perennials were planted on the estate grounds in Torresdale, and that it was Marielle Gray's remains buried beneath them. The preliminary reports indicated the young woman had probably died in childbirth. Byrne recalled the small makeshift surgery he'd found among the catacombs, the room where Violet was probably born. He tried to banish the image of the dried blood on the floor.

Although they would never know for certain, it was likely that Luther had been leaving the white flowers at the crime scenes in tribute to Marielle.

"For years I didn't understand the feelings," Rachel said. "When Marielle disappeared, I knew she wouldn't just leave without telling me."

Rachel Gray buttoned her coat, slipped on a pair of gloves. "I haven't really slept for the past three years," she added. "I'm not sure that I ever will."

"You will," Byrne said.

She fixed him with a look of determination, far older than her years. "I'm not giving up looking for my niece."

Byrne understood. "Nor will I."

He opened his arms. Rachel stepped forward, fell into his embrace.

When she pulled away Byrne reached into his bag, removed a large padded envelope. He handed it to her.

"What's this?" she asked.

"A lullaby."

As she drove away, Byrne turned to the house, a house he'd first heard about from Ray Torrance. He thought about the videotape he had just given the young woman, the tape Ray played for him, the video recording made in the kitchen of this house, many years ago.

The testament of a little girl named Bean.

81

The fog misted along the Delaware River like a ghost.

Jessica knew they would one day talk about Violet, but not for a while. They both knew that in this life they'd chosen there would be great victories, and heartbreaking losses.

They stood in silence on the Race Street pier for a long time, watching a barge troll slowly upriver. Jessica was just about to say something when her cell phone rang.

She held up a finger. Byrne nodded, took a few steps away, giving her privacy. Jessica looked at her iPhone's screen.

It was her husband. She answered.

"Hey," she said. "I'll be on my way in—"

"It's Carlos!"

Talking on the telephone, especially a cell phone, was one of her son's favorite things. His enthusiasm for it never waned.

"Hi, sweetie," Jessica said.

"I made supper!"

Uh oh, Jessica thought. This was never good news coming from someone younger than six. "You made supper?"

"Uh huh."

"What did you make?"

"Macaroni and cheese."

The thought of her son trying to wield a huge pot of boiling water was one of Jessica's myriad kitchen nightmares. "All by yourself?"

"No," Carlos said. "Sophie helped me."

Jessica's heart suddenly ached for her home. She wondered if Violet would ever know the love of a real family.

"Okay," Jessica said. "Macaroni and cheese sounds really good."

"The box says it serves four! That's us!"

"Yes, honey," Jessica added. "We are four."

"Love you, Mom. Hurry up!"

"Love you too. On my way."

Jessica clicked off, put her phone in her pocket. She turned to tell Byrne of her son's culinary adventures, but he was gone. Jessica looked down the pier, found him. He turned and waved; she waved back.

A few moments later Byrne crossed the street, and disappeared into the neon of the Philadelphia night.

EPILOGUE

The first thing the hunter heard was the whisper of the Maxima Crossbolt, followed by the soft rustle of nylon fabric against the bark of a birch tree.

The man fell without another sound.

When the man had spotted him, and fired his weapon three times, the report of the 9mm Colt Defender echoed across the valley.

The hunter waited a few moments, crept forward. He crouched down, felt the man's neck for a pulse. There was none. He took out his cell phone, snapped pictures of the body, the area.

The hunter kept a low profile as he moved along the ridge.

The letter from the lawyer's office had come in the mail almost six weeks after the funeral. He hadn't expected it; the deed to the cabin, along with its contents. He had not yet become proficient with the crossbow, though he suspected he would, in time.

As he neared the house, he saw the little girl sitting in the window of what looked to be a study. She turned the pages of a picture book. Even in this short amount of time she looked to have grown. He'd forgotten this about children.

The hunter glanced at the large room on the right. Martin Léopold — Eduard Kross — sat near a fireplace. The woman called Astrid served him tea out of a sterling pot.

The hunter turned to the vista behind him. The painting he had seen in Eduard Kross's library was a beautiful, realistic depiction of this valley, with the unmistakable image of St. Alexander's in the distance.

It took him a while, but eventually he recognized the view.

As he prepared to wait for the cover of night, Kevin Byrne looked down at the crossbow. Two arrows remained.

He would not need more.

ACKNOWLEDGMENTS

With heartfelt thanks to:

Jane Berkey, Meg Ruley, Peggy Gordijn, Christina Hogrebe, Danielle Sickles, Rebecca Scherer, Christina Prestia, Donald Cleary, and everyone at the Jane Rotrosen Agency;

Michael Pietsch, Reagan Arthur, Josh Kendall, Pamela Brown, Wes Miller, Theresa Giacopasi, Ben Allen, and my new family at Little, Brown;

Chuck McGroarty, Capri D'Amario, Frank Jacovini, Bob Dellavella, Pamela Bernzweig Kiner, John Rybas, Kathleen Franco MD, Lt. Edward Monaghan, Kathleen Heraghty, Heike Haddenbrock, and Joe Ruggiero;

Carole Wallencheck, Raidene Hebert, Rebecca Katzenmeyer, Jo Ann Vicarel, and Greg Fisher;

Acknowledgments

Mike Driscoll, Pat Ghegan, Dom Aspite, and the men and women of the Philadelphia Police Department;

Daniel Mallory, Christina Zoldak Sheppa, Larraine Parker, Colin Tomele, Lt. Tom McDevitt, and Michael J. Caticchio;

And, as always, Dominic Montanari—my most steadfast champion, my greatest friend.

ABOUT THE AUTHOR . . .

Richard Montanari is the internationally bestselling author of *The Echo Man, The Devil's Garden, Badlands, The Rosary Girls, The Skin Gods, Merciless,* and more. He lives in Cleveland.

. . . AND THE NEXT BYRNE AND BALZANO BOOK

The Doll Maker finds detectives Kevin Byrne and Jessica Balzano investigating the macabre murders of a succession of children, each one's body posed and waiting with an invitation to a tea dance in a week's time. With the killers at large, the detectives must find the link between the murders before another innocent child is snatched from the streets.

Following is an excerpt from the novel's opening pages.

He knew the moment she walked in.

It wasn't the way she was dressed—he had been fooled by this more often than he had been right, and he had been right many times—it was, instead, the way her heels fell on the old hardwood floor, the weight of her stride, the way he knew she'd put a thousand sad stories to bed.

He remembered her from Raleigh, from Vancouver, from Santa Fe. She was no one he recognized. She was every woman he'd ever met.

The bar was long and U-shaped. He was seated on one of the short sides, next to the wall, his right shoulder against the paneling. This helped to hide from the world the large scar on his right cheek. As little as he cared about anything, he was still self-conscious about his scar, a birthday present from his father and a Mason jar of moonshine. Besides, with one shoulder to the wall, he was always protected from that flank.

The bar was almost empty. It smelled of overcooked fish and Mr. Clean.

The woman sat two stools to his left, leaving an empty seat between them. As she dropped her purse to the floor, wrapping the strap around an ankle, the juke spun a new song, a tune by Lynyrd Skynyrd. Or maybe it was the Allman Brothers. He wasn't big into seventies southern rock. Oddly enough, considering his job, he didn't care much for music at all. He enjoyed the silence. There was precious little of it these days.

It was clear that the woman expected him to summon the barkeep, offer her a drink. When he didn't, she did. The barman took his time. Had the woman been ten years younger, or five years prettier, the barman would have flown.

When he finally made his way down the bar the woman looked over, giving it one more chance. When she looked back she said, simply:

"Seven and Seven."

The barman dawdled, returned, slid a napkin onto the bar in front of the woman, put down the watery cocktail, waited. The woman picked up her bag, then fished out a rumpled twenty, dropped it onto a wet spot — a spot the barman, if he'd given a shit, would have wiped down.

The man made an elaborate process out of straightening out the wet bill. Eventually he came back with the change. All singles. He dropped them into the puddle on the bar.

Asshole.

He wished he had time to deal with the bartender.

Two songs later the woman slid one stool to her right, uninvited, bringing her almost empty drink with her, rattling the cubes.

"What's your name?" she asked.

He glanced over, got his first good look. Her eye shadow was electric blue, her lipstick far too red for a woman her age, which he pegged at forty-five, maybe more. She looked like a woman who slept in her makeup, only bothering to wash her face when she took that infrequent shower. Her foundation spackled a landscape of acne scars.

"Jagger," he said.

She looked surprised. They always did.

"Jagger?" she asked. "Really? Like *Mick* Jagger?"

"Something like that."

She smiled. She shouldn't have. It ruined what little about her face there was to like. In it he saw every regret, every Sunday morning, every gray towel and yellowed bed sheet.

But this was still Saturday night, and the lights were low.

"You got as much *money* as Mick Jagger?" she asked.

"I got enough."

She leaned closer. Her perfume was too sweet and too heavy, but he liked it that way.

"How much is enough?" she asked.

"Enough for the night."

Something lit her eyes. It helped. Maybe she wasn't so banged up after all, despite the fact that she was turning tricks in a hole like this. He nodded at the bartender, dropped a fifty on the bar. This time the barkeep was prompt. Odd, that. In a flash he was back with refills. He even wiped down the bar.

"But can you *go* all night, that's the question," she said.

"I don't need to go all night. I just need to go until the meter runs out."

She laughed. Her breath smelled of cigarettes and Altoids and gum disease.

"You are funny," she said. "I like that."

It doesn't matter what you like, he thought. *It hasn't mattered for more than twenty years.*

She drained her Seven and Seven, tapped her plastic nails on the bar. She turned to face him again, as if the idea had just come to her. "What do you say we buy a bottle and go have some fun?"

He glanced over. "*We?* You pitching in?"

She gave him a gentle slap on the shoulder. "Oh, stop."

"I've got a bottle in my truck," he said.

"Is that an invitation?"

"Only if you want it to be."

"Sounds like a plan," she said. She slipped off the stool, toddled a bit, grabbed the rail to steady herself. These were clearly not her first two drinks of the evening. "I'm just going to visit the little girls' room. Don't you *dare* go anywhere."

She flounced to the far side of the bar, drawing meager attention from the two old codgers at the other end.

He finished his beer, picked up the bills, leaving the barkeep a thirty-nine cent tip. It didn't go unnoticed.

A few minutes later the woman returned, heavier on the eye shadow, lipstick, perfume, breath mints.

They stepped into the cold night air.

"Where's your truck?" she asked.

He pointed to the footpath, the trail that snaked through the woods. "Through there."

"You're parked in the rest area?"

"Yeah."

She looked at her shoes, a pair of cut-rate white heels, at least one size too small. "I hope the path ain't muddy."

"It isn't."

She slipped an arm through his, the one opposite his duffel. They crossed the tavern's small parking lot, then walked into the woods.

"What's in the bag?" she asked.

"All my money."

She laughed again.

When they got to the halfway point, far from the lights, he stopped, opened his duffel, took out a pint of Southern Comfort.

"For the road," he said.

"Nice."

He uncapped the bottle, took a drink.

"Open your mouth and close your eyes," he said.

She did as she was told.

"Wider," he said.

He looked at her standing there, in the diffused moonlight, her mouth pink and gaping. It was how he planned to remember her. It was how he remembered them all.

At precisely the same instant he dropped the razor blade into her mouth, he poured in a third of the bottle of Comfort.

The steel hit first. The woman gagged, choked, bucked. When she did this the blade shot forward in her mouth, sliced through her lower lip.

He stood to the side as the woman coughed out a gulp of blood and whiskey. She then spit the blade into her hand, dropped it to the ground.

When she looked up at him he saw that the razor had sliced her lower lip in half.

"What did you do?" she screamed.

Because of her destroyed mouth it came out *whan nin you noo?* But he understood. He always understood.

He pushed her into a tree. She slumped to the ground, gasping for air, hacking blood like some just-hooked fish.

He circled her, the adrenaline now screaming in his veins.

"What did you think we were going to do?" he asked. He put a boot on her stomach, along with half his weight. This brought another thick gout of red from her mouth and nose. "Hmm? Did you think we were going to *fuck?* Did you think I was going to put my cock into your filthy, diseased *mouth?*"

He dropped to the ground, straddled her.

"If I did that, I'd be fucking everyone you've ever been with."

He leaned back to admire his work, grabbed the bottle, downed some Comfort to ward off the chill. He took his eyes off her for a second, but it was long enough.

Somehow the razor blade was in her hand. She swiped it across his face, cutting him from just below his right eye to the top of his chin.

He felt the pain first, then the heat of his own blood, then the cold. Steam rose from his open wound, clouding his eyes.

"You fucking *bitch*."

He slapped her across the face. Once, twice, then once more. Her face was now marbled with blood and phlegm. Her ruined mouth was open, her lower lip in two pieces.

He thought about taking a rock to her skull, but not yet. She'd cut him, and she would pay. He killed the bottle, wiped it clean, tossed it into the woods, then ripped off her tank top, used it to sponge his face. He reached into his duffel.

"That is one nasty cut," he said. "I'm going to close that wound for you. There's all kinds of bacteria out here. You don't want to get an infection, do you? It wouldn't be good for business."

He pulled the blowtorch from his bag, a big BernzOmatic. When she saw it she tried to wiggle out from under him, but her strength was all but sapped. He hit her in the face again—just hard enough to keep her in place—then took a lighter from his pocket, lit the torch, adjusted the flame. When it was a perfect yellow-blue point, he said:

"Tell me you love me."

Nothing. She was going into shock. He brought the flame closer to her face.

"*Tell* me."

"I...na...yoo."

"Of course you do."

He went to work on her lip. Her dying screams were swallowed by the sound of the blowtorch. The smell of charred flesh rose into the night air.

By the time he reached her eyes she was silent.

The clouds had again pulled away from the moon by the time he emerged from the woods, the quarter-mile pass-through that led to the rest area where he had parked.

When he had parked his truck, earlier in the day, he had positioned it as close to the path as he could. There had been three other rigs closer, but he figured he was near enough.

The other trucks were now gone.

Before stepping into the sodium streetlights of the massive parking lot—which held a fueling station and an all-night diner—he looked at his clothes. His jacket was covered in blood, large patches that appeared black in the moonlight. He took off his down jacket, turned it inside out, put it back on. He picked up a handful of leaves and wiped the blood from his face.

A few moments later, when he came around the back of the diner, he saw a woman standing there. She saw him, too.

It was one of the diner waitresses, standing by the back door, her powder blue rayon uniform and white sweater looking bright and clean and sterile under the sodium lamps. She was on break, using an emery board, sanding her nails.

"Oh, my goodness," she said.

He could only imagine what he must look like to her.

"Hey," he said.

"Are you okay?"

"Yeah," he said. "You know. I'm good. Ran into a low branch back there. Cut me pretty fine, I reckon."

He was lightheaded, and not just from the watered down Scotch and flat beer and warm Comfort. He had lost blood.

The waitress glanced over his shoulder, back. She'd seen him come out of the woods. Bad for him, worse for her. The night was getting deeper. As exhausted as he was, he knew what he had to do. She would get the short ride, but she'd ride.

He turned, scanned the parking lot, looked at the steamed windows of the diner. No one was watching. At least, no one he could see.

"You don't happen to have a Band-Aid or anything do you?" he asked.

"Maybe." She unzipped and ransacked her purse. "No, sweetie.

Best I can do is a Kleenex, but I don't think that'll help. You're bleeding pretty good. You should go to the hospital." She pointed at a blue Nissan Sentra in the lot. "I can take you if you want."

He chucked a thumb toward his rig. "I've got a first aid kit in my truck," he said. "You any good with that stuff?"

She smiled. "I've got a whole passel of younger brothers and sisters. Always getting in scrapes. I think I can manage."

They walked to the far end of the lot. More than once he had to slow down, dizzy. When they got to the truck he unlocked the passenger side first. The waitress got in.

"The kit's in the glove box," he said.

He closed the door. On the way to the driver's side he unsnapped the closure on his knife sheath. It was a six-inch Buck, razor sharp.

He opened his door, pulled himself into the cab, angled the mirror toward his face.

The whore had sliced him good.

While the waitress lined up the gauze and the foil-wrapped alcohol swabs on the dashboard, he pushed back the mirror, glanced around the lot. No other drivers, no one coming out of the diner.

He would do it now.

Before he could slip the knife from its sheath he noticed something in the parking lot, right near the entrance to the path. It was a small red wallet. It matched the red vinyl of the waitress's purse. For any number of reasons, he couldn't leave it there.

"Is that yours?" he asked.

She glanced to where he was pointing, put down the first aid kit, looked in her purse. "Oh, shoot," she said. "I must have dropped it."

"I'll get it."

"You're a doll."

He stepped out of the truck, walked across the lot, his head throbbing. He had a few Vicodin left. He reached into his pocket, pulled out the vial, chewed them dry, trying to recall if he had an inch or so of Wild Turkey left in the truck.

He picked up the wallet, thought for a moment about opening it, about learning the waitress's name. It didn't matter. It never had.

Still, his curiosity got the better of him.

As he opened the wallet he felt the hot breath brush the back of his neck, saw the long shadow pool at his feet.

An instant later his head exploded into a supernova of bright orange fire.

Cold.

Lying on his back, he opened his eyes, the pain in his head now a savage thing. The world smelled of wet compost and loam and pine needles. Snow whispered down, catching on his eyelashes.

He tried to stand up, but couldn't move his arms, his hands, his feet. He slowly turned his head, saw the whore's dead body next to him, the scorched holes where her eyes used to be. Something—some animal—had already been at her face.

"Stand up." The voice was a whisper near his left ear.

By the time he managed to turn his head, no one was there.

"I...I can't."

His words sounded distant, as if they belonged to someone else.

"No, you cannot," came the soft voice. "I have all but severed your spinal cord. You will never walk again."

Why? he wanted to ask, but knew instantly that he could no longer make a sound. Perhaps it was because he *knew* why.

Time left, returned. It was morning somehow.

He looked into the gently falling snow, saw the axe, the bright steel wing glimmering in the splintered dawn like some silent, circling hawk.

Moments later, when the heavy blade fell, he heard them all — as he knew he would on this day — every dead thing beckoning him toward the darkness, a place where nothing human stirred, a place where his father still lay in wait, a place where the screams of children echo forever.

At just after six a.m., as every other day, Mr. Marseille and I opened our eyes, dark lashes counterweighted to the light.

It was mid-November, and although the frost had not yet touched the windows—this usually comes to our eaves in late December—there was a mist on the glass that gave the early morning light a delicate quality, as if we were looking at the world through a Lalique figurine.

Before we dressed for the day we drew our names in the condensation on the windowpane, the double *l* in Mr. Marseille's name and the double *l* in mine slanting toward one another like tiny Doric columns, as has been our monogram for as long as we both could remember.

Mr. Marseille looked at the paint swatches, a frown tilling his brow. In the overhead lights of the big store his eyes appeared an ocean blue, but I knew them to be green, the way the trees appear after the first draft of spring, the way the grass of a well-tended cemetery looks on the Fourth of July.

On this day, beneath our drab winter overcoats, we were dressed for tea. My dress was scarlet; his suit, a dove gray. These were the colors of our amusements, you see, the feathers by which we cleave our places at the table.

"I don't know," Mr. Marseille said. "I just don't know."

I glanced at the selections, and saw his impasse. There had to be a half-dozen choices, all of which, from just a few feet away, could be described as yellow. Pale yellow, at that. Not the yellow of sunflowers or school buses or taxicabs, or even the yellow of summer corn. These were pastel shades, almost whitish, and they had the most scandalous of names:

Butter Frosting. Lemon Whip. Sweet Marzipan.

Mr. Marseille hummed a song, *our* song, almost certainly turning over the words in his mind, perhaps hoping for a flicker of inspiration.

I soon became distracted by a woman with a small child, passing by at the end of our aisle. The woman wore a short puffy jacket and shockingly tight denim jeans. Her makeup seemed to have been applied in haste—perhaps reflected in a less than well-silvered mirror—and gave her an almost clownish look in the unforgiving light of the store. The child, a toddler at oldest, bounced along behind the woman, deliriously consumed by an oversized cookie with brightly colored candies baked in. A few moments after they passed from view I heard the woman exhort the child to hurry up. I don't imagine the little boy did.

At the thought of the mother and child I felt a familiar yearning blossom within me. I scolded it away, and turned once more to Mr. Marseille and his assessments. Before I could choke the words, I pointed at one of the paint swatches in his hands, and asked:

"What's wrong with this one? Candlelight is a delightful name. Quite apropos, *n'est-ce pas?*"

Mr. Marseille looked up—first at the long, empty aisle, then at the myriad cans of paint, then at me. He replied softly, but forcefully:

"It is *my* decision, and I *will* not be hurried."

I simply hated it when Mr. Marseille was cross with me. It did not happen often—we were kindred and compatible spirits in almost all ways, especially in the habits of color and texture and fabric and song—but when I saw the flare in his eyes I knew that this would be a day of numbering, our first since that terrible moment last week, a day during which a young girl's blood would surely be the rouge that colored my cheeks.

*　　*　　*

We rode in our car, a white sedan that, according to Mr. Marseille, had once been advertised during a football game. I don't know much about cars — or football, for that matter — and this was not *our* car, not by any watermark of legal ownership. Mr. Marseille simply drove to the curb about an hour earlier, and I got in. In this manner it *became* our car, if only for the briefest of times. Mr. Marseille, like all of our kind, was an expert borrower.

The first thing I noticed was that the front seat smelled of licorice. The sweet kind. I don't care for the other kind. It is bitter to my tongue. There are some who crave it, but if I've learned anything in this life it is that one can never reason, or truly understand, the tastes of another.

We drove on Benjamin Franklin Parkway, the magnificent divided thoroughfare that I've heard is patterned, after a fashion, on the Champs-Élysées in Paris. I've never been to Paris but I've seen many photographs, and this seems to be true.

I speak a cluttered French, as does Mr. Marseille — sometimes, for sport, we go for days speaking nothing else — and we often talk of one day traveling from the City of Brotherly Love to the City of Light.

The trees along the parkway were deep in their autumn slumber, but I've been on this street in summer, when the green seems to go on forever, bookended by the stately Museum of Art at one end, and the splendid Swann Fountain on the other. On this November morning the street was beautiful, but if you come here in July it will be breathtaking.

We followed the group of girls at a discreet distance. They had attended a showing of a film at the Franklin Institute, and were now boarding a bus to take them back to their school.

Mr. Marseille had thought of making our invitation on Winter Street, but decided against it. Too many busybodies to ruin our surprise.

At just after noon the bus pulled over near the corner of Sixteenth and Locust. The teenage girls—about a dozen in number, all dressed alike in their school uniforms—disembarked. They lingered on the corner, chatting about everything and nothing, as girls of an age will do.

After a short time, a few cars showed up; a number of the girls drove off in backseats, carpooled by one mother or another.

The girl who would be our guest walked a few blocks south with another of her classmates, a tall, lanky girl wearing a magenta cardigan, in the style of a fisherman's knit.

We drove a few blocks ahead of them, parked in an alley, then marched briskly around the block, coming up behind the girls. Girls at this age often dawdle, and this was good for us. We caught them in short order.

When the tall girl finally said goodbye, on the corner of Sixteenth and Spruce, Mr. Marseille and I walked up behind our soon-to-be guest, waiting for the signal to cross the street.

Eventually the girl looked over.

"Hello," Mr. Marseille said.

The girl glanced at me, then at Mr. Marseille. Sensing no threat, perhaps because she saw us as a couple—a couple of an age not significantly greater than her own—she returned the greeting.

"Hi," she said.

While we waited for the light to change, Mr. Marseille unbuttoned his coat, struck a pose, offering the well-turned peak lapel of his suit jacket. The hem was a pick stitch, and finely finished. I know this because I am the seamstress who fitted him.

"Wow," the girl added. "I like your suit. A *lot*."

Mr. Marseille's eyes lighted. In addition to being sartorially fastidious, he was terribly vain, and always available for a compliment.

"What a lovely thing to say," he said. "How very kind of you."

The girl, perhaps not knowing the correct response, said nothing. She stole a glance at the Walk signal. It still showed a hand.

"My name is Marseille," he said. "This is my dearest heart, Anabelle."

Mr. Marseille extended his hand. The girl blushed, offered her own.

"I'm Nicole."

Mr. Marseille leaned forward, as was his manner, and gently kissed the back of the girl's fingers. Many think the custom is to kiss the back of a lady's *hand*—on the side just opposite the palm—but this is not proper.

A gentleman knows.

Nicole reddened even more deeply.

When she glanced at me I made the slightest curtsy. Ladies do not shake hands with ladies.

At this moment the light changed. Mr. Marseille let go of the girl's hand and, in a courtly fashion, offered her safe passage across the lane.

I followed.

We continued down the street in silence until we came to the mouth of the alley; the alley in which we parked our car.

Mr. Marseille held up a hand. He and I stopped walking.

"I have a confession to make," he said.

The girl, appearing to be fully at ease with these two polite and interesting characters, stopped as well. She looked intrigued by Mr. Marseille's statement.

"A confession?"

"Yes," he said. "Our meeting was not by accident today. We're here to invite you to tea."

The girl looked at me for a moment, then back at Mr. Marseille.

"You want to invite me to tea?"

"Yes."

"I don't know what you mean," she said.

Mr. Marseille smiled. He had a pretty smile, brilliantly white, almost feminine in its deceits. It was the kind of smile that turned strangers into cohorts in all manner of petty crime, the kind of smile that puts at ease both the very young and the very old. I've yet to meet a young woman who could resist its charm.

"Every day, about four o'clock, we have tea," Mr. Marseille said. "It is quite the haphazard affair on most days, but every so often we have a special tea—a *thé dansant,* if you'll allow—one to which we invite all our friends, and always someone new. Someone we hope will *become* a new friend. Won't you say you'll join us?"

The young woman looked confused. But still she was gracious. This is the sign of a good upbringing. Both Mr. Marseille and I believe courtesy and good manners are paramount to getting along in the world these days. It is what lingers with people after you take your leave, like the quality of your soap, or the polish of your shoes.

"Look," the young lady began. "I think you've mistaken me for someone else. But thanks anyway." She glanced at her watch, then back at Mr. Marseille. "I'm afraid I have a ton of homework."

With a lightning fast move Mr. Marseille took the girl by both wrists, and spun her into the alleyway. Mr. Marseille is quite the athlete, you see. I once saw him catch a common housefly in midair, then throw it into a hot skillet, where we witnessed its life vanish into an ampersand of silver smoke.

As he seized the girl I watched her eyes. They flew open to their widest: counterweights on a precious Bru. I noticed then, for the first time, that her irises had scattered about them tiny flecks of gold.

This would be a challenge for me, for it was my duty—and my passion—to re-create such things.

We sat around the small table in our workshop. At the moment it was just Nicole, Mr. Marseille, and me. Our friends had yet to arrive. There was much to do.

"Would you like some more tea?" I asked.

The girl opened her mouth to speak, but no words came forth. Our special tea often had this effect. Mr. Marseille and I never drank it, of course, but we had seen its magical results on others many times. Nicole had already had two cups, and I could only imagine the colors she saw; Alice at the mouth of the rabbit hole.

I poured more tea into her cup.

"There," I said. "I think you should let it cool for a time. It is very hot."

While I made the final measurements, Mr. Marseille excused himself to make ready what we needed for the gala. We were never happier than at this moment, a moment when, needle in hand, I made the closing stiches, and Mr. Marseille prepared the final table.

We parked by the river, exited the car. Before showing our guest to her seat, Mr. Marseille blindfolded me. I could barely conceal my anticipation and delight. I do *so* love a tea.

Mr. Marseille does, as well.

With baby steps I breached the path. When Mr. Marseille removed my scarf, I opened my eyes.

It was beautiful. Better than beautiful.

It was *magic*.

Mr. Marseille had selected the right color. He often labored over the decision for days, but each time, after the disposing of the rollers and trays and brushes, after the peeling away of the masking tape, it was as if the object of his labors had always been so.

Moments later we helped the girl—Nicole Solomon was her full name—from the car. Her very presence at our table made her absent from another. Such is the way of all life.

As Mr. Marseille removed the stockings from the bag, I made my goodbye, tears gathering at the corners of my eyes, thinking that Mr. Shakespeare was surely wrong.

There is no sweetness in parting.

Only sorrow.

I returned to where Mr. Marseille stood, and pressed something into his gloved hand.

"I want her to have this," I said.

Mr. Marseille looked at what I had given him. He seemed surprised. "Are you sure?"

I was not. But I'd had it so long, and loved it so deeply, I felt it was time for the bird to fly on its own.

"Yes," I said. "I'm sure."

Mr. Marseille touched my cheek and said, "My dearest heart."

Under the bright moon, as Philadelphia slept, we watched the shadow of the girl's legs cast parallel lines on the station house wall, just like the double *l* in Anabelle and Mr. Marseille.

MULHOLLAND BOOKS

You won't be able to put down these Mulholland Books.